THE LEFT HAND

BOOK ONE IN THE VICTOR WELLS SERIES

JORDAN ALLEN

For Britton, who didn't look at me like I was crazy when I said, "I think I'm going to write a book." Your support means more than you know.

1

Sparks flew on impact, blue and bright like miniature bolts of lightning. The air smelled of electricity, and adrenaline rushed through my veins.

Gio was already sweating. He grunted as he tried to force his electrified saber down, but I didn't budge. We locked eyes for a brief moment. He was scared, just like our last match. It hadn't lasted more than a minute, and even though Gio was two years older and therefore two years more experienced, I didn't expect anything different this time.

I forced him off and took a step back, careful that my foot didn't leave the round dais we fought on, and twirled my saber, electricity coursing up and down the length of the triangular blade. A group of spectators jumped back as my swinging blade came perilously close to paralyzing one of them. Temporarily, of course.

I watched Gio as he mirrored each of my steps. Had he fixed anything since last time? I focused on him, searching for a weakness.

His grip was the same: strong on the forehand but weak on the backhand. He kept his weight centered, though his body exhibited a slight backwards lean. He was ready to retreat, not attack.

He expected to lose.

I twirled my saber again and exhaled. Another boring match.

The crowd began to clap and yell, urging us to engage. It'd been thirty seconds and our blades had only made contact twice. Grandfather had said I could only fight if I was done in time to make it to Senator Supart's event tonight.

I advanced quickly, forcing Gio to the right. Two moves and the match would be done. I'd feign a thrust, he'd meet me with a backhand to block, and I'd change directions hard, making sure to catch the tip of his blade with mine to create maximum torsion at the hilt. His grip wouldn't hold, he'd lose his saber, and that would be it. It would almost be too easy.

But then, I shouldn't have expected more of him. His DNA was only in the high eighties.

Gio stood at the defensive. Ready but scared, sweat beading around his temples.

I plunged my arm forward.

Blue lightning raced down my blade as the tip flew through the air like an arrow toward my opponent's shoulder. He took the bait, bringing his blade up to parry. Our blades collided in a shower of sparks. His saber flew free from his grip and clattered to the ground.

The crowd roared its approval. The clock continued to count. Fifty-one, fifty-two.

Gio raised his empty hands, a defeated look on his face.

I glanced around. A few people to my right held up a sign with my name on it. I saw a few more of them scattered throughout the crowd.

I smiled and checked the clock. There was plenty of time before I needed to meet up with Grandfather, and that was sure to be boring. At least here I wouldn't fall asleep.

This didn't have to end yet, did it?

I stepped back and motioned to Gio's saber with my own. The crowd yelled its approval.

I'd give him another chance—not that things would end any differently, of course, but it just wasn't satisfying for a match to be over so quickly. Besides, giving second chances was the Noble thing to do, right?

Gio stooped to pick up his blade.

I twirled my saber again and nodded.

Gio faced me.

I awaited his advance.

He lunged and I reacted.

I dodged his blade easily and batted it away with a casual flick of the wrist.

While Gio collected himself, I searched the crowd. Alex was supposed to be around here somewhere.

The building hosted multiple daises, each one surrounded by a small crowd of people. The crowd encircling me was by far the largest, and with all the waving signs and loud cheering, it wasn't easy to find Alex.

I sidestepped another lunge and moved to the opposite side of the dais.

Where was he? Alex never participated in the saber fights, even though his DNA was definitely Noble enough for him to do so, but he was usually here, either watching me or sneaking off to watch a few of the girls fight. Well, he didn't do *that* much anymore, not since Daphne.

I forced the thought of her out of my mind and glanced back at Gio. He was ranked second, just behind me. Although "just" was overstating it a bit. My Noble DNA registered in the nineties. I could spare another second or two searching for Alex.

Despite my best efforts, though, I didn't find him in the rowdy crowd.

Something moved in the corner of my vision. Gio. I turned to meet him, but I was half a second too late. An electric shock exploded up my arm, like a swarm of bees all attacking at once. I was too stunned to even cry out in pain, but the sensation disappeared instantly. My left arm fell completely limp—paralyzed.

The crowd gasped.

"Ha!" Gio said as he retreated, a surprised smile on his face.

An electronic buzzer sounded, signaling the end of the first round. I couldn't believe it. I couldn't remember the last time someone had even come close to touching me in a one-on-one fight. Several months at least. Maybe a year?

Gio eyed me as he fist-bumped and high-fived everyone around him. I remained where I stood. There was no need to go over to my trainer for advice, or to rest for a moment. I didn't need the former, and I didn't deserve the latter.

I matched Gio's stare. There would be no second chances in the next round. I exhaled a frustrated breath and checked the luminescent numbers of the giant time clock. With the mandatory five-minute wait between rounds, I'd be cutting it close, and I couldn't be late. Nobles weren't late.

Finally, the bell sounded. Gio approached with more confidence than in the first round, but not with more skill. Even with my paralyzed arm he was no match for me. Fifteen seconds in he lay on his back, his sword arm and left leg temporarily paralyzed. I held my saber inches from his face until he uttered the match-ending phrase.

"I yield." He was one of the few people I knew who had a British accent, which meant his family had money and he had studied saber fighting. Too bad it didn't do him any good.

The crowd burst into applause. I de-electrified my saber and extended the tip to Gio's good arm. He grabbed it, and I pulled him to his feet as his trainer jogged over to support him.

"Good match," he said.

I nodded in reply. It was my worst match of the year. I pushed my way through the people who had flooded the dais, ignoring the slew of congratulations that met my ears. I was once again thankful for the exit that was connected to the locker room. I wouldn't have to fight my way out of here, or talk to any members of the overexcited crowd. There was nothing worse than repeatedly being told "great job" when you knew you didn't deserve it. Maybe a Sinister would enjoy that, but not me, not a Noble.

Just before I reached the locker rooms, my face and name appeared on a large screen occupying the majority of the far wall.

The word "winner" was emphatically displayed in all caps, and a polite smattering of applause sounded throughout the building. I opened the door and walked quickly inside.

Another tournament victory. With an asterisk. How could I have let him hit me? It'd been stupid to draw out the match, and worse, to let myself get distracted.

Anger began to well up inside me, but I pushed it back down. There would be time to think about my mistakes later. For now, I needed to hurry.

2

I stepped through the door, blinking as my eyes adjusted to the brightness. The afternoon sun glinted off the crystalline windows of the surrounding buildings. Most were a single story tall, though some were two. Each building looked nearly identical to the next. All were made entirely of polished steel, tinted glass and concrete, giving the street before me an almost sterile feel. The complete absence of people didn't help either.

Everyone else was still inside—most matches went at least five rounds, if not more—which was a good thing. I didn't know if I could handle more "congratulations" while my paralyzed arm hung limply at my side. Gio was probably ecstatic. Months of perfect matches and I let him catch me in the arm. Ridiculous.

I turned my back to the street and pulled the door closed until I felt the latch engage. My left arm swung useless at my side. I stared down at it. Boredom. I blamed it on boredom. Maybe one of these days I'd fight someone who could last longer than a minute. But it wouldn't be any time soon. My next match was in a couple of days. Since Gio was out of the running, I was fighting the kid ranked number five. Gio had beaten him in two rounds.

Maybe I'd fight left-handed.

I placed my right hand on the glass panel of the scanner mounted to the right of the door handle. Not everyone had access to this door, but after a handful of late-night phone calls to the building owner asking to be let in or out, he had decided to just program my DNA into the system.

I watched as beads of white light snaked around the outline of my hand.

Come on, hurry up.

A soft green light pulsed from the scanner, and the DNA-controlled locking mechanism clicked into place. I had stayed much longer than I'd planned, and the Capital was about as close as the nearest train station, which meant I'd have to run the entire way if I wanted to get there on time.

I guess there was one upside to not exerting effort in my matches: I was fresh for the two-mile dash I was about to run. But Alex wasn't. Hopefully by now he had made his way over to the Capital, or his father had sent someone to pick him up.

I pulled out my phone and pressed on Alex's icon. It didn't even ring. Straight to voice mail. But I wasn't surprised. Alex's father became very irritated when he turned off his phone, which was exactly why he did it. I wasn't worried. Rebellious or not, Alex would be at the Capital tonight. Maybe he was already with Grandfather?

I pocketed my phone, shrugged the leather strap of my saber sheath over my shoulder, and took off at a jog. I cut straight across the empty street, the rhythmic tap of my feet the only sound breaking the silence. My left arm dangled at my side, not quite in sync with the rest of my body.

I ran for a few blocks, trying to make up for lost time, but if I stayed in the Flats, it wouldn't be enough, and the nearest train station was over a mile in the wrong direction. I glanced at my watch again and cut through the next alleyway toward the center of the city, toward the Heights.

Immediately the scenery began to change. Instead of steel and glass, the buildings here were older, but generally well maintained. The red brick from years past had become a washed-out mix of pink and brown. I briefly caught my distorted reflection as I passed the first cracked window and came to a stop at the mouth of a long alley.

Generally, I stayed on our side of the Innerbelt, but I'd promised Senator Supart I'd be there. On time. And my only option to make that happen was to cut through the Heights. Grandfather wouldn't approve of this shortcut, but it wasn't illegal, just ill-advised. Well, maybe ill-advised for someone like Gio. I'd be fine. Plus, if Grandfather knew how many times I'd used this shortcut, well... maybe it was better he didn't know.

I checked the street in both directions and headed down the alleyway.

About a hundred yards in, the alley ended in a brick wall, blocking the way like an antiquated gatekeeper. I slowed to a walk as I approached it. It wasn't a real wall. It was a hologram, almost completely indistinguishable from the brick of the surrounding buildings, but if you looked at it just right, it would shimmer.

Grandfather said walls like these were in place more to keep Noble kids from straying into the Heights than to keep Sinisters from coming out, but I wasn't so sure. Only a Sinister would mistake a hologram for the real thing.

I took a step forward, feeling nothing as I passed through the projection, and was met immediately by a series of weathered caution signs and a rusting ten-foot-tall metal fence. Fortunately, someone—not me, of course—had cut a slit in the links that was easy enough to slip through, even with a paralyzed arm.

In front of me, the Innerbelt stretched out to either side until the gradual curve of its black and silver tracks disappeared from view. My vision blurred as one of the train carriages shot down the tracks almost faster than I could follow. Its speed masked its size. The brief flash of white was roughly the size of my house, probably carrying hundreds of people toward the Capital or some other destination. I checked my watch. Too bad I couldn't hitch a ride.

The customary whoosh of air filled the vacuum left by the speeding carriage. Now was my chance. I took off in a sprint and leapt onto the first track, almost losing my balance as I landed on the strips of plastic separating the giant magnets that propelled the carriages forward. *Stupid arm.*

Once on the other side, I unslung the leather sheath from my shoulder and knelt down to unzip it. A series of metallic clicks gave way to the dull polish of my blade. I picked it up and tapped the concealed button on the butt of the handle. A spark of lightning arced across the blade, electrifying it.

I slung my bag back over my shoulder and headed down the nearest alleyway. Like flipping a switch, the urban scenery changed. The well-kept cityscape and clean walls of the Nobles became a forest of graffiti. I was officially in the Heights now, the Sinisters' territory, but this shortcut would take me through a kind of buffer zone where people didn't live. I probably wouldn't run into any Sinisters, but if I did, I'd be ready.

Sinisters.

Most people, including Grandfather, said Sinisters weren't evil. They just didn't have a tendency for good like Nobles did. And they couldn't—it was written in their DNA, just as clearly as it was written in mine that I was Noble, and that I was good. I almost felt bad for them, or some of them at least.

I exited the alley and turned onto a main street. Cracked roads wound their way through the dilapidated neighborhood. Boarded-up windows dotted the high-rise buildings like old Band-Aids attempting to cover wounds that wouldn't heal. The whole area felt claustrophobic, the towering, crowded structures hanging ominously overhead, blocking out the afternoon sunlight.

Tall buildings were mostly absent from the Flats. It was rare to see anything over two or three stories there, hence the name.

My journey through the Heights was quick and uneventful. The only movement other than my own was some loose trash rustling in the breeze. But even so, as I turned down another alley, a familiar scene came into view and I felt compelled to pause for a moment.

Unlike the jumbled graffiti found throughout the Heights, this alley displayed an organized sea of color. The features of the person in the mural weren't easily recognizable, but the white coat was a dead giveaway. A very old, very ugly Victoria Rosewood peered over the alleyway like a sentinel guarding the Flats. In each hand she held a vial filled with people. One hand was bathed in light—the Nobles. The other hand was covered in shadows—the Sinisters. The words "The Great Experiment" had been scrawled along the bottom of the mural.

I stared at the haggard representation of Dr. Rosewood, our city's savior. She was the only person currently living who had been granted a life extension. Some Nobles, if sick, could have healthy replacement organs grown, but the cutoff age was seventy-five. There was a good chance Dr. Rosewood's life would more than double that. What would happen to her when the Experiment was over?

Alex had his theories, but I didn't have time to think about it. I needed to get going. A quick glance at my watch granted me some relief: I was back on schedule.

I tore my eyes and thoughts away from the mural and continued onward. Forty seconds later, I was back in Noble territory.

The walls were clean. The sun shone a little brighter. I breathed a little easier.

Too bad the whole city wasn't like this.

3

I checked my watch again, my breath coming in short puffs. What was it now? A mile left? And was my arm supposed to be numb for this long? It'd been so long since I'd been hit that it was hard to remember.

I dodged a group of teenagers standing in a circle and picked up speed. The streets had become more and more crowded as I neared the Capital. Well-dressed people strolled casually along, some obviously on their way to tonight's event.

Sometimes I hated how connected Grandfather was. It definitely had its perks, but even though he wasn't directly involved in politics anymore, I still had to go to things. Actually, I had to go to everything. And I usually had to be early.

Up ahead, the road was partially blocked by a group of Followers. A dozen of them stood across the road like a dotted line on a page. And they weren't the benign type of Followers either. They weren't dressed like their rock-star idols or favorite athletes. They were dressed completely in black—shirts, pants, and trench coats. And they wore masks, eerie ones that blurred their features but left the eyes sharp. They were Bounty Hunter Followers.

"Great," I huffed.

Should I try and make it past them? Or should I cut down a side street and then have to push myself to make up for lost time? For the most part, Followers weren't very athletic. I could probably push my way through. But still, twelve to one wasn't good odds, even for me.

I tried to gauge their overall fitness as a group, but before I could make up my mind, they made it for me.

"Get him!" one of them yelled, pointing in my direction.

Like a swarm of drunken birds, they broke from their line and ran straight at me in something resembling a formation. The Bounty Hunter would not have been proud.

"Oh, come on!" I said to no one in particular.

I cut a hard left into the nearest alleyway, keeping one eye on my pursuers. They followed at a sprint, some of them keeping pace while others were already slowing down. Did one of them have an inhaler out?

I smiled. I'd lose them in no time.

I burst out of the alley and turned right. After about a hundred feet, I veered left into an alleyway I didn't recognize. I cast a glance over my shoulder, trying to gauge my lead. Five seconds, and still no sign of anyone. Perfect.

I'd get through this alley, hang a right, and cut back over to the street I was originally on.

I turned my attention back to the path in front of me and quickly realized my error. There was no exit. It was a dead end, and not one with a holographic wall.

I slowed as I reached the end and turned just as the first of the Followers made their way into the alley. It looked like only half of their ranks had managed to not give up along the way.

My heart continued its rapid beat. Followers were usually peaceful, imitating their heroes and whatnot, but then again, most of them didn't Follow someone tasked by the government to find and bring the most dangerous Sinisters to justice.

I needed a plan. I didn't want to hurt them—they were Nobles too. But did they feel the same way about me? Alex had told me stories of people who had done crazy things in the name of being "true" Followers.

The group slowed their approach and spread out to block my exit completely. I took a moment to analyze them. Five on one. Better odds. Not ideal, but better. Now if I could only get my left arm to start working.

I reached over my shoulder, unsheathed my saber, and charged the blade with electricity in one smooth motion. The Followers paused and looked at each other, an unspoken message passing between them. They pressed forward.

"Wait! Stop!"

The Followers turned as another trench coat-clad person rounded the corner into the alley.

"Wait!" he shouted again, waving his arms and looking a bit like a bird that was incapable of flight.

The Followers in front of me relaxed, but in a disappointed sort of way.

I let the blade of my saber dip, but kept it out.

Running the last twenty feet in one of those slow jogs that makes walking look fast, the newcomer finally came to a stop in front of us. His chest rose and fell in rapid succession and he stabilized himself by placing one hand on his hip and the other on the alley wall.

"Oh good," he gasped between breaths. "Nobody got hurt."

He wore a mask, but I recognized that voice. And that wheezing. Both belonged to Alex.

He was a Follower. I should have known! Alex had never been one for convention, and running around with a group of Followers was definitely not in accordance with expectations, especially for the son of a senator. Not to mention Alex's fanboying over the Bounty Hunter bordered on worship.

I de-electrified my saber and slid it carefully back into its bag. "Alex, what are you doing here?" I asked.

"I'll tell you in a second," he said with a wave as he slumped to the ground, still breathing heavily. "But what"—he paused to breathe —"were you guys thinking?" He nodded at the other Followers.

The tallest one answered. "What? We weren't going to hurt him."

Alex laughed, but started coughing. He pulled out an inhaler and took an overly long draw on it. "Ahhh, that's the stuff," he said as his breathing returned to normal.

I had tried to get him to stop saying that, but five years later and here we were.

"Anyway," Alex continued. "I wasn't worried about him. I was worried about you guys! Do you know who that is?"

The black-clad group all peered at me in unison. Or at least I assumed they did. It was difficult to tell with those unnatural masks on.

"It's Victor Wells," Alex said.

A chorus of understanding met my ears.

The Follower closest to me spoke up. "How can you be sure?"

"Several years of best-friendship, that's how," Alex said, pushing himself to his feet. "But for you skeptics, let's see how he stacks up to this." He whipped a shiny white card out of his pocket. My new ID card. I patted my pocket, only to find the zipper open.

Alex brought the card up to his nose and started reading from it. "Victor Eugene Wells."

"That's not my middle name," I said.

"DNA Status: Noble." He looked up. "Obviously. You've got a saber on your back." He looked back down. "Sixteen years old. Black hair. Green eyes," he continued. "Five feet, ten inches tall. A hundred sixty pounds." He paused. "Five-*ten*? Really? Were you wearing lifts the day you got this?"

"Give me that," I said, swiping the card out of his hand. "And now that you know my basic statistics," I said with a sarcastic smile, "nice to sort of meet you all." I checked my watch. Great, behind schedule again. "Now, what do you say we get out of this alley?"

"Sounds like a great idea," Alex said. "And I think it's about time to take these masks off. We're all friends here, aren't we? No need for intimidation."

I agreed. While I knew that underneath the masks lay a group of nerdy Noble teenagers, something about their look was unsettling.

Alex slid off his mask, revealing a crooked smile, sandy blond hair, and a full face that suggested a figure unaccustomed to rigorous exercise. The other Followers followed suit, and I was met with a series of round, youthful faces. Much less frightening than a half dozen pale, blurred visages. Alex was clearly the oldest of the bunch, but definitely not the most out of shape. All the black did a great job hiding a little pudginess.

"Why don't you guys head back to the main street?" Alex said. "Victor and I have somewhere we need to be."

"Can we at least show Victor to the others?" the tall one asked.

I gave Alex a questioning look. Kind of a weird request.

The tall one continued. "It's just that we finally had someone cornered, you know? Just like Kratos. The other guys would want to see that we finally caught someone."

"Wait a second," I said. "Like who?"

"Kratos," Alex said. "You know, the Bounty Hunter?"

"Nope," I said. "I just call him 'the Bounty Hunter' like everyone else. Why Kratos?"

"That's what the best intel says his real name is," Alex said matter-of-factly.

"The best intel?" I raised a skeptical eyebrow.

"Absolutely," Alex said. The other Followers nodded their heads in agreement. "Not to mention it sounds awesome, right? Kratos the Bounty Hunter. Could he have a cooler name?"

The youngest Follower of the bunch spoke up. "Soooo," he started timidly. "Can we show them?"

Alex looked my way.

"Do we really have time for this?" I asked, checking my watch again.

"Come on, we're probably ahead of schedule," Alex said. "I mean, look how much running we just did."

I scanned the hopeful faces of Alex's group. A few minutes wouldn't hurt.

"Fine," I said.

"All right!"

"Yes!"

"You guys go on ahead," Alex said, motioning for them to calm down. "We'll be right behind you."

We exited the alleyway and made our way down the street.

Up ahead, the rest of the Followers waited for us to arrive, perched on the sidewalk like a bunch of overweight crows. They stood beneath a billboard of Dr. Rosewood, a much younger Dr. Rosewood than the graffiti from earlier. The words "Safety in Order," her slogan for the Great Experiment, drew almost as much attention as she did. As we neared Alex's friends, a couple of them hastily hid their inhalers. A few appeared to be wearing glasses over their masks. *Nice.*

"So, um, what happened to your arm?" Alex tried to suppress a smile.

"Just practicing keeping my arm still." I did my best to keep my tone light.

"I knew it! You got hit!" Alex punched me in the arm. Regrettably, I still didn't feel anything. "Oh man, I can't believe it," he continued. "When's the last time that happened? Did you lose the match too?"

"I don't know, over a year? And of course not," I said. "We just had to go a second round."

"Come on, who was it? Someone new, or did Daphne make a surprise guest appearance?"

My head snapped up, and I locked eyes with Alex.

"Sorry," he stammered out, "I shouldn't have mentioned—"

"Maybe we should get going," I said, checking my watch.

Alex paused, the silence uneasy between us. "We've got at least a few minutes, right?" he said timidly, nodding toward the waiting group. "Plus," he said, his tone returning to normal, "you gave them your word. Come on, I'll introduce you."

Begrudgingly, I followed him over to his band of fellow Bounty Hunter worshipers. I mean, Kratos Followers.

"Awesome!" one exclaimed.

"Good work!" said another.

"Just like the Bounty Hunter himself!" shouted a third.

"Now, now everyone," Alex said, "this is Victor. Masks off. We've known each other for years."

Alex's um, friends, all fixed me with a stare. Obvious lack of physical prowess aside, they still gave me the chills. Those unnatural masks...

But one by one, the masks came off. Most of the kids appeared to be between twelve and fifteen years old. I forced a smile. While I appreciated the work the Bounty Hunter did, he wasn't someone I'd want to invite over for dinner. I was sure these Followers would have died for a chance to meet Kratos in person.

Looking at the group in front of me, I couldn't imagine what would happen if they saw him in public. Their masks were the best I'd ever seen, and their costumes were more detailed than I thought possible, all the way down to his signature black gloves. Given the chance to meet him, I'm sure there would be chaos. Or a mass fainting. It'd probably depend on whether or not they all had their inhalers with them.

Most Followers weren't nearly so dedicated. Musicians and performers were commonly Followed, as were political figures and sports stars. Basically, anyone famous. I think Alex had even mentioned a Followers convention at one point. But regardless of how nerdy or strange it was, I was still a Noble, and so were they. I'd treat them as such.

"You guys had me on the run. And your masks are spot-on," I told the group, surveying them all, keeping a smile fixed on my face.

The real Bounty Hunter, Kratos, apparently, was tasked by the government to hunt down the worst of the Sinisters. He wore a mask similar to the ones Alex and his friends used. To my knowledge, no one had ever seen him without it.

Once, a few years ago, he had stopped by a saber tournament to pay someone a visit. There was something *different* about him, something foreboding and dangerous. Alex and his friends might wear the mask, but none of them could match the cold, hard eyes of the man tasked with hunting the very worst society had to offer.

"So, introductions," Alex was saying. "Victor, this is Jacobsy, Frentoff, and Brons—"

The arrival of a sleek black car cut Alex's words short. Cars were a rarity, even amongst the more affluent Nobles. The Followers grew silent as the front passenger window rolled down. My grandfather leaned his head of white hair out of the window and looked over the group, his expression unreadable.

"A fitting place to congregate," he acknowledged, nodding to the billboard behind us. "Bounty Hunter Followers, I take it?" He had the inexplicable ability of staying informed about teenage fads, no matter how wild or obscure.

Everyone nodded.

"Yes, thanks to Dr. Rosewood's research, your hero captures those the government deems a threat," he said.

The group remained silent.

He turned to me. "Well, Victor, I do believe it is time for us to be on our way. Alex, you too."

I smiled, grateful to be rid of the group.

Alex feigned shock as we made our way to the car.

A formidable man stepped out of the driver's seat and opened the door for Alex and me.

"Thanks, Freddy." I slumped into the large back seat.

Alex gave a pathetic wave to his friends and fell into the seat beside me.

Freddy took his place behind the wheel, and the car took off.

I wasn't fond of automobiles, mostly because of the accident that killed my parents, but Grandfather insisted we continue to use one— something about "facing our fears" or "healing requires acceptance."

The partition between the front and back seats descended, revealing the wrinkled smile of Ulysses Wells.

"I thought I might find the two of you out evading your social duties," he said.

"'Duty' might be a little strong," I said.

Grandfather thought going to the public city meetings was important. Maybe he was hoping I'd be like him and my parents, but there was no way I'd go into government. All the meetings and events were boring, not to mention a waste of time.

"And we"—I looked over at Alex, who stared determinedly out the window—"well, *I* wasn't evading anything. I was on my way, at least until I ran into Alex."

A smile itched at Alex's face.

"Your parents were fond of these types of things, you know," Grandfather said with a smile. "Perhaps with time you'll enjoy them more yourself."

That, I seriously doubted. And although Senator Supart was a family friend and I'd be there tonight because he asked us to come, it didn't mean I'd enjoy tonight, whatever tonight was.

"So how did you know where to pick us up?" I asked. "I thought for sure we were going to be late."

"Your new ID card," Grandfather said.

"It's got a GPS chip in it," Freddy chimed in.

"Oh yeah, that's right," I said, vaguely remembering Freddy had mentioned it when he gave me the new one. I'd have to be more careful with my whereabouts. They could have easily seen that I'd taken a shortcut through the Heights. Luckily, they must've only tracked me down once I was back on our side of the city. Otherwise Freddy would have said something by now.

Grandfather nodded to a bag hanging from one of the ceiling hooks. "Yes, well, I've brought a suit for you to change into, Victor. Unfortunately, Alex, you'll have to remain..." He paused, eyeing Alex's costume. "In whatever it is you've decided to clothe yourself with today, until we meet up with your father later this evening."

"Unfortunately?" Alex gave him a look of disbelief. "I'm dressed like the Bounty Hunter!"

"We noticed." I snorted.

"How awesome I am? Thanks," Alex said with a shrug. "Even the Sinistrali are scared of him."

Grandfather's look hardened. "I've never been a fan of that term."

I took a deep breath and held it. *Here we go.*

"What, Sinistrali?" Alex asked.

"Yes. It implies that all the members of the Left Hand, the Sinistrali, as you call them, are Sinisters. Or at least that Sinisters are sympathetic to what they do."

It was unpopular in some circles, but Grandfather had a rare quality that even the most Noble of the Nobles often lacked: he gave most Sinisters the benefit of the doubt. "They're not all bad," he would often say. I tried my best to emulate him, but it wasn't easy.

Freddy turned to enter the conversation, something that didn't happen often. "Are you saying Sinisters aren't sympathetic to the Left Hand?" he asked, his gruff voice straining to be polite. "And Nobles could be?"

"I'm saying it's misleading and dangerous to assume. Not to mention unkind."

Freddy grunted and turned back around without another word. He mostly kept his opinions to himself, but I wished that he wouldn't.

Grandfather was right—not all Sinisters were bad—but I had to agree with Freddy. I couldn't imagine a Noble killing another Noble. Only Sinisters would target and kill Nobles. Rosewood's research had proven as much. Things like that were in their nature.

But it wasn't worth fighting about, and besides, the Left Hand hadn't been active in years.

I caught Alex glancing back and forth between Grandfather and Freddy. He began to fidget, uncomfortable in the silence.

"All I know," he said, "is that if the Bounty Hunter ever gets ordered to go after the Left Hand, they better watch out. You know he can fly, right?"

"Wouldn't that be something," Grandfather said, a smile playing across his lips.

"It's true! Look!" Alex reached deep into his many layers of black clothing and pulled out his phone. "This is from last month, when he caught what's his name from the Heights."

A shaky, out-of-focus video appeared on the screen, showing a nondescript dark blob falling from the sky and landing softly on the ground.

"All right," I said, "I'm convinced. Wait, no, can you play it again?"

Alex pushed replay. I squinted at the screen. "Yep, just like I thought. It's a little tough to tell, but I think this is footage from our first-grade video project." I elbowed Alex. "Come on, that could be anything. And when was the video shot? A hundred years ago?"

"Believe what you want," Alex said. "I have it from a very reliable source—"

"Like the 'Theories of the Bounty Hunter' thread you follow?" I asked.

"Maaaybe," he said. "But there's definitely something different about him. I mean, Victor, you're really good with a saber, but even you don't have a perfect record." He motioned to my arm. "The Bounty Hunter does. Even the guys with T1ID haven't lasted long."

"He has been of great service to society, there's no arguing against that," Grandfather said, then nodded to my arm. "Dare I say someone got the best of you today?"

"Come on, Grandfather, I thought you knew me better than that."

"Forgive me," he said with a smile.

"No, it was like Gio showed up ready to lose," I said. "I got bored and lost focus for a moment, that's all. It won't happen again."

"I'm certain it won't," Grandfather said. "Oftentimes we learn the most through failure." He gave me a small smile before turning back to the front to talk to Freddy.

I stared out the window, the blurred reflections in the glass-paneled buildings letting my mind wander. I caught a glimpse of Alex in the window. His Bounty Hunter mask lay facedown in his lap.

Kratos the Bounty Hunter. He wasn't sent after petty criminals. The regular police could deal with them. He was sent after those who possessed the gene T1ID.

Years of history lessons flashed through my mind. Dr. Rosewood had first found the gene in a frozen sample of Hitler's DNA. It had since been identified in the genetic code of every terrorist or tyrant who had been analyzed. More recently, just after the Great Experiment started, Brovecheq and Qinsari had been caught, each of their genomes containing T1ID. Brovecheq had blown up a school full of Sinister children and brought down a building in the Heights before he was caught. Qinsari had opened fire in a Noble hospital with a homemade gun. Noble or Sinister, you feared the carriers of TiiD. Rosewood's research allowed Kratos to identify and bring carriers of TiiD in before they acted. Thousands of lives, both Noble and Sinister, had been spared since this discovery.

Suddenly, the car tires screeched. I lurched forward, my train of thought effectively wrecked. A small yelp escaped Alex as he slid off his seat, and the car came skidding to a halt.

Through the windshield, I saw a lone person in front of the car. He appeared disheveled; his hair was tangled, his clothes ragged and worn, his skin the sallow color of malnourishment. He walked across the otherwise deserted street, in no apparent hurry. Clearly, he was a Sinister. But what was he doing here in the Flats?

He held something in his hand, something large, rectangular and red. Then he threw it.

The brick arced through the air and exploded against the reinforced glass of the car, leaving nothing but a small, red dust mark on the windshield.

The Sinister let out a yell of frustration that even the electronically silenced cabin couldn't suppress. He pointed at the buildings to his right and continued to yell, but his words didn't reach our ears. Freddy tried to maneuver away from the man, but he moved to block our path. He pointed again, and this time I followed his gesture. A graffiti message marred the walls of the nearest building.

"Nobles are the problem. Sinisters will rise."

Freddy rolled down his window and pulled out his concealed stunner.

"Move or I'll shoot."

The man paused. His face contorted, showing deeper lines of anger than before. His words grated through the window like a rusty hinge. "You Nobles think you're so much better. You oppress us! You'll get what's coming to you. I guarantee it!"

Freddy eased the car to the left, and this time the man didn't move, so Freddy closed the window and sheathed his stunner.

Alex climbed back into his seat and decided to buckle himself in.

Grandfather poked his head back through the open partition. "Everyone okay back there?"

I nodded and Alex grunted in the affirmative as he tried in vain to straighten out his trench coat.

"I know not all Sinisters are bad," I thought aloud. "But some are. Wouldn't it just be better if people like that guy weren't around?"

"Remember, Victor," Grandfather said, the wrinkle lines on his forehead becoming more pronounced as he spoke, "not all Sinisters are like the man we just saw."

"But some *are*," I replied.

"And don't they deserve second chances?"

"Maybe some do," I said. "But there are definitely some who don't."

Grandfather frowned, studying me for a moment before turning back to the front of the car.

I knew the reason for his frown: the Pendletons. But nothing I had said was wrong. In fact, most Nobles would agree with what I said, especially in *their* case.

The Pendletons had been a high-profile family. All of their DNA registered in the nineties. Augustine Pendleton had been a senator, a member of the governing body of the city. He and his wife, Patricia, had been like second parents to me when I was younger. And then there was their daughter, Daphne.

I could still picture her in my mind: thirteen years old, long dark hair, extremely talented, maybe my equal in the saber fights. She had been my good friend, maybe my best friend. But that was four years ago.

One day, the Pendleton's DNA scans started registering them as Sinisters, and soon afterwards, a government investigation exposed the Pendletons as frauds. News stories ran for months. "Prominent Noble family is actually Sinister." "From Nineties to Nobodies."

In my mind's eye, I could still see Daphne with tears running down her face, screaming that it wasn't true. Her family had tried to fight it, saying there had been an error in the system, but it was no use. You can't hide who you really are. The truth always comes out.

Their whole family had been immediately exiled to the Heights, and there they had remained. Mrs. Pendleton passed away after the first year. Grandfather had gone to the funeral, but I didn't think I could handle it. I had been too angry. I was still too angry.

I shook my head, trying to force the memories out of my mind, but much like an old scar, they couldn't be forgotten.

Yes, some Sinisters *did* deserve second chances, but the Pendletons weren't among them.

"Victor, you all right over there?" Alex asked.

"Fine." I continued to stare out the window for another moment before turning to face him.

"Oh, I gotcha." Alex nodded knowingly. "Not looking forward to being up on stage with Jeffry's dad. I hear ya. I hate when my dad speaks and he wants me up there."

"Yeah," I said, bringing my mind back to the present, "I won't be able to get my usual nap in."

"No, you won't," Grandfather said. "And the time for napping has passed. We're here."

4

Our black car pulled up to the entrance of the Capital district. Unlike in other parts of the city, ours was not the only car on the road. Half a dozen were lined up with us to go through the checkpoint.

"Windows down," Freddy said as we pulled up.

The electric motors whirred as the windows slid down into the door panels.

Two men and two women approached the car, DNA scanners in hand. They all wore standard government uniforms, white clothes with blue piping and helmets with mirrored visors.

Grandfather frowned at the scanners. He'd never cared much for the scans, even though his DNA ranked exceptionally high on the Noble scale.

I didn't mind them. Grandfather said that the old scanners pricked your finger or palm, but the current ones could read the DNA in your blood through your skin.

Plus, if your Noble percentage was high enough, you could expect a little preferential treatment.

"ID card," the man at my window said. A similar request was made to Alex, Freddy and Grandfather in turn.

I fished out the thin piece of plastic and handed it through the window.

"Thank you."

The Capital district was one of the few places that Sinisters weren't allowed to go. Everywhere else, there were no restrictions. Not that they liked to spend much time in the Flats, but you had to agree with Dr. Rosewood. Safety in order.

"Your hand, please."

My arm had finally regained feeling. I stuck it out the window, placing my hand on the thin screen in the officer's hands. Immediately, an outline appeared, snaking its way around each of my fingers. A series of attributes and characteristics appeared adjacent to the handprint. *Intelligent, brave, athletic, strong-willed, decisive.* The information DNA held, the information Dr. Rosewood had been able to glean from it, was incredible.

At the top right corner, a small circle began to fill up, but stopped just short of completion. The screen emitted a faint green glow.

"Ninety-two percent? Looks like we've got a future leader on our hands."

"We'll see." I gave the officer a practiced smile.

Those words had become a common remark, and my response was the same every time. Ever since I was little, I'd been told I was destined for something more than saber fights. But I wasn't sure. Unlike my parents and grandfather, I didn't see the appeal of the senate. And I definitely didn't see the appeal of being president.

I glanced across the car at Alex. The government worker on his side of the car seemed a bit flustered. Alex had decided to put his mask back on before having his DNA scanned. I smiled to myself and looked back out my own window as the officer retreated

Alex's DNA registered about as high as mine did, yet his actions and mannerisms were suggestive of someone slightly less refined, or perhaps just more rebellious, than the scanner indicated. But his refined side was in there somewhere.

"Victor."

Alex's whisper caught me off guard. As did his proximity. I found myself almost face-to-face with him.

"Why are you whispering?" I asked.

Alex nodded to the front of the car. Freddy had left the partition down.

"Do you think they'll talk about the war front tonight?" he said.

Ah, the war front. Hence the whispering.

"No idea. I still don't know what's going on tonight. Do you?"

"Something important, a big announcement or a debate or something." Alex waved a hand dismissively. "But I mean, the Experiment's almost up. Just a couple of months left, right? Maybe they're starting to decide what they're going to do with the city. What do you think? Stick with the Noble-Sinister model or start all over?"

"I don't know," I said. "Things seem to be working pretty well so far."

"I think they should trash it," Alex said.

"Seriously? They say things are safer than they've ever been."

"Yeah, but it'd be fun to start over, right? New rules, new laws. Maybe I'd finally be able to order more than two dozen donuts at one time."

"You can eat twenty-four donuts in a sitting?" I asked, raising an eyebrow.

Alex smiled. "Come on man, have you seen the donuts I get? Of course I could." His face turned serious. "But think about it—what if the Heights weren't off-limits at night? What if the Heights were safe? That's like half the city that we've never set foot in. A new set of rules would be awesome."

I disagreed. Until Dr. Rosewood figured out how to change people's genomes so that everyone was Noble, I was content having the Sinisters stay right where they were.

I looked back out the window. Off to the right sat the second-tallest building in the area, a government building known as the Ixlir Building, named after one of Dr. Rosewood's early colleagues. Most people called it "the meeting place." I knew senators spent a good deal of time there because it was there that government officials and other prominent members of society would meet to discuss important issues. Some said it was the most important place in the Capital. And at five stories tall, it dwarfed most of the other buildings in the area. However, it looked minuscule compared to the building several blocks over.

I leaned back in my seat and looked up through the glass roof of the car. Dr. Rosewood's research tower shot through the sky like a tall, skinny mountain of steel and glass. It was the one building in the area that resembled the architecture of the Heights. Fifty stories tall and containing multiple research labs, it was there that Dr. Rosewood spent her days doing what some thought was the most important work that had ever been done.

But apparently, not everyone agreed, and that brought conflict, within the city and beyond it. Neighboring cities that weren't part of the Experiment wanted to intervene. More than once, a nearby city had laid siege near the border. The most recent war had been going on for over a year. We kept them at bay, but I wasn't sure how. Freddy had some experience there but didn't like to talk about it, so most everything I knew about the war front came from Alex, and I was pretty sure what he said was about as reliable as his idea that the Bounty Hunter could fly.

The research building disappeared from view, blocked by an immaculately decorated building adorned with lights and crowded with the colorful outfits of the Nobles who would be in attendance tonight.

"Here we are," came Freddy's voice from up front. The car slowed to a stop.

Four women dressed in floor-length blue gowns approached the car. Apparently, this was a bit more formal than I was expecting. Each woman placed a hand on one of the car's windows. I could just see the faint outline snaking its way around the handprint of the hostess at my window. A list of words appeared, backwards to my eyes. The standard faint green glow emitted from my window and the doors opened.

I reached for the bag containing my suit and allowed the woman to escort me through a sea of people toward the building that housed the auditorium. The woman who escorted Freddy brushed past me, heading for another group of people who had just arrived. Up ahead, Freddy stood alone, taking in his surroundings while periodically checking my and Grandfather's positions. As was often the case, Freddy was here in bodyguard capacity only tonight.

He was a good man, a friend, but I wished he'd be a little more lax with his responsibilities. However, a brief survey of the crowd showed no fewer than a dozen people like Freddy—men built like boulders and trained in military fashion. I always found the enhanced security here odd. There would be no Sinisters to contend with. Only the best of what society had to offer would be in attendance. And wasn't that the ultimate point of the Experiment, to take away the need for security?

I took a step forward but paused, noticing the absence of my trench-coated friend.

"Where'd he go?" I muttered. He didn't need babysitting, but I wouldn't put it past him to make a run for it. I sometimes wished I had his disregard for the expectations of others.

I looked around and found him without much trouble. Alex still stood next to the car. It looked like the woman who had opened his door was refusing to show him inside until he removed his mask. Stifling a smile, I caught his eye and begrudgingly, he complied.

A few familiar faces stood out in the crowd of people. I supplied hurried greetings to friends and acquaintances as my hostess guided me inside to a changing room.

I emerged a few minutes later, my street clothes exchanged for a crisp, silver suit, a pressed white shirt, and a red vest. The hostess took the suit bag now filled with my jeans and a T-shirt and left me to wander around until the event started. I searched the crowd, looking for Freddy. I found him inhabiting the most strategic position, equidistant between me and Grandfather with his back to a wall and his eyes on the exits. I started toward him, but was intercepted by the rustling of a trench coat.

"I just heard he's going to be here!" Alex said.

"Who?" I queried.

"Kratos! Oh man, I hope I get to meet him! Will it be weird if we're wearing the exact same outfit?"

"Um, I—"

"Alex!" someone called out.

We both looked for the source. A portly man with graying hair and a large mustache stood across the hall, holding a suit bag. It was Senator Trabue, Alex's father.

"Well, crap," Alex said, looking crestfallen. "I was hoping he'd forget that I was supposed to be here tonight, like last time. That was much better."

Senator Trabue motioned Alex over, and Alex reluctantly shuffled toward his father. Alex's dad was a good man and very Noble. He worked harder than any other senator I knew of, but that also meant he didn't have a lot of time for Alex. Sometimes Alex would go over a week without seeing or talking to him. I missed my parents terribly, but to have them alive yet absent all the time would be torture. Maybe that's why Alex was out Following today.

Begrudgingly, Alex went off to change clothes, and I took a spot next to Freddy along the wall.

"Senator Supart asked me to be here tonight, so here I am," I said. "And you know this never happens to me," Freddy gave me a sidelong glance, "but I'm not sure exactly what kind of event this is." Freddy shook his head and smirked. This happened all the time. I continued. "Alex says it's debate or a big announcement or something. Care to fill me in?" I looked up at him with a smile.

Freddy was ex-military. He'd had spent years in his previous line of work as a go-between for the Flats and the city to the south called Ville, a kind of neutral pseudo ally, but he'd also spent some time at the war front. What his job entailed was a mystery, and despite years of prodding, I hadn't found out any of the specifics.

"This is a political event," Freddy replied evenly.

"And here I was thinking Senator Supart was inviting me to a really fancy saber tournament," I said.

Freddy didn't react.

"But it's more than a simple political event," I continued. "The clothes." I gestured to my silver suit, white shirt, and red vest. "The decorations." I pointed to the brightly lit room in which we stood. A lush crimson rug covered the white marble floor, the light fixtures were encased in various combinations of semi-transparent porcelain and gold, and dozens of bouquets adorned the room. "Everything points to something special," I said. "I heard something about an announcement or a debate?"

"Yes."

"Yes?"

"Indeed."

"You know, Freddy, I sometimes wonder where you learned your incredible conversation skills," I said, eyeing him.

"Military."

"Uh-huh. Did your training involve limiting your sentences to five words or less?"

"No, it involved self-control." The corner of his lips twitched.

"Well, I'll send Alex over after I tell him you're on a first-name basis with the Bounty Hunter. Good luck stonewalling that."

"I'll wait for him here," Freddy replied, unconcerned.

"Contractions count as two words."

"That's good to know."

I laughed as I walked off. Freddy and I often had these little contests, especially at gatherings like this. Time passed more quickly that way.

Ahead of me, there was a disturbance in the crowd. Silence spread across the room like a power outage. The crowd parted, and for a fleeting second, I thought Alex had returned still wearing his trench coat. But it wasn't Alex. The man was too tall, too confident, and too cold to be Alex. This was the man Alex Followed. This was the real Bounty Hunter.

The whole room watched in uncomfortable silence as he strode through, never stopping, never making eye contact. The tension grew with each footstep until he finally disappeared through the guarded doors at the end of the large gathering hall. The moment the door closed, the hall erupted in chatter. It was rare for the Bounty Hunter, I mean Kratos, to attend an event like this.

If Kratos was here, tonight must actually be important, unlike most of the events we went to. And since Freddy was being his usual tight-lipped self, Grandfather would have to be the one to fill me in.

He stood along the opposite wall talking to a man I didn't know. I waded through the sea of suits and ball gowns, catching snippets of speculative conversation. Apparently I wasn't the only one who didn't know the nature of tonight's event.

I stopped short of Grandfather, not wanting to interrupt the ongoing conversation.

"... for the good of the public at large. Our friends to the south—"

"A rather generous descriptor of the leadership of Ville, don't you think?" Grandfather said.

"They could be great allies, Ulysses! Should the need ever arise—"

"If luck prevails, the need never will."

"I'm not sure it's wise to trust in luck," the other man said, "especially with people like Mr. Kane running around the Heights. Some in the senate believe he is part of the Sinistrali. He may even—"

Grandfather held up a hand.

"Julius, you know my thoughts on the subject."

A hand closed on my shoulder and I turned to see Senator Avardi Supart, strawberry-haired and freckled, standing beside me.

"Ulysses! Victor! I was hoping I'd find you here," he said with a smile on his face. "Thanks for being early."

Grandfather turned and, catching sight of the two of us, smiled warmly and extended a hand.

"Avardi," Grandfather said. "The man of the hour. How are you, my friend?"

The man with whom Grandfather had been conversing gave a polite nod and excused himself.

"I apologize for interrupting your conversation," Avardi said as he shook Grandfather's hand.

"Not a problem. Julius was trying, as usual, to convince me of some of his ideas. But tell me, Avardi, how are you? The rumors say the debate between you and Dr. Rosewood promises to be quite a show."

So that's what was going on tonight, a debate. I didn't envy Avardi for a second. While Dr. Rosewood was extremely important, she didn't have a reputation for warmth. Those graffiti-covered billboards in the Heights weren't completely inaccurate.

"We'll see," Avardi replied. "It's more for the president's benefit than anything else. The Great Experiment is coming to a close. He wants to hear the arguments and judge the pulse of the people before coming to a decision."

"Ah, of course," Grandfather said. "A wise man, President Keltan."

"Agreed." Avardi nodded. "But enough about that." He turned to me. "I heard about your victory over Gio today." He pulled me into a one-armed hug and ruffled my hair. It'd been this way for years. I'd learned to stop struggling and just let it happen. "Congratulations!" he said. "The perfect record is still intact."

"Thanks," I muttered, taking a step back and doing my best to flatten my hair.

"Now, I know he's a couple of years younger than you," Avardi said, "but watch out. Jeffry's been practicing."

"I'm going to have to watch out if he keeps growing," I said. I'd seen a few of his fights. He wasn't half bad. And at thirteen, Avardi's son already matched me in size and weight.

"Lora and I are going to have to watch our grocery bill," he said with a chuckle as he checked his watch. "Oh, it looks like it's time for me to go. But before I do"—he leaned in close—"I've got something to give you after I get done speaking tonight."

"Like, in front of everyone?" I asked.

"Oh no, in private." He gave me a reassuring smile. "Grab me afterwards. It's important, so don't forget, okay?"

"You got it," I said, a little perplexed. He'd never done anything like that before.

"Great." He turned to Grandfather. "Ulysses, always good to see you. We'll talk after the event?"

"As always, my friend. We'll see you inside."

With a nod, Senator Supart made his way toward the doors at the end of the hall.

5

"And now, ladies and gentlemen, for tonight's debate, we are pleased to welcome Senator Avardi Supart." The announcer paused as polite applause rang through the packed auditorium and Avardi stepped up to his podium. As the applause died down, the announcer continued. "And the esteemed Dr. Victoria Rosewood."

The crowd erupted. Dr. Rosewood entered the stage from my left. I had never been this close to her before. Nearly a hundred years old and she looked like she was thirty. She strode up to her podium dressed completely in white, appearing almost angelic. And to most of our city, she was.

The lights of the auditorium dimmed and zeroed in on the senator and Dr. Rosewood. Their faces appeared on the huge screens that covered the walls of the room. Dr. Rosewood was statuesque, no perspiration, no wrinkles, her lips pressed together in a soft smile. Avardi looked less comfortable, sweat already beading on his face.

"And finally," the announcer finished, "it is my great pleasure to introduce our moderator for the night, our very own President Grayson Keltan."

A spotlight illuminated the front row, directly in front of the two podiums. The most powerful man in the city appeared beneath the light, silver hair glinting and white teeth shining as he smiled and waved amid unanimous applause. He was well liked and respected. People from all sides of the political spectrum spoke highly of him, including Grandfather.

"Thank you both for being here tonight," President Keltan's warm voice boomed over the speakers. "As you know, we've gathered to hear your arguments about the permanence of the Great Experiment. One for"—he motioned to Dr. Rosewood—"and one against." He gestured to Avardi.

All the movement and talking in the auditorium ceased, everyone's rapt attention on the podiums. The Experiment would soon come to an end, and President Keltan would have to make a decision.

From what I knew, the Great Experiment worked. The goal was safety. Safety in order. Rosewood had achieved that. And compared to all other cities, ours was the safest and the most stable. Yeah, I wished it was a little more favorable toward the Sinisters—well, some Sinisters—but there seemed to be little reason not to adopt the Noble-Sinister division permanently. What else could you say about it? Facts were facts.

I looked at the back of Avardi's thinning red hair and Dr. Rosewood's carefully manicured image as President Keltan continued talking. I tried to settle myself a little deeper into my seat. This was going to be a long night.

"And now for the arguments," President Keltan was saying. "Senator Supart, we'll start with you. After you've finished, Dr. Rosewood will have a chance to counter, and I'll ask any additional questions at the end as I see fit. Senator Supart."

The large screens in the room filled with Avardi's face.

"Thank you, Mr. President, and good evening," Avardi said. He then looked out over the audience. "We've all benefited from the Great Experiment." He nodded to Dr. Rosewood. "The Flats are safe, our children are safe, but in this system..." He paused. "In this system, safety will not last."

Boos resonated throughout the auditorium. I sat up a little

straighter in my chair. Maybe tonight would be more interesting than I thought.

Dr. Rosewood held up a long-fingered hand. The boos died.

"Let him speak. He will say his piece, and I mine." She turned to look at the senator. "Please, continue."

Senator Support gave a surprised nod and continued.

"Thank you, Dr. Rosewood." He nodded in appreciation before turning back to the dimly lit audience. "We are endangered both from the outside and from within. Neighboring cities threaten us with war because of what we've done in the name of safety. The Heights are full of Sinisters who are tired of feeling oppressed and second rate. We can't hold off our neighbors forever, and if a substantial part of our population revolts, safety will cease."

His words were met with silence. Avardi was a good man with a good family, but his views were unpopular. How could he think giving up on the Experiment was a good thing? It would sacrifice our security. What would he propose, that we just let the Sinisters wander around unrestricted, free to do whatever they wanted? Sure, some would be fine and no harm would come of it. But what about people like the Pendletons? Augustine had been a senator. A senator! He had infiltrated our government, and if that happened on a larger scale, no one would be safe.

Avardi continued to speak.

More boos issued from the crowd.

Rosewood didn't intervene again, but instead stood politely by, waiting her turn. Avardi's tone had changed, his words coming faster. It happened every time Grandfather and I had dinner with the Supart family. Avardi was just getting started, and I'd probably heard it all before.

I tried to get a little more comfortable as I changed my focus to the audience and peered out into the darkness. Alex was out there somewhere, probably eating a box of donuts or sleeping. Oh, how I envied him.

A smattering of applause issued from the crowd. A moment or two late, I joined in and looked back to the dual podiums. In my periphery, I caught sight of Freddy standing just off stage. His eyes narrowed slightly. With two fingers, he pointed at his eyes and then pointed at Avardi. I turned my attention back to the front, lest Freddy have a reason to say more than five words to me later.

"Thank you, Senator," President Keltan said. "Dr. Rosewood, the floor is yours."

I perked up, as did the rest of the audience. How would she respond?

"We all appreciate your impassioned words," Dr. Rosewood started. "Your contributions to this city have not gone unnoticed." She lifted her hands and started a polite applause that rippled through the crowd. "That being said," she continued as the clapping died out, "you misunderstand the scope of the Great Experiment. Crime in our city has dropped dramatically since I started the Experiment fifty years ago. Murder has been eliminated in the Flats. The—"

A renewal of applause cut her off. She smiled, an expression not often seen on her billboards, and looked down at her podium until the clapping died out.

"The Flats is, statistically speaking, the safest city to live in. And that will not change."

More applause.

"This city's senate is responsible for placating any who come against us, but we must be strong from within. Imagine a city where all people are Nobles. In the future, that city exists. Look how far we've come since the beginning of the Great Experiment! Look at how much more we know. Over the next fifty years, that knowledge will only grow. I believe that I will be able to change genetic makeup, even after birth. A Sinister will become a Noble, and once that is reality, safety will truly reign."

Cheers and clapping, yelling and whistling filled the air. I couldn't help but join in. What she was saying was unprecedented. The auditorium became so loud I almost couldn't hear my own clapping.

Dr. Rosewood held up her hands to quiet the audience.

"But it is up to you to decide," she said over a few scattered claps. "As a scientist, I am here to present facts. In one months' time, a vote will be held to determine our fates. My hope is that we do what is best for our children and our children's children. Thank you."

With a wave, she stepped away from her podium and made to leave the stage amid tumultuous applause. Without a backward glance, she disappeared from view.

President Keltan waited for the noise to die down before speaking.

"Another warm round of applause for Dr. Rosewood and Senator Supart," he said, putting his hands together as the audience joined in. "Thank you both for your words. The decision before us is one of great weight, something that will impact our lives for generations. I do not take this matter lightly. Thank you once again for your confidence and trust."

President Keltan paused as the applause rose again.

"I was notified several minutes ago," he continued, "that Dr. Rosewood had something to attend to in her lab and would not be able to stay for questions. This being the case, Senator Supart has some closing remarks on behalf of the senate which he has told me are unrelated, but of the utmost importance."

There's more? The mood in the auditorium immediately became restless. I slumped back down into my chair, only to receive another stiff glance from Freddy. I straightened up and looked to Avardi, the back of his neck drenched in sweat. Poor guy. People would be talking about what Dr. Rosewood said for weeks.

"Thank you all for your time this evening. As is customary at these meetings, I have a few things to share on behalf of the senate before we end the night, as well as an announcement."

Great. I stared out over the audience. Anytime someone shared something on behalf of the senate, it was bound to be boring and long-winded.

I looked up to the ceiling. It was my favorite pastime in these types of meetings. Nothing helped me go to sleep better than a couple minutes of staring up at the ceiling.

It had been adorned with several peculiar patterns, most of them geometric in nature. Sharp, colorful lines crisscrossed and made angles, each line constructing a dynamic piece of the larger overall artwork. Closer to the stage, the pattern became more detailed. Starting at the back, I looked over each section until I was almost looking straight up. The patterns were pretty cool. Far more interesting than listening to the business of the senate anyway. Although…

I tuned in to see if he'd moved on to anything exciting.

"… 22.3 percent of senators voted to…"

Nope. I tuned back out.

The pattern that covered the ceiling directly above the stage was the most intriguing. It was a series of intricate circles that all came to a point immediately above center stage. It was flawless, except for what looked like the almost finished form of a square that intersected several of the most centrally placed circles. The four lines, one of which didn't quite connect to the others on one end, weren't like the other lines that covered the ceiling. These were thicker and more rugged than the rest. I wouldn't consider myself an art expert, but the thick, dark lines seemed to ruin the display of color.

Suddenly, before my eyes, the almost-square started to close itself, the fourth line growing longer on its short end. I blinked. It had to be an illusion. I pulled my eyes away from the ceiling and looked at the ground, massaging the stiff spot in my neck for a moment before returning my gaze upwards.

The line continued to grow.

"But tonight, there is another matter that we must address." Avardi's voice took on a stronger tone. The background sounds of people coughing and shifting in their seats stopped.

It really is moving, I thought to myself. The black lines seemed to have depth. A flurry of white flecks danced across the lights of the stage just below the square. Dust. Dust coming from the black lines.

They weren't the lines drawn *on* the ceiling.

They were cuts *in* the ceiling.

And the final cut was reaching its end. A perfect square.

"Tonight, we must talk about a group that has been dormant for several years now. We must talk about the Left Hand."

You could have heard a pin drop, but I barely noticed. I kept my eyes fixed on the ceiling. The cut moved steadily. Mere inches remained. I looked from the almost-square in the ceiling and drew a mental line straight down.

Avardi. He was directly underneath it.

Two inches remained.

I looked around. Someone had to have noticed.

I couldn't get Freddy's attention.

"For many, if not all, this will be a difficult truth," Avardi continued.

One inch remained.

Out of all the times for Freddy to not be watching!

The square closed.

6

I leapt out of my seat, adrenaline fueling my movements. The ceiling let out a mighty groan as the giant slab of cement and plaster fell from its place. I dove, colliding with the senator, and we both flew away from the podium.

The slab exploded on contact, crushing the podium under its weight. A barrage of plaster dust, cement rocks, and wooden splinters ricocheted into the crowd. Pieces of debris pelted my back and legs like a swarm of bees on a rampage.

Panic ensued. Screams filled the air. Hundreds of people scattered.

I remained where I was, mentally checking myself for any serious injuries. Incredibly, I was okay. And if I was okay, then Avardi should be too.

"Avardi!" I rolled off of him and pushed him onto his side. His body was stiff and his eyes were wide. I grabbed his shoulder. "Are you okay?"

He said nothing.

"Are you hurt?" I asked.

He shook his head, his face almost as white as Dr. Rosewood's outfit. Was he in shock? I quickly checked him out. No blood. He was breathing. He'd be okay.

I picked myself up and looked to where the podium had once stood.

Now it was a pile of rubble.

"Avardi," I said firmly, "are you all right? Can you stand?"

He ignored me, and instead pointed at the remains of the podium. It looked as if he were trying to say something, but he couldn't seem to get it out.

"Yes, I know, it fell," I said, motioning to the ceiling. "We need to get you out of here."

I extended my arm.

He ignored it, continuing to stare and point at what was once his podium.

The hole in the ceiling gaped open above us like a foreboding cloud. Plaster dust hung in the air, irritating my throat. I coughed, trying to clear it. My mind filled with questions. Who would do this? Who would attack Nobles? Who would attack Avardi? There was no way Sinisters could get in here, was there?

I stumbled forward as Avardi suddenly accepted my outstretched arm, grabbing the corner of my jacket to stabilize himself.

I turned to face him. "Are you okay?"

"The office!" he said, staring intently into my eyes. "Go to the office!"

"What?" I said. "The office? I don't understand."

Had he hit his head when I tackled him?

He didn't respond, and turned away from me. He had to be in shock. He wasn't making any sense. I kept an eye on him as I looked around for Grandfather and Freddy. Twenty feet away, Freddy was fighting his way against the flow of hysteria toward us. I couldn't see Grandfather. Freddy pushed his way through the last couple of people, relief registering on his hard face as he saw both of us on our feet.

"Are you hurt?" he said, placing two meaty hands on my shoulders.

"I'm fine," I said, "but Avardi needs help. He sounds like he's in shock.'"

Avardi had wandered over to what was left of the podium. He stood there, almost like he was lost, staring at the debris.

"He'll be okay in an hour or two," Freddy said. "Any injuries?"

I could only imagine he'd seen things like this before. I dusted some bits of plaster off my jacket.

"Maybe a few bruises," I said, "but nothing serious."

I looked up at the giant projection screen. The camera hadn't been turned off and was still recording, sending the scene out live to many of the Nobles who weren't in attendance.

"Victor! Avardi!" Grandfather shouted, making his way through the dust and debris. We rushed over to meet him.

"Everyone's fine, Mr. Wells," Freddy said as Grandfather neared. "The senator appears to be in shock." He nodded toward Avardi, who had remained where he was with a semi-blank look on his face.

Grandfather thanked Freddy. "I'm sure police and a medical team are on their way," he said before wrapping me in a hug. "Are you okay, Victor?"

"Yeah," I said, "but who would do this?"

Grandfather coughed in the haze. "I don't know, son," he said, surveying the wreckage.

Avardi took a few tentative steps toward the crushed podium. He looked up into the black void above. I followed his gaze and started. I could have sworn something moved. Avardi didn't seem to notice and returned his gaze to the ground, taking a few steps backwards.

"Did you see that?" I pointed.

"See what?" Freddy said, following my finger.

Just then, a silver sphere fell from the void, landing with a metallic clink on the remains of the podium. We all watched as it bounced down the pile of rubble, coming to a stop on the dust-covered wood of the stage.

The ball was about ten inches in diameter and was made up of several individual pieces of metal that had been fused together, like swatches of fabric on an old-fashioned soccer ball. The silver sphere spun slowly in place, almost like it was looking for something.

Then it started rolling.

Avardi stood fifteen feet way, oblivious. The ball rolled straight for him, but stopped five feet short.

"Senator!" Freddy yelled, rushing toward him. But Avardi didn't seem to hear him.

A plate on the front of the ball slid open. Freddy froze mid-step.

"Senator!" he yelled again. "Run!"

But the senator didn't run. Instead, he turned toward us, finally catching sight of the metal ball.

A thick, black material shot from the ball and caught Avardi in the chest, throwing him backwards. He screamed in pain, smoke issuing from his body as he fell to the ground.

Finally, a group of police officers appeared at the far end of the stage.

"Officers!" Grandfather yelled, motioning to them. "Senator Supart has been injured!"

Then the silver ball exploded. Shrapnel flew through the air. Grandfather cried out, and I turned to see him cover a gash on his cheek, a few drops of blood falling onto the wooden floor of the stage. Freddy rushed over to help, but Grandfather waved him away.

"I'm fine! See to Avardi!"

Freddy changed directions, running over to Avardi's writhing body. He moaned, his fists clenching, his legs kicking, trying to outrun the pain. I knelt beside him. The officers rushed toward us. The front of Avardi's suit had been mostly burned away, the skin underneath already erupting in horrible red boils.

"Acid," Freddy muttered under his breath. "Victor," he said, tearing away the remains of the senator's ruined shirt, "there is a container of water off the side of the stage. Bring it. Quickly."

I dashed off, passing a few policemen on my way. I found a large jug and grabbed a passing officer to help me carry it back.

"Get a medic over here now," Freddy said to the officer, unstopping the jug as he gave the flustered man orders. The white-faced policeman ran off as Freddy poured a liberal stream of water onto Avardi's heaving chest. The senator arched his back in pain, but then relaxed, welcoming the cool water on his skin.

I stepped back as the medical team finally arrived.

"Rest, Senator," Freddy said, a hand of restraint on Avardi's shoulder. He set the water jug down as a medic removed the rest of the senator's shirt and jacket. The nearest officer gasped. Grandfather let out a low moan.

"What is it?" I tried to peer around the group of people huddled over Avardi, but couldn't get a close look.

"He'll be dead in a week," Freddy said.

"From acid burns?" I asked in shock.

"No." Grandfather stood up and ran his hand through his white hair, giving me a clearer view of Avardi's chest. "No, not from acid burns."

The burns weren't random. They formed a pattern, or rather, a symbol. Two concentric circles enclosed by what was clearly the form of a hand. I gasped. I knew what that was. Everyone knew what that was.

"The Left Hand." Freddy shook his head. "Poor sap. Nothing we can do for him now."

The Left Hand was a terrorist group that had formed a few years after the Great Experiment started. Their actions were sporadic, random, and seemingly motiveless. Nobles were targeted exclusively. Several people had been killed over the years, mostly politicians, some scientists. The Left Hand had taken responsibility for all of them.

The last attack had been over ten years ago, but I still remembered the frenzy it caused, even as a child. If I remembered right, Dr. Rosewood had been injured, and one of her research partners had been killed. She had never been a primary target. However, if past victims were any indicator, her time was limited.

Sweat covered Avardi's forehead. He let out a moan. The medical team worked quickly to dress Avardi's wounds and covered the symbol in a transparent paste. Finally, Avardi's legs stopped kicking, and his body relaxed.

Grandfather grabbed me by the arm and pulled me backwards.

"Let them work, son. There's nothing we can do for him now."

I couldn't tear my eyes away from his chest. The burns, the pain, the symbol. Less than a week to live.

"Why would this happen?" I asked. "Why him?"

Tears stung my eyes.

"I don't know," Grandfather said. He took a short breath, like he was about to start talking, but instead he merely exhaled and shook his head.

I glanced at Avardi, his eyes shut tight in pain.

His wife was about to become a widow, and his son was about to become fatherless.

"What if he left the city?" I said. "I mean, there's got to be a way to save him, right?"

"I don't know," Grandfather said wistfully. "No one has ever survived a Marking, and I don't know if being outside the city is any safer than being inside it. War and anarchy is no place for a family."

"What about the city to the south? What about Ville?" I asked. "They don't have the same system we do, but—"

Grandfather cut me off.

"I don't think that is such a good idea either," he said. "The leadership of Ville says they are neutral, but I don't know how kindly they'd take to bringing a Marked man into their city. Besides, put yourself in his shoes. Wouldn't you want to spend as much time with your family as possible? You, more than most, know how important that is."

I didn't answer. I did know. What I wouldn't give for just one more day with my parents. But running and living was better than giving up, wasn't it?

A figure approached, his black trench coat swishing as he walked over and knelt next to Avardi. Kratos's cold eyes swept over Avardi's body, unfeeling and calculating.

"You," he said, pointing at the nearest officer, "document the man's injury." The officer nearly tripped in his haste to follow orders.

A more seasoned officer appeared. "Everyone, please remove yourselves from the crime scene. I've been told that's the Left Hand's symbol, but let's not jump to conclusions or spread any rumors."

"I don't deal in rumors," Kratos said, looking between Avardi's body and the rubble pile. "This is the Left Hand." Silence settled over our group. The Bounty Hunter removed his gloves and began to pick through the debris.

"A silver ball, about ten inches in diameter, was dropped from the hole in the ceiling," Freddy said. "It Marked the senator."

Kratos looked to Freddy and acknowledged his words with a nod. He turned back to the pile of debris and spoke again. "Officer, escort these people outside."

7

The pressure on my shoulder increased as Freddy slowed our pace. We hadn't quite reached the street, and it didn't look like we were going to. Cameras and flashing lights surrounded us. Freddy attempted to clear the way, but fought in vain to stop the swarm of reporters.

My mind swam with images of the senator's branded body. How could this happen? Had a contingent of Sinistrali really made it inside the Capital? As far as I knew, no Sinister had ever set foot inside the Capital before tonight, yet somehow the Left Hand's minions had bypassed all the scanners, all the security, and had enough time to cut a hole in the ceiling. Historically, they had a flair for the dramatic, but this was something else. And why would they be after Avardi?

Despite Freddy's protests, the media pressed around us, microphones in hand, questions at the ready.

"Mr. Wells! Mr. Wells! How do you feel about your grandson saving the senator's life?"

"Victor! You're a hero! What's going through your mind?"

"How did you know the ceiling would fall like that?"

After a few more moments of halting progress, Freddy caved.

With a sigh, he let go of my shoulder and brought the three of us to a halt.

"Mr. Wells, how did you know an attempt would be made on the senator's life tonight?"

I stared down my nose at the end of a microphone.

"Keep it short," Freddy whispered before walking past the reporters to retrieve our car. Grandfather stepped backwards, giving me complete freedom. The gathering of reporters waited expectantly.

What do I say? My heart was still pounding from the adrenaline. I was sure I was covered in plaster dust and bits of debris. But I was just as much in shock as everyone else. The Left Hand was back.

"Mr. Wells?"

Grandfather nodded encouragingly.

"Oh, yeah," I said. Another handful of microphones appeared next to my face. I took a breath and began from the start. I told them about the crack in the ceiling, how it moved, how nobody noticed. The questions kept coming.

"Why tackle the senator off the stage? Why not yell instead?"

"I didn't really think about it." I shrugged. "I just tried to do something before it was too late."

"Was the symbol of the Left Hand branded on the Senator's chest, or is that just speculation?" one of the reporters asked.

"It—"

A scream cut through the crowd. More followed. In unison with the cameras that surrounded me, I looked for the source. I caught sight of Freddy running toward me, leaving our car with the trunk open. Fifty feet in front of me, the crowd parted like an invisible force was throwing them aside. People fled in opposite directions. In their wake rolled a small steel ball.

It came straight toward us. The moment the reporters caught sight of it, they ran. Microphones dropped. Cameras were left behind.

A thought kept me from fleeing. *Someone else is about to be Marked.*

The image of Avardi writhing in pain flashed in my mind.

I looked around. Who could it be? They had to be close. All the reporters had scattered except one, but none of them would merit a

Marking anyway. There were no other politicians nearby. Except Grandfather.

The ball continued toward us.

I grabbed Grandfather's arm, dragging him out of the path of the metal sphere. The ball switched directions and followed us.

"Ulysses, Victor, over here!" Freddy's deep voice carried over the chaos like the warning sound of an approaching train. The ball rolled toward us, now only thirty feet away.

Freddy intercepted us, grabbing Grandfather and protecting his body like a human shield.

Freddy pushed me away. "Run to the car. Don't stop!"

I switched directions, pivoted hard, and ran the other way. I cast a glance over my shoulder. Freddy and Grandfather ran, but the metal sphere seemed to have disappeared.

Somewhere nearby, a woman screamed and pointed. I followed her outstretched finger. Fifteen feet away, the metal ball rolled across the pavement.

It was following *me*.

Shock flowed through me, stronger and more encompassing than a blow from an electrified saber. But I couldn't let it paralyze me. So I ran, zigzagging through the already panicked crowd. The ball followed my every move, forcing me back toward the buildings I had just come from.

The ball moved to my left. I ran right. Adrenaline surged in my veins, but I couldn't outrun it. I raced alongside a building, my heart thumping in my ears.

This couldn't be happening. It didn't feel real. It couldn't be real.

Up ahead, another wall blocked my path. I made to go right, but the steel ball blocked me, urging me forward. A wall to my left, a wall in front of me, and the steel ball to my right. Dread washed over me. It forced me onward, until the two walls came to a corner.

I was trapped.

I came to a painful stop, slamming my palms against the cool, smooth concrete walls. My lungs burned. My vision threatened to swim.

Why me? It didn't make sense.

I turned to face the steel ball as it rolled closer, finally coming to a stop ten feet away. I could make out Freddy in the periphery of my vision running and yelling.

"Don't stop! Keep moving!"

My face grew hot, the sickly feeling of terror washing over me like hot wax.

I bounded laterally, but the ball spun in place, matching each movement.

Behind the ball, Freddy sprinted toward me, jacket in hand.

A steel plate on the front of the ball slid open.

Freddy yelled again, but I didn't hear him. There was only the small dark opening on the ball. There was no escaping it.

Freddy threw his jacket with precision, smothering the ball just as acid erupted from the sphere. The front of the jacket disintegrated with a menacing hiss.

The sphere of steel looked dead. Relief flooded my body.

I couldn't believe it. The jacket had saved me. Freddy had saved me! I looked to him, the concern on his face turning slowly into a smile.

But then the ball rolled forward, and a new panel opened up. My heart skipped a beat. I closed my eyes and braced for impact. A few people nearby screamed...but nothing happened.

I opened my eyes and ran my hands over my chest, searching for the sting of acid. But there was none, and there didn't need to be. Acid wasn't the only way to Mark someone.

A symbol, a death sentence, covered my chest, painted by the light projecting from the metal ball at my feet. I stepped to the left and then to the right. The ball tracked my motion, keeping the Left Hand's symbol projected squarely on my chest. Two concentric circles enclosing a left hand.

I looked up to find half a dozen cameras focused on me, along with a small crowd of people. I made out Freddy's face in the gathering, along with Grandfather's, one twisted in anger, the other disfigured by sadness.

Freddy stepped forward, lifted a massive boot, and crushed the metal sphere. The light went out, but the cameras remained, as did the small crowd of people. Their faces registered both shock and sorrow.

The Left Hand had struck again.

8

I had been Marked.

I sat on the street curb watching people leave. The reporters had tried to resume their interviews, but after a broken camera and possibly a broken nose, courtesy of Freddy, they all backed off. Everyone was on edge. I heard at least one passerby say something about "leaving before a mass Marking occurred." Several people made hurried stops on their way out to express their condolences. Some I knew personally, others were acquaintances of Grandfather. It occurred to me that they were saying goodbye.

It was odd, to say the least. I was perfectly healthy, yet terminally ill. They all expected me to be dead within the week. Soon, Grandfather would be alone, having outlived his entire family.

I had been *Marked*. The word repeated through my mind like a chisel chipping away at my resolve.

I knew Grandfather was somewhere talking to the chief of police, organizing a contingent of officers for round-the-clock surveillance, but did it even matter? People before me had had security guards, and the Left Hand had gotten to them. No one had survived a Marking. It was a promise, and the Left Hand never broke their promise.

Avardi, and now me. We would both be dead before the week was through.

I ran my hands through my hair and let out a long, slow breath. *Why Mark me?* I wondered. It had to be a mistake. The steel ball had to have been meant for someone else. Someone important. Like Grandfather.

Immediately, I felt guilty.

I couldn't think like that. No one deserved to Marked. Maybe the Left Hand would retract it. Did they do that sort of thing? Or would they send their Sinistrali to kill me just to maintain their perfect record? And really, what was the life of one Noble kid worth to them?

A shadow fell over me, followed by a rustle of clothing and a grunt as Alex sat down next to me. He said nothing.

After several moments of silence I spoke.

"Thanks," I said.

"For what?" Alex asked.

"For being here. Even when we were younger, after my parents died, you were always here."

"Yeah, well you've always been one of those needy friends," he said flatly.

I couldn't help but smile. It was just like Alex to make light of something serious, but I needed him to know how much it meant to me.

"I've never known how to repay you," I started, "and—"

Alex held up a hand. "It's what friends do, right? You've been there for me too, remember? Like that one time Jessica Ketley walked into the boys' bathroom with an electrified saber while I was still in the stall. And you just happened to have your saber bag on you when you walked in. You remember that?"

I chuckled. That was one of the many tight spots Alex had somehow gotten himself into over the years.

"Still your best fight, in my opinion," Alex said. "But it looks like you've got company."

I turned to see Freddy approaching at a brisk pace.

"Alex." Freddy nodded. "Victor, there's one more person who wants to see you."

I really didn't think I could handle another pity-filled person saying goodbye. I started to object, but Freddy retreated without a word and was replaced a moment later by Jeffry Supart. His face was covered in brown freckles that matched his hair.

"Hey, Jeffry," Alex said.

He didn't respond. His eyes were red and puffy.

"Jeffry, I'm so sorry about your dad," I said, and despite my own situation, I meant it.

Jeffry opened his mouth to speak, but no words came out. Instead, he took a step forward and hugged me. "Thank you," he managed to mumble out. Then he stepped back, looking at the ground awkwardly. "Dad could have died tonight, but he didn't. At least now I've got a few more days with him. I'm sorry you got Marked too," he finished. I nodded and Jeffry retreated the way he had come.

I watched him go. I knew the pain Jeffry would soon be feeling. It had been five years since my parents were killed—a freak car accident at a Noble outreach site in the Heights. After their deaths, things were difficult, but I got through it. I was sure Jeffry would too.

Grandfather approached, a few policemen trailing behind him.

"Victor, we'll be heading home soon. I've arranged for a contingent of policemen to stake out our home tonight. The Supart family will be afforded the same care," he added. "Freddy, I'll need you to brief the police force on the layout and security measures of our residence. We'll be leaving in five minutes."

Five minutes later, I stood between Grandfather and Freddy in a circle of police officers.

"We've just received word from a group of our boys that the Wells residence is clear," the commander said. "Freddy, as ex-military and a trusted friend of the Wells family, you'll be assigned to Victor around the clock. We'll have a group of guys head over by train and another contingent of men follow you home in one of the cruisers. The house will be under round-the-clock surveillance, with group reports coming directly to me every hour." He paused to look at me, then locked eyes with Grandfather. "We'll do our best to keep your grandson safe, Mr. Wells. If the Left Hand really is back, maybe we can even catch a Sinistrali if they try anything."

"Your efforts are very much appreciated, Officer."

"Of course," the officer said. "Victor, in here, please."

The officer walked me over to our car. I placed a hand on the window. The customary trace outline appeared, scanning my DNA. I waited for the faint pulse of green and the click of the locking mechanism, but it never came. The space around my hand emitted a faint red glow with the reading, *Denied. Noble Access Only*.

"Must be a glitch," I said, lifting my hand off the window and replacing it.

The officer stood by wordlessly.

Again, a faint red pulse.

The officer grew impatient.

"Mr. Wells."

"Yes, Officer?"

Grandfather approached, and I placed my hand on the window again. Red light. I looked to the circle in the corner of the screen. It was less than half full.

"I'll have to get that checked out," Grandfather said, frowning.

"Mr. Wells, if you please? We are on a timetable."

"Oh yes, of course." Grandfather placed his hand on the window. A second later the locking mechanism clicked open.

"Thanks," I said, climbing into the back seat. Alex made to follow.

"Hold on there, young man." The officer grabbed Alex's sleeve, halting him mid-step.

Grandfather placed a hand on his shoulder. "I apologize, Alex, but you won't be coming with us. I won't allow you to unnecessarily place yourself in harm's way." He gave Alex a look of appreciation and sympathy. "I'm sure your father agrees. He's waiting for you just over there."

Alex's face fell.

"Like he would even care," he muttered. He turned to me and raised his voice loud enough for Grandfather to hear. "See you tomorrow."

Grandfather didn't object.

Alex made to walk away and join his father, but suddenly halted and gawked at an approaching person. A person in a black trench coat.

"I'd like a word," Kratos said quietly. The officer in charge looked to Grandfather, who nodded and then stepped aside. Kratos placed an ungloved hand on the front passenger window, bracing himself as he peered into the back seat. He opened his mouth to speak, but I was surprised to hear Grandfather's voice instead.

"So the rumors are true," he said with interest. "I always wondered."

I looked into the front right window, following Grandfather's line of sight. The window had scanned the Bounty Hunter's DNA. I couldn't read any of the listed attributes, but it didn't matter. My eyes darted to the circle in the corner of the window. It was full.

I was taken aback. I had always thought the rumor was just one of Alex's exaggerations about Kratos. Nobody was perfect. But the man standing in front of me *was* perfect. His DNA was perfect. He was perfectly Noble.

At least Alex had picked someone good to Follow.

The Bounty Hunter slid into the seat next to me and shut the door behind him, the dim light of the car's interior hiding the blurred features of his mask.

"Victor," he began, "no one has ever escaped the effects of the Mark."

My heart sank. Kratos, a man more privy to the Sinister happenings in the city than anybody else, didn't think there had been a mistake. My Marking was real. Permanent. I searched his eyes for some shred of hope, but there was nothing. I guess I shouldn't have expected a pep talk from a man wearing all black.

"But I've studied them," he continued, "the Left Hand. They

watch you, watch your patterns, and strike when they know exactly where you are and what you're doing." He paused. "They work much like I do, but they work to kill." The Bounty Hunter looked down.

Hearing his words was like falling through the ice of a frozen lake. A chill began to encompass my body. I could fight, but it was only a matter of time before the cold got to me and dragged me down into its depths.

I waited for more. Kratos continued to stare at the floor.

"Why tell me this if they've never been beaten?" I asked.

"Because never is a strong word," he said, eyeing me, "and we all need exceptions to fight for." He reached for the door handle, but hesitated. "I'll be in touch."

The door swung open and he was gone.

9

The ride home passed in silence. Freddy drove stone-faced as usual while Grandfather faced the window, his brow crinkled, his eyes shut lightly in thought. The silence gave me time to think. I replayed the brief meeting with Kratos in my mind, but it only raised more questions.

Was he going to help? Did he really think the Left Hand could be beaten? And if so, how?

The car bounced over the curb as Freddy steered it into the driveway and parked. Grandfather opened his eyes and faced me.

"You're going to beat this," he said. I saw a steely determination in his eyes, something that had been absent from everyone else I had talked to after the Marking. His resolve gave me hope. No one had survived a Marking, but that didn't mean no one could, right?

I did my best to muster a smile.

"Thanks, Grandfather."

Freddy popped open the doors and grunted as he hoisted himself out of the car.

"Let's go," he said. "Captain Revore and his crew will be inside waiting for us."

I exited the car and headed for the front door, Freddy and Grandfather right behind me. I placed my hand on the glass panel next to the door when I arrived. The familiar line of light snaked around each of my fingers. Instinctively, I reached for the handle and pulled, but the door didn't move. The glass emitted a faint red light.

I tried again. Another pulse of red light.

"Try your card," Grandfather instructed.

I reached inside my pocket and pulled out my ID, placing it flat against the door. A light snaked around it. The outline around the card grew solid and turned red. The circle in the corner was nowhere near full.

Twice in one day?

Grandfather stepped forward, a dark look crossing his regal features. He placed his hand on the glass and the lock clicked open. He held the door and stood to the side.

"Hmm," he muttered as he stared at the floor.

The door closed with a click behind us. We walked into the living room, where four policemen dressed in battle-ready black stood waiting for me.

Grandfather sat at the table and motioned for me to sit down next to him. "This is Captain Revore"—he indicated the officer standing to his right—"and he has been assigned to complement and bolster Freddy's current security efforts."

Captain Revore was a large man, about the same size as Freddy, with a thick mustache that reminded me of the end of a broom. He also kept a close-cropped beard and had a no-nonsense air about him. With Grandfather's introduction out of the way, he took over.

"Good to see you, son," he said as he extended a hand. I took it. "Those were some admirable actions today, saving that senator's life. That's something any man can respect." He turned to Grandfather. "You've done good, Ulysses."

"Thank you, Captain."

"Now, we're not sure why you were Marked, Victor, but we're here to make sure the Left Hand doesn't keep its promise." He fixed me with a stare. "Today, you acted like a true Noble. In order to stand a chance at surviving the week, it is likely that your Nobility will be called upon again. Do exactly as I say and be prepared. You may survive this yet."

"And where is your team now, Captain?" Freddy asked.

"Three of them are completing a sweep of the house. Once they've finished, I'll introduce them and brief you on our plan. Until then..." He dropped his militant air for a moment. "Relax—you've had a difficult night."

I nodded but didn't say anything. It wasn't like relaxing was going to improve the situation.

"Thank you, Captain," Grandfather said as Captain Revore strode out of the room.

I sat at the table staring at my hands, but not really seeing them.

I could feel Grandfather's eyes on me. I turned to face him. The corners of his mouth were turned downward like tree branches straining under the weight of too much snow.

"How are you doing with all of this?" he asked.

"I'm okay," I said, trying my best to sell it.

"There's no reason to give up hope." Grandfather placed his hand on my shoulder and gave it a squeeze.

"Captain!" one of the officers yelled from a back room. "I've got something!"

From the opposite end of the house, another voice called, "I've found something too!"

My heart sank. What had they found? Listening devices? Cameras? Whatever they were, it meant the Left Hand had been planning to Mark me. It wasn't a mistake.

"Bring them here!" Captain Revore yelled, reentering the room with another officer.

Seconds later, the two officers appeared, each holding something tightly in a closed fist. Captain Revore turned to us and introduced the incoming men, pointing at each one as he said their names. "Carter, Wilkes, and"—he gestured to the man behind him—"Harvesty."

All three were large, burly men with close-cropped haircuts and bulging muscles. Harvesty looked especially imposing as he glared maliciously around the room. I was just glad he was on our side. I'd hate to run into a Sinister who looked like him.

"Carter, you first," Revore said.

"It's small, Captain, but our equipment managed to pick it up." He opened his gloved hand.

"I don't see anything." Revore bent down and squinted until his face was inches from the man's palm.

"Then you won't see this either." Wilkes offered his seemingly empty hand as well. I stood up and looked, craning my neck to see what Wilkes had, but it must have been too small to see without enhancement. I looked up to see Harvesty nod to Wilkes and then, like a bad dream, it happened.

Wilkes sucker punched Revore in the gut, and Carter's elbow came down hard on the back of Revore's head. Harvesty reached inside his vest, pulled out a short metal spike, and deftly drove it between Revore's shoulder blades. Revore screamed in pain. A flash of light emitted from the spike, and he dropped to the floor.

I felt like I was caught in a whirlpool, the cold feeling of pure terror threatening to drag me under and drown me.

Harvesty gave Revore a look of disgust. "Where is it?" he asked me, stepping over the body.

I couldn't tear my eyes away from Revore's lifeless form.

"He's not dead, boy, just stunned. No orders to kill him. But you"—he reached back and pulled a pistol from inside his belt, swinging the barrel around until it was pointed at my chest—"the Left Hand has no restraints on killing you."

It was as if the air had been sucked out of the room. I couldn't breathe. This man had a gun. A real gun. Those had been banned years ago.

"No!" Grandfather yelled.

Harvesty moved with blinding speed and drove the butt of the gun into Grandfather's face. His shrapnel wound from earlier tore open again, and blood ran down his face. Grandfather groaned in pain and slumped back into his chair.

Anger flared to life inside of me. Harvesty turned his gun on Grandfather.

"You'll stay out of my way, or I'll—"

I vaulted forward with the same speed and precision that had made me victorious on so many occasions. Harvesty didn't have time to react. My right fist collided with his outstretched hand, the gun flying out of his grasp, and my left fist slammed into the right side of his jaw. The gun clattered to the ground, but Carter was on it before I could react, and Harvesty recovered remarkably fast from the blow to his face.

Harvesty held out his hand, and Carter placed the gun back in it. I stayed where I was, desperately wishing I had my saber. Grandfather remained slumped in his chair, cradling his cheek.

"You're a fighter," Harvesty said with a grim smile showing bloodied teeth. He spit a glob of red saliva on the ground, then massaged his jaw. "You get one shot in, no penalty. But try that again..." He gestured menacingly with the gun. "Now, where is it?"

"Where's what?" I said. What could he be talking about?

"Don't be stupid, boy," Harvesty snarled. "The senator gave you something earlier tonight. Hand it over."

"Why do you want it?" I said, playing for time.

Harvesty smiled.

Carter stepped forward. "Because we don't want the whole world knowing who our boss is, now do we?"

Harvesty looked over at him, his expression murderous. "You idiot!" he hissed.

Realization dawned on Carter, followed by fear. His eyes went to Harvesty's gun. Harvesty's gaze lingered on Carter for a second before he turned his attention back to me. "Tell me where you hid it," he said quietly. "Now."

The back door burst open. Freddy stood framed in the doorway for a split second, still dressed in his suit from earlier. I felt a surge of hope at his entrance.

"Stay where you are!" Harvesty said, taking a step back and simultaneously swinging his gun toward Freddy.

"Freddy, no!" Grandfather yelled.

But Freddy dove to the right, disappearing behind a couch. He reappeared on the other side, bounding forward with powerful steps, a heavy decoration in hand, ready to use as a weapon.

A gunshot rang out.

Freddy appeared to move in slow motion. His eyes went wide. His hand rose to his chest, where a red bloom of blood was spreading across his jacket. Freddy wavered for a moment, as if confused, and then collapsed.

With a cry, I stumbled over to him. "No, no, no," I said, attempting to stop the blood flow.

Freddy looked into my face, his eyes slowly losing focus.

"Come on, Freddy." I put more pressure on his chest, but there was so much blood. My hands were covered in it. The pool of red continued to spread across the floor.

Freddy coughed and sputtered, his lungs crying desperately for air. He reached up and grabbed me by the shoulders, and for one lucid moment, we locked eyes. His expression was fierce. He nodded, then the pressure around my neck lessened and his arm fell limp. His eyes closed. His body exhaled one final time, and he was gone.

Slow footsteps made their way across the room, coming to a stop behind me just as the tears started rolling down my face.

"Now that you know I'm serious," Harvesty said, "where is it?"

10

I felt the cold metal of a gun barrel on the back of my neck.

Harvesty—I wanted to kill him.

"Get up, boy," he said.

I got to my feet, shaking with rage, and turned to face him. He stared at me with sharp, unforgiving eyes that seemed almost inhuman. They were evil.

"Now tell me," Harvesty said slowly, "where it is. Where did you hide the information the senator gave you?"

I stared back into his eyes, defiant. My mind began to work, to push my anger to the side and analyze.

"Answer me!" Harvesty yelled.

"He didn't give me anything!" I said. They were here because they thought I had something—information on the leader of the Left Hand? Was this all a mistake? Was Freddy dead because Harvesty thought I had something I didn't?

"Oh yes, he did." Harvesty leaned in closer. "And you're going to tell me exactly where it is," he finished, emphasizing each word. He smiled. It was a cruel expression.

I tried to keep myself from glancing at Freddy's lifeless body. His last moments, his last look, they had been courageous. He had given me a look I'd seen many times when I was younger and had just lost a match. It meant to never give up, to keep fighting.

Somehow, we had to survive this. We had to survive the Left Hand. For Freddy.

"I know you don't want to talk," Harvesty said, "but there are ways we can fix that." He took a step over to Grandfather and pointed the gun at his leg.

"The senator didn't give me anything!" I shouted.

Harvesty took a quick step toward me and jammed the barrel of the gun against my forehead. "Don't lie to me, boy! Or I will do things to you to make you wish you were never alive."

With his free hand, he reached behind his head and tugged. I watched in horror as his face seemed to come off, revealing someone who looked completely different underneath. Black hair replaced the brown. Low cheekbones replaced high ones. Pale skin replaced a rugged tan. And a few days' worth of stubble replaced a clean-shaven chin.

He tossed the mask to the side and, like a wild animal about to kill its prey, grinned. "I want my face to be the last one you ever see." He kept his gun steady. "Now, where is the information?"

My mind raced. Where could I lure him that I'd have the advantage? No doubt he would follow me anywhere I went—

A knock sounded at the door, and Wilkes and Carter started.

"Ignore it," Harvesty growled, not taking his eyes off me.

There was another knock. Then another.

Harvesty rolled his eyes. "Carter, check that out. See if it's one of ours."

Carter dutifully stepped over to the door. "There's no one there," he said, puzzled.

Another knock sounded. Carter, with a hand on his stunner, peered out the windows on either side of the door.

"Wilkes," Harvesty growled, eyeing Carter with some distaste, "get over there and help Carter figure out who it is." Wilkes hurried over, stunner in hand.

Another knock.

"I can't see anyone either."

Knock.

And then silence.

Wilkes and Carter looked at each other and shrugged, making to step back toward us.

And that was when the door burst open, a black trench coat following in its wake.

The door smashed Wilkes into the wall. Carter didn't hesitate to attack, but the Bounty Hunter ducked Carter's right hook with ease, dealing him two swift jabs to his unprotected ribcage and throwing his face into the doorframe. He fell to the ground but pushed himself back up almost immediately.

Harvesty touched his shoulder and spoke rapidly into his microphone. "Backup, come in. Backup, come in." He kept his gun leveled at me and one eye on the Bounty Hunter.

Kratos blocked a punch from Carter, stepped back, grabbed the open door, and swung it forcefully into Wilkes's head.

"Send all additional units to my location!" Harvesty said quickly.

Carter rushed Kratos, who sidestepped him and used his momentum to throw him headlong into the wall. He bounced off the wall and turned, trying to attack again, but he was too slow. The Bounty Hunter came down hard, his right fist connecting with Carter's cheekbone. An audible crack sounded, and Carter collapsed. Kratos stepped over the unconscious body, heading for Harvesty.

"Stop," he said, his gun still pointed at me. "I'll shoot. And as you can see, I'm not afraid to do it." He motioned to Freddy's body.

Kratos froze, two unconscious bodies strewn about his feet. A grin spread across Harvesty's face. He had a gun. An actual gun. All he had to do was hold out until more of the Sinistrali showed up.

"Mr. Harvesty, what would you have us do? Perhaps we can come to some sort of arrangement?" Grandfather pleaded.

What could we do? Even Kratos the Bounty Hunter couldn't dodge bullets.

Harvesty laughed. "You think a washed-up senator can give me more than the Left Hand? You have no idea what's in store." Harvesty backed up a step, attempting to keep the three of us in his field of view.

"Do *you* know what's in store?" Grandfather asked.

Harvesty's eyes bulged. He swung his gun around, aiming it at Grandfather's legs.

"Another word and you won't ever walk again, old man."

Grandfather pursed his lips.

"That's close enough!" Harvesty turned his gun on the Bounty Hunter, who froze with a foot in midair.

Captain Revore stirred on the ground at Harvesty's feet, moaning in agony. A look of disgust crossed Harvesty's face as he lifted a foot to silence Revore once again.

A split second was all I needed.

I threw my shoulder hard into Harvesty's stomach. He grunted as the air rushed out of his lungs and stumbled backwards. Grandfather moved with a speed that defied his age and dove for Harvesty's feet. Then I launched myself at him again, wrestling his gun arm for control. We hit the ground, and the gun careened across the floor.

The Bounty Hunter rushed forward and kicked Harvesty in the head, silencing him.

I reached down and helped Grandfather up, looking over at Freddy's body.

We had to survive.

"More Sinistrali will be on the way," Kratos said, eyes darting to the door. "You need to leave, immediately. Go t—"

"No," I said, cutting him off. But I could hear the footfalls of heavy boots running toward the open front door. "What about you and, and—"

Kratos locked eyes with me. "They're after you. Go. Now."

I looked at Grandfather and opened my mouth to speak, but he spoke first.

"We'll be okay," he said. His jaw was set, his eyes determined. "Find a way to get in touch when you're safe. I'll take care of Freddy. Now go."

"There he is!" A man dressed identically to Harvesty rushed

through the door. Kratos lifted his arms and drew an X in the air in front of him, a faint hiss accompanying the movements. Four more men pushed through the doorway. The first man launched himself at Kratos, but seemed to slow down in midair, a misting of gray beads appearing around him. Confusion barely had a chance to cross his face before Kratos's powerful right hook caught him in the temple. He fell unconscious to the floor.

The Bounty Hunter drew three more invisible X's in the air, a hiss sounding with each one. He looked over his shoulder to see me standing there, immobile. "Go!" he shouted.

The living room window nearest me shattered. Four men kicked their way through the remains of the broken glass and clambered into the room.

"Now, Victor!" Grandfather shouted. Before I could blink, he threw himself at the newcomers. He took a hard punch to the side and stumbled. The man closest to him fired his stunner, and Grandfather fell to the floor. Instinct took over. I ran to him.

Kratos thrust out one arm, and with a hiss, I was almost stopped dead in my tracks. Small droplets of gray materialized before my eyes. It felt like running into a pool of water.

"Go!" Kratos commanded. "I'll take care of him!"

More Sinistrali advanced, blocking Grandfather from my view. I couldn't leave him.

A flash of stunner fire flew by my face. It was from the Bounty Hunter. "I said *go!*"

He hurled the stunner in his hand at the man nearest me, catching him in the face. The strange hissing noise continued, and Kratos's multiple foes recaptured his full attention. He battled six men at once. They fired their stunners, but the blasts seemed to dissipate just before they reached him, somehow evaporating when they hit the invisible X. With each blast, more of the gray beads appeared and fell to the ground.

I wanted to fight, but I had to trust him. There was no other option.

I ran. Blood pumped in my ears as I hurtled down the hall. A glass picture frame exploded near my head, showering me in tiny shards. I turned the corner. I had to get outside and down the street to Alex's house.

The sliding glass door was up ahead. Twenty more feet. I grabbed a decorative vase off the wall and chanced a backwards glance. A black-clad man thundered around the corner, crashing into the wall but recovering quickly. Ten more feet.

I hurled the vase at the door. Glass exploded in front of me, peppering my face like a thousand miniature hailstones as I jumped through them. My feet landed on the soft grass, and I was outside. In practice, I never ran, I always fought, I always won. I had to force my legs onward against my instincts.

The sun had already set. I streaked across the darkened lawn, my mind straining for a plan. The road. Alex's house. Four doors down. His father was a senator. That meant bodyguards and protection.

"He's gone out the back!" My nearest pursuer blundered through the shattered door, doing his best to keep up. But I had the advantage, especially at night.

I changed directions and forced my way through a hedge, blocking myself from view, and then turned left. Adrenaline fueled my body. I sprinted flat out, making it to the road in a matter of moments. I glanced left, catching sight of a group of five or six Sinistrali jogging alongside the house. Ducking down, I ran in a crouch in the opposite direction, doing my best to stay clear of the streetlights.

I didn't let up. Looking behind me, there was no one, but I stayed low just in case. I passed my neighbor's driveway at breakneck speed. Almost there.

Alex's house. A ten-foot-high iron gate encircled the house like a moat would a castle. I turned down the driveway, pausing only for a moment to place my hand on an access screen next to their mailbox. The DNA scanner was agonizingly slow.

"Come on, come on, come on!" I waited, breathing heavily, for the affirmative beep of the machine. A tone sounded, and I took off toward the gate, but it didn't move. I rushed back to the scanner, catching sight of a group of Sinistrali running my way.

How did they find me so quickly?

I slapped my hand on the scanner again, then ducked behind the machine as a wave of stunner blasts illuminated the air around me. A tone sounded again, and I stole a look at the results—the screen glowed red. Sinister.

What was happening?

I slammed the scanner in frustration. I had to move. Another round of stunner blasts punctuated the air. I ducked behind the scanner, hesitated for a second, and made a decision.

The train station. Lots of people all the time. It was close, a few blocks down and a couple streets over, and I knew a shortcut.

I looked up the road and caught a glimpse of the men about a hundred yards back, stunners out. Another punch of adrenaline coursed through my body, and I shot out of Alex's driveway, sprinting across the deserted road. A yell from one of the men was drowned out by the wind rushing in my ears.

If I could just make it to the end of the street, I could double back and use the neighborhood access route to the train station. If I could get there unnoticed, I might be able to lose them. It was a small, gray shed that shared its back wall with the train station. A door inside the shed led directly into the station. That was my shortcut.

But it had a scanner.

I slowed for half a step, searching desperately for a solution, before remembering that this scanner was different. The DNA of the local residents had been programmed into it—no Noble or Sinister restrictions, just DNA.

If I could get to the shed, I might stand a chance.

My legs ached and my lungs burned, each breath searing my throat as I gulped it down. I put on another burst of speed, but adrenaline couldn't sustain me forever. Stunner fire tickled the air around my body and lit up the street in flashes of blue. The last several shots were dangerously close.

House after house flew by, a flurry of blues, grays, and reds. I rounded the corner and the train station loomed before me. It was a massive domed structure made completely of matte gray soundproof steel which spanned the length of several streets. It was a several-minute walk in either direction to get to an actual entrance, but there it was, forty yards away: my shortcut.

My feet pounded on the pavement, their quick rhythm breaking the nighttime silence of the empty street. I hurdled over a flower bed and skidded to a stop, dropping to my knees just to the side of the shed. I was hidden from view, but could still see most of the street. The scanner stood two feet to my right, but I couldn't reach it without exposing myself.

The fastest of the Sinistralis rounded the street corner, looking about wildly for any sign of me. He slowed to a jog and then stopped, letting the rest of the group catch up. One of them pulled out a portable screen from a large pocket on his vest. He consulted it and hurriedly gave orders. The group split into four smaller units. Two units went left, each taking one side of the street. The other two units went right.

They began to search around each house. My breath came in shallow gasps and sweat poured down my face. I figured I had less than a minute before I had to move.

The nearest unit of bad guys was seventy-five feet away, and they were making their way around the perimeter of a house three doors down from where I was hiding.

I watched them, trying to pick an opportune moment to scan my hand and slip inside the shed unnoticed.

As soon as they go around the far side of the house, I'm moving, I thought.

I waited, hands sweaty, heart racing.

The last member of the nearest unit disappeared behind the side of the house. I moved from my hiding spot, but stayed in a crouch, pressing my moist hand onto the scanning plate. I heard another small beep, but it didn't come from the scanner. One of the Sinistrali reappeared on the street holding a screen.

"He's here!" he shouted. I dropped back to the ground and hid myself from view. I tugged on the door, but I had pulled my hand away too soon. The door remained locked.

How did they know where I was? They couldn't see me, or they would have shot me already.

The man with the screen was joined by several more members of the Left Hand.

"He's here somewhere!" he said, looking around. The other units converged on his position.

A hot, sickly feeling washed over me. I tasted vomit in the back of my throat, but forced it back down.

I had to get out of here.

Staying in a crouch, I reached my hand upward and placed it on the scanner until the locking mechanism clicked, opening the shed door. The moment I did so, another beep emitted from the portable screen carried by one of the Sinistrali. Six heads turned my way.

They were tracking my scans.

"There!"

I ducked. Stunner blasts slammed into the shed door. I wrenched it open, and another gunshot pierced the night air. Splinters burst from the door, showering me in toothpick-sized pieces of wood. I ducked inside the door, slammed it behind me, and took off at a sprint, bursting through the opposite side of the shed into the station.

I wove my way through the masses of people like a confused spider. My mind raced. I ducked down, trying to blend in with the crowd.

People milled about, some waiting to board the trains and some staring expectantly at the giant departure and arrival clocks, waiting for others to disembark. There were three main lines of people matching the three different train lines: Sinister, Noble, and Noble Elite. Scanners were everywhere. Both the Noble lines required a scan for anyone trying to board. Any Noble could ride the Noble line, while government officials and the wealthy frequented the prestige and privacy of the Elite line. But Sinisters only had one option, the Sinister line. There were no scanners there.

I took in the scene, and the final parts of a plan clicked into place. The muffled sounds of splintering wood and men yelling reached my ears. The Left Hand would be here in a matter of moments.

I took off at a sprint, running toward the Noble Elite train line. Several people grunted and exclaimed angrily as I shoved past them. I glanced down at my clothes. I needed to find someone in a gray suit.

With a loud banging of a door, the Left Hand barreled through the final barrier into the terminal. The man at the forefront had his portable screen out. I turned my back to them, head swiveling to find someone who fit what I was looking for.

There, I thought, catching sight of a man wearing a gray suit. *A real gun won't be used here,* I told myself. *Just stunners.* The Left Hand only killed who they Marked, no additional casualties. At least that's what I'd thought until I met Harvesty.

The vision of Freddy's lifeless body assaulted me again, but I pushed it away.

I shoved past another couple of people until I was I was standing right in front of the man I had chosen. I was almost at the front of the line. I looked discreetly over my shoulder, ignoring a dozen angry glares from everyone I had bypassed. The Sinistralis fanned out, searching the busy platform for any sign of me. The man behind me cleared his throat. I took a step forward and placed my hand on the glass pane of the scanner. I immediately ducked down. The sound of a sharp beep cut through the air, and I quickly turned to the man behind me.

"Sorry."

And then I bolted.

"The Elite terminal," the man with the screen shouted. Half a dozen black-clad men converged on the Elite line.

"There he is!" another one yelled.

A crunching sound carried above the chatter of the nearest groups, and three bodies hit the floor amidst a cry of pain from the unsuspecting victim. I cringed at the sound, but kept going.

"It's not him!"

I continued to run. I had to go somewhere they couldn't track me. The Sinister line had no scanners. I'd be safe there. Well, safer.

I looked up at the monstrous departure clock. Thirty seconds until the next Sinister train departure.

I pushed my way through the crowd of people, a stream of muttered "sorry's" left in my wake. The Sinistralis still hadn't spotted me, but the next Sinister train was about to leave. I wasn't going to make it, not unless I moved a lot faster. If I didn't make the train, I was done. There would be nowhere left to run.

Abandoning all pretense of stealth, I stood up to my full height and ran.

"Move!" I yelled, throwing the first couple of people aside. A path began to clear in front of me.

Fifteen seconds.

"There he is!"

I stole a backwards glance. Two of them were close. Too close. They locked onto my location in an instant and thundered after me. People screamed, some thrown aside and some scattering away from the path of the charging men.

A woman to my right absorbed a stunner shot and fell to the ground. I jumped her body and kept running. My muscles screamed at the effort.

I broke into a clearing and pushed my legs to move faster. The clock reached single digits.

A charge of electricity flew by my ear, leaving a trail of static in its wake. I vaulted over the unguarded turnstile. Twenty more feet.

The doors stood open, beckoning to me. The occupants stared on with looks of confusion.

I zigzagged, two stunner shots barely missing their mark.

The doors were still open.

I dove, passing through the train car doors, stunner shots lighting up the air around me.

The clock registered 0:00.

The doors closed. Stunner blasts continued to come but dissipated as they reached the glass.

Slowly, the train started to move, and I looked out the window at my pursuers. The Sinistralis could do nothing but watch as I sped away to temporary freedom.

11

I stood behind the closed door, my chest heaving. I caught my reflection in the glass. Ragged didn't even begin to describe it. Plaster dust was still visible in my hair and on my jacket. Dried blood had found its way underneath my fingernails and in the creases of my palms.

Freddy's blood.

Emotion that had been shunted to the side as I fought to survive came rushing to the forefront. My breath caught in my throat. My eyes burned with tears.

Freddy was gone.

Harvesty had killed him. And what for? Some kind of information Avardi had never given me? We hadn't even met up after his speech! The Left Hand had seen to that too.

I pounded my fist against the glass of the train door, startling the nearest occupants. A few indistinct mutterings met my ears.

I had to keep calm. I wasn't safe yet, especially here, on a train full of Sinisters. I wiped my eyes and forced myself to stand upright. I didn't have time to mourn. I had to think.

The Left Hand was following me, tracking my DNA. Scanners were no longer an option. What now?

I surveyed the rest of the train car as I searched for ideas.

My surroundings were familiar, yet different. Black crevices in the floor and ceiling created an intricate series of squares and rectangles, just like in the Noble trains. The perimeter of the train car was made of floor-length glass windows. However, unlike the Noble trains, these windows didn't appear to stream the news or TV programs. I couldn't place it, but everything here just seemed a little darker, dirtier, and more, well, Sinister.

Maybe it had something to do with the people. None of them looked as ragged or deranged as the brick-throwing Sinister from earlier, but it would be best to avoid them all the same. Thankfully, it looked like they wanted to avoid me too.

A soft "ding" sounded, and red light shone out of several crevices in the floor and ceiling to form a small square. Text scrolled across several of the large windows: *Exiting to Granville Street.*

"Too close," I whispered to myself. Granville was still in the Flats. Scanners would be everywhere.

I made my way to a vacant section of the train. I watched as glass walls seemed to grow out of the lighted crevices until a fully enclosed cube had been created. Another "ding" sounded, and the newly created cube was released from the rest of the train car, almost like breaking a square off a chocolate bar. Transportation cars like this would continue to break off into individual pieces, sending people to their respective locations until all the stops had been made and there was no more train left.

The trouble was, I had no idea where any of the train pods would go. I assumed at some point they'd start going into the Heights, but wherever I ended up, I'd be completely lost.

I stood there, trying in vain to stop the cascade of thoughts running through my mind. I was sure the Left Hand was plotting their next move, but there was nothing I could do. I was headed to the Heights, a place rampant with Sinisters and with little to no Noble presence. But what choice did I have? I closed my eyes and clenched my teeth. I needed to do something. Anything.

I pulled out my phone and unfolded two sections from the back, doubling the size of the screen. It turned on, and the latest news announcement popped up.

The screen zoomed in on a dark-haired news reporter. Grandfather's picture appeared in the corner of the screen. I turned up the volume.

"...turn of events. Hours ago, the former Senator Wells had cause to rejoice, his grandson having saved the life of Senator Supart during his speech after the debate." My picture joined Grandfather's on the screen. "However, stunning new information has come to light. The government has just uncovered information that Victor Wells is not a Noble, but is, in fact, a Sinister. Much like the Pendleton family from four years ago, the authorities are unsure how he was able to avoid detection for so long. But, unlike the Pendletons, Victor Wells is not only Sinister, but also carries the gene T$_{\text{II}}$D. Victor's guardian, the former Senator Wells, was unavailable for comment."

Ice washed over me. T$_{\text{II}}$D?

No, this was a dream, I told myself, a very bad, very twisted dream.

I quickly thumbed down the volume and turned my body to shield my face. Thankfully, no one paid me any attention.

The reporter continued. "There is speculation that Victor's parents, most likely his mother, had been hiding their true lineage all along. However, due to their unfortunate deaths in an accident several years ago, we'll probably never know the answer."

I stopped listening. My mom? It couldn't be true. There was no way. My parents had been good people, not Sinisters. They were Nobles.

I acted Noble. My DNA was Noble. I felt Noble. I *was* Noble.

Wouldn't I know if I was a Sinister? Wouldn't I know that I was a T$_{\text{II}}$D carrier?

Or was this how it worked? My current life was a facade, my future actions somehow sealed by my genetic code?

On my phone, the newscaster continued to speak. "President Keltan is here with us to make a statement. President?"

President Keltan stepped into the frame. "Yes, thank you, Kelly," he said before turning to look directly into the camera. "Tonight's events have been devastating and confusing for us all," he began. "Our top analysts will be working around the clock to find out how Victor Wells was able to fool the scanners for so many years, but the public can rest assured that all efforts will be expended to bring Victor Wells in."

"Will that include the Bounty Hunter?" Kelly asked.

"As you know, all official Bounty Hunter missions are classified," President Keltan said. "But the law does forbid the Bounty Hunter from pursuing minors. That's all I'll say about that. We've instructed the police to be particularly vigilant, considering a carrier of TɪɪD is running unchecked through the city. I am confident we will find him and bring him in before any harm is done."

"Do you have any words for Victor Wells, Mr. President?"

"I do," he said, pausing briefly. "Victor, you saved a man's life earlier this evening. I know there is good in you. Turn yourself in before you or others are injured. Dr. Rosewood has volunteered to help your situation, and possibly even remove or permanently deactivate your TɪɪD gene."

"Can she really do that?" Kelly Straunton asked.

"Dr. Rosewood is hopeful, but it remains to be seen," he said.

"Wouldn't that be something! Well, thank you for your time, Mr. President," Kelly said with a respectful nod. President Keltan returned it and exited the screen. She turned back to the camera. "Well folks, you heard it here first. Are we up for another Dr. Rosewood miracle?" She paused and flashed a brilliantly white smile. "Reporting live from the Capital, this is Kelly Straunton. Tom, back to you."

I shut my phone and let it hang limply in my hand as I struggled in vain to comprehend what I had just heard. My mind felt like it had been paralyzed by a saber strike.

TɪɪD. I had DNA in common with tyrants, mass murderers, and serial killers.

I grappled with the idea in my head. It wasn't possible. I searched for any plausible explanation, but came up with nothing. DNA didn't suddenly change.

Another set of lights lit up near my feet, and I was forced to take a few steps forward as another pod of glass formed and broke off from the rest of the train.

Outside, the train flew past an unfamiliar landscape, reminding me of my immediate problem. I was on a Sinister train. I would have to worry about everything I had heard later. I needed a plan. I needed help.

Help. But from who? And after that news announcement, would anyone help me? Or would they turn me in?

Several more lines in the floor lit up around me. Another exit. I took a couple steps to the side and glanced toward the train's other occupants. Sinisters. I couldn't trust any of them. Had any of them seen the news report? Would they turn me in or congratulate me for being one of them? For the moment, they all seemed to be minding their own business.

I just hoped it stayed that way.

I closed the extra screens on my phone and brought up my contacts, searching for help.

Alex? Maybe his father? I couldn't get past their gate earlier, but I could call.

I pulled up Alex's number and brought the phone up to my ear. I waited. No ring. I clicked on Alex's number again.

Nothing.

I looked around. Was there some sort of interference? The train didn't travel through tunnels and I didn't see anything that could stop the signal. I slapped the phone into my other palm and gave it a few good shakes. I was about to redial when I saw a word at the top corner of the screen.

Blocked.

Blocked? I should have seen this coming.

Phones worked much the same as everything else did, by DNA. Most Nobles would set their phones to only receive calls from other

Nobles. If a Sinister tried to call a Noble number, it wouldn't even dial, and I was registering as a Sinister.

Anyone I knew, any friends I had, were Nobles. I didn't know any Sinisters.

I fought off the sinking feeling in the pit of my stomach.

Wait, I *did* know a Sinister.

Daphne.

Going to her, a liar and a deceiver, for help? The thought almost made me sick. It was a ridiculous idea, but did I have any other options?

I closed my eyes slowly and exhaled, thinking. I balled my hands into fists. My fingernails dug into my palms. I wanted to yell out in frustration. There was no one else.

When Daphne's family had been forced out of the Noble society, Grandfather had put Daphne's new number in my phone. I could still remember the day he did it. He said he'd put it there "just in case." I had let him do it, but silently vowed never to call.

I searched my phone frantically for her number. Had I deleted it? My eyes came across an entry labeled *Do not call.*

I knew it was hers.

I tapped the icon and her number appeared on the screen. I hesitated. The number was several years old. Would it even work? Would she take my call, or would she be just as angry at me as I was with her? It didn't matter. I needed help, and I was desperate.

I watched the landscape outside fly by in unfamiliar snapshots. At some point, I would have to get off the train, and by the looks of it, soon. More than half the train had already broken away.

It was time to call.

My thumb hovered over the video call button. No, I wasn't ready for that, not yet. I tapped the audio call icon and waited.

It rang. My heart started to beat a little faster.

Please answer.

It rang again.

Please answer.

Finally, a click sounded, but no one spoke.

"Hello?" No answer. "Daphne? It's Victor. Victor Wells." I fought to keep my voice level, to keep the desperation out of it as I spoke.

A slow intake of breath met my ears. A crisp female voice sounded on the other side, a mature voice. "What do you want?"

I hesitated. A forgotten flood of emotions spilled into my mind. We had been friends once, best friends. But that was all in the past now. I was halfway surprised that she hadn't hung up already.

"What do you want?" she repeated, her words growing sharper with each syllable.

"I need help."

"And you called me?" she asked with a snort. I stared out the glass window. Multistory buildings flew by almost without registering. I didn't have time to beat around the bush.

"My DNA has changed and I'm being hunted." There was a long pause. I kept talking. "I'm on the run. Grandfather might have been taken by the Sinistrali, but I'm not sure."

I could hear the muffled sound of conferring voices. Another set of gaps in the floor lit up and I was forced to move closer to a few of the remaining Sinisters on the train. "Where are you now?" came Daphne's voice.

"I'm on the Sinister line." Another large set of gaps in the floor and ceiling lit up. The remaining Sinisters stepped inside the blinking lights. I read the text on the glass. *Just passing Hilltop Village.*

"Is the train crowded?"

I looked around. "No, the last few people just got off. Why?"

She ignored me. "Walk to the front right corner of the train."

Obediently, I walked there, stabilizing myself with the straps on the ceiling as the train flew around another corner.

"Okay."

"Now take four paces to your left."

"Done. Now what?"

"Stay there," she said. "That train pod will take you to the center of the Heights. Zeno will meet you there."

"Who's Zeno?" I asked.

"I have to go. Don't move from that spot."

"Wait—"

"I'll send a picture. Go with Zeno."

Click.

Frustration fought against relief. Go with Zeno. That was it?

I balled my fists and fought to calm myself. I needed to keep it together. I was going into the Heights. I would find Zeno and he would take me to Daphne.

And then what?

I had no idea.

Freddy had sacrificed himself for me, as had Grandfather and the Bounty Hunter. I couldn't give up. I had to survive.

I stared at my reflection in the window in front of me. Looking back at me was a confused boy wearing a dirty suit with no plan, no weapons, and no allies. I took a deep breath and closed my eyes. I needed a miracle.

12

All I knew was that I was deep in the Heights. Sections of the train had peeled off until my lone train pod remained, shuttling me through the silent night. Buildings loomed above me on either side, finally closing in overtop of me as the pod slowed to a stop inside the terminal. I peered through the glass. Was Zeno already here?

Although it was the middle of the night, only about a quarter of the lights functioned on the platform, most with a flicker. It appeared dark and dirty, exactly what I expected this far into the Heights. The lone form of a man stood on the otherwise deserted train platform.

My mouth had become dry. I forced a swallow and checked my phone one last time before I exited.

A picture of Zeno stared back at me on the screen. He wasn't exactly the muscle I'd expected. He looked...well, nerdy. The picture showed an immaculately kept rectangular afro and thick pair of glasses atop a head that sat on a rather thin neck.

I shoved my phone in my pocket and stepped cautiously onto the platform as the glass walls receded in front of me. The man, hopefully Zeno, didn't move. The lights flickered above him, making it difficult to see what he looked like. My heart raced.

"Zeno?" I called out, my footsteps slowing.

The man held a finger to his lips and looked around, but beckoned me forward. I caught every other movement beneath the fluttering lights. I walked slowly toward him. Could I trust Daphne? Would this Zeno character actually help, or would things go south?

The light above the man stopped flickering and stayed on. Immediately, I froze. No glasses. No afro.

My heart hammered in my chest. I stared at my opponent standing fifteen feet away. He was black like Zeno, lightly built, and about my height. But that's where the similarities ended. The face didn't match at all. Shorter hair, no glasses, and a bone structure that was completely different from the picture.

That wasn't Zeno.

Had the Left Hand somehow figured out where I was going? Was he Sinistrali?

I evaluated the man before me. He didn't look like he was carrying any weapons, but those could be concealed easily enough. My only exit was past the man, and if he had taken down Zeno, if he was Sinistrali, I'd almost certainly have to fight him to get to it. And if I could surprise him, all the better.

I took a casual step forward.

"Daphne told me she'd send someone. Man, am I glad to see you." I let relief sweep over my features like I was meeting an old friend. I forced an exhausted smile across my face and extended my hand. "I'm Victor."

The imposter smiled and took it. "Ze—"

I thrust my hand downward and rammed my opposite elbow into his nose.

He yelled in pain and threw his head back, both hands flying to his face. I took a quick half step forward, positioning my right leg behind his. With all the force I could muster, I threw both of my hands onto his chest and used his momentum against him, throwing him against the terminal floor with a thud.

I dealt him a quick blow to the stomach and took off in a dead sprint in the only direction available: out of the terminal and into the Heights.

"Wait!"

The imposter's voice bounced around the empty terminal like a gunshot in a cave. I paid it no heed. I cast a backwards glance as the imposter pushed himself to his feet.

Adrenaline fueled my movements, but my mind felt paralyzed. *Come on! Something, anything! Think!*

I couldn't call anyone Noble. Police would detain me and bring me in. My only hope was Daphne, assuming she hadn't been compromised too.

I glanced back. Fake Zeno had started to run after me.

I just needed to outrun him, get him off my trail and hide. Then I could call Daphne. That's what I had to do.

Seventy yards away, the exit loomed in front of me, a poorly lit rectangle that was almost smothered by the blackness of the night beyond. And in the middle of the rectangle appeared the silhouette of a man.

"That's him!" the imposter yelled, now jogging after me, slightly bent over, one hand on his stomach and the other pointing at me.

My internal alarms were blaring. I slowed my sprint to a jog and tried desperately to come up with a plan. I was essentially in the middle of a long hallway with someone on either side. I was trapped.

The man silhouetted in the exit stepped into the light, and I stopped dead in my tracks. He was huge, at least six and a half feet tall. Black-skinned and bald, he wore a tank top through which every one of his sharply defined muscles could be seen.

"It's all right," he said with a British accent, "we're not going to hurt you." He held out his empty hands.

I highly doubted that, but his accent took me aback. As far as I knew, Sinisters were banned from international travel. Had the Left Hand actually recruited Nobles?

"You're Victor Wells, aren't you?" the man asked.

I hesitated, weighing my options. I could lie. I was just a Noble kid who got on the wrong train. But the Sinistrali knew what I looked like.

"Yes," I said. I stood up straight and stared ahead in defiance.

Behind me, the irregular gait of the imposter continued to draw closer. My body tensed, waiting for some sort of impact, the blast of a stunner or a swift punch to the kidney, but it didn't come. He came to a labored stop behind me, barely out of arm's reach.

"Dang, man, Daphne said you might pack a punch." He cupped his bleeding nose with one hand. "But I guess that's my bad. Dax, a little help, please?"

"Wait, you know Daphne?" I asked.

The behemoth, Dax, started forward.

"Wait!" I held out my hand.

Miraculously, he stopped.

"Oh," he said, breaking out a wide grin. "I see what's going on here."

"Enlighten me," I said and turned to the imposter. "You know Daphne?"

"Bro, first, take the seriousness down a notch. Second, welcome to the Heights. This is Dax"—he motioned with his free hand—"and I'm Zeno. We hope you enjoy your stay."

"Daphne sent me a picture. You look nothing like Zeno."

I kept my knees bent, ready to spring into action, regardless of how futile it would be.

"That was the plan." Zeno turned. "You know, Dax, this new material is so comfortable, I forgot I had it on."

"A little too comfortable, perhaps? Looks like you didn't reinforce the nosepiece like I suggested."

Nosepiece? What was he talking about?

"Hey man, there wasn't supposed to be a need. The whole purpose of wearing one of these is so you don't get clocked in the face. But I could use a hand."

Dax started forward again. I held out my hand. Again, he stopped.

"First, how do you know Daphne? Who are you, really?"

The imposter sighed. "I'm Zeno," he said slowly, "but I'm in disguise." He motioned to his face. "I'm wearing a mask, which I will take off as soon as my nose stops bleeding. Dax, you got anything for this?"

Dax nodded and took a tentative step forward. I nodded slowly and took a step to the side, careful to stay out of reach of both of them. My heart pounded in my chest. I could run. Dax had his back to me. I could make a break for it. But to where? I didn't even know if I could trust Daphne and Augustine.

Dax reached into his pocket, pulled out a small syringe, and squirted the contents into Zeno's nostrils.

"Ahhh," he said in relief. "That's better. Thanks, my man!" Zeno wiped his nose and patted Dax on the arm. "All right, time for the big reveal!"

With a flourish, Zeno reached behind his ear and tugged. It was like déjà vu.

The real Zeno appeared before my eyes, rectangular afro and all, except for the glasses. In his hands he held a limp, lifeless silicone silhouette. A mask.

"Cool, right?" he said, smiling. "I would have brought one for you too, but—"

"Where did you get that?" I asked, cutting him off. It looked almost exactly like the one Harvesty had been wearing. I balled my hands into fists. I had to be ready to fight.

"I made it," Zeno said, confusion showing on his face. "Why, what's wrong wi—"

"Did you make one for Harvesty too?" I asked.

Zeno looked bewilderedly at Dax, who shrugged.

"Who's Harvesty? Did he have a mask like this?" Zeno asked, holding up the silicone form.

"He's Sinistrali," I said quietly. "And he just attacked me and my grandfather. I barely escaped."

"What?" Zeno looked to Dax. "The Left Hand showed up at your house? What'd you do, forget to tell Daphne that on the phone? How'd you—"

"We should go," Dax said, cutting Zeno off. "Now."

I scrutinized the man. He looked more tense than he had a moment before. His knees were slightly bent, his hands clenched into fists. His posture matched mine. He was ready to fight.

"You think?" Zeno said. "We're in Tyrann Kane's part of town, and the Left Hand could be here any minute!"

Great. Add Tyrann Kane to my list of problems. If the government had a list of people they thought were part of the Left Hand, Tyrann Kane had to be at the top.

"I came straight here from the station," I said. "The Sinistrali who were following me only saw that I boarded a Sinister train. There's no way they could know where I'm at, right?"

"Let's not underestimate their resourcefulness," Dax said. "We should leave. Now."

"Agreed," Zeno said. "But first..." He paused as he turned to face me. "You wouldn't happen to have one of those snazzy new ID cards, would you?"

"Why?"

It was in my jacket pocket, but I wasn't about to give it up, at least not to them. I knew Daphne had sent them, but besides the fact that they were here and scared of the Left Hand, what else did I know about them?

"GPS tracking," Zeno said. "And the Left Hand could be using it to track you. Hand it over." He held out his hand.

I hesitated. I knew all Sinisters weren't bad, but that didn't mean they could all be trusted.

"Look man, I'll take you to Daphne, but not if you've got something on you that can lead a whole team of Sinistrali right to us. Your choice."

If I handed my ID card over, it meant that I was trusting them. I was going to trust a couple of Sinisters I had just met in the Heights in the middle of the night.

"Right," I said, reluctantly placing my card into Zeno's outstretched hand.

"There you go," he said. "Be right back."

Zeno sprinted back to my empty train pod and tossed the card inside. He got down on his hands and knees, and after a moment he stood back up. The glass panes closed once more and the pod shot off back down the tracks. Zeno came back at a jog.

"Let's see them follow that," he said with a smirk.

"How'd you do that?" I asked. I'd never seen anyone manipulate a train pod before.

"It's all just science and stuff, bro." Zeno tossed the mask back over his head and tugged it into place. I still didn't know how he got his afro to disappear underneath it. He smiled at me. "And I know science and stuff."

"Right then, let's go," Dax said, glancing at the exit before locking eyes with me. "Victor, stay close and keep quiet. In this part of the Heights, you'll be safe with me, but I'd rather not run into anyone, understand?"

I nodded and Dax took off at a fast jog, his quiet footfalls belying his incredible size.

I stayed right behind him, and Zeno brought up the rear. We exited the terminal and turned left. Dax led us on in silence for a few blocks. It was too dark to make out much of my surroundings. Tall, neglected buildings seemed to be the status quo. The occasional street lamp bordered the road, but most of them were broken or merely flickering dimly in the darkness.

Finally, Dax came to a stop. A set of small tracks cut through the road and a collection of personal transports sat off to the side. Each transport was composed of a clear plastic standing platform and a pair of metal poles sticking out of the base with grips to hold on to and steer.

Dax walked over and picked up three transports with almost superhuman ease and placed them on the tracks. Each personal transport floated several inches off the ground, suspended, I guessed, by the same mechanism the trains used, albeit on a smaller scale.

Dax placed a finger to his lips and motioned us to come close, speaking fast.

"Zeno, you take the lead, Victor, you're in the middle, and I'll follow from behind." Dax turned to me. "Victor, you ridden one of these before, mate?"

I shook my head.

"Right, they're easy enough. Each platform has a pair of poles for balancing and speed control. To go forward, push the bars forward. To slow down, pull the bars backwards. You'll get the hang of it," he said as he stepped onto his platform.

I did likewise.

"Stay close to Zeno," he said. "I'll follow until you're in the clear."

"Thanks, Dax, you're the man," Zeno said, and they exchanged a fist bump. It was a distinctly Noble gesture, mostly because that's what you did to start every saber fight—a fist bump with your saber hand.

"Remember to have these back before tomorrow," Dax said. "And Victor"—he turned to me—"see you around."

I nodded and attempted a smile.

Dax nodded to Zeno. "Right then, let's go."

We each jumped onto a platform.

Zeno looked back at me. "Ready?"

I nodded. "Yes."

He leaned forward and shot down the tracks. I took a quick glance back at Dax, who gave me an encouraging nod. I pushed the bars forward and flew after Zeno.

The wind rushed past me and the knot in my chest loosened ever so slightly. I was on my way to Augustine's. On my way to Daphne. A hundred thoughts fought for attention in my mind. What would happen when I got there? Could they even help? Would Daphne be angry with me? Would I even be around long enough for it to matter?

But one question sounded in my mind louder than the rest: could I trust them?

13

Zeno hauled his platform off the tracks and stashed it next to a derelict wooden shed that leaned precariously to one side.

"There's room for yours too, bro," he said.

I hauled my platform off and placed it next to his. It was nearly pitch-black outside. Stars twinkled above us, but there seemed to be fewer of them here. Up ahead, a few streetlights fluttered on and off, failing to completely illuminate the way.

"No more need for this," Zeno said, reaching behind his ear once more. The real Zeno emerged a moment later, his rectangular afro somehow still a picture of perfection. He winked and slung the mask over his shoulder. "Come on, we don't have much further to go. Stay close."

He took off at a jog toward the semidarkness of the streets. Flanked on either side by old brick buildings, some with lights, some without, we made our way toward the Pendletons. Or at least I assumed that's where we were going. It was hard to imagine anyone living here. Nothing was clean. The ugly sound of decaying matter squished beneath my shoes more than once, despite my best efforts to avoid it. Intact windows seemed to be the exception, not the rule.

Welcome to the Heights, I guess.

We ran in silence, but the further we got into the, um, neighbor-hood, the less silent things became. The sounds of glass breaking or people shouting broke the still night air, but Zeno didn't flinch. Apparently, this was commonplace here. I shouldn't have been surprised, but how could people live like this?

Zeno turned right and the street descended, coming to an end at a relatively large building made from crumbling brick. It reminded me of an events center, and that's exactly what it was. Upon reaching the entryway, Zeno slowed to a walk. Old newspapers and bits of trash covered the ground. Faded posters and signs for concerts coated the decaying brick walls. The musky smell of mildew hung in the air like fog on a still morning.

Zeno cast one last look over his shoulder before opening the front doors. He stood to the side and ushered me in. I approached cautiously.

"Come on, bro, get inside."

But I hesitated. What awaited me beyond those doors?

"I promise this isn't the place where I take people and kill them," he said, visibly straining to keep the door open. "Come on, man, I can't hold these doors forever. I'm not Dax."

I stepped inside, and Zeno closed the door behind us. A series of lights came to life, illuminating a room that would have put most Noble houses to shame had it been in mint condition. Instead, layers of dust and grime coated the walls.

"Is this it?" I asked, looking around. My voice echoed in the cavernous atrium. "Is this where Augustine and Daphne live?"

"Yep, and me too."

I gave Zeno a questioning look.

"Well, at least for the time being. I'm looking for my own place, you know, something a little smaller, more modern. But for now, Augustine's got a room for me."

"Does anybody else live here?" I asked. Several hallways branched off in different directions. This place was huge.

"Every once in a while there's a homeless person, but usually it's just us."

"But, I mean, look at this place. It's—"

"Massive?" Zeno said. "Yeah, if Augustine had his way, it'd be full, but you know, it's not a perfect world down here. Not everyone agrees with his way of thinking." Zeno shrugged. "Come on, they're probably waiting for us."

Zeno turned and walked on. I followed him, our footsteps echoing through the wide, vacant halls.

What had he meant by "Not everyone agrees with his way of thinking?" Were the Pendletons outcasts, even here? Zeno, admittedly, seemed more like a Noble than a Sinister, but it could all be a trick. I hadn't seen the Pendletons in four years. Who knew what I was in for, actual help or more trouble? I needed to prepare. I had to survive.

I followed Zeno around two more corners before we stopped at a door. He turned and faced me. This must be it.

"All right man, are you ready?"

Honestly, I wasn't sure. There were so many thoughts going through my mind. Everything felt uncertain.

"Look, I know it's been a long time since you last saw Augustine and Daphne," he said, "but you can trust them." He paused and fixed me with a serious stare. "I did."

"What do you mean, 'I did'?"

"That is a story for another time, but suffice it to say, my man, that I, like you, am a Noble."

Zeno, a Noble? I chewed on that. I guess it wasn't a huge stretch to believe—the way he acted, the fact that I wasn't dead or a hostage. Both were good indicators. But if he was telling the truth, the real question was, what he was doing here?

"Why should I believe you?" I asked.

"Bro, come on. I mean, Sinisters aren't all bad, but have you ever seen one look this good?" he said, motioning to his entire person with both hands. "And unfortunately, tech skills like this"—he paused and held up his mask—"aren't learned in the Heights."

He had a point, about the tech skills at least. If Zeno was a Noble and he was here with the Pendletons, what did that mean?

Zeno looked at me and squinted.

"Yeah," he said with a nod, "I think it's about time you talk to Augustine and Daphne."

Zeno turned to the door and rapped his knuckles two times on the wood.

Immediately, my heart rate climbed. A deluge of old feelings returned—friendship, betrayal, anger.

I needed to stay calm. I needed to evaluate the situation and figure out my next move. But if Zeno was telling the truth, maybe there was a sliver of hope.

I heard a soft metallic click, and Zeno pushed the door open. Light illuminated the darkened hallway. Across the room, two people stood at the end of a table.

14

Zeno shut the door behind me. I had stepped into silence. Daphne and Augustine stood before me. I took them in, and the memories came flooding back. Family parties, Sunday dinner at their house, Christmas afternoon. The Pendletons had been like family.

Augustine appeared much as I remembered him, tall and thin with a full head of dark hair. However, he looked tired, older. More pronounced wrinkles flanked his eyes, and a smattering of silver had made its way into his hair. He hadn't changed much, but I couldn't say the same for Daphne.

She was beautiful—taller, with piercing gray eyes and sharp features. Long, dark hair cascaded past her shoulders, outlining the hard look that rested on her tanned features. The younger, carefree Daphne was gone. Years of living in the Heights probably did that to a person.

"Victor!" Daphne said, her expression softening as she walked over to me.

I took a reflexive step back, the heel of my dress shoe catching the closed door behind me. Daphne stopped in her tracks, a look of confusion crossing her face.

"Victor, we're glad you made it," Augustine said quickly. "Zeno sent us a message saying the Left Hand showed up at your house. Are you hurt?"

"I'm fine," I said. I shifted my eyes to Daphne, who had fixed me with an unreadable stare. I looked back to Augustine. He smiled wearily.

"Good, I'm glad. And what about your grandfather?"

An image of him lying on the floor unconscious flashed into my mind.

"I'm not sure," I said. "One of the Sinistrali stunned him, but they were there for me and I ran." I felt ashamed saying it.

"Any of us would have done the same thing," Augustine said kindly. "I'm sure your grandfather will be okay. Like you said, they were after you." He paused. "But it's good to see you. It's been a long time."

I shifted my weight from one foot to the other. It *had* been a long time, but I needed answers.

"Thanks for sending Zeno," I said, looking at Daphne. "But why bring me here at all?"

"You called me, remember?" Daphne said with her arms folded.

"I think he's asking about our motives," Augustine said, eyes on me. "He's not sure if he can trust us."

Daphne looked pointedly at me.

"Look, the last time I saw you guys, you were being escorted out of the Flats for hiding your DNA status and—"

"And it was just as much of a lie then as it is now," Daphne said.

"Am I just supposed to take your word for it?" I asked.

"No, you're not," Augustine said. "But I'll ask you to hold your frustrations for a few minutes longer." He turned to Zeno. "Could you go grab the two scanners?"

"You got it, boss. And not that this isn't going to be a lot of fun, but I'm going to visit Gina first. You can ask Victor about that." Zeno rubbed his neck and winked at me. He lowered his voice and leaned in. "Give them a chance, man." And then he walked out the door.

"Zeno said no one else lived here," I said. "Who's Gina?"

Augustine let a guarded smile cross his face. "'Gina' is an interface that runs all the electronics in this place, but judging by the way Zeno was rubbing his neck, I assume he's talking about his spinal realignment device. Also named Gina," he added. "Somehow you're responsible for his need to visit her?"

"He showed up wearing a mask and forgot to take it off," I said.

"I see." Augustine smiled wearily. "Well Victor, we've got a few minutes before Zeno gets back. Sit, make yourself at home. Daphne, you too."

Daphne didn't move.

I stayed where I was.

"I'll stand," I said.

"Suit yourself," Augustine said. He reached into his pocket and pulled out a screen and began working on it. I glanced over at Daphne, but quickly looked away. The silence was uncomfortable at best.

I took stock of my surroundings. The room was immaculate—well lit, plush carpet, nicely furnished—nothing like the dusty hallway we had come from.

Augustine pushed a button on his screen and spoke. "Zeno, are you on your way?"

"Just about," he grunted. An audible cracking sounded over the speaker.

Augustine grimaced at the sound. "The quicker the better. Please." He went back to tapping on his screen.

It had only been four years, but he looked like he had aged a decade. I tried to gauge him, Daphne, and Zeno. Did they really think they could explain the last four years away?

Two knocks sounded at the door. I stepped forward to let the door swing open.

Zeno's rectangular afro preceded his entrance. He carried a black canvas bag at his side, which he set on the table in front of Augustine. "I'll tell you what, guys, Gina is a miracle worker. Do I look taller to any of you?"

"Thanks, Zeno, please take a seat." Augustine nodded at the chair in front of me. Zeno looked back and forth between us and shrugged, plopping down in his chair.

"Come on, you'll want to sit for this." Zeno patted the chair next to him.

Some of the tension in the room eased.

"Victor, I said you didn't need to take our word for what happened to us, so I'm going to give you some proof. Please, sit down. The chairs are comfortable, I promise."

Augustine motioned to the seat next to Zeno. Reluctantly, I stepped over and sat down in the chair.

"Good man," Zeno said, clapping me on the shoulder.

Augustine reached into the black bag and pulled out two scanners.

"These are DNA scanners, as you've no doubt noticed." He slid them both across the table toward me.

"If I use these, the Left Hand will be here in minutes," I said. "They're tracking my DNA. That's why I came to the Heights—no scanners."

Augustine leaned forward in his chair, letting his elbows rest on the tabletop. "Smart." He nodded appreciatively. "However, Mr. Zeno here is something of a technological virtuoso. That scanner"—he indicated the one on my right—"hasn't been updated in almost a decade. However, that scanner"—he pointed to the one on the left —"was synced to the government mainframe..."

"Thirty minutes ago," Zeno offered.

"Perfect. Neither one is currently connected to the government's main system, so neither one will allow your DNA to be tracked. You follow?"

"Okay," I said. "And how do I know you're not lying to me?"

"What possible reason could we have for inviting the Left Hand into our home?" Augustine said.

Zeno turned to me. "Come on bro, they're safe, I promise. Plus, I wouldn't risk my neck in Tyrann's territory for nothing."

He had a point, they both did.

"All right," I said, "what do you want me to do?"

"Place a hand on each scanner," Augustine said. "What follows will be fairly evident, I think."

"That's it?" I asked.

Augustine nodded. "That's it."

Slowly, and with both skepticism and curiosity, I placed a hand on each scanner. The green lines snaked their way around my fingers, undulating with their calculating light. Everyone watched me intently, waiting.

At the same instant, both screens gave off a pulse of color. The one on the right radiated red along with a warning: *TɪɪD IDENTI-FIED*. The one on the left glowed green along with the regular list of attributes. The green circle in the corner of the screen read 92 percent. The red circle on the other scanner read 14 percent.

My skepticism started to melt away. "They're different," I said slowly. "Why?"

"One readout is from today, and the other is from when you were a boy," Augustine said.

"Okay," I said, trying to make sense of it, "but DNA doesn't change, so that means there's just been a mistake, right?" A flutter of hope danced in my chest. Mistakes could be corrected.

Augustine smiled bitterly. "Unfortunately, no."

The flutter disappeared.

"Then what does it mean?" I asked. "Somebody changed my DNA readout? On purpose?"

Augustine locked eyes with me for a moment, his face a mix of emotions.

"Yes," he said quietly, looking down at his hands. He pushed himself to his feet. "It means that someone in one of the government's three DNA databases changed what shows up when your DNA is scanned."

My heart felt like it had stopped beating. Why? Why would someone do that?

Augustine walked around the table and pulled both scanners to himself, placing a hand on each one. I stared at the two different scanners, watching the lights trace Augustine's handprints.

"But it also means that you're not a Sinister," he said, "and you don't have TⅡD either, if it's any consolation."

The two scanners glowed again, each showing a different result. Ninety-six percent. Twenty-two percent. Augustine sat back down.

I continued to stare. Ninety-six percent Noble. Higher than me. Higher than anyone I knew, well besides the Bounty Hunter. And what he was saying, what he was showing me, was that I wasn't a Sinister. And he and Daphne weren't either. None of us were.

Was this all a setup? Some elaborate plan to bring me here? *And then what?* I asked myself. It didn't make sense.

I stared at the scanners again.

One hand 96 percent. The other 22 percent.

I wanted to accept it, but I couldn't. It was the best worst news I'd ever received. I wasn't a Sinister. But it also meant that society was flawed and corrupt—a lie. The hot feeling of shame boiled up in my stomach.

"Four years ago, you weren't hiding anything," I started slowly. "You weren't trying to cover up your DNA." I looked up at Augustine. "The same thing that's happening to me, happened to you."

"Yes," he said, his gaze strong and unblinking. I looked at Daphne, who stared at the floor.

Zeno fidgeted in his chair. "He's telling the truth, man. I wouldn't be here if he wasn't."

I had been angry at the Pendletons for so long, but I had been wrong.

"Victor, you haven't changed, but your readout has," Augustine said. He placed the scanners back in the bag. "Someone wants to lock you out of Noble society. The question is why. And who."

"Victor shows up and suddenly this matters again?" Daphne muttered.

Augustine closed his tired eyes and turned to Daphne. "We don't need to have this discussion now."

"Or ever, apparently," she said. A pained expression grazed Augustine's face. I wasn't sure what that was about.

"So if none of us are Sinister," I started, "why can't we just go to the DNA centers and sort everything out? We could show them the scanners and—"

"Because each of the three DNA center locations is kept secret. That was privileged information, even inside the senate. And besides, it's not that simple—"

"But someone you know had to know, right?" I said. "You used to be in the senate. Couldn't you just convince—"

"Do you think I haven't tried?" Augustine said, cutting me off. He glanced at Daphne, who stared at the floor. "No one would talk to us once the news broke, and no one will talk to you either," he continued. "There are no doors left for us to open, but maybe there are for you." He paused. "Can you think of any reason this would happen? Is there anyone who would want to do this to you?"

I racked my brain, but nothing came. The closest thing I had to an enemy was Gio, and at worst, we were friendly rivals. Plus, why would someone change the DNA readout of a sixteen-year-old?

"Victor?" Augustine said.

"Yeah, sorry. I have no idea." I shook my head. "No one comes to mind. This morning I was a Noble. After I was Marked, I started reading Sinister."

"No, Victor, there's no Noble, no Sinister, there's just you."

I looked up, confused.

"But that's for another time," he said, waving his hand. "I didn't think you'd have any enemies."

"And what about the Left Hand?" I asked. "Do you think they're connected?"

Augustine stared at the floor for a few moments before responding.

"The Left Hand has a perfect record going back decades," he said, bring his gaze back up to meet mine. "If they have the necessary information to do that, I imagine they could change a DNA readout. And given the fact that they showed up at your house, I'd say it's a pretty good bet."

I fought against the cold shiver that made its way up my spine.

"Do you think it was the Left Hand who changed your readouts?" I asked.

"The thought crossed my mind in the beginning," Augustine said, "but no. I have to believe it was someone else. The Left Hand never threatened us." He glanced at Daphne before continuing. "Unfortunately for us, who and why remains a mystery." He paused. "But that's all in the past now. We need to focus on the present, and I think that something must have happened yesterday, something we missed." He locked eyes with me. "I need to you to tell me exactly what happened. Don't leave anything out."

"From the beginning?" I asked.

"From the beginning."

Daphne was looking at me now, her expression difficult to read. I took a deep breath, gathered my thoughts, and began. No one interrupted. They all listened closely, and I told them everything.

"And then I jumped on the Sinister line and called Daphne," I said. "Zeno met me and brought me here."

Augustine sat with his fingertips together, a thoughtful expression on his face. He stayed that way for several seconds. Daphne had listened intently, but hadn't said a word. She stood with her back to the wall, arms folded like before.

Finally, Augustine shook his head and spoke. "And you're sure Senator Supart didn't give you anything?"

"Positive," I said.

Zeno leaned back in his chair. "And they think that Senator Supart figured out their boss's name? Man, if he had that"—he blew out a mouthful of air—"who knows what the Sinistrali would do to get it back."

"Do you think it's possible?" Augustine asked, looking at Zeno.

"I don't know, boss. It *would* explain why he and Victor were Marked." Zeno yawned and checked his watch. "But what do you say, take another crack at it in the morning?"

"Yes, I think that's a good idea," Augustine said. "I need to think on this."

"Think about what?" I said. "We need something else to go on.

Avardi said he wanted to see me after he got done speaking. Maybe me getting Marked is related to that? Maybe we could get ahold of him and he could tell us something that would help us out."

"And how would you do that?" Daphne asked. "What are the chances his phone is like yours and doesn't take Sinister calls?"

She fixed me with a glare. The flames of guilt returned.

"I...don't know," I said beneath her withering glare.

"Wellllllll," Zeno said, drawing out the word and looking back and forth between us, "I could let you use my untraceable, ultra-cool, custom phone which defies all labels, which I built with these hands"—he held them up—"but you really think the Left Hand won't be listening to his phone calls?"

"Oh, right," I said, grateful for the excuse to escape Daphne's gaze. "Couldn't you engineer a way around that?" I asked. "With those hands?"

Zeno cracked a smile.

"We'll figure it out tomorrow," Augustine said. He scooted his chair back and stood up. "For now, we need to get some rest."

"What about me?" I asked.

"What about you?" he said.

"Here?"

"Of course," Augustine said with a confused smile.

I thought I heard Daphne mutter something under her breath. It sounded suspiciously like the word "idiot."

"But I've been Marked, and the government still thinks I'm a TiiD carrier. My being here puts you all in danger and—"

"And this is the best place you could have come to hide from the Left Hand," Augustine said, walking to the door. "And the government, for that matter. Now follow me. I'll show you to your room."

Augustine held the door open for me.

I pushed myself away from the table and stood up, relieved by his answer.

"Night," Zeno said, remaining in his chair.

"Night." I caught Daphne's eye. Her glare hadn't fully subsided.

"Night," I said to her. She didn't respond, and I headed out the open door.

Augustine closed the door behind me, and I followed him into the dingy hall beyond. We took a few turns and passed through a series of doors, walking in silence most of the way.

A strange series of emotions ran through my head, each poignant in its own right. Relief that I was still Noble, guilt for how I had thought about the Pendletons, and confusion at why all this was happening to me. Not to mention Daphne—she was clearly not happy with me.

A few moments later, we arrived at the mouth of a short hallway.

"You can take the last one on the right," he said.

Each of four doors on the right side had a glass pane that had been covered from the inside. As we approached the room, I could make out the glue residue from the now absent vinyl letters. *Events Center Manager.*

"We converted the offices to sleeping quarters," Augustine explained. "You'll find a bed and bathroom, and I believe there is another set of clothes for you, something that won't stand out so much." He nodded to my suit. "Daphne will come get you in the morning. Stay with her and don't wander around. Most people around here are harmless, but not everyone is. Daphne knows who's who. Stick with her."

He turned to leave. My mind still buzzed with everything I had learned, but there was one thing we hadn't talked enough about.

"Mr. Pendleton."

"Yes, Victor? And Augustine is fine."

"Have you heard anything about my grandfather? When I checked on the train, the news hadn't mentioned anything."

Augustine brought his hand up to his chin. "Hmm. It could be that yours is such a big story that it overshadowed everything else, but I could do some checking."

"Do you think I could try calling him?" I asked. "He took some hard hits, and I just want to make sure he's okay."

Augustine viewed me with a mixture of sadness and pity. "I'm sure Zeno would let you borrow his phone for a few minutes. I'll be right back."

He gave me a tight-lipped smile and walked off. Two minutes later, he returned carrying a phone that looked nearly identical to mine. "Zeno said that the only person able to track this phone is him. Just type the number in and call."

"Thanks, Augustine," I said, taking the phone. I dialed Grandfather's number and pressed the call button.

The line was silent. No rings, no static, nothing. I pulled the phone away from my ear to make sure it had connected. It had.

"Strange," I mumbled.

I ended the call and dialed again.

Nothing.

"If what you told me earlier is true," Augustine said, "it could be that he's at a hospital recuperating. I can't imagine him being there for more than a night though. Maybe we can try again in a day or two?"

"Yeah, sure," I said.

"We'll keep an eye on the news too, okay? Don't worry, Victor, I'm sure he's fine."

"Yeah, me too," I said, but without conviction. Augustine hadn't been there. The Left Hand didn't care about my grandfather. They certainly hadn't cared about Freddy.

"We'll work on this more tomorrow," he said. "Now try and get some sleep." He patted me on the shoulder and turned to leave.

"Augustine?" I said.

He stopped and turned to face me.

"Yes?"

"Thanks for everything," I said, and I meant it. Who knew where I'd be if not for him and Daphne and Zeno?

Augustine smiled softly and nodded.

"Have a good night, Victor."

"You too," I said.

He turned and disappeared down the hallway. I pushed open the door to my room and stepped inside to find a well-made bed, stocked dresser, and a personal bathroom. I grabbed some clothes and headed for the bathroom, pausing when I caught myself in the mirror.

Everything had changed. Everything. But I was still Noble. Just like the Pendletons.

I splashed some water on my face. It mixed with the salt and dirt on my skin and dripped a gray residue into the porcelain sink. I dried off and made my way to the bed, not knowing what tomorrow would bring.

15

I woke slowly, pulling the covers up over my head, letting the warmth of the sheets lull me back to sleep.

My eyes shot open.

Yesterday's events came flooding back in a deluge of color. The Left Hand, the Pendletons, the fact that I wasn't a Sinister and neither were they.

"Grandfather," I whispered to myself.

I jumped out of bed and grabbed my phone. Headlines scrolled across the screen. "Gene of Terror." "First Dual Marking in History." I thumbed past them, searching for any mention of Grandfather. There was nothing.

Nothing.

Did that mean he was okay? Then again, there was nothing in there about Freddy either.

So much had happened. Things that were irreversible. Freddy. I could see his lifeless body falling to the ground. It didn't feel real. How could someone be there one moment and be gone the next?

A shallow, shuddering breath broke through, and I wiped at my eyes. I needed to get up and get going. I couldn't sit here and think about that.

Ten minutes later, I was clean, dressed, and had no idea what I was supposed to do next. Supposedly, Daphne was going to come get me, but who knew how long it'd be until that happened?

I opened the door and headed down the hallway, doing my best to remember where Augustine had taken me, but failing miserably. Two minutes into the complex web of dusty hallways and I had no idea where I was. Surely I'd run into someone at some point, though, right?

I took the next right turn and found myself standing in front of a set of double doors. I pushed my way through and stopped in my tracks. I stood at the top of a vast auditorium. Rows and rows of empty seats culminated in a large stage in the center of the room. And on the stage stood Augustine, his voice filling the cavernous room even though his audience was small.

"... can, and you will, but you must not give up!" He spread his arms wide. "Think of the progress you've made. Things will only improve from here."

Twenty or thirty people sat scattered throughout the first several rows of seats. They ranged in age from early grade school to senior citizenship. What was going on here?

I made my way down several flights of stairs as quietly as I could, aiming to get closer to the stage without causing a stir. I settled myself into a seat a few rows behind the next closest person. Augustine walked about the stage, which was littered with a handful of chalkboards, each one filled to the brim with his hurried, all-caps script.

The boards taught everything from math to reading and writing and history. It was a school, I realized. Was this what Augustine had been doing since he'd been forced out of the Noble society? Teaching what looked like a ragtag band of Sinisters elementary-school concepts?

"Very good! Okay, Cordone, can you tell me the—"

A door to the left of the stage banged open, stopping Augustine mid-question.

"Augustine Pendleton, the great teacher," a voice echoed from the doorway. A bald man wearing a tailored maroon suit and powder blue shirt strode onto the stage. The audience grew tense. Several people close to me quickly stood up and made to leave. "Please don't leave on my account," the man said. Immediately, those leaving returned to their seats. Except for one.

"How very unwise."

In a flash of movement, the man reached inside his jacket and pulled out a stunner, firing a single shot. The fleeing man collapsed. No one moved to help. No one spoke. The air grew thick with fear. Augustine turned to face the newcomer, his posture defiant, but not confident, his mouth tight and closed.

"Aug, old friend, I see you've garnered quite the turnout," the newcomer continued and faced the audience with an insincere smile draped across his face.

"I think you're stretching the bounds of our relationship," Augustine said.

"Nonsense. What's the old saying? An enemy of my enemy is my friend? A foe of the Nobles is a friend to me, which is why I'm concerned about my other friends here in attendance." He motioned to the small crowd. The audience straightened in their chairs.

"I'm no one's foe."

"Yes, yes, I know, you're a teacher." The man leaned in and raised an eyebrow as he spoke. "A teacher spreading dogma in direct opposition to the Noble government, which is why you and I get along so well."

Augustine's voice grew weary. "What do you want, Tyrann?"

Tyrann? I knew of only one man by that name, and judging by everyone's response to his entrance, it had to be the fabled Tyrann Kane, master of the Heights. A tingling made it's way down my spine. I eyed his stunner. My first instinct was to run, but there was no way I could leave. I shrunk in my chair. I'd just have to wait it out.

"What do I want?" Tyrann said, taking a step towards the front of the stage. "Aside from ridding the city of Noble swine? Well, we'll get to that, but first, forgive my lack of manners. It's not just me today, my dear friend. It's a family affair!" Tyrann spread his arms wide, and two girls followed him onto the stage, each the polar opposite of the other. One wore black everything—clothes, makeup, fingernails. Her hair was black, too, but had a small stripe of pink running through it. The other wore white pants, a white shirt, and shiny golden gloves that extended just past her elbows. And she was beautiful, her hair a sparkling shade of silver that framed her fair-skinned face.

"Augustine, you remember my daughters, Pria and Printh," he said, motioning first to the angel and second to the goth.

"Of course." Augustine gave each of them a curt nod. "Now, if you'll excuse me, I'll be free in fifteen minutes." Augustine turned to face the class again, most of whom shifted uncomfortably in their seats.

"As I previously said, I am worried about my other friends here this morning. This cannot wait."

"I'm sure it can wait fifteen minutes."

"I do wonder, Aug, if you really even care about these people?" He spoke slowly and deliberately, his pauses only increasing the drama. He turned and faced the small crowd, his gaze scanning the faces until it focused in on me. He smirked. "Are you doing this for all the right reasons?"

Augustine's expression turned murderous. He tried to interject. "Tyrann, I w—"

Tyrann continued speaking like he was driving a car and Augustine was a fly in his path. I had seen this style of speaking before in the senate. It had never worked well amongst the Nobles, but the Sinisters held on to every word.

"I know that some of you may fear the nighttime sweepers, the war front, and the Noble-Sinister inequalities, not to mention the end of the so called 'Great Experiment.'"

"Tyrann, I'd ap—"

"But I want to talk about something far more pressing and dangerous," Tyrann continued, pacing back and forth along the stage, his eyes dangerously alight. He paused and turned to face the audience. "I want to talk about T11D." More uncomfortable shifting followed his words. "As our friends in the audience may know," he continued, "TⁱⁱD is found in those special individuals who have the disposition of being inclined toward mass murder, genocide, and—"

"Tyr—"

"And," Tyrann said loudly, "killing for fun." He let a smile crawl across his face. "I don't need to remind you of Brovecheq, do I? Hundreds of Sinisters dead—men, women, and children alike. I'm a saint by comparison, wouldn't you agree?"

Several heads nodded in hurried agreement. I stared on in horror. How could someone, anyone, think like that?

"Your point, Tyrann?" Augustine said.

"Who among you have loved ones?" Tyrann said, focusing on the audience. "Go ahead, don't be shy."

Everyone in attendance raised a hand.

"Yes, I thought so."

"Why are you here, Tyrann?" Augustine said loudly.

"Why, I'm here to take care of my friends. I'm here, my dear Augustine, because I can't imagine that you are keeping these fine people's best interests at heart while secretly harboring a carrier of TⁱⁱD."

Augustine's face fell as Tyrann pointed at me. My heart seemed to stop beating. Printh remained gothic and motionless on the stage. Pria feigned surprise and placed a hand to her mouth. As one, the audience turned to follow Tyrann's finger, their collective gaze landing on me. Gasps assaulted the tension-filled air.

"Victor Wells is here!" Tyrann bellowed.

The Sinisters attempted to scatter. A wicked smile crept across Tyrann's face. He whipped out his stunner and fired a shot into the air.

"Stop!" he yelled.

Almost immediately, the auditorium became still. Tyrann kept the stunner out, swinging it at his side as he began to pace once more.

"Cowards, all of you!" he said. "Victor Wells is here, yes. I assume you are all frightened of the teenage ex-Noble." He let the stunner fall limp in his hand, suspended by his trigger finger. "Perhaps he is here like Brovecheq. Perhaps he is here to kill us all. However"—he paused and pointed his stunner at me—"I for one am interested in seeing who he will become. Friend or foe?

"You all remember Qinsari," Tyrann continued, staring up at the rafters. He smiled and shook his head as if he were recalling a happy memory. "A true hero. All the Noble children screaming, the hospital in ashes... Ah, it was a wonderful day." He continued to stare off into the rafters. We all remained silent.

You could learn a lot about a person in a short amount of time.

I had learned that Tyrann Kane was crazy.

All of a sudden, his head snapped back down, anger contorting his features.

"And if any of you breathe a word of Victor Wells's whereabouts to anyone," he whispered, his voice carrying throughout the auditorium, "I will not rest until justice has been served!"

No one moved. No one breathed.

"Victor Wells is mine," he said, his voice back to a whisper, "and as long as none of you meddle in my affairs, we will make an ally out of him yet."

His posture relaxed and he pocketed his stunner.

"You're all free to go," he said simply. Augustine looked ill in the background, his gaze directed at the floor, his hands balled into fists.

The Sinisters scrambled. Friends and family members tripped over each other in their attempts to escape.

Within seconds, the room was empty.

A malicious smile crept onto Tyrann's face. It was the first real expression I had seen on the man. He looked around the now empty auditorium. "Well that was fun, wasn't it?"

Augustine looked up, a weary expression on his face. "Don't you know what I'm trying to do here?" he said.

Tyrann held up a finger. "Yes, yes, change the Sinisters, teach them to be good, rainbows and all that nonsense, but how boring! Besides, business comes first, Aug, and there are a few things we need to discuss."

Augustine sighed and started to make his way toward the unconscious man Tyrann had stunned earlier.

"He can wait," Tyrann said. "I can't."

Augustine stopped in his tracks, clenching his fists.

Tyrann began to walk toward the door behind the stage. "Come, I don't have all day," Tyrann said happily. "And Mr. Wells." Tyrann looked at me and paused. "It's not every day a man gets to meet a carrier of TⁱⁱD. Join us."

He turned and disappeared through the door. I caught Augustine's eye. He nodded, and I followed him across the stage. I couldn't even begin to guess what would happen next.

"I assume you know why I'm here."

Augustine stood five feet from Tyrann, arms folded. "I don't presume to know your dealings, Tyrann."

We had moved to the cavernous room just behind the stage filled with tables, chairs, and a massive projector screen on one wall. Pria and Printh leaned against the far wall ten feet apart from each other, not talking. Daphne and Zeno had entered the room moments before. Both stood behind Augustine.

"So hostile so early in the morning," Tyrann said. "I'll make a point of showing up later in the day."

"Maybe then you could come alone, or not at all," Daphne countered. Her gaze hadn't strayed from Pria, almost like she was trying to bore a hole into the side of her head. Augustine gave Daphne a look of warning, but said nothing.

After seeing Tyrann's antics in the auditorium, I couldn't believe she'd talk to him like that. I couldn't believe any of us were talking to him at all.

Tyrann smiled. "Ah, but I do enjoy my visits here."

"What we'd enjoy is getting all this over with," Zeno said, appearing more impatient than anything.

"Yes, Mr. Zeno. I agree! Down to business."

"And what business might that be exactly?" Augustine said.

"As you well know, Mr. Zeno extracted Victor from the very heart of my favorite little neighborhood last night. And I seem to recall a deal we made—"

Augustine cut in. "These were special circumst—"

"The short and long of it is this," Tyrann cut in, his voice suddenly razor sharp. "Compensation must be made."

Augustine stood quietly, his face closed and unreadable. Daphne scowled. Zeno's casual air seemed to have left him.

"Though I must admit," Tyrann continued, "bringing Victor Wells here—it's almost like you're trying to get on my good side. I have a feeling he and I could make a great team."

"Team?" I said.

"Oh yes," Tyrann said with a nod. "The Nobles are a scourge—power hungry, oppressive, but weak. Of course you know all of this already, having lived among them for so long." He paused and we locked eyes. There was no light in them, just trickery, malice, and hate. "The Nobles must be stopped," he continued. "Your intimate knowledge of their society will be an invaluable asset. Not to mention, shall we say, that killer genetic code of yours."

He was talking like I would join forces with him. He was crazy.

I looked to Augustine. He gave a slight shake of his head and held a finger to his lips. The message was clear, but I disagreed. Tyrann was powerful and power respected power, not weakness.

"Here's the thing," I started. Augustine's eyes went wide. Surprise registered around the room. "I have my own agenda, and it's not spending time helping you."

"Is that so?" Tyrann said slowly.

"Yes," Augustine said, "Victor will make his own choices."

"Or has his DNA made them for him?" Tyrann countered. "Well, I can see this will be fun! You should know, Mr. Wells, I won't give up so easily. But I'm getting off track." He waved his hand. "Back to business." His turned his gaze on Augustine. "There is still a price to be paid."

"Which you could waive," Augustine said.

"And I would have considered that until you enlisted the help of one of my inner circle."

"Come on," Zeno said, "Dax came with me as a favor, not to spite you."

It took me a moment to process what had been said.

"Dax works for you?" I said.

Tyrann turned to me. "Absolutely. In fact, everyone in the Heights works for me," he said, turning back to Augustine, "even if they don't know it. Waiver denied."

"Name your price, Tyrann." Augustine's words were sharp.

Tyrann stared at Augustine for several long moments before speaking, glancing back at me before continuing. "I apologize, Mr. Wells, but I do think you'll appreciate what comes next." He looked back to Augustine. "You can have Mr. Wells in exchange for a detonator."

I watched the color drain from Augustine's face.

"And what makes you think you could take me?" I asked.

"Ha! I'm sure you would put up a good fight, but you misunderstand the situation." Tyrann pulled out his stunner. "You see," he said to Augustine, "I'm prepared to take Victor from you by force, breathe out a series of threats which you know I am all too willing to make good on, and then force you to trade me for what I want." He paused and smiled benignly. "But why don't we skip the in-between and make this easy on ourselves? Mr. Wells in exchange for a detonator."

A detonator. The words repeated in my mind. Just over a day ago, I was in a completely different world. People didn't talk of detonators. And why would Augustine have one?

"You're Tyrann Kane," Augustine said. "Why not get them from somewhere, anywhere else?"

"Because, Aug, you know as well as I do that the Noble scum have put a net of disablers over the entire city. I need a detonator that will work. And I seem to recall a slightly more youthful Augustine Pendleton seizing a cache of detonators after the best bomb maker in the Heights was killed. It's a shame you abandoned your attempt to clean up the Heights. You might have had even better toys to bargain with."

I looked back and forth between the two men. Augustine's eyes were wider than usual and his cheeks were the color of nausea. Tyrann smiled.

Augustine took a step toward Zeno.

"Excuse us, Tyrann," Augustine said. "We'd like to speak in private for a moment."

Tyrann continued to smile and waved a hand in assent. He had been expecting this.

I was a little confused. I waited for Augustine and Zeno to move, but neither of them made to leave, and there wasn't anywhere to hide. Daphne threw an undisguised look of irritation toward her father.

A strange, almost inaudible hiss sounded in the cavernous room. I looked around, searching for the source of the noise, but couldn't find anything. That was, until my eyes landed on Zeno. He held a can of what looked like old-fashioned hairspray, which he swung in an arc around himself and Augustine. The hiss sounded familiar, but I couldn't place it. And I had no idea what he was doing. Augustine stood there with his back to us all. Zeno finished up, and then opened his mouth to talk, but no sound came out.

I looked over to Daphne, hoping for an explanation, but she avoided my gaze. Pria matched Daphne's look of annoyance but said nothing.

It seemed to me that I was the only one in the room who wasn't sure what was going on. After a few moments, they appeared to be done talking, and Augustine turned to face us, still silent. He lifted his hands and parted an invisible veil that I couldn't see. As soon as he did so, the air around him became opaque, tiny gray droplets appearing from nowhere. He swept them aside, and they all fell noiselessly to the ground, where they dissolved into nothing, emitting that same faint hiss as they did so.

"I have stockpiled a small cache of pistols, real pistols," Augustine said. "They're yours and Victor stays."

Tyrann stood silent for a moment, considering the offer.

"Hmm. And the detonator?" he asked, his voice softer than before.

"Not part of the deal."

Tyrann remained silent.

Augustine spoke again. "This is a good deal, Tyrann. There's no need for us to fight."

"You're right," he said, "but it seems we must. No deal." He paused and turned to me. "Come now, Mr. Wells, I don't live far and the place is very well fortified—scanners, stunners, etc. Your scan must be less than forty percent to get in. You'll love it."

"I thought I made myself clear," I said. "I'm not coming."

"Have it your way."

Tyrann raised his stunner and pointed it directly at my chest. I watched his finger, tensing myself to dive out of the way.

"Tyrann!" Augustine said.

Tyrann removed his finger from the trigger. "Yes, Aug?"

"The detonator," Augustine said, looking and sounding much like a deflated balloon. "It's yours in exchange for Victor."

Tyrann did an about-face, a malevolent grin stretching from his lips to his eyes like the exaggerated face painting on a clown.

"Wonderful!" He stepped forward. "However, the price has gone up. Your pistols?"

Augustine stepped back. "You can't—"

Tyrann held up a finger. "The price of negotiation, Augustine. You rejected my offer, but you come from a place of weakness."

Augustine's jaw tightened.

"However," Tyrann drew out the word, "I am feeling, what's that word you sometimes teach about? Generous? In addition to the detonator, I only require one pistol, not your entire cache. Let's just say that you owe me one."

The whole room turned to Augustine, waiting for his response. He stood there, lips pressed tightly together in frustration. Finally, he nodded.

Tyrann's face lit up. "I knew you'd see reason, old friend!"

Augustine nodded to Zeno, who left the room. He returned promptly, carrying an off-white cloth sack that clanked as he strode across the room. Zeno unceremoniously handed the bag to Tyrann and then stood there, allowing him time to inspect the contents.

"Well, everything appears to be in order," he said as he closed the bag. "Aug, everyone, it has been a pleasure."

Augustine's pale cheeks surged with blood. Daphne looked murderous.

"And Mr. Wells, you're welcome to join forces with me at any time." He smiled and allowed his daughters to exit before leaving the room. "Until next time," he said. And with a swing of the door, he was gone.

16

"Do you know what he's going to do?" I asked.

"No," Augustine said with a sigh, "not for certain. There are always rumors floating around, some farfetched, some not so much." He slumped into a nearby chair. "Either way, it's worrisome. And with his hatred for Nobles..."

Silence fell over the room. With each passing moment, my guilt grew. If not for me, Tyrann wouldn't have a detonator.

"I'd always heard people whisper about Tyrann Kane," I said. "I knew he was bad, but I didn't know he was crazy."

"Crazy is an understatement, bro," Zeno muttered. "Dude wishes he was a T1D carrier and idolizes the Left Hand. I wouldn't be surprised if he had a book about Qinsari that he read every night before going to bed."

"And that's what makes him particularly dangerous," Augustine said. "He believes in Dr. Rosewood's research just as much if not more than most Nobles. There's no reasoning with him. If he could exterminate all the Nobles tomorrow, he wouldn't hesitate."

"Then what about you guys?" I asked. "I mean, you're not actually Sinisters. Does he know that?"

"He's aware of what we think," Augustine said, "but he doesn't believe it. He thinks we're rebelling against the Nobles and doing our best to undermine them." Augustine shook his head. "But I suppose we should be thankful—otherwise we might not still be here. In some deluded way, he thinks of us as different players on the same team."

"And what about his daughters?" I asked.

"Don't even get me started," Daphne muttered, kicking at a spot on the ground.

"They're not extreme like their father is, but I wouldn't underestimate them. I'll leave it at that," Augustine said, keeping an eye on Daphne.

"So what now?" I asked. "Not that Tyrann isn't a problem, but—"

"The Left Hand," Augustine said, slumping into a chair. "Yes, of course."

"What are we going to do?" I said.

"Victor, I stayed up all night thinking about it. Unless Senator Supart gave you something—"

"He didn't."

"Then I'm not sure we have much else to go on," Augustine finished.

"So that's it?" I asked.

"I don't know what to tell you, Victor. We no longer have any Noble contacts and we don't have access to the Capital. What else do you want me to do?"

"Why am I not surprised?" Daphne muttered, looking down at the ground.

Augustine gave Daphne a pained look, but she wouldn't meet his gaze.

My mind fought furiously for a solution. There had to be something more we could do. And did we actually need access to the Capital?

"Look," I said, an idea striking me, "the Left Hand doesn't make mistakes, right? If they Marked me and we don't know why, we're just missing something." I looked over at Zeno.

"What are you thinking, bro?" he said.

"The Left Hand has to be after me because of something that happened at the debate, something other than me saving Senator Supart."

"Right," Zeno said slowly.

"So," I said, "the whole event was broadcasted, wasn't it? Couldn't we comb through whatever footage there is and see if we can find what we're missing?"

Zeno began to nod, and then a smile took hold of his face. "My man, I can do you one better. It's going to take some time, but these hands"—he held them up and wiggled his fingers—"are about to do something awesome. Augustine, I'll need your help with this one."

Augustine nodded. "What did you have in mind?"

"We're going to give Gina a little update."

"And what about us?" Daphne asked.

"Stick with Vic." Zeno winked at me. "And don't get into too much trouble."

Augustine pushed himself to his feet. "And stay here. After this morning, I don't know how safe it is to have Victor out and about."

I hoped that whatever Zeno was cooking up would work. Maybe it was a long shot, but we couldn't give up.

I looked over at Daphne, who was ignoring me completely. Her phone was out and her fingers flew across the screen. Augustine and Zeno had left five minutes ago, and we were alone in the room. I could sense the tension between us. She had hadn't said a word, but we would need to start talking soon.

"Daphn—" I started, and her phone buzzed.

"We're leaving," she said, snapping her phone shut and pocketing it. "Now." She stood up.

"Leaving?" I asked.

"Yep."

"As in, going into the Heights?"

"No, we're going to the Flats to do a little shopping," she said with a wry look. "Now, quit asking stupid questions and follow me."

If she was going to be short with me, I could be short back. The sooner we got whatever was going on between us out of the way, the better.

"Hold on a second," I said. Daphne paused, one foot out the door. "What's your deal?"

I knew this was going to blow up, and maybe I was forcing it, but the sooner it happened, the sooner we could move on. At least I hoped so.

"What's my deal?" Daphne said slowly, her voice dangerous.

"Yeah," I said, "your deal. You're clearly not happy to see me. Well, you were for a minute, and now you're not, so what's your deal?"

Daphne stared at me for a moment, a look of incredulity on her face, before speaking. "My deal is that I agreed to help you and probably saved your life. So you can do what I say and deal with it. Understand?" She turned on her heel, grabbed her bag, and strode out the door.

That had *not* gone according to plan.

I dashed out of the room to keep up. "So where are we going?" I asked.

"Out."

I let loose an exasperated sigh, which she didn't acknowledge.

"At least a hint would be nice," I said. "Don't forget that a terrorist group *and* the government are after me."

Daphne didn't look at me, but continued her quick pace down the hallway. "Wow, life must have been really hard for you for the last few hours."

I trailed a half step behind her. Her dark hair and bag swayed back and forth in time with her footsteps. I didn't know what to say. Hours of difficulty versus a lifetime. I kept silent as we made our way through the maze that was the events center.

After a series of turns, we came to a set of glass doors. Beyond them lay the Heights. Daphne set down her bag and checked her watch.

"So, for real, where are we going?" I asked. "I mean, I'm all for coloring outside the lines, but I'm also all for not dying."

Daphne turned to face me. "Vic, do you trust me?"

"Yeah," I said slowly. She was a Noble, like me.

"Then realize that immediately after saving your life, I'm not going to make you lose it, okay?" She stared intently at me. "And to help us with that..." She reached inside her bag and pulled out a floppy, silicone-looking thing. One of Zeno's masks.

"Is it going to fit?" I asked, taking it out of Daphne's outstretched hands.

"Of course it is," Daphne said. "It's made for you."

"Seriously?" I said. "Zeno made one for *me*?"

"Zeno's like that."

I pulled the mask over my head. It seemed to fit perfectly and was surprisingly light and comfortable. I could see how Zeno forgot it was on. I'd have to apologize to him about that again later.

"So what's Zeno's story?" I asked, feeling my face with my hands. It even felt like skin.

"That's his story to tell," Daphne said. "And quit playing with your face."

"Sorry," I said. "Who do I look like?"

"Someone that's not you. Now let's go. And try to keep quiet."

She turned her back to me and pushed through the doors that led to the street, her brown hair turning golden in the sunlight. I caught the door before it closed and walked after her. It felt good to have a conversation with her, regardless of how short it was. Progress was progress. And even though she still had something against me, trusting her was surprisingly easy.

I followed Daphne down streets of crumbling brick and scattered trash. Most were sparsely populated by Sinisters. The whole place felt dirty, including the people. Several buildings showed distinct signs of break-ins, robberies, and neglect.

"Are there a lot of officers in the Heights?" I asked, careful to keep my voice low. I hadn't yet seen any patrolling the streets.

"Depends."

"On what?"

"On whether or not there's anything here worth policing. Riots, public disturbances, fugitive Nobles," she said, eyeing me. "You know, things like that."

"Then why aren't there any here now?"

"Because they haven't figured out where you're at yet," she said. "Honestly, Victor, I think you were smarter when we were kids."

I could have sworn she started smiling before she turned away.

We continued onward, taking the occasional turn. We came to an intersection, and Daphne held up her hand and came to a stop. She craned her neck around the corner before proceeding. A group of ten or so children played in the otherwise deserted intersection. Daphne didn't wait for them to pass.

"Come on," she said, stepping out from around the corner.

"Daphne!" shouted one of the children. "Look, everyone. Daphne's here!"

The group of kids immediately abandoned their game and ran over to her as she walked toward them. I kept my distance as they swarmed her. The youngest looked to be three or four years old and the oldest couldn't have been more than ten. They were all dirty, their clothes didn't fit, and some didn't wear shoes.

Daphne unzipped her bag and reached inside. With her free hand, she motioned me over. I took a few tentative steps forward.

"Hi, everyone!" she said, pulling out what looked like a fistful of colorfully wrapped candies. She got down on one knee. "Are you all being good?"

They all responded in unison. "Yes, Daphne!"

Daphne smiled. Most Nobles wouldn't even think to interact with a Sinister child, much less smile at them. I willed my face to assume a grin and waved at the small group. A few of them gave me uncertain looks and waved back.

"I'm glad to hear it!" Daphne said. "Here you go—one for you and one for you." She handed each of them a piece of candy.

The oldest one, however—a boy—refused.

"What's wrong, Berg?" Daphne asked.

Berg looked down at the ground. He was a tall and skinny kid, probably a little too skinny.

"Come on Berg, you can tell me," Daphne said gently.

"Well," he said, "I tried to do good, but Ma said I can't. She said I'm a Sinister so there's no use in me goin' about tryin' to be good all the time."

Daphne hesitated and looked back over at me. I wasn't sure what she wanted me to do, so I kept a smile on my face. Unfortunately, his mom was right.

Daphne turned back to the boy. "That's okay, Berg," she said with a soft smile. "It's tough to be good all the time, but the harder you try at it, the easier it gets. Just remember, you get to choose, okay? And if you want to do good all the time, it can be our little secret. Deal?" She held out the piece of candy to him.

He looked at the candy, then up at her. A smile took hold of his face as he reached for it. "Deal," he said.

One of the little girls piped up. "Daphne, who's that? Your boyfriend?" Immediately, she and the other little girls broke into a fit of giggles.

"Who, him?" Daphne said, pointing a thumb toward me. The little girls nodded. "Oh no," she said, shaking her head, "that's just Dorth."

The little girls laughed. I raised an eyebrow. *Dorth, really?*

"That's kind of a silly name," the youngest one said.

"It's kind of a stupid name," Berg said. Then his eyes got wide and he looked up at Daphne. "See? Sorry." He held out his piece of candy and looked back at the ground.

"No, Berg, it's okay." She closed Berg's fist and looked back at me. "It *is* kind of a silly name, huh?"

He nodded.

"And we all make mistakes, but all we have to do is keep on trying, right?"

The kids nodded. Berg continued to stare at the ground.

Daphne got down on one knee and lifted his chin. "Right, Berg?" she said gently. "We just have to keep on trying."

Berg nodded and Daphne stood up.

"Well, Dorth and I have to go," she said.

A chorus of childish dissent filled the empty streets.

"Do you have to?"

"But you just got here!"

Daphne reached into her bag one last time.

"Yes, we really have to go, but if you all promise to be extra good, I'll give you each another piece of candy. Can you do that?"

All ten vigorously nodded their heads, even Berg, and I stood by smiling as Daphne handed out more of the brightly wrapped candy, making sure to slip an extra piece to Berg.

"All right everyone, be good!"

"Bye, Daphne!"

The children waved and went back to their games. Daphne made her way to the other side of the street. I jogged a couple of steps to keep up.

"Dorth, huh?" I asked, turning to her with a smile. She didn't return it, and instead I saw anger on her face.

"What was that back there?" she said.

"What was what?" I asked, mystified.

"You! Do you hate children or what?"

"What? No, of course not," I said. "What are you talking about?"

"I'm talking about you, standing there like you thought they might attack you at any second. They don't bite, Victor. They're no different than Noble kids."

"Hold on a second," I said, grabbing her arm and bringing both of us to a stop. "I thought I did pretty good. What did you want me to do, pick one of them up and play with them? They're just a bunch of Sinister kids."

"Exactly," she said, "they're just kids. And even with your parents dying, you had a better childhood than they do."

———

We came to a stop at a section of tracks that cut across the street, stretching out in each direction until towering buildings blocked them from sight. A large, tarp-covered dumpster sat near the tracks and looked to be overflowing with garbage.

Daphne walked over and pulled the tarp off with a flourish, revealing a handful of personal transports like the one I had come in on last night.

"You know how to ride one of these, right?" she said, pulling one from the stack. We hadn't said a word about our last exchange, but her anger seemed to have dissipated somewhat.

"Yeah, I rode one back with Zeno and Dax," I said as I started toward the dumpster. A thought stopped me mid-step. Last time I rode these, I had been with Dax. Dax worked for Tyrann...

"Can anyone use these?" I asked.

"*I* can."

Somehow I doubted that.

"The Left Hand isn't waiting for us just down the road, you know," Daphne said as she muscled her platform onto the tracks.

In all likelihood she was right, not that I wanted her to know that.

"So let's say I agree with you," I said, making my way toward the stack of platforms. "But for the sake of preparation, what would we do if the Left Hand *was* just around the next corner?"

Daphne jumped onto her platform. "Are you always this paranoid?"

"Just since my last death threat," I said.

"Well, if a group of Sinistralis were waiting right over there, I'd push you off your platform and go as fast as I could in the other direction." She gave me a sarcastic smile. "Now come on."

Daphne shot off down the tracks without a backward glance. I jumped on my platform and sped after her, winding through a forest of dilapidated buildings that blocked out the sunlight.

After several minutes of making our way along the darkened tracks, the sunlight finally managed to make it through a gap in the buildings. Daphne continued through it without slowing down, but I couldn't help myself. Being in the Heights was like visiting a foreign country.

A set of tracks the size of the Innerbelt ran perpendicular to the track we rode on. They were huge, but unlike the Innerbelt, the tracks were straight. They appeared to go on for miles, and they headed south.

I knew that somehow the Heights and the Flats were connected to Ville. Was this it? Did the tracks stretch all the way down there? In school, we had learned virtually nothing about the only other city that was somewhat friendly to us. They were part of the Great Experiment, just not in the same way we were. For the most part, the whole city was an enigma. Why would they need such a large set of tracks?

I switched my gaze from the enormous offshoot to my own track. Daphne had put some distance between us. I pushed the bars forward on my platform and sped after her into a tangled mess of rundown brick buildings.

Five minutes later, Daphne held up a hand and slowed her progress. I came to a stop next to her and looked around. No station, no landing platform, just buildings that rose up on either side of the tracks, creating a stifling, tunnel-like atmosphere.

"Come on." Daphne hopped off her platform and made a beeline toward a washed-out red door. The building it belonged to had a series of boarded-up windows and missing bricks—it looked like all the other buildings in the area.

"What is this place?" I asked as I abandoned my platform. "Does someone live here?"

Daphne reached into the bag hanging from her shoulder and pulled out an antique metal key.

"More or less," she said, glancing back at me.

I heard the click of the lock, and the door swung inward on noiseless hinges.

17

I could only describe it as a lair. Dim light filtered into the room, illuminating the particles in the air and a light layer of dust on the floor.

"How about some lights, Gina?" Daphne said.

"Gina's here too?" I asked as the lights flickered to life. Tables littered with electronics, wires, and sketches occupied one side of the room. A digital map of the Heights adorned the far wall. Fluorescent dots of different colors marked specific buildings, and a series of sabers and silicone heads hung on the wall beside it. Clearly, Zeno had a hand in all of this.

I couldn't help wandering over to the most intriguing thing in the room. It looked like a refrigerated wine rack in miniature, except that instead of wine, small vials of a crimson liquid were displayed, each with a handwritten label.

"Don't touch anything," Daphne said.

I retracted my hand. "Is that blood?"

"Yep," she said as she scoured one of the nearby tables.

"Why?" I said.

Daphne moved a pile of wires and gadgets and then turned to face me. "Access. What do you think I've been doing for the last four years? My dad might have given up, but I've been trying to figure out who changed our DNA status and why. Those answers don't come from the Heights."

I thought I was coming to understand Daphne more. I couldn't begin to fathom what she'd had to live through, what she'd had to do, to be where she was now.

"So you're saying all of that"—I pointed in a circular motion—"is Noble blood? And you use it to get into the Flats?"

Daphne nodded. "Mostly the Sinister-restricted areas."

My mind spun with questions. There were areas all over the Flats that were off-limits to Sinisters—clubs, restaurants, office buildings. I never would have guessed that someone from the Heights could get into those places.

"How did you get it all? I mean, that's a lot of blood from a lot of different people," I said, looking through the glass.

"You'd be surprised at the people that come into the Heights," she said.

I turned to find Daphne closer to me than I had anticipated. In her hand she held what looked like a gun, but with one difference. Where the barrel would normally be was a needle.

"Whoa, what is that?" I took a step backwards.

"Oh, don't be such a wimp," Daphne said. "It's just a needle. "

"And why would we need that?" I said.

"Do you trust me?"

"Yes," I said, "but this would be an ideal time for an explanation."

"Look, here in the Heights, it pays to be prepared," she said. She reached into her bag, fished out a glass vial, and loaded it into the gun. "You said the Left Hand is tracking your scans, right? Well, what if we were able to scan your DNA, say, somewhere near your house, when you were actually still here?"

"You could do that?" I asked.

"Not without a sample of your blood."

I stared at her. It was a brilliant idea. Potentially lifesaving too. Daphne was turning out to be a very interesting person.

"So how do we do this?" I said, offering up my arm.

"Now you're catching on," she said with a smile. "You'll want to sit down for this." She motioned to a chair by the table.

I took a seat. "Does anyone else use Noble blood to get into the Flats?"

Daphne grabbed a rubber cord and tied it around my arm.

"Tyrann and his men do," she said. "That's actually where I got a lot of this." She nodded to the cabinet.

"Seriously? Tyrann Kane gave you all that blood?"

"*Gave* maybe isn't the best word," she said slowly. "Now hold still."

A small jolt of pain made its way up my forearm as the needle penetrated my skin. The vial began to fill with blood.

I opted to look around the room instead of staring my arm. A picture of Dr. Rosewood and President Keltan hung on the wall.

"Almost done," Daphne said. "And that's it." She withdrew the needle. "Put a finger on that." She nodded to my forearm, where a small dot of blood had started to gather.

"So," I said as I placed some pressure on my arm, "if you've been working on this for four years, what have you found out?"

Daphne labeled the vial of blood and placed it in the refrigerator with the rest.

"Not as much as I'd hoped." She pulled out her phone and her fingers danced across the screen. "I'm supposed to be meeting with someone in a few minutes to get some information. Something that might help both of us." She shoved her phone back into her pocket. "Let's go."

"We're leaving?" I asked. "What, no grand tour? This is awesome!"

"Try telling that to my dad," Daphne muttered. "Now come on—Brick and Jonny told me the guy would be there at one o'clock." She crossed the room, opened the door, and held it for me.

"Brick and Jonny?" I asked, making my way back outside.

"A couple of Tyrann's men who owe me a favor," she said, locking the door behind her. She pocketed the key and stepped onto her platform. "Try and keep up."

I jumped on my platform, pushed the two bars forward, and chased Daphne down the tracks.

18

Daphne came to a stop so fast I almost collided with her. She jumped off her platform and wrenched it off the tracks.

"What's going on?" I asked.

"That."

She motioned up the tracks. Another person on a platform flew toward us, her silver hair billowing out behind her. I jumped off my platform, but not in time to pull it off the tracks.

"Well hello, hello!" Tyrann Kane's daughter slowed to a stop in front of us. She had changed her outfit from earlier, trading in her white for orange pants, a blue shirt, and white, elbow-length gloves that sparkled in the sunlight.

"Pria!" Daphne said, a tone of mock excitement in her voice. "What are you doing here?"

Tension filled the air like a thick fog.

"Just out for a ride," she said, displaying a dazzlingly white smile. An expression of distaste crossed Daphne's features as Pria stepped off her platform.

"Where's your bodyguard of a sister hiding?" Daphne asked.

"Oh, you mean Printh? Off running errands, I suppose. I might have to go catch up with her. Daddy won't be pleased to learn that you're using his toys again." Pria gestured to the platforms.

"Yes, Pria, we're well aware that you, Printh, and Tyrann are the royal family of this part of the city and we're all your lowly subjects," Daphne said. "But I'm surprised that you're out here alone, so vulnerable, such an easy target. Your 'daddy' has a lot of enemies."

"I can take care of myself," Pria said coolly. "Besides, you're no threat to me, even if you want to be."

I turned my snort into a cough about a half second too late, my mind flashing back years into the past. Even as a twelve-year-old, Daphne was poised, relentless, and aggressive in saber matches. Other than me, she had hardly met her equal in younger years, and after seeing the contents of her lair, I would bet that she hadn't quit practicing.

"You disagree?" Pria said, turning to me, her pale eyes narrowed. "And I know it's you under that mask, Victor. You don't have to be so shy." She smiled unabashedly at me.

I looked over at Daphne, whose eyes were fixed on Pria.

"Yes," I said slowly. "I disagree."

Pria raised her eyebrows, waiting for me to elaborate.

"I've seen Daphne fight," I continued. "You wouldn't stand a chance."

I thought I saw Daphne straighten beside me.

"Tsk tsk, Victor. I seriously doubt that. And such a forward opinion from a complete stranger."

"The curse of Nobility," I answered.

"Curse indeed," she said, her face taking an ugly turn for the first time. "Fortunately for you, you are no longer Noble. In fact, you're the furthest thing from it. TɪɪD?" She let loose a giggle. "How exciting for you!"

"Don't you have somewhere to be?" Daphne cut in, her voice flat.

"You're quite right, but I do enjoy spending time with my peasants." She smiled and her eyes flashed at Daphne. "I'll let the platforms slide today, but next time, I won't be so kind."

"You're too generous."

"You'd do well to remember that," she said, her eyes aflame. Then, like a switch had flipped, her demeanor changed and she smiled, her words almost sounding sincere. "Daphne, it's always such a treat running into you. And Victor"—she fixed her large eyes on me—"I've heard you're quite the swordsman. Maybe we can get together sometime and you can show me something, without the mask." She raised an eyebrow, smiled, and sped off down the tracks.

Daphne scowled, and we both watched as she disappeared into the distance, her silver hair flowing in the wind behind her like the tail of a comet.

"Well she's just a ray of sunshine, isn't she?" I said.

"You don't know the half of it," Daphne mumbled, "but come on. I should be getting a text any minute. There's a place a couple minutes down the tracks where we can wait for it to come in." She threw her platform back onto the tracks. "Let's go."

"Hold on a second," I said. "If I didn't know any better, I'd say you two have a history."

"Let's just say I've seen a pattern in my life where my friends abandon or betray me." She looked pointedly at me.

I didn't know what to say. An awkward silence hung in the air between us.

"Look, Daphne, I'm sorry."

"For what?" she said, her eyes locked on mine. A series of thoughts swirled around in my head—things I should have said or done differently. She didn't flinch. Her eyes were fierce and unyielding.

"I'm sorry for not being there for you."

The words seemed to burn as they came out, an admission of my wrongdoing and selfishness. I could see color begin to well up in her cheeks. Feelings suppressed until now rose to the surface.

"Look, I know that you were just Marked and your life is completely upside down," she said. "But sorry isn't going to cut it."

I nodded. Whatever came next, I was sure I deserved it. She had been my best friend, and a Noble, and I had abandoned her.

"I know," I started. "I'm rea—"

Daphne cut me off, her voice rising. "You *know*? You have no idea! Our family undergoes a horrible tragedy, and instead of support, we don't speak for four years! Four years! Did you even know my mother died after we were exiled to this place? Your grandfather came to the funeral *without* you."

I stood there on my platform, the afternoon still, the air taking on a chill that hadn't been there before. She was right. Grandfather had told me when he found out that Mrs. Pendleton had died. He had even invited me to the funeral, but I didn't go. A rock of guilt sat in the pit of my stomach, growing larger by the second.

"Sorry," she said, turning away. "I know you've been through a lot."

"No, I'm sorry," I said, not meeting her eyes.

Daphne opened her mouth, but I held up a hand.

Daphne's phone buzzed, but she didn't answer it, and instead continued to stare at me. She stood there in the shadows of a derelict building, one foot on her platform and the other on the tracks. Who knew what pains she had had to endure? There was more I needed to tell her, more I needed to do to make things right, but what could I say? What could erase four years of neglect?

"I know that's not good enough," I said. "I was angry and selfish. I thought you were a Sinister, and I know that's no excuse, but I promise you, as a Noble, I'm going to make it up to you."

"But that's half the problem, Victor!"

I looked at her, uncomprehending.

"Look," she continued, "I'm just Daphne and you're just Victor. No Nobles, no Sinisters, just people." Her phone buzzed, but she silenced it. "You believe us, right?"

"Yeah," I said slowly. "I mean, the whole thing with the scanners and how we're not Sinisters makes sense."

"Well that's only half of the story." She took a deep breath. "Victor, it's all a lie. Nobody is Noble or Sinister. The government didn't just mess up on you, they messed up on everybody."

"What do you mean they messed up on everybody?"

"I'm saying that there is no such thing as Noble or Sinister, Victor.

There are only people, people who make good choices and people who make bad choices. That's it. Decisions determine destiny, not DNA."

The wind rustled around us, filling the silence as I grappled with what she was saying. It was crazy, wasn't it? You were either born Noble or you were born Sinister. Period.

"Is it really so hard to believe?" she asked. Her phone buzzed again, but she ignored it.

"But what you're saying sounds crazy," I said. "I mean, your DNA is everything,"

"Look, when you do something good, does your DNA compel you to do it, or do you make a conscious decision to do something good?"

"I don't know," I sputtered. "I guess I make a decision. But I make the decision because I'm Noble and Nobles act a certain way."

"Okay, so what about Dallin Fratdorf? You remember him, right?"

My stomach tightened. I did remember. Dallin had tormented us. Once, when I was five, he had taken his saber and paralyzed both of my legs, and that wasn't even the worst of it.

"Yeah, I remember," I said.

"And what's he doing now?" Daphne asked.

Everyone in the Flats knew what he was doing now. He was on track to become the youngest senator in the city's history.

"He's better now," I said slowly.

"He changed, Victor! He changed and started making better decisions. If DNA controlled everything, why didn't he make great choices as a kid? If DNA controlled everything, we wouldn't be able to improve or grow—everything would be set from birth."

I fought to wrap my mind around what she was saying, but the truth was that I had seen what she was talking about over and over again. I'd even seen it in myself. If I was as Noble as I thought I was, I wouldn't have been so angry at Daphne and her family for all these years. I would have called. Things would have been different.

I looked away from Daphne and down at my feet. Could it be that everything I knew, my whole life, everyone's life, was a lie? My mind wanted to fight it, but what she said rang true.

Daphne's pocket buzzed again.

"The meeting isn't for another fifteen minutes," she muttered as she pulled out her phone. A puzzled expression came over her face, and she held her phone up to her ear. "Hello?" She paused. "Wait, what?" Another pause. "On our way." Daphne jammed her phone into her pocket and jumped back onto her platform.

"Come on, we've got to get back," she said.

"What about your meeting?" I asked, following suit.

She paused and looked at me. The look in her eyes told me that something wasn't right.

"It'll have to wait," she said. "Alex Trabue is here."

19

We burst through the doors of the events center in a full-on sprint. I followed Daphne through the dusty hallway, slipping as we raced around the corners.

Alex was here? It sounded ridiculous, impossible even. But the bigger question was why? Alex might not be a conformist, but he always had a purpose behind what he did.

We took another turn and headed down several flights of stairs, onto the stage, and into the room beyond. I beat Daphne to the door and threw it open to find Augustine sitting at a table with none other than Alex Trabue, who had a donut in one hand and was in the process of slurping a drink through a straw.

"Alex!"

He looked at me with mild confusion. "Victor?" he said slowly, as if he wasn't sure whether it was me.

"Mask," Augustine said.

"Oh yeah," I said. I reached behind my ear and tugged it off.

Recognition blossomed across Alex's face. "I thought that sounded like you!" he said. "Good to see you man! Cool mask!" He stood up and took another bite of his donut.

Daphne entered through the open door behind me. Alex's

eyes grew wide. He inhaled part of his donut and erupted into a coughing fit, his face turning red. Augustine looked at Alex, his hand half-raised, like he was unsure whether he should offer Alex some water or slap him on the back. I walked over and chose the latter, giving him a few good thumps. This was not the first time he had almost choked on a donut after seeing a pretty girl.

After a moment, he recovered and took a long draw from his straw.

"Thanks," he said as he exhaled. He looked up at me and mouthed the word "wow," and then looked over at Daphne, who still stood in the doorway. I was pretty sure she saw him do it.

"Alex, what are you doing here?" I asked. "I mean, it's good to see you, but haven't you been watching the news?"

I was almost surprised that he appeared happy to see me. Alex was a Noble, or rather, he was a good person who believed in the system. The system was saying that I was a Sinister, and a deadly one at that. Everyone else would be avoiding me.

"How could I not?" he said. "Your face is everywhere. It's like being at a saber competition, but instead of everyone clapping when your face shows up, everyone gets terrified. It's kind of nice for a change." He paused. "I'm just kidding, but don't worry, Augustine showed me the scanners. Besides, we've been best friends for as long as I can remember. Noble or Sinister, I'm here for you."

I made sure to not look at Daphne.

"Thanks, man," I said.

He nodded.

"Alex, you said you had some information for us?" Augustine said. "Something that we needed to know right now?"

"Oh yeah!" Alex said, his face lighting up.

"Should Zeno be here to listen to this?" Daphne asked.

"He's on his way," Augustine said, "but I wouldn't be surprised if he was listening in." He looked at me and pointed up. "Gina."

I nodded in understanding. Apparently, she was everywhere.

He turned to Alex. "Go ahead."

Daphne walked over to Alex and gave him a hug. "It's so good to see you," she said.

I watched in mild shock. Daphne hadn't so much as shaken my hand. Alex turned a shade of red I'd only ever seen a severe sunburn achieve.

Daphne let go and took a few steps back.

"That was good, I mean, it's good to be, I mean, it's good to see you too," Alex stammered, smiling dazedly at Daphne.

"So what's this news?" she said, bringing him back to reality.

"Right," Alex shook his head, "the news." He looked to me, his red face turning serious. "Victor, Kratos is after you."

"Who's Kratos?" Daphne said.

"The Bounty Hunter," I said, my voice barely above a whisper. I felt like the temperature in the room had suddenly dropped thirty degrees. I didn't know what I had expected Alex to say, but it definitely wasn't that.

Augustine sat forward in his chair and fixed Alex with a stare.

"Are you certain?" he asked. Alex nodded vigorously. "How do you know this? That's very privileged information. President Keltan is the only one who knows the full extent of the Bounty Hunter's—"

"Kratos's," Alex corrected.

"Yes," Augustine said, "Kratos's missions. Even the senate doesn't find out until afterwards."

"Right, this is the good part," Alex said, his smile returning. "Kratos came to my house last night!"

"What?" I said.

"Yeah!" Alex said, obviously elated by the memory. "He showed up and asked me some questions about you—why you would go to the Heights, what kind of person you were, you know, stuff like that. That's how I knew he was coming after you."

Alex smiled like he had just given us wonderful news, but his response was met with silence.

"Come on, guys. Kratos was in my house! In my bedroom! Cool, right?"

"I've heard that the Bounty Hunter works in this way," Augustine said quietly. "There are rumors that he visits the friends of whoever he's tracking in order to get information out of them."

The door behind me opened, an afro filling up the space.

"Kratos?" Zeno said as he entered the room. "Is his name common knowledge in the Flats nowadays or what?"

"Alex," Augustine said, "this is Zeno. Zeno, this is Alex Trabue."

"Good to meet you," Alex said, taking a step forward.

"You too, bro." Zeno held out a fist. Alex bumped it and smiled. Even in the Flats, it wasn't a gesture that he did often. "Seriously though, do people in the Flats know his name?"

Alex shook his head. "There are a few of us who figured it out, but that's about it."

Zeno nodded appreciatively. "That's some good detective work, my man."

"Thanks," Alex said.

Augustine sat in his chair, clearly thinking.

"So you were able to figure out where Victor was going," Daphne said, her brow creased. "What did you tell the Bounty...I mean, Kratos?"

Alex shrugged. "Nothing."

"Wait, seriously?" I asked. I was pretty sure Alex would have given Kratos anything—his ID card, his allowance, his computer, his first-born child.

"Seriously. I swear. I was kind of in shock when I realized he was in my room. I, um, couldn't get much out, so he left." He shrugged his shoulders and gave Daphne an awkward smile. The red in his cheeks intensified.

Alex's ineptitude in high-pressure situations had often frustrated me. Maybe that's why he never took up saber fighting and hadn't had much luck with pretty girls, but today I was grateful for his poor nerves. Although I did find myself wishing it was me Daphne had hugged instead of him.

Augustine stood up. "Well, Alex, that's good news for us."

A thought struck me. "Wait, what about the law that says Kratos can't go after minors?" I asked. "Technically, he shouldn't be able to come after me, right? Even if they do think I have TɪɪD."

"Yeah," Zeno said slowly, "I'm pretty sure if Kratos is showing up at Alex's house, that law is being ignored. Wouldn't be the first time."

Suddenly, the room was bathed in a bright red light that originated from a huge screen on the back wall.

"What's going on?" I asked.

"Easy, bro," Zeno said. "I told Gina to track any mention of the Left Hand on the news. It's just an alert." He approached the screen. "Gina, what do you have for me, girl?"

The screen came to life, and President Keltan appeared wearing a blue suit and a somber expression. "It is with the greatest regret and deepest condolences that I tell you all that the inevitable has happened. Senator Avardi Supart was killed by the Left Hand. We're still collecting data from the site, but we know that an explosive of some sort was used. Our thoughts and prayers go out to his family."

The screen went black.

Avardi is dead? Already?

My vision blurred as tears sprang to my eyes. I turned away.

Immediately my thoughts turned to Jeffry. I could vaguely imagine what he was feeling right now. Having your parents die in an accident was one thing. Having one of your parents murdered was something else. Not to mention it had only been two days since Avardi's Marking. He had been Marked mere minutes before me. How much longer did I have before they were here, plotting their next move while I took my last?

"Victor, are you okay?" Augustine said. I hastily rubbed a hand across my eyes.

"Um, yeah." I coughed and sniffed. "Look, I understand if you want me to leave."

Augustine looked at me in confusion.

"What are you talking about, bro?" Zeno said.

"I was Marked a few minutes after Avardi," I said. "How do we know the Sinistrali aren't waiting outside for me?"

"Because I have Gina watching all the cameras," Zeno said matter-of-factly.

"And even if they were, it wouldn't change our decision," Augustine said.

I stared at him and he gave me a tight-lipped smile. How could I have ever thought he was a Sinister? "Thanks," I said quietly. "So if Kratos is after me, we should really get to work figuring this out, right?" I looked over at Zeno. "You said you were going to give Gina an update?"

"Bro, update is an understatement. I'm talking Gina 3.0. We're skipping 2.0 and going straight to the next level. And the best part"—he paused and smiled—"is it'll be ready by morning."

20

"Femi, Trezel, and Sharmet—did you get them?" Alex asked. "They *always* have their phones going, and I'm sure they were there. I don't know if Gina can hack it, but Trezel has a camera embedded in her nose."

Zeno wrinkled his face in disgust. "For real?"

"Don't ask me why," Alex said, throwing up his hands. "The last time I asked her, she wouldn't tell me. And then her virtual avatar attacked my virtual avatar for like a month. And then there was that whole thing with her friend Mykail..."

I stopped listening for a moment and let my head slip through my hands until it made contact with the table. I had barely slept last night. Alex and I had stayed up talking about everything—Sinisters, Nobles, the Left Hand, Daphne, Zeno, Augustine, Kratos, Daphne again. It felt like my head had barely touched the pillow when Zeno woke us up to let us know Gina was ready.

Zeno peered up at the projector. "Femi, Trezel, and who?"

Sharmet appeared on the screen.

"Dang, Gina, if you're so smart, why don't I see the video up there then?"

More text rolled across the screen almost instantaneously: *Video acquired.*

"Mm-hmm," Zeno said, "that's what I thought."

Three new boxes showing the same event appeared, each one playing on a loop. It was incredible. Hundreds of soundless video clips played before us. Somehow Zeno had figured out how to steal any video that had been shot the night Avardi and I had been Marked. So far we hadn't learned anything new. All the videos showed the same thing. A piece of the ceiling falling, the podium being smashed to bits, and then everyone scattering in terror.

We had video of everything from every angle from before the ceiling dropped, but it was those few seconds right after it happened that we couldn't find. Whatever we were missing, it had to take place then.

"Nope," Zeno said, "same thing as before. We need someone who was seated further to the right."

"Can you pull up a shot of the audience?" I asked.

A single image took over the giant projection screen.

"Thanks, Gina," Zeno said. "Can you zoom in right there?" He pointed and the picture magnified.

"Third one from the right," I said. "Purple hair. Priscilla Poyfort. Try her. I doubt anyone else around her recorded anything."

"Gina, you heard the man," Zeno said.

Alex and I had debated where the name Gina had come from. I thought it was an acronym. Alex said it was an ex.

"Hey, I was going to ask you," I said, "why call the system Gina?"

"It's easy to yell and it's got a nice ring to it, you know? Like this. Gina!"

Yes?

"Nothing, go back to doing whatever it is you do in your off time."

You never give me any off time.

"Oh yeah, that's right. You got that video for us yet?" Zeno said.

Which one?

Zeno looked at me.

"Priscilla Poyfort," I said.

Video acquired.

"Perfect. Play it," Zeno said.

A close-up shot of a heavily made-up face took over the projection screen.

"Come on, Gina! We're on a time crunch here. Fast-forward past that. Yeah, and that too." A series of self-absorbed expressions and a fair amount of primping finally gave way to a perfect shot of the podium.

"Angle looks good," I said.

"Yeah, let's see if she holds through till the end. Gina, play that on double speed."

It looked like the camera jerked a little bit, but stayed pretty steady, even as people around her scattered.

"This could be it," Zeno said. "Let's get Augustine and Daphne in here. Pause that, Gina."

Moments later, Daphne and Augustine pushed through the doors.

"Find anything?" Augustine asked, his voice weary.

"We might have something. Take a look," Zeno said. "Go ahead, Gina. And slow it down."

The video began to play.

On screen, I collided with Senator Supart. The section of ceiling smashed the podium into a pile of debris. The camera jumped, but stayed mostly on target.

Dust partially clouded the view. I watched myself get to my feet. The senator stayed where he was and instead began to point, just like I remembered.

"What's he pointing at?" Daphne asked.

"What's left of the podium?" I answered.

"Dude looks terrified out of his mind," Zeno said.

"With good reason," Augustine said.

On the screen, I offered my hand to the senator, who continued to point at the pile of rubble.

Everything was happening exactly as I remembered it. Nothing new.

"I wish we could see what he was pointing at," Daphne said.

"I looked," I said, remembering back. "There wasn't anything there. He just kept pointing for a second and then finally grabbed my hand to get up. But this has got to be it, right? I mean, we've got footage of everything else except for this."

As if to prove my point, the senator reached up hastily and accepted my outstretched hand, grabbing my jacket to stabilize himself. Moments later, Freddy appeared on the scene. And that was it. We had seen this part before.

It had happened exactly as I remembered it. No variation.

"Wait," Daphne said. "Can you play that back?"

Gina rewound the footage.

"There, start right there. And can you slow it down even more?"

"What are you seeing, Daph?" Zeno asked.

"It could be nothing but..." She trailed off as we watched the clip move forward frame by frame.

In super-slow motion, the senator reached for my hand, and with the other grabbed my jacket. A flash of white light radiated from my jacket where the senator touched it. By the next frame, the light was gone.

My heart started to race.

There was a sharp intake of breath from Alex.

"Holy..." He stared at the screen. "So does the senator have superpowers? And did he transfer them to Victor's jacket? That's why Victor was Marked? The Left Hand wants superpowers?"

"What? No, man, it was a data transfer!" Zeno said.

"Ohhhh," Alex said. "Yeah, that makes more sense."

"Wait," I said, "that flash of light. That was a data transfer?"

"I think so," Zeno said. He adjusted his glasses and took a few steps closer to the screen. "Gina, play that part again, and blow it up."

The picture magnified and the clip restarted. I watched the senator's hand as he reached for my jacket. Then came the flash of light. The video stopped.

"This sort of thing is tricky, you know?" Zeno said. "I've heard of things like this—clearly not something I designed. I mean, come on, guys, a flash of light, really? I mean, if you're trying to be covert, you shouldn't be shooting off a flare—"

"Zeno!" Daphne said.

"Right," Zeno said, turning from the screen to face us. "This sort of thing does exist. I'm like, ninety-six percent positive it was a data transfer. A little gimmicky with the light, but I bet it got the job done."

"Wow," Daphne said, "that's pretty positive. You usually don't go over eighty-five."

Maybe I hadn't noticed it before, but they seemed to be very comfortable with each other, and for some reason it irked me a little bit.

"Yeah, Daph, gotta account for statistical error and whatnot."

A memory flashed to the forefront of my mind. "Before Avardi went out on the stage, he did tell me that he had something for me after he got done speaking."

"Boom!" Zeno said. "There you go."

"So if you're right," I said, "if it really was a data transfer, maybe that's what the Left Hand is after?"

"If so," Augustine said, "it might be exactly what we need to find out what happened to all of us."

"Please tell me you have it with you," Daphne said.

I took one last look at the screen. My heart raced. Nervous adrenaline coursed through my veins.

"I'll be right back," I said.

21

I looked at the jacket in my hands. A dead man's last act was to transfer information to it. I turned it over in my fingers.

"So how do we get the information out?" I asked.

"Let me take a look," Zeno said, taking a few steps closer. He glanced up at the projector screen. "Gina, can you zoom out just a little bit? Yeah, that's perfect."

It looked like the flash of light occurred when Avardi touched the inside of the jacket just beneath the front right pocket.

"So it should be," Zeno mumbled to himself and flipped the jacket inside out, "right here."

Everyone crowded around. On the inner lining was a chalky silver smudge about two inches in diameter. Zeno waved his hand over it and touched it.

Nothing happened.

"Just as I suspected," he said.

"What?" I asked.

"The info is DNA matched, or at least I think it is. Would it have been easy for Senator Supart to get some of your DNA?"

"Well yeah," I said. "We had dinner at his place pretty frequently."

"Then I'm ninety-nine percent certain this is matched to your

DNA. It's what I would do if I had a super-secret message and I didn't want it going to a bunch of Sinistrali thugs."

"What happened to statistical error and whatnot?" Daphne asked.

"He wouldn't have transferred the data to Victor without knowing he would be able to open it." Zeno locked eyes with me. "It's all you, bro."

"So what do I do?" I asked.

"My guess is that you just have to touch it."

"And then what?"

"And then," Zeno said, "hopefully the material detaches from the suit and coagulates into an encoded data card."

"So this spot here is going to turn into a data card? And what do you mean 'coagulates'?"

"The particles should come together and form a card. In order for the material to get into your suit, it had to disassemble and work itself into the fabric, you follow? Some data cards are made up of millions of tiny, individual pieces that are all attracted to each other in a specific way, almost like a self-organizing puzzle. When the right DNA comes in contact with it, the puzzle pieces get activated and the whole thing reassembles itself."

"Okay," I said slowly, "so then this encoded card comes out and we somehow get the information off of it?"

Zeno stepped over and grabbed a small black device off the table. "Bro, you underestimate my technological powers. This is a universal data reader." He indicated a small slit in the side of the box. "My own design," he said as he patted the top of the box. "This baby has a port for any kind of information that could come out."

I looked down at the faint silver outline.

"Well let's see what secrets the senator uncovered."

I placed my palm over the splotch of silver. A blast of white light shot out between my fingers. I could feel the jacket vibrating underneath my hand. And then all at once, it stopped.

22

"What is it?" Alex asked.

A sparkling silver card glittered in my hand. It seemed to pulse with its own energy, almost like it was alive. I held it up to the light, examining it. "This has to be what the Left Hand was after," I said, "but I've never seen anything like it. Zeno, are all data cards li—"

The rigid card began to droop in my fingers, like a thin layer of plastic being exposed to a flame.

I looked at Zeno. "Uh, Zeno, is it supposed to do this?"

His eyes widened. I tried to straighten the card, but it started to melt, becoming a hot, glittering silver ooze that coursed down my fingers.

"Zeno! What's happening?"

I tried to shake the card off, but it stuck to my fingers and continued to melt. Droplets made their way down my palm and onto my wrist. I grunted in pain as it scalded my skin.

I wiped my hand on my shirt, trying desperately to remove the burning plastic, and then the pain was gone. And so was the card.

"What happened? What was that?" I glanced at my shirt, but there was no silver on it anywhere. Zeno took a quick step over and grabbed my left arm by the elbow, turning my arm so he could see the underside. I could only stare in disbelief.

There, on the inside of my palm, from the tips of my fingers all the way up my forearm, were streaks of silver. A pattern. The plastic from the card seemed to have incorporated itself into my skin.

"Hmm, that was unexpected," Zeno said, his eyes curious behind the glasses.

"You think?" I said.

Zeno shrugged. "Pretty cool, right? I've never seen one in person, but—"

"What? No! What is it, and what are you—ouch!"

Zeno had taken his index finger and poked me in the arm, right in the center of the largest streak. I tried to tug my arm away from his grasp, but he held it firm.

"Easy, bro. Watch," he said, nodding to my arm.

Augustine, Alex, and Daphne each took a step closer.

The silver streak rearranged itself and formed a new pattern. It was an odd sensation. It felt like the individual skin cells of my arm were being shuffled around and momentarily displaced to make room for the silver substance, like an itch that continually changed places.

"Have you seen anything like this before, Zeno?" Augustine said, his brow furrowed.

Zeno paused, the beginnings of a smile creeping onto his face.

"It's a fluid tattoo!" Alex said, peering at my arm.

"I don't know," Daphne said, stepping over and taking my wrist in her hand. I felt a shock go up my arm that had nothing to do with the recent changes to my skin tone. She bent over and examined it up close as my heart raced. "No, it's not a fluid tattoo," she said. "They're outlawed in the Flats and they don't look quite like that. And why would the Left Hand be after a tattoo?"

Alex's face fell. "Oh yeah."

Zeno took a step back and smiled. "Well guys, remember when I said that this little box could read anything we found on the card? *This* just might be the only exception. It's a biokey."

"Ah," Augustine said, comprehension dawning across his face. I looked back and forth between Alex and Daphne. Both shrugged their shoulders in return.

"And what exactly is a biokey?" I said.

"It's a key that's alive," Zeno said.

"Right, but what is it? What does it do?" Daphne asked.

"Years ago, simple DNA was used as a key," Augustine said. "If you wanted to store something precious or sensitive in a safe, you put a biometric scanner on it, and a fingerprint or a strand of hair was the passcode. But there was a problem. To get past the scanner, all you needed was a piece of that person's DNA, and you know as well as I do that that's easier to get than it should be. A more secure key needed to be built, and this was the result." He pointed at my arm.

"Okay, but couldn't someone just, I don't know, cut off my arm and take it to the safe?" I asked. I figured the Left Hand would have no trouble turning me into an amputee.

"That's part of what makes this so cool," Zeno said.

I raised my eyebrows in question. "That's what you're going with, cool?"

"Yeah, cuz if you die, it dies, and then it's useless."

"Then why not just steal the safe?" Daphne asked.

"Because you know how safes are these days—they could be anything," Zeno explained. "This safe could be like a paperweight or a sentimental object. And the biokey is attached to it. It can't be hacked. If you force it open, the information will deteriorate. The only way to find it and open it is with the biokey."

"So Victor's arm is a biokey. What now?" Daphne asked.

The screen suddenly blinked red.

Left Hand activity noted. View feed now?

Zeno turned from the group and spoke at the screen. "Of course, Gina! Show us the feed, girl!"

We turned to watch as a familiar face appeared on screen.

"And the feud between President Keltan and Dr. Rosewood continues. Find out what was said later tonight," Kelly Straunton said. "In other news, I'm reporting live from the Capital."

In the background, things were a mess. Police lights everywhere. People crying.

"Minutes after the closing of the emergency meeting of the senate," she continued, "two members of the city's decision-making body were marked by the Left Hand. Senator Joan Hammoth and Senator Greg Talhalf. Both are currently in police custody. The senators were Marked in a similar method to Victor Wells. Thankfully, no one was hurt and they'll be able to enjoy their last few days with their families.

"Surprisingly, Dr. Victoria Rosewood issued a statement minutes after the dual Markings."

A quote appeared on the screen, which Kelly Straunton read.

My condolences to the families of Senators Mammoth and Talhalf. We've feared the Left Hand for long enough. I'm working on something to bring their identities to light. More updates to come.

The quote disappeared, and the camera returned to Kelly.

"If I know anything about Dr. Rosewood, this should make the Sinistrali shake in their anonymous boots." She flashed a dazzling smile. "Back to you, John."

"Thanks, Kelly. To add to the turmoil, a section of the Innerbelt has been shut down temporarily. A portion of a vacant building was apparently jettisoned onto the tracks a little over ten minutes ago. Once again, a group known as 'The Bombers' has claimed responsibility. If you're traveling along the southeast rim, expect dela—"

"I think we're good there," Zeno said. "Thanks, Gina."

Don't mention it.

The screen went black.

Zeno turned to Augustine. "Have you heard anything about Dr. Rosewood's project?"

"I was about to ask you the same question," Augustine said. He stepped away and motioned to Zeno. They started conversing in quieter tones the rest of us couldn't hear.

Alex still stared at the black screen, his mouth hanging slightly open and a look of horror on his face. "Two more?" he said. "And a section of the Innerbelt is out?"

"They're not related," Daphne said. "And it's basically worthless protesting. The Bombers only ever scrounge up enough money to cause a disturbance once or twice a year, and the longest it's taken the city to clean up the tracks has been an hour and a half. They cause a headache for an afternoon, but that's all they do."

"Wait a second," I said. "Daphne, do you know The Bombers?" I had almost forgotten about her lair.

She stole a look at her father and Zeno, who were still occupied in whispered conversation.

"Maybe," she said quietly.

I raised my eyebrows.

"Okay, yes, I know them," she said, "but they're small-time."

"Shutting down the Innerbelt is small-time?" Alex asked. "What's big-time look like?"

"I believe we have more important things to worry about," Augustine said, stepping back to the rest of us.

"Right," I said, shaking Daphne's underworld contacts from my mind. "We need to find the safe that correlates with this thing." I held out my arm.

"Where would a senator hide something the Left Hand would kill him for?" Zeno asked. "Any insight into that one, boss?" He looked at Augustine.

Augustine shook his head. "There are a whole host of possible places, but nothing in particular sticks out. I would have to guess that—"

"Oh my gosh," I said, bringing my hand to my head. "I know where it is!"

"Seriously?" Daphne said.

"Yeah! Avardi told me, right before he got Marked," I said, remembering the confusing scene. "Gina, can you pull up the footage of me and Avardi after the ceiling fell, but before he was Marked?"

Text rolled across the black screen.

Anything for you.

"And how come you treat him so good, girl? *I* am your creator!" Zeno said.

Sorry, busy pulling up requested video.

"Oooo, girl, I'm going to do some programming work on you! Getting sassy in your advanced age, you old bag. Remind me to make you more pleasant," Zeno said.

I'm beautiful the way I am.

"Unbelievable," he said, turning to Alex. "Man, you see what I have to live with?"

The video came to life on the screen, and Alex was spared from responding. The remains of the podium could be seen. The dust was still settling. On the screen I pushed myself to my feet.

"Can we get some sound with that, Gina?" I asked.

Scattered screams emitted from unseen speakers. Avardi was still on the ground, pointing at the pile of debris. My arm was outstretched.

"Here it comes," I said.

The video showed me stumbling as Avardi accepted my outstretched arm.

"Are you okay?" I heard myself say.

Avardi stared at me intently.

"The office!" he said. "Go to the office!"

"That's it," I said.

"Of course," Augustine said, one hand rubbing his chin. "All senators have a personal train car that doubles as their official office. The rumor is that's the preferred place to hide things from prying eyes."

"Makes sense." Daphne nodded. "I got to ride on one when I was younger. They're mobile, protected, and monitored."

"Exactly!" I said, feeling triumphant for the first time in days. "What better place to hide something?"

"Are you sure that's what he meant though?" Alex said. "I mean, he looked crazy. 'Office' sounds a lot like 'off this.' Maybe he just wanted to get 'off this' stage."

"I think the video was pretty clear," Daphne said.

"Yeah, bro," Zeno said. "'Go to the office' is about as clear as it gets."

"All I'm saying," Alex held his hands up, "is that I know I say some crazy stuff when I'm hungry. Speaking of, are we going to eat soon? And where do you get donuts around here?"

Zeno shook his head and let out a chuckle.

"So we've got to go to Senator Supart's office," Augustine said contemplatively, ignoring Alex's last comment.

"Right," I said.

It wouldn't be easy. The huge train system that circled the city wasn't composed entirely of public transportation. Police cars, cargo cars, and mail cars were interspersed as well. Just about anyone or anything could be transported to the other side of the city in a matter of minutes.

I absentmindedly scratched my arm. The odd sensation returned, and I looked down to see the silver of the biokey rearranging itself in my skin. Weird.

"I'm going to say something I don't think I've said in years," Augustine said. "I think we've just gotten lucky."

"Lucky?" Daphne asked. "Seriously? We've got to find the train car, which probably has security on it, and then break into it, most likely while it's on the tracks, find the safe, and escape with whatever's in it. I don't think that qualifies as luck."

"You're forgetting what happens when a senator passes away," Augustine said. I could see hope in his eyes. A plan was beginning to take shape.

"What happens when a senator passes away?" Alex asked.

"Their office is sent off to be cleaned," I said, vaguely remembering Grandfather's explanation to me after my parents passed away.

"Exactly," Augustine said. "Senator Supart's train car will be sent off to be cleaned, inspected, photographed, and cleared of any sensitive material. Once the whole process is complete, the family will be able to retrieve their belongings."

"Is the safe going to make it through all of that?" I asked.

Augustine looked to Zeno.

"Not sure, boss," Zeno said. "My guess is no. They won't be able to unlock the safe, but I doubt it'll go unnoticed."

"So we'll need to get to it before it gets found," I said.

"Exactly." Augustine nodded.

"Do we know which train car belonged to Avardi?" I asked.

"That'll require a little bit of research," Augustine said. "Zeno, do you still have access to those feeds all along the Innerbelt?"

"No," Zeno said, rubbing the back of his neck. "I lost the police feeds when the passwords changed a while back. I can put Gina to work on it, but I don't know if she'll be able to break through the government firewall. Any thoughts?"

Augustine and Zeno continued to talk for a moment.

I glanced down at my arm again and took it in. Silver and flesh seamlessly melded together. It was the key, a legitimate key, to something worth killing for.

The sound of a vibrating cell phone caught my attention.

Daphne pulled hers out of her pocket. Her eyes darted back and forth across the screen. "Perfect," she muttered, a grim smile creeping across her face.

"Who is it?" I asked.

Daphne cast a furtive glance at her father. He and Zeno were still talking.

"The people I was supposed to meet up with from earlier," she said softly, her fingers dancing across the screen. She gave one last emphatic tap and shoved the phone back in her pocket. "They want to meet up now."

"And you're going to go?" I said. "What about planning? It seems like you know the Heights and the people in it better than anyone here."

"That is one hundred percent true, but if this is what I think it is," she said, keeping one eye on her father, "it'll be worth it."

"Okay." I locked eyes with her. "I trust you."

She smiled. A strange fluttering in my stomach caught me off guard, but in the midst of all the chaos, it felt nice.

Zeno and Augustine finished their conversation, and Zeno made for the door.

"I've got to let Zeno know," Daphne said. "Zeno!"

The fluttering feeling disappeared all too quickly.

She jogged over and caught him at the door.

I couldn't hear what they said, but after some whispered conversation, she waved and dashed through the open doors at the back of the room. Zeno made his exit at a much more leisurely pace.

"Where's she going?" Alex said, watching longingly as she left.

I shrugged. I didn't want to say anything with Augustine still here. I had the feeling he didn't approve of her extracurricular activities.

"I would imagine she's off to get some information from an unsavory individual," Augustine said almost absentmindedly from the table he had reseated himself at.

"Information?" Alex asked.

Augustine looked up from what he was doing and took a deep breath. "Yes," he said with a sigh. "Although I'm not sure how much good it will do us." He leaned back in his chair and interlocked his fingers behind his head. "See, when we first arrived in the Heights, I was desperate to know what happened to us, to figure out why our DNA readout had been switched. It drove me crazy. I asked the same questions you did, Victor. Who could have changed our DNA? I spent all my time and most of my resources trying to make sense of everything.

"I learned some interesting things that changed how I viewed people, but everything came to a dead end. After Patricia died, I just didn't have the heart to continue, so I gave up and turned to other things, like teaching." He paused. "We're all in charge of our own destiny," he continued, "and I thought if I could help people here see that, things might change." He shook his head and sat forward on his chair. "However, Daphne wasn't satisfied. She never gave up hope that we could figure it out and fix things. I don't think she and Zeno know that I know what they're up to, but I do."

I wasn't quite sure what to say. What he said filled in a lot of gaps though. It explained the events center—all the screens, scanners, and projectors. He must have been going to great lengths to figure out who had kicked his family out of Noble society.

The back doors opened, and Zeno stepped back through them.

"I set the system to search for the train," he said. "Gina needs a few hours, at least. What do you say, boss? You have a plan?"

"A few thoughts," Augustine replied, "but I'll need all of you to help me figure out how to approach this." He looked at Alex and me. "The more ideas the better."

"Agreed," I said, making to join him at the table. "I think—"

A sharp pain shot through my arm. I stared in horror as the silver on the inside of my arm and palm started to move, the silver dots vibrating. The configuration changed in unison, almost like a swarm of silver bees. I grabbed my wrist in pain as the individual dots of silver scurried through the confines of my skin. A few moments later, the pain subsided, replaced by a persistent itch.

I breathed a sigh of relief.

"Victor!" Augustine said, rushing to my side.

"Bro, what happened?" Zeno said.

"I don't know," I said, showing him my arm. "You tell me."

Four distinct groupings remained. A cluster of tiny silver dots almost entirely covered my index finger. Another cluster of larger, more dispersed dots covered my palm. The next bunch of silver dots covered my wrist. These were bigger still, and there looked to be at least twenty of them. The largest dots were on my forearm. There were two of them.

Zeno squinted at my arm through his glasses. "Four groups. Two, four, forty-six, and this last group is on the move."

Sure enough, the smallest of the silver dots seemed to be combining with one another at regular intervals. We watched until there was a huge, unbroken silver mass that covered the majority of my fingers.

"There!" Alex said.

"What?" I asked.

"One of the dots on your palm just squished together with one of the other ones."

I could hear Zeno muttering under his breath. "Forty-six, but now forty-five." He paused, staring at my arm, and then his eyes lit up. "It's a clock!"

"What?" I asked.

"Bro! It's a biokey timepiece," he said, turning to face the table. "I think we're being put on the clock."

"What do you mean?" Augustine asked.

"All right, look, see the four groups? These ones are seconds. When they all combine, then one of the dots on his palm will combine with the bigger dot...and there it goes." Another of the palm dots was absorbed into the larger dot.

"That would make the palm minutes, the wrist hours, and the forearm days?" Augustine said.

"So I've got two days, four hours, forty-ish minutes, and some seconds until what?" I asked.

Augustine looked at Zeno.

"Now guys," Zeno said, "I'm no expert, but my guess is that it's an expiration date."

"As in the biokey dies if we don't get to the safe in time?"

"'Fraid so, my man."

Augustine nodded slowly and spoke. "We've got some planning to do."

23

"I don't know, Alex. I don't think multiple drones carrying a body double of Victor are the way to go," Augustine said. He sat with his fingertips on his temple, staring at the ground somewhere near Alex's feet.

"You sure?" Alex said. "Think about it. T11D-carrying Victor Wells, suspended in the air by some drones, flying through the Flats. It would cause a panic, wouldn't it? And then Victor could use the distraction to get on the train."

"And how would I get off the train?" I asked.

Alex hesitated before answering. "More drones?"

"Let's keep thinking," Augustine said. Alex looked crestfallen. It was his fifth, and in his opinion, best idea of the last hour.

I ran a hand over my face. "So I need to get inside the train car, search it, and figure out a way off without getting caught," I said. "Zeno, what about one of your masks? Could you make me look like, I don't know, someone who has access to the train?"

"My man, I like where your head's at," Zeno said. "And yes, I most definitely could do that. But then what? There would be multiple scans and probably one of those new ID badges involved."

"Couldn't you just make all of that?" I asked.

"Bro, I'm flattered, but given our timeframe, that's an impossible order, even for me," he said.

"Hmm, let's take a look at this," Augustine said, sitting up straight. "Gina, can you please pull up a map of the route of Senator Supart's train car?"

Of course. And thank you for being polite.

"Girl, I swear, I'm going to deactivate you," Zeno said.

An intricately detailed diagram of the proposed route appeared on the screen, complete with three-dimensional buildings, the lake that bordered a section of the Innerbelt, and labels over each of the stops the car was supposed to make.

"Now, once we locate the senator's car," Augustine said, "we'll be able to follow it through each of the checkpoints."

The back doors banged open, and Daphne walked in. Augustine paused as she motioned to Zeno. He pushed himself up and met her by the door, where they spoke in whispers. Judging by their body language and Zeno's expressions, he didn't appear too happy with what she said, but nodded his head nonetheless. It was easy enough to pick up on the meaning. *Not ideal, but we'll take it.* They broke up and joined the rest of us.

Augustine smiled. "Welcome back."

Daphne nodded.

I caught her eye. "Did you get it?" I mouthed.

She shook her head and mouth the word "Later," then looked up at the screen.

I followed suit, my mind burning with questions.

"As I was saying," Augustine continued, "the car makes a series of stops. The first one is here." He pointed to a spot along the track, and a red dot popped up on the screen. "This is the photography station. Protocol dictates that the senator's car is on its way there now. While it's parked, it will be filled with people. Everything in the car will be meticulously documented and photographed. It'll be there all night and then leave again in the morning.

"In between checkpoints, the car will be empty. Ideally, that's when Victor would search the train—while it's in transit. The best-case scenario would be to do it tomorrow morning when the car is leaving the photography lab. If we can't get to it then, there are four more stops the car will make over the next two days," Augustine explained. "The next stop is the crime lab, here, followed by the sweep lab and the sterilization lab, here and here."

Gina highlighted each stop on the diagram as he spoke. There were now four red dots on the screen, all located at different points around the Innerbelt. "As long as we get to it before the sweep lab, we'll be fine." Augustine pointed at the third red dot. "The sweep lab removes all sensitive material—all government documents, all paperwork, all digital traces..."

"And the safe," I said.

"Right, anything electronic in nature. After that, the train car is sterilized, stripped down, and repurposed."

"But we still don't have a way on?" Daphne asked, standing up and moving closer to the screen.

"Well, Alex had some cool drone ideas," I said. "But no, not yet."

"Not to mention we still have to figure out which train car is the right one," Zeno said. "I've got Gina working on it, but we don't have anything yet."

"Okay," Daphne said slowly as she studied the map. "So assuming we get a lock on the senator's car, maybe... Gina, can you show me the buildings surrounding the first checkpoint?" The buildings came into greater detail. "Okay, perfect. And what's the distance in height between the tallest building and the tracks below?"

Approximately 247 feet.

Zeno slapped his hand to his forehead. "Of course! How did I not think of that?"

"Think of what?" I asked.

"Oh man, this is the bomb," Zeno said. "Bro, man, I can't even... You're going to love it!"

"You think it would work?" Daphne asked, turning to him. "And could he learn fast enough?"

"Would you mind filling us in?" Augustine asked, smiling politely between Daphne and Zeno.

"Daphne's thinking that Victor could jump off one of these buildings," Zeno said, "and land on top of the senator's train car." He smiled and let loose a chuckle. "And I think it would work! He could do it just as it's leaving the checkpoint too. Bro, I've got some cool stuff that could cut through the car's outer shell and—"

"Hold on a second," I said, cutting him off. "You want me to jump"—I pointed at the screen—"off the top of a building and land on top of the train car a few hundred feet below?" I looked back and forth between Zeno and Daphne. "And survive?"

Zeno leaned back in his chair and smiled. "Ah, I see you don't know about my special spray."

Daphne rolled her eyes.

"Oh," Augustine said with surprise. "That could actually work."

"Wait, seriously?" I asked.

"Absolutely." Zeno winked at me. "Don't worry, my man, I will teach you my ways."

Completely baffled, I didn't know what to say.

Augustine stood up and moved back over to the diagram. "Gina, how long will it take the cars to travel from checkpoint to checkpoint?"

A list of times appeared.

"Okay," he said, more to himself than everyone else. "Zoom in here." He pointed and Gina obliged. A raised section of the Innerbelt came into greater focus. "Perfect." Augustine turned and faced me. "That would be the perfect exit point."

Zeno and Daphne nodded in unison.

"Agreed," Daphne said. "Then Victor could jump off the tracks there and we can be waiting for him a few blocks away in the Heights."

Zeno's smile grew, and a crazy glint appeared in his eye, which did nothing to comfort me.

"Can you teach him in time?" Augustine asked.

"In time for when?" Zeno asked.

"Tomorrow," Augustine said. "Assuming we've identified the right train car, the best time to do this will be right after the photography lab."

Zeno checked his watch. "We've still got a good chunk of daylight left. As long as Gina finds the car for us," he said, turning to me, "I think it'll be more than enough time. Tomorrow it is!"

"Wait a second," I said, "so that's it? This is the plan?"

Daphne and Zeno looked at each other and then at Augustine.

"Yes," Augustine said with a nod. "This is the plan."

"Bro, how much time is left on that biokey of yours?" Zeno asked.

I pulled up my sleeve and counted.

"Two days, zero hours, and thirty-ish minutes," I said. I was a little worried at how quickly everyone had decided on the free-fall option, but I also knew we needed to act, and act quickly. I glanced at the diagram again. Assuming I survived the drop, the plan made sense. I'd be landing on top of an empty train car, bypassing scanners, ID cards, and people. "Is Gina going to be able to find it in time?" I asked.

"She's never failed us before," Zeno said, "but she's got some serious work to do."

"Can you speed her up at all?" I asked. "If we don't find it tonight, could our plan still work, but at one of the other stops?"

Augustine stared up at the screen for a moment before responding. "It would be more difficult, but yes."

"Bro," Zeno said, patting me on the shoulder, "have a little faith in my girl, and put your focus on learning how to use the spray."

"Agreed," Augustine said. "I'll arrange all of the finer details while you're out, and we can tinker with the algorithms when you get back."

"Sounds good to me, boss," Zeno said before grabbing my arm. "Come with me, bro. I'm going to teach you how to jump off a building and not die."

24

Zeno had disappeared briefly, returned carrying a bag, and headed straight out the door, an almost giddy smile on his face and a rather noticeable skip in his step. I bid everyone a hasty farewell and trailed Zeno out the door and onto the street. I was about to demand some answers about surviving a free fall when a terrible stench reached my nostrils.

"What the—" I started, finding the ground littered with decaying refuse, and then I saw the graffiti, graffiti that hadn't been there yesterday.

Turn him in. Or else.

The prospect of jumping off a building momentarily left my mind.

"Zeno, what's all this about?" I said, coming to a stop. The words were dark red, the color of blood.

"Oh yeah," Zeno said, looking nonchalantly over his shoulder, smile still on his face, "I was watching that on the cameras earlier."

"Why didn't you say anything?" I said.

"Bro, it's nothing you need to worry about. Harmless locals, that's all."

I knew the message was about me. I didn't know why Zeno

seemed to not care about it, but something about the blood-red words "or else" painted on the side of my temporary residence gave me chills. The harmless locals were serious.

"I thought Tyrann told them to not interfere with me being here," I said.

"Tyrann may scare them," Zeno said, "but they make their own decisions, right? They did some pretty good protesting when we first got here, but luckily, nothing came of it."

We walked in silence as I contemplated his words. *They make their own decisions.* Zeno's words sparked something that I hadn't had much time to think about.

"Do you think people can change?" I asked.

He looked at me with a raised eyebrow.

"Like Sinisters," I said. "Do you think Sinisters can change?"

Zeno stopped walking and faced me. "That's a heavy question, man. What do you think?"

"I don't know," I said. "I mean, it's completely different from what I've thought my whole life. When Daphne first told me, I thought it sounded crazy, but now..." I paused and exhaled a deep breath. "I don't know."

Zeno stared at me, almost like he was measuring me somehow. "Your grandfather, he's a good person, isn't he?"

"Yeah," I said, caught off guard. "The best person I know."

"You know how I can tell?" Zeno said. "Most Nobles wouldn't even entertain the idea that this whole Noble-Sinister thing isn't real, but you're considering it."

"What changed your mind?" I asked.

"Who said my mind needed changing, bro?" Zeno asked. "Nah, I'm just kidding. There were a ton of reasons. You remember my scanners, right? When I worked with the Bounty Hunter—"

"Wait, you worked with Kratos?" I said, surprised. But it made sense. Zeno's skillset probably made him an ideal person to be part of the Bounty Hunter's team.

Zeno nodded.

"Yeah, and I saw and heard things that didn't quite match up, you know? It kind of left me feeling unsettled right here." He patted his stomach. "And not because I was hungry, bro. But I trusted it. The more I researched it and the more I observed people around me, the more things made sense, which was not a popular opinion in my former line of work. I heard about Augustine and decided we should talk. And now here I am, standing with you in the middle of a street in the Heights."

Zeno, Augustine, Daphne—they had all sacrificed so much.

"And bro, come on, if you didn't believe it too, you would have left a while ago."

Daphne had asked me if I believed her, if I trusted her. I locked eyes with Zeno. He was a good man, like my grandfather. He had never come right out and said it, but Grandfather had always hinted that he didn't agree with the Noble-Sinister divide, and after these last couple of days, I wasn't sure if I believed it either. And I trusted Zeno and Daphne and Augustine. When the rest of the world had given up, they hadn't abandoned me.

"I hope that helps, bro."

"Yeah, definitely." I somehow felt much better, more settled, even though I was about to do something completely insane. I rubbed my hands together. "All right," I said, focusing on what we were about to do, "how am I going to survive this fall?"

"Good man," Zeno said, clapping me on the shoulder, his grin from earlier back on his face. "First things first. We need to hurry. Let's go." He started walking. The bag at his side clanked against his leg as he increased his speed. "Police shouldn't be coming this way for another two hours." He adjusted the bag and looked at me. "And you're gonna need all the practice you can get."

"That's what you keep saying." I eyed the bag swinging at his side. I wasn't completely sure what was in it, but I assumed it would prevent me from falling to my death. My stomach growled and I remembered I hadn't eaten dinner. I was beginning to think this was a good thing. "Will the police stick around here for long?"

"Nah, probably half an hour, maybe forty-five minutes."

"So why aren't we just waiting until after they leave?"

"Sweepers," Zeno said.

Of course. We had been warned about the Heights after dark. Sweepers cleaned the streets by picking up and disposing of anything that wasn't concrete or asphalt. Weeds, trash, dogs, cats—anything. Humans included. Everyone knew about them. Alex had told me once that sweepers supposedly left a trail that smelled like bleach.

"Do many people stay out after dark down here?"

Zeno gave me a sidelong glance. "There's always a few, but bro, they're crazy. Some people say the sweepers have a pattern, but I haven't ever looked into it. Never had a need to, you know? I've always stayed inside. No temptation, no consequences, right?"

"What about Daphne?" I asked. "Does she have meetings with her, um, contacts often?"

Zeno shifted his bag uncomfortably as we walked, almost like he wasn't sure whether he should say anything.

"Daphne showed me your lair," I said.

"First off, *lairs* are from the stone age, my man! Ours is more like a headquarters," Zeno said. "I mean, bro, did you see all the cool stuff in there? And to answer your question, Daphne might have, on occasion, stayed out a little later than I would recommend."

"And?" I asked.

"And she's still here, isn't she?" Zeno shook his head. "Maybe she's just been lucky, but man, the stories you hear about those things down here, they'll give you nightmares."

There was something in the way Zeno said it. I could tell he disapproved, and maybe he was even a little mad at Daphne for taking a risk like that.

I tried to imagine the sweepers in my head. Monstrous metal machines trolling the streets at night, snatching up anyone brazen enough to challenge them. I couldn't imagine what it would be like to live knowing that every night you were under house arrest.

We walked in silence for several blocks, leaving me to stew in my dark thoughts. I could only hope that whatever information Avardi had for me in his safe was worth all this.

"You've been quiet, bro," Zeno said. "What's on your mind?"

"Well," I began, not sure what to say.

"Wait." Zeno held out his hand and shut his eyes. "Okay, don't tell me. I got it. The answer to your question is no."

"No?"

"No, there's nothing going on between me and Daphne," he said.

"I didn't, I wasn't..." I sputtered.

"Come on, bro, I see the way you look at her."

That fluttering feeling from earlier returned for a brief moment. I didn't know what to say. I mean, I was a Marked man. Were Daphne and I even a possibility at a time like this? I definitely wouldn't *mind* going down that path...if I lived for longer than a few more days.

"Vic, bro, it's okay. No worries, all right?" Zeno fixed a small smile on his face.

I walked beside him in a slightly uncomfortable silence. But me and Daphne? Was he saying she had a thing for me too?

It was time for a subject change.

"So, Zeno, did you, uh, grow up around here?" I asked, breaking the silence.

"Around here?"

"Well no, I mean, clearly you weren't raised a Sinister."

Zeno glanced at me. "You sure?"

"Pretty sure?" I said slowly.

"I'm just giving you a hard time. Yeah, I was raised in the Flats, same as you." Zeno came to a stop. The buildings towered over us like fading torches in the setting sun. Red and orange hues fought against the elongated shadows that covered most of the road. "This one should do," Zeno said. "Can you give me a foot up?"

I looked at him in bewilderment.

He pointed to a fire escape that hung a few feet out of reach.

"We're not using the elevators?" I asked. I knew the buildings around here were old, but they couldn't be *that* old.

"Come on bro, what fun would that be?" Zeno grinned.

I cupped my hands and Zeno stepped up.

"I was thinking more along the lines of easier, faster..." I grunted.

"Then I am happy to report that we're going all the way to the top," he said.

I peered up. It had to be at least fifty stories. Zeno didn't look to be the athletic type. He was thin, but not muscular. He didn't move with the practiced grace of a fencer or the confidence of an athlete. Yet the thought of a five-hundred-foot climb didn't seem to daunt him in the slightest.

With a metallic clang, Zeno slid the fire escape down to me.

"You ready?"

I grasped the cold metal with both hands and pulled myself up. "I'm going to go with mildly unprepared."

Zeno chuckled to himself and started to climb.

I wasn't used to being up so high. I stood a few feet back from Zeno's precarious position. Zeno stood so close to the edge that a hard gust of wind could have pushed him off, but he appeared completely unconcerned with his nearness to certain death. He turned to look at me, a giant grin on his face.

"All right, man, when we find the senator's train car, you've got to get inside, but first you've got to get *to* it. I'd love to be the one to do this, but you know, you're the biokey." He gestured to my arm. "Lucky for me, you need a teacher. So, like we talked about earlier, there's no way that you'll be able to sneak onto the train while it's still at the station. Way too many people. Way too much security. You'll have to do it as it's pulling out." Zeno tugged a screen from his pocket and unfolded some of the extensions from the back, doubling its size.

"When the train leaves the station," he continued, a graphic on his screen offering a diagram of his words, "it does so slowly. Once it's a certain distance from the station, it speeds up considerably. You'll need to get to the senator's car before that happens." Zeno closed his screen and put it back in his pocket. "And that's why we're here. The only way for you to get to the train is by flying onto it."

I swallowed hard. Zeno's bag wasn't nearly large enough to contain a personal carrier drone, or anything like that.

"You seem a little skeptical, bro." Zeno smirked.

"What's in the bag?" I asked, not smiling.

"You know a little bit about the Bounty Hunter, right?"

"A bit."

"Have you heard that he can fly?"

I remembered what Alex said. "Yes."

"Well, it's complete crap."

"Ha!" I said. Alex would be disappointed. "So then what are we doing up here?"

"We're up here because the Bounty Hunter *appears* to fly. But he flies only in a downward direction."

"Isn't that just called 'falling'?"

"Now you're catching on." Zeno reached into his bag, pulled out a pair of gloves and threw them over to me. "You ever seen gloves like this?"

They were black and extended almost to the elbow.

"They look like the gloves Kratos wears," I said.

I turned them over in my hand. I hadn't noticed before, but there seemed to be a small hole in the wrist area. The forearm area appeared to be bulkier than the rest of the glove. The gloves were also suspiciously heavy. Each one weighed at least a pound and a half.

Zeno nodded. "I'll let you in on a little secret, my man. I invented those."

"You invented heavy gloves?" I said, weighing them in my hands.

"Heavy gloves? Please." Zeno grabbed one of them from me. "Years of research, tons of trials, and then boom! A brand-new molecule of my making. Cool, right? This thicker area of the forearm is where it's housed. The molecule's got a long and complicated name that I never could pronounce but—"

"I thought you invented it," I cut in.

"Regardless, for now we'll call this stuff 'Zeno's special spray.' Kratos uses this stuff all the time."

"Seriously?" I asked.

"Absolutely."

"So, what does it do?"

"What does what do?" he said, tilting his head to point his ear in my direction.

I sighed. "What does *Zeno's special spray* do?"

"Ah, that sounds nice." He winked. "I'm glad you asked. I'm sure you remember the day we traded you for a detonator? Remember when Augustine and I stepped aside to speak, and I sprayed something all around us? You might have even seen it when Kratos showed up at your house and fought the Sinistrali."

The memory returned. The hiss. The gray beads.

"Let me guess, your special spray?" I said. Zeno smiled.

"Mm-hmm. The molecules in the gloves are absorptive. They intercept and capture energy. Sound, kinetic, heat, everything. Make sense?"

I nodded.

"All right, so you might be wondering, 'Zeno, just how strong are your super-cool molecules?'" He reached into his bag, pulled out an identical set of gloves, and slid one onto his hand. "How about a demonstration? Daphne told me you've used one of these before." He pulled a saber out of his bag and tossed it to me. He then stuck a bare arm out and sprayed some of his spray around it. "Whenever you're ready, take a swing at my arm. Don't hold back."

"Are you serious?" I felt a little awkward. Zeno stood there with his arm out in front of him, completely defenseless.

"Absolutely. I want you to be able to trust the spray. And to do that, you've gotta know how strong it is." He nodded to his arm.

I couldn't give it my best shot. Every bone in his hand would be broken.

I brought the saber down in a soft arc onto his hand—except it didn't make contact. It hung suspended in the air several inches above his skin. I applied more pressure. The saber hardly moved. It was like cutting through frozen butter with a cold knife. Small gray beads appeared in the air and fell to the ground as I pushed harder. I grunted with exertion. More beads appeared and Zeno moved his hand out of the way. My saber slipped through the space his hand had occupied and caught on the other side of the spray. I pulled my saber out of the invisible barrier, a few gray beads materializing as I did so.

Zeno looked pleased. "And that was some of my weaker stuff. What do you think? Satisfied?"

I walked around the spot where Zeno's hand had been and prodded the invisible mass. A few more gray beads materialized.

"So I'm going to use your special spray to"—I looked at Zeno —"fall without dying?"

Zeno pulled on his other glove and motioned me over to the edge of the roof. "I prefer the term 'guided falling.'"

I walked closer to the edge of the rooftop and glanced fifty stories down to the ground below. My heart pounded in my chest. I took a step back.

Zeno held up his hands so I could see his palms. "You see the small hole in the middle of the wrist?"

"Yep."

"That's where the special spray comes out. All you have to do to release the spray is go like this." He closed his hand and made a fist, but he moved his thumb up on top of his index finger, almost like he was pressing a hidden button there. A small hiss accompanied the movement.

I mimicked the motion, and the familiar hiss sounded. I made the movement several times in quick succession. Each time another hiss sounded. My heart continued to pound in my chest.

"So how exactly does this keep me from dying?" I said, looking at my hands.

"When you're falling through the air, you're going to let out bursts of spray directed toward the center of your chest. That way, you'll keep from spinning, and it'll slow you down. It's pretty intuitive once you're doing it."

"So what do you want me to do, jump off the building and hope for the best?"

"Nah, man," Zeno said, taking a few steps back, "we'll fall together. I'll be there the whole way, teaching you when you should give a burst and what to do on the landing. Cool?"

Not cool, but necessary. I nodded. I was going to jump off a building. A hot, sticky feeling began to boil up inside me. Fear. Terror. But I had to do this.

"You see that building out there, the tallest one in the distance?" He pointed to the horizon.

"Mm-hmm," I said, keeping my mouth shut, lest something come out. Like vomit.

"See how it's kind of blue on the top half and changes colors about halfway down?"

"Uh, yeah?"

"Try and keep your eye on that."

"Why?"

I should have seen it coming.

Zeno collided with me, and I left my feet, my torso flying out over the empty space just past the edge of the rooftop. Everything seemed to go in slow motion. I kicked out, reaching desperately for the ledge of the roof, for anything that would keep me from falling. My arms flailed wildly, grasping for something that wasn't there.

Time sped back up. The air whooshed past me at increasing speeds. Adrenaline surged through my body, and I heard a loud laugh to my left.

Zeno. Of course.

"Bro, use your gloves!" he shouted.

I closed my fists in the way Zeno had shown me. Immediately, I felt as if the top half of my torso, including my face, had been hit with a pillow. The air exploded with gray beads.

I was flung backwards, head over heels, and began to spin wildly out of control. All my thoughts vanished except one. *I'm going to die.*

I felt my legs go through a dense cushion of air, and my spinning stopped.

Zeno appeared in the air by my side. "Spray it at your chest!"

The ground sped toward me.

"Spray it at your chest!"

I brought my arms down, closer to my chest, and rotated my wrists inward.

"Now!" Zeno yelled.

I closed my hands, and my chest and stomach passed through a dense cushion of air. I shot upward, the ground seeming to retreat in a shower of gray.

Zeno came flying up past me a moment later. "Again!" he shouted, his voice almost lost in the wind.

I closed my hands again, and Zeno fell past me, plummeting toward the earth.

Then up he came once more. "Again!"

We were like two bungee jumpers flying through the air, passing each other every time we rebounded. I was flying...well, falling with guidance.

Zeno appeared by my side again, but the ground couldn't be more than seventy feet away now. "Spray until we hit the ground! Now!"

I closed my hands, and the strange pillow sensation washed over me. My speed decreased. I kept spraying. Gray beads peeled out from under me as I descended.

"Good," Zeno said at my side. "Good, keep spraying. Just before you hit the ground, adjust the spray so it cushions the top half of your torso."

Forty feet. Twenty feet. Ten feet.

"Now," Zeno said.

We adjusted our spray, and the dense invisible cushion caught me in the shoulders, pushing me upright. I landed hard and unsteady, but on my feet. I stumbled a couple of steps and then fell to my knees. My hands were shaking uncontrollably.

"What were you thinking?" I yelled.

"I was thinking, 'If your friend jumped off a building, would you?' And then I thought, 'Nah, Victor's not that kind of guy,'" Zeno said.

"How about, 'Hey, Victor, if you don't figure this out, you'll likely die anyway, so get out there and do it'? I think that would have worked."

"Think about it this way, man," Zeno said, completely disregarding my anger, "you're not dead. I think that counts as a win."

"Yeah, but yo—"

"And," Zeno talked over me, "you liked it. You were enjoying yourself."

"Bu—"

"Don't try and deny it. I saw."

I regarded him with an icy stare. But he was right. At least at the end when I was getting the hang of it. Never before had I felt such a rush.

"And think about this," he continued. "That is as bad as it'll ever be, bro. You'll never have to deal with a jump worse than that."

Again, he was right. Or at least I hoped he was. I looked back up to the rooftop. Tomorrow, my jump would have to be perfect. I wouldn't have multiple chances to get it right.

I walked over to the ladder, grabbed the first rung and started to climb.

"Hold on," Zeno said, nodding down the street, "I called Gina for some help."

A faint buzzing noise filled the street behind us. A small, four-wheeled contraption sped toward us.

He nodded at the roof. "It takes too long to climb."

The device stopped at Zeno's feet. He picked it up, walked over to the fire escape, and placed it on the metal supports of the ladder.

"It's held on by magnetized wheels," he said, flicking a switch and letting go of the machine. It hung on to the bars. "It'd take about a thousand pounds of force to pry it off. Here, put these on."

Zeno threw me another pair of gloves.

"Do you specialize in glove making?" I asked.

"No, my man, I just specialize in cool. Now grab on to the handholds. The gloves have metal in them—they're magnetized to the machine. They'll do all the holding for you while it carries you to the top."

"And we couldn't have started with this?" I said.

"No way, man. Can't have you taking my incredible genius for granted. Now you'll appreciate it."

"Thank you for that life lesson," I said.

"Don't mention it."

I reached for the handholds, the magnetism between the gloves and the contraption accelerating my movements. My hands connected to the machine with a metallic clink.

"You know what, Zeno?" I said.

"What?"

"You're kind of a nerd. A nerd who makes gloves. You're a glove nerd."

"Don't forget mask nerd and general nerd, bro! And you should be careful what you say before hooking yourself up to one of my gadgets."

Zeno stepped over and slapped a small red button in front of my face, and the contraption shot off and shuttled me to the roof.

25

The sun blinked at me as it hovered just above the horizon. I had flown up the rails of the fire escape at least twenty times on Zeno's little contraption. No fatal injuries had occurred, although I was pretty sure I had a bruise on my forehead from disengaging the magnetized handholds. Apparently the only way to hit the button that released them was to head-butt it.

Zeno had accompanied me up to the rooftop several more times to give me pointers and help me get more comfortable in free fall but had left over an hour ago. His only condition was that I come back before nightfall. The side streets would be free of police, and the main streets would be clear of sweepers.

Once I got over the initial shock and terror of falling through the air, I began to envy the Bounty Hunter. Nothing before had given me such a sense of freedom, soaring through the air, falling from incredible heights with no consequence. This was how he traveled.

I sat on the rooftop with my legs dangling over the edge as I stared out over the Heights. The moon was starting to make its ascent to replace the sun. The streets below still had functioning street lamps, and some of the bulbs had begun to flicker on, but the streets were oddly still. On the whole, I had expected more people, but since

Zeno left, I hadn't seen a soul. Maybe people just weren't taking any chances with the sweepers.

I tightened the straps on my gloves and looked down at the shadow-covered road below. It was probably time to head back. I knew Augustine and Zeno would be smoothing out the plan, but I couldn't help wondering what Alex and Daphne been up to this whole time. I smiled to myself thinking about it. I hoped Alex had kept himself together, but I knew better than to expect much.

Out of the corner of my eye, something moved. I refocused and saw a figure a few blocks away jogging down the street. The figure passed beneath a streetlight, and I caught a gleam of long brown hair and a small bag draped across her back.

Daphne.

And I was fairly certain she wasn't running toward home.

I swung my legs up onto the rooftop and took a few steps back. I paused briefly, collecting myself, and then took off in a sprint, taking a flying leap off the corner of the building in the direction Daphne was headed.

I peaked, and for a moment I hung almost motionless in the air, not moving up or down. There was only one word for it.

Freedom.

I plummeted toward the earth.

I kept my eye on Daphne as I fell, sending intermittent bursts of spray toward my torso until I touched down. My landing was significantly smoother than my first attempt, and I sprinted after her. She had stayed on the same street as me, but was a few blocks up. As far as I could tell, she was alone.

Up ahead, Daphne cut across the street and headed down an alleyway. I picked up my pace, but I decided not to get her attention. I doubted that she would approve of me following her, but where was she headed at this hour? Another secret meeting? Did she always go to these things alone? And what if she needed help?

I turned right down the alleyway Daphne had taken and rounded the corner just in time to see her vanish down another side street. By now, the sun had completely disappeared behind the buildings.

Nightfall was setting in. I sniffed the air for the smell of bleach, just in case, but it smelled like regular old air. Where did Alex get all of his "information"?

I rounded another corner and slowed my pace. Daphne wasn't more than twenty feet away, but I could barely see her in the increasing darkness. I did everything I could to keep quiet and keep pace with her.

I almost jumped when she broke the silence.

"What do you want me to do?" she said, her voice frustrated and sharp. I thought for a second she was talking to me, but she never turned around. Daphne passed beneath one of the flickering streetlights, and I could see she was holding her phone up to her ear. She wore all black and had a small, narrow case slung over her shoulder.

"I don't think Gina can find the senator's train car without complete access," she said and then paused, waiting for the reply. I guessed she was talking to Zeno. "Right, and if that's the case, then we don't really have another option, do we?" she continued. "I don't like it either, but she's not going to get the password before morning. I can. And it's not like this kind of opportunity comes along ev—"

Zeno must have cut her off. She balled her fists and picked up her pace. I followed.

We were in a part of the city I hadn't seen before, which wasn't really saying anything since I had only been a couple of places, but even in the dim light, this street looked even dirtier and more abandoned than the rest. Cracks littered the road like a complex series of spiderwebs. Plants had managed to break through the surface and covered big chunks of the road.

"Zeno, I'll be fine," Daphne said as she disappeared around a corner. I took the opportunity to make up some ground. The overgrowth on the road dampened my footfalls as I jogged. I stopped at the corner and peered around it. Daphne had come to a stop, one hand on her hip and the other holding her phone.

"Yes, it's a sure thing," she said. "She's never beaten me. I'll be back in an hour with the password."

A brief moment of silence and then Daphne responded, "Zeno!

Look, I know! This is Victor's life we're talking about. And maybe even our lives. We don't have time to wait for Gina. I'm doing this. Bye." She hung up the phone and shoved it into her pocket. She let out a big huff of air and composed herself. She looked down the far end of the street, checking to make sure she was alone.

I quickly yanked my head back around the corner before she saw me. Clearly, Zeno didn't agree with what Daphne was doing. What kind of risk was she taking?

From around the corner, the sound of knuckles on glass met my ears, followed by the metallic sliding of a door hinge.

"What do you want?" a man said, his voice deep and menacing.

"I'm here for the first fight," Daphne said.

"Who are you here to see?"

"Myself." She said it like the man was an idiot.

"Of course."

A brief pause accompanied the man's words, followed by the sound of metal on metal and finally the click of a locking mechanism.

Daphne was here for the first fight, whatever that was, and she was here to see herself? I was positive that the case on her shoulder held a saber. After seeing her lair, I knew she hadn't quit practicing. Was I about to find out just how good she was?

I waited another thirty seconds and then turned the corner, looking for a glass door. There wasn't one. But I could have sworn I had heard her knock on glass. I looked up and down the street. To my left was a lone window with some faded lettering on it. All the other ones were broken.

Here goes nothing.

I knocked on the glass, careful to keep my face out of the dim wash of light from the street lamp. The section of wall below the window slid silently into the ground, revealing not the rest of the window, but the bottom half of a glass door. It swung outward, and I was met by a man whose clothes looked like they were centuries old. He was dressed in a brown leather jacket and black pants, and I noticed a couple of small daggers hanging on his belt. He was about Alex's height, but thin and scrawny.

"What do you want?" he said in a surprisingly deep voice.

"I'm here for the first fight," I said, repeating Daphne's words.

"Who are you here to see?"

I sized him up. I could probably take him. Would it be better to lie or just knock him out? I eyed the daggers at his belt. I was defenseless.

"Who are you here to see?" he asked again, impatient this time.

I took a chance. "The best female fighter you've got," I said.

It had sounded better in my head.

"You and everybody else," he said with a smirk. He stood aside to let me in.

The door shut behind me, and I was plunged into darkness.

"Follow the stairs to the end and take a right at the bottom."

Hands outstretched in the darkness, I felt around for a handrail and started my descent.

26

It looked like a scene from a history book. Rows of blinking fluorescent lights carpeted the ceiling, reflecting off the now dormant railway tracks and casting odd shadows across the walls. A dead subway car sat stationary on the old metal rails. It had been gutted and graffitied. Most of the walls were covered in colorful graffiti too.

In school, I had learned that subway systems were the precursor for the Innerbelt, but that decades ago, all the subways had caved in. Obviously, this wasn't the case. There were hundreds of people scattered across the defunct station, and I doubt they would all be here if the place was liable to collapse.

When Daphne said she was here for the first fight, I was expecting something different—a ring or a court maybe. Not hundreds of Sinisters milling about an antiquated subway station.

On that note, where *was* Daphne?

Not wanting to attract too much attention, I headed for the back wall, walking past people who looked nothing like the majority of Sinisters I had seen so far. Most of them resembled the guy who'd let me in here—darker colors, a lot of leather, but thankfully no free-hanging weapons.

Once situated against the back wall, I scanned the room. It was huge, and I'd never seen so much graffiti in my life. Even the streets above weren't tagged like this place was. I looked at the picture nearest me. It looked like a ball was emitting light. The graffiti people appeared to be screaming. If I didn't know any better, I would say this was a picture of a Marking, my Marking. It sent a chill down my spine.

I took a few steps over to the next part of the graffiti. The rays from the ball connected to a large, white building. The Capital? I looked around me. Were these people not just anti-Noble, but pro-Left Hand? I could feel myself start to sweat.

I needed to blend in. I still wore my black gloves from earlier, and several people in the crowd wore something similar, but that wouldn't be enough. I needed to hide my face.

Twenty feet to my left, a scuffle broke out in the crowd. I headed straight toward it. People on both sides were shoving and yelling at each other. A few hats had been knocked off, and I scooped one off the ground as I walked by and put it on.

It was an olive-green bowler that I was able to tilt down over my eyes. The smell was so terrible it stung my eyes and nose, but I kept it on anyways.

"Scoundrels and ladies!" a voice boomed over a set of unseen speakers. A smattering of whoops and applause sounded throughout the subway station. "Welcome to the biggest fight of the evening!" More applause. The center of the room was beginning to clear out, opening a space for what was to come next. "I hope all your bets have been placed. Tonight's fight promises to be good. You know the rules. The fight starts when the fighters get to the center of the floor." The applause and yells became louder and more intense. "Tonight's match will be a clash of kingdoms, a battle of royalty! After a brief hiatus, we have once again, the only as of yet undefeated fighter—the Exile!" A roar from the crowd drowned out the magnified voice as a masked figure emerged from the broken-down subway car. "And the scrappy and ever-resourceful Duchess of the Heights." Another roar from the crowd. Another masked figure descended the staircase.

I squeezed my way to the front for a better view. Daphne—the

Exile, as the announcer called her—stood alone in the middle of the room, her brown hair tied in a bun on the back of her head, an electrified saber at her side. But she didn't *look* like Daphne. She wore Daphne's clothes, but the face didn't match.

And then it dawned on me. She was wearing one of Zeno's masks. Clever. I wished I had been too.

Hundreds of people formed a large U that left the area around the subway tracks open. The crowd grew silent as the Duchess approached the center of the floor, saber in hand. Both Daphne and her opponent sported dueling blades. Instead of the double-edged sword or rounded saber, each blade was made up of an equilateral triangle—three equal sides with a blunted pyramid on the top. The edges of the blade were blunted as well. A hit would bruise, not cut. No severed limbs would result, just pain, and if the blade was electrified, temporary paralysis.

"Fighters approach the center and cross your blades!" The speakers boomed and the crowd tensed with excitement. Directly across from me stood a man who watched the two fighters intently. He didn't yell and he didn't cheer. He was dressed differently, maybe overdressed. He wore a black suit and a black shirt, and he was tall.

He looked like he had money, Noble money. Was it possible? If there were good Sinisters, like Daphne said, it made sense there were bad Nobles too. I followed the tall man's eyeline. He watched the Duchess without blinking, which was a feat in and of itself.

She wore a dazzling white suit that almost seemed to sparkle in the underground light. It was snug, but covered in protective padding. Daphne's clothes hadn't changed from before. All black, no padding, and full range of motion intact. She was counting on her skill rather than her gear. Daphne stood in the center of the room, twirling her saber idly as she waited for her opponent to approach.

The Duchess came to a halt before her. They crossed blades as a mutual signal to begin the fight. Electric sparks jumped from blade to blade, and the scent of electricity and metal started to fill the air.

The Duchess struck first. A quick leap forward and a thrust.

Daphne parried the blow, knocking it to the side. She brought her left fist around, aiming at her opponent's head. The Duchess blocked with a free hand and leapt backward. The crowd cheered. It was immediately apparent that Daphne was the superior swordswoman. She moved comfortably across the floor, her movements fluid, practiced, and precise.

Any erroneous contact—punching, kicking, elbowing—none of it was allowed in the Flats. But we weren't in the Flats. I shouldn't have been surprised.

Daphne landed a punch that sent the Duchess stumbling sideways. I yelled along with the rest of the crowd and pumped my fist. I heard a soft hiss come from my glove and realized I had inadvertently released some of Zeno's spray. The person nearest me gave me a disgusted look and backed up a couple of steps.

The sound of metal on metal rang through the air. Daphne took a step forward. The Duchess took a step back. Daphne attacked. A quick thrust. Blocked. She jumped deftly to the side and parried a blow, but did so aggressively, throwing her opponent off balance. Taking advantage of the situation, Daphne caught the Duchess in the stomach with a kick that sent her flying into the crowd.

The crowd was going crazy, especially near where the Duchess had fallen. She still hadn't gotten up. I couldn't even see her from where I was. It was as if the rowdy spectators had swallowed her and were determined not to let her go.

Daphne yelled at them, and after a moment, the Duchess resurfaced as if she were being regurgitated by a giant beast. Several hands pushed her back onto the floor. The once-clean suit was now dirty and ripped, and she tested her shoulder rotation gingerly before proceeding. Apparently even the spectators could get in on some of the action.

Daphne attacked and stepped back, trying to draw the Duchess back to the center of the room, but she wasn't going for it. Even from where I stood, the Duchess looked beaten. Her chest rose and fell with each labored breath. Daphne, by comparison, looked like she hadn't even broken a sweat.

The Duchess stabilized herself with her saber. Daphne backed up a few steps and relaxed, giving her opponent time to regain some composure. The crowd booed. Daphne adopted a fighting stance and nodded at the Duchess, who ignored her and began searching the crowd.

Daphne straightened her back to more boos.

I looked back to the Duchess. She wasn't staring at Daphne, but somewhere past her. The Duchess shook her head and then nodded. I traced her line of sight as best I could.

It was the man I had seen earlier. Tall and composed, wearing a suit. He nodded and discreetly pointed in my direction. I lowered the brim of my hat. The moment I did so, the man next to me elbowed me in the ribs, trying to get a better position. I grunted against the pain, but managed to hold my ground.

Who had he been pointing to? I looked back to the man and watched him nod to the Duchess.

Immediately, she attacked. Displaying a blinding flash of speed, she jumped laterally to the right. Daphne took the bait and moved left. The Duchess didn't stop but rocketed straight toward Daphne, bringing down her saber in a double-handed swing toward Daphne's head. She blocked the blow but retreated a few steps, moving toward me. The Duchess didn't relent. Another hard over-head swing before Daphne could fully recover forced her to backpedal. The Duchess dashed forward and thrust again. Daphne set herself into a lower stance to absorb the blows without being driven further backwards. She didn't want to get any closer to the crowd than she had to.

The man next to me elbowed me again and tried to shove me out of the way. I grunted in pain and pushed my shoulder into him, but he was heavier than I was.

Hands reached out from the crowd, each one grasping for a piece of the action. But no one wanted it more than the man next to me. He threw one final elbow and dove out into the ring at Daphne. At the same moment, the Duchess pounced. The man grabbed hold of Daphne's free hand and tugged. She had just enough time to regain her footing and block the Duchess's downward swipe. The man wouldn't let go. Daphne struggled to stay on her feet. The crowd booed at the man, but he wouldn't relent.

I had to help. I kicked out and caught the man in the gut. With a yelp, he let go of Daphne's arm and covered his stomach. The crowd cheered and several spectators reached out and dragged the man back to the sidelines.

Daphne regained her footing and spun away from the pressure of the Duchess's sword. The man fought his way free and tried to jump out again, but this time, mine weren't the only hands that came to stop him. He was immediately restrained by everyone around him. I looked at his face. He was angry, crazed even. And his eyes were fixed on a point across the room.

I followed his gaze. He was looking directly at the tall man in the suit. His face was mostly impassive, but his brow furrowed slightly. He shook his head slowly, and the man next to me yelled in anger.

The guy next to me was a plant. The tall man had planned it.

Daphne twirled her saber around in her palm and turned to face the Duchess, a cold fury in her eyes. Then she advanced. Her blade was a blur of gray and crackling blue electricity.

The Duchess couldn't keep pace with Daphne's superior skill, and two hard strikes later, the Duchess's electrified blade flew out of her hand, clanging to the ground several feet away.

The crowd roared. I did too. Daphne held her opponent at saber point.

She had won, just like she knew she would.

A loud disturbance somewhere to my right caught everyone's attention, and the crowd started to part. A figure approached the floor, walking through a hallway of Sinisters, blue sparks dancing at her side. She wore a suit similar to Daphne's—it was all black, but so was her hair. However, a small streak of pink could be seen among the black.

I only knew one person with hair like that: Tyrann's gothic daughter, Printh. She entered at a right angle to Daphne and the Duchess.

"And it looks like we have a latecomer to the fight!" The announcer's voice reverberated off the tile-clad walls, and the crowd roared.

Two on one? They were going to allow this? In practice, I sometimes fought two on one, but I hardly ever won. All it took was for one opponent to engage you completely, and the match was over. Daphne didn't have many options.

She looked back and forth between her two opponents again. Printh stopped where she was, electrified saber in hand, poised to pounce. Daphne made a decision. She kicked the Duchess hard in the chest, sending her flying backwards. Daphne took another swing at her with her saber, but the Duchess was quick, expertly dodging the blow. Printh made her move, and the Duchess scrambled around Daphne to get her saber.

Daphne barely had time to turn as her blade clashed with Printh's saber. She spun out of it and feigned a swing. Printh jumped to the side and Daphne gained a little space.

Daphne sprinted toward the Duchess. Printh followed. Daphne jumped, bringing her saber down in a powerful arc. The Duchess rolled out of the way and sprung back up to her feet, saber in hand. Then Printh attacked.

Daphne engaged, then the Duchess joined the mix. There was nothing she could do.

Printh landed a kick that caught Daphne in the chest. She absorbed the blow by rolling through a backwards somersault. She came to her feet and blocked the Duchess's renewed attack, but it was clear her strength was failing. Printh saw an opening and swung her saber at her abdomen. Daphne braced for impact, but Printh stopped an inch short, hovering the electrified blade just before contact.

I could see Daphne's face contorted with exertion as she held off the Duchess's blade. Her eyes darted to Printh. She noticed the blade poised inches from her stomach. She was beaten.

27

Printh nodded to Daphne and raised her saber. The Duchess backed away too. The match was over. Daphne tossed her saber to the ground. The crowd yelled and screamed, some in protest, others in glee.

"What an ending!" came the disembodied voice over the speakers. "The perfect record is no more!" More boos and yells from the crowd. "Ladies and scoundrels, make way for the champion of tonight's fight so the Duchess can collect her prize!"

The crowd parted along the path that led to the stairs. The Duchess walked toward the stairs somewhat unenthusiastically as Printh melted into the crowd and disappeared. Turning off her saber, the Duchess reached up under her mask. A moment later, silver hair cascaded down past her shoulders, but the mask was left in place. A few whistles made their way above the tumult.

"Take off the mask!" someone shouted, but I didn't need the Duchess to do that to know who was behind it.

Pria. It made sense. Printh had come to her rescue, but I guessed that she wasn't happy about it. Pria might have officially won the fight, but we were all losers, me most of all. I had been so caught up in the fight that I had almost forgotten why Daphne was here in the first place—the password. She wasn't getting it. Zeno would be furious, and unless Gina pulled out a miracle, we wouldn't know which train car I was supposed to land on tomorrow.

Daphne stared at Pria, her face a mix of regret and anger, but Pria wouldn't meet her gaze, choosing instead to stare down at the ground as she made her way to the front.

"We have our winner!" the announcer's voice boomed amidst a renewal of cheers from the crowd. Most people followed Pria over to the stairway, but I turned my attention to Daphne. She had picked up her saber, and I could tell by the look on her face that the fight had carried far more baggage than I knew. She had known it was Pria all along. She had thought she was going to win and get the password. Now, the whole trip down here was for nothing.

The crowd started to thin as some of the Sinisters filtered out of the subway. It was time to go. I didn't think Daphne knew I was there, and I preferred to keep it that way. Clearly, she could take care of herself, but I got the feeling she would go crazy if she found out I had followed her. I kept my distance.

A group of people passed in front of me and momentarily blocked her from my view. By the time they passed me, Daphne was gone.

A few yells made their way to me over the buzz of the dispersing crowd. I turned to see Daphne sprinting across the floor, shoving people aside. Several steps ahead, someone else was running. It was the tall man in the suit I had seen earlier. Daphne was chasing him.

I broke into a run, weaving in and out of the throng, doing my best to keep up without my hat flying off.

The tall man headed for the exit, and Daphne wasn't gaining much ground. All the people milling about didn't make things easier for her. The tall man flung open the door and dashed up the staircase. Moments later, Daphne disappeared from view too. I fought my way to the stairs and raced up them two at a time.

I burst through the door into the alleyway. Daphne and the tall man were about fifty yards away. Daphne was gaining, but not enough. In addition to her sword, she now had a slim carrying case around her shoulder. Suddenly, she ducked down, scooped something off the ground, and threw it. The object connected with the back of the man's right leg, and he went down. Daphne jogged to a halt and pointed her saber at the man's head.

She turned to look when she heard my footsteps on the weed-covered ground. I lifted my bowler so she could see my face. Surprise was followed immediately by disapproval. I came to a stop at her side.

The tall man on the ground rolled over on his back to face us.

"You lost. No information, that was the deal," he said, his voice surprisingly even.

"Daphne, what's going on?" I whispered, trying to make sense of the situation.

"We had a deal," she said through gritted teeth.

"And clearly you forgot how this side of things works," the man said. "Or did you just want to spend more time with me?"

Two seconds with this guy and I already didn't like him.

"What kind of deal?" I asked. "And what is that smell?" I almost had to plug my nose it was so strong. The aroma reminded me of a hospital room.

"He placed a bet on me tonight," Daphne explained. "If I win, he wins a lot of money and I get information. If I lose, I get nothing. As for the smell"—she paused—"it's probably the only thing that covers up the stench of someone like him. How much of the fight did you see?"

"All of it," I said. "I couldn't believe they let Printh come in like that!"

"It's the Heights," Daphne said with a scowl.

"I saw *him* sending signals to Pria during the match," I said.

"Is that so?" she said dangerously, thrusting her saber forward until it was just under the man's chin.

"And to the guy in the crowd who tried to take you down," I said.

Daphne twisted the tip of her saber, moving it ever so closer to the man's Adam's apple. "I'm starting to get the feeling that you're a worthless, cheating dirtbag."

The man held up a hand. "Now, I don't know about worthless, bu—"

"I was favored to win that fight three to one. If you really wanted to make a lot of money, you'd have bet against me and fixed the fight."

The man on the ground remained silent.

It made sense. Calling him a dirtbag was being kind, in my opinion.

"You were never planning on giving me the information in the first place, were you?" Daphne said viciously. "Isn't that right, Chairman?"

"Chairman?" I asked.

"Self-appointed nickname," Daphne said. "They never work out well."

"Two things," the Chairman said from the ground. "I wouldn't call it a nickname, and as far as the match goes—"

Daphne cut him off.

"Before you finish that, I'll make you a deal," she said, her eyes rock hard in the moonlight. "For every lie you tell me, I'll paralyze one of your limbs. I'm sure you don't live near here, and I hear this isn't the safest part of town, especially for a Noble."

"It would be difficult to walk out of here a paraplegic." The Chairman motioned to Daphne. "Please, continue."

"Did you fix the match?" She enunciated each word, and at the end of her question, she pressed a button on the hilt of her saber. Electricity flowed up and down the width of the triangular blade.

"Yes," he said, staring down his nose at the blue sparks, "I did."

Daphne retracted her saber a few inches. "Good. Next question. What's your name?"

The man hesitated. The blade reappeared beneath his chin.

"I'm afraid 'the Chairman' will have to suffice." He sat up, supporting himself with both palms on the ground.

"Your choice," Daphne said.

"I'll save you the trouble." He reached out and grabbed Daphne's saber. With a grunt of pain, his arm immediately fell limp. "What other questions do you have for me? I have a few more things to take care of before the night is through."

Daphne's brow furrowed. "Last question. What is the password you promised me if I won?"

"If I tell you, can I ask you a question?"

"What do you mean, *if*?" Daphne countered.

"What's the deal with your friend here?" he continued, motioning to me. "Are you two a thing? And why is he wearing that ridiculous hat? Are you into that sort of thing?"

Daphne shook her head and maneuvered her saber dangerously close to the Chairman's throat. "The password. What is it?"

"Yes, of course." He looked slightly crestfallen at the reply. "I've got it somewhere in here." He used his good hand to tap his right temple.

"I'd be happy to beat it out of you." Daphne smiled.

"I don't think there will be a need for that. The password is very sensitive information. It grants you access to the train system's mainframe and cameras, among other things."

"Great, now what is it?" Daphne said. "Keep in mind that if it doesn't work, I will hunt you down, and we can repeat this little scenario."

"I believe you. You seem a very determined woman," he said. "And I like that."

I was starting to hope Daphne would hit him just to make him shut up.

"Strike two," Daphne said, cocking her saber arm back.

The Chairman held up his hand. "Hold on a moment. The password is *truenoble*. All one word, lowercase."

"T-R-U-E-N-O-B-L-E?" Daphne said, spelling it out.

"Yes, now am I free to leave, or would you like me to escort you home? It's been such a lovely evening and all."

"You're free to leave, but Mr. Chairman..." she said as he pushed himself sloppily to his feet.

"Yes, my dear?" He put on his best seductive smile.

"Don't lie to me again."

Her saber flashed in the moonlight and caught him across the thigh. He groaned and collapsed again.

"Pitiful," she said as she turned to me. "Let's go."

We began walking away from the Chairman, when an abrupt scream rent the night air. And then another. And then another. A couple hundred yards away from us, a man yelled in abject terror and nearly tripped over himself as he tried to flee down the street.

"Run!" he shouted at us as he flew by.

I looked to the end of the alleyway. At least ten people sprinted past, pushing and shoving each other in a bid to reach the front of the group. One of them tripped and fell. No one stopped. No one reached down to help. They just kept running.

A metal pincer suddenly shot into view and grabbed the fallen man by the ankle, jerking him out of sight. He screamed at the top of his lungs—until the sound was cut short.

My insides turned to ice. There was only one explanation.

"Sweeper," Daphne said. She grabbed my arm, pulling me away. "Come on! There!" She dragged me after her, leaving the Chairman on the ground, helpless.

"What about him?" I said.

"Leave him!"

"What?"

"He deserves it. Come on!"

Daphne dashed up the alleyway. I looked back. The Chairman's face was expressionless. He glanced over his shoulder and then looked back to me. He knew what was coming, and we didn't stand a chance if he was with us.

I ran after Daphne. An old metal fire escape hung off the side of a dilapidated building. We leapt up onto it and climbed desperately for the top.

"Come on, Victor!"

I looked down the alleyway just as the metal monstrosity came into view. It looked like an urbanized sea monster. Its rubber tracks spanned nearly the entire width of the street. Its multiple metal pincers shot out from its body with precision, picking off stragglers and picking up trash in equal measure.

Daphne shot up the fire escape ladders almost as fast as Zeno's ladder-scaling contraption. I did my best to keep up, but the sweeper was gaining on us. Only a few people in the alleyway remained, including the Chairman. There was no way we'd make it to the top of the building.

Glass shattered above me. Tiny shards rained down on my head.

"Victor. In here!"

Daphne jumped through the broken window. We were only five stories up, but sweepers stuck to the streets, right?

"Come on!" Daphne yelled. I forced myself to climb faster. The sweeper continued to gain. Now, the Chairman was the only person left in the alleyway. A single metallic arm reached out and snatched him up, retracting swiftly into the body of the machine. Just like that, the alleyway was empty, but it didn't stop there. It headed straight toward us.

I jumped the last two rungs and threw myself through the window.

"Victor!"

Daphne stood at the opposite side of the room in the doorway, motioning frantically to me. I raced toward her. We barreled into the hallway, and Daphne slammed the door behind us. I was breathing hard, adrenaline coursing through my veins. I looked at her.

"Are we safe he—"

The door splintered as a metal pincer tore through it.

"Run!"

We tore down the hallway. Daphne led the way.

"We need to get higher," she said, her breath coming in gasps. "We'll be safe on the roof."

Daphne reached the end of the hallway and threw open the door to the stairs. We bounded up them and didn't stop until we reached the top.

The night air felt cool on my sweat-drenched face.

Daphne stood with her hands on her knees, catching her breath, the threat of the sweeper finally gone.

"We'll be safe up here," she said between breaths.

We had almost been taken. It had almost been the end for us. It *had* been the end for everyone else.

"All those people," I said, my breaths shallow. "And the Chairman."

We had left him behind. He wasn't a good person, clearly, but it didn't sit right with me.

"Some say you don't survive getting taken by a sweeper, but rumor has it they go to the war front," Daphne said, straightening up. "Either way, we got what we needed." She walked toward the edge of the roof, surveying the streets below.

My mind was reeling. Just like that, a dozen people were gone. Even if they *were* sent to the war front, they'd still die.

"Don't feel too bad." Daphne continued to watch the streets below. "They knew the risks of being out, same as we did." Her gaze hardened as she turned to me. "Speaking of, what are you doing here?"

"I should say the same thing to you," I said.

"I was trying to get information to save your life," she said. "What's your excuse?"

"I was learning how to use these"—I held my gloved hands up —"and I saw you. I didn't know where you were heading, so I followed you."

"You're lucky no one recognized you." She crossed her arms.

"That's why I put on a disguise." I pointed at my head. "Did you not see my cool hat?"

"You look ridiculous."

"Well, regardless, I owe you."

For a moment, her features softened. "Yeah, you do. But don't breathe a word of this to anyone, especially Zeno."

"I can't even tell them how great you fought?" I asked.

Daphne smiled bitterly. "I lost."

"Because they cheated," I said. "And for a moment there, I still thought you were going to win."

"Only a moment?"

I smiled. "Has Printh ever swooped in to save the day before?"

"No," Daphne said, "that was a first. I feel terrible for Pria. Tyrann already thinks she's worthless compared to Printh. He probably won't talk to her for a week, and she'll probably never talk to me again."

"And that's a problem?" I said, remember their last exchange. "You two didn't strike me as being the best of friends."

"We used to be," she said softly.

"And after a stunt like that?" I said. "Working with that Chairman guy to fix the fight against you? You still want to be her friend?"

She turned to me. "She's not a bad person."

"She's a Sin—" I started, but then stopped. I couldn't keep thinking like that. Daphne, Zeno, Augustine, even my grandfather and Alex had shown me that labels didn't matter.

"If you actually got to know Pria, you'd be impressed," Daphne said. "Did you know that when we first met, she wanted to be a doctor? She wanted to spend her life helping people... Unfortunately, she was raised by Tyrann Kane."

The weight of her words almost crushed me. I used to envy some of my friends because they were being raised by their parents, not their grandfather. But to have a parent like Tyrann Kane, I couldn't even imagine.

"We need to get back." Daphne turned away and looked to the streets below. "The coast should be clear. You ready?"

I paused, still thinking about Pria. She wasn't Sinister, she was just a teenager, like me.

"Um, yeah," I said, "but what about the sweepers? I mean, they don't just disappear after ravaging one street, do they?"

"This is not my first time," she said. "Stay close and you'll be fine."

28

The return trip was uneventful. It passed quickly and mostly in silence, but I couldn't get the look on the Chairman's face out of my head, or the screams of the people as we left them for the sweeper.

I shook my head. Daphne had saved my life. And because we had the password, she might have saved it again.

We arrived back at the events center. Trash and an assortment of new rotten food and refuse greeted us, as well as some new graffiti. More of the same "turn him in" threats. Regardless of what Zeno said, the locals worried me.

We walked through the doors, and I followed Daphne as we made our way into the big room behind the stage.

"Zeno," she said. "Zeno!"

He walked out from behind an opaque glass panel he had been writing on. "Daphne, where have you been?" He spotted me. "And bro! What part of *before* dark did you not get?"

"He followed me," Daphne said.

"Is that so?" Zeno said through squinted eyes.

I nodded.

"And she didn't beat you up for it, huh? Man, lucky you."

"Zeno," Daphne said. "I've got it."

"It?"

"The password to the Innerbelt! It's 'truenoble.' Lowercase, all one word."

"Seriously? I'll set the search. We should be able to find the car in the next couple of minutes." Zeno dashed off through the door.

It was happening. We were that much closer to finding the senator's car, that much closer to potentially saving my life.

Thirty seconds later, Zeno was back. "It's going. Let me call Augustine." He looked over at the huge projection screen and spoke to it. "Gina! Call Augustine and tell him to come here. It's urgent."

Text appeared on the screen.

As you wish.

"I don't tell her this enough, but Gina's a pretty cool system, right?" Zeno said, looking at me and smiling.

"Yeah," I said, "but I was going to ask you, why just text and no voice?" Zeno had created the Bounty Hunter's gloves, the spray, and who knew what else, but he couldn't build a personal assistant that talked? Even I had something better than that back home.

"Well, it used to have a voice, but it got out of hand..."

"Out of hand?"

"Let's just say I wrote a program so it could learn how to talk, and it chose the wrong people to learn from. It spoke mostly in expletives."

"Seriously?"

"Seriously." Zeno nodded gravely. "Augustine had a fit. I don't think I've ever see him get so mad at technology before." A small grin crossed his face, and his eyes became unfocused as he recalled the memory. He shook his head, and his eyes refocused. "Speaking of, Gina, where is Augustine at, girl? You *did* tell him, didn't you?"

Of course I did. Are you questioning my loyalty?

Zeno sighed.

"Where's Alex?" I asked.

"Oh, right." He turned back to the screen. "Hey, Gina, get Alex here too."

Augustine came through the doors at a brisk walk. "Zeno, what's going on?"

A soft tone sounded and the giant projector screen turned on. Text rolled across it.

Train car located.

"That's what's going on."

"Where?" Augustine practically yelled at the screen.

"Come on, Gina," Zeno said impatiently. "Show us where it's at."

A video feed appeared. Gina manipulated the picture so that the senator's train car was highlighted on the image.

"It's parked at the photography station," Augustine said. "Second car from the back."

Alex stumbled into the room, rubbing his eyes against all the light. "Hi, everyone," he mumbled.

"We found the train car, bro!" Zeno said, thumping him on the back.

"Ow!" Alex flinched and rubbed the spot where Zeno hit him.

"Okay, this is exactly what we wanted," Augustine said, his eyes alight. "Everything else is in place for tomorrow. This was the last piece."

Alex, still squinting against the light, let out a huge sigh. "I got out of bed for this? Why couldn't someone just tell me in the morning?"

"I think it's time for all of us to get back to bed," Augustine said. "Or at least *get* to bed." He nodded at Daphne and me. Alex trudged back out of the room, holding one hand over his eyes. He bumped into the doorframe twice before making his way through it.

"Night, Alex," I said.

"Night," he slurred. "And don't let me forget my snacks tomorrow. Watching you do hard stuff makes me hungry."

"We won't forget, Alex," Augustine said. "Now get some sleep." He turned to me. "Are you okay? You look like you've had quite an evening."

I looked over at Daphne. She stared at the floor.

"Yeah, I'm good," I said. "It's just been a long night."

Getting pushed off a building and almost taken by a sweeper in the same night was enough to make anyone look haggard.

"Good. Are you ready for tomorrow?"

"I think so." I held up my hands and looked at Zeno's gloves. I had almost forgotten I had them on. I felt confident using them, but tomorrow would be a whole different story. I'd have to land on a moving train. "I feel pretty good about using them," I said. "I mean, I haven't died yet."

"Yes, well, you'll do great," Augustine said. "But I do think we should get some rest."

"Yeah," I agreed, stifling a yawn.

"You remember how to get to your room?" Augustine asked. I nodded. "Good, then get some sleep. We'll leave early in the morning."

I nodded goodnight to Augustine and Zeno and headed over to the door, where Daphne stood. She pushed the door open and we headed down the hall together, our footsteps echoing in the silence.

"So the Chairman came through for us with that password," I said.

"Yeah, he did."

"Do you feel bad that we left him for the sweeper?" I asked.

Daphne hesitated before answering.

"Honestly, no. He was a creep and a liar. I don't think we need any more of those in the world," she said.

She was right, but it still didn't sit right with me, leaving him there to be taken by the sweeper without doing anything.

We continued our walk in silence until we arrived at my door.

"I guess this is goodnight then," I said.

"Yep."

Daphne reached over and gave me a quick hug. It was over far too soon.

"What was that for?" I asked.

"I saw how jealous you were when I hugged Alex earlier."

"So that was a pity hug?"

"No, that'll come after we see who's better with a saber between the two of us, and I win."

"I think you've got that backwards."

"We'll see." She turned to leave, but stopped. "Hey, Vic?"

"Yeah?"

"I'm glad you're here." She gave me a half smile and disappeared through the door opposite mine before I could respond.

I was left standing in the doorway, replaying that smile over in my mind. After a few seconds, I went into my room and closed the door behind me. I felt like a weight had lifted, like the rift I had made between Daphne and me was finally closed. It felt good.

I took a deep breath as I sat down on the bed. I knew sleep wouldn't come easy, not after everything that had happened tonight. But I had to focus on what tomorrow would bring. I forced Daphne's hug and her final smile out of my mind and went over the plan again and again in my head as I stared into the darkness, the details becoming fuzzier the more tired I became. Finally, my eyes closed, and the last thing I remembered before falling asleep was Daphne's smile.

29

"Mic check, Victor. This is Augustine. Can you hear me?"

"It's like you're right here with me," I said. The earpieces Zeno had cooked up worked great. I looked upward and grasped the next rung. Twenty more feet. If only Zeno would have let me bring his ladder-climbing contraption.

"Daphne? Alex?" Augustine said.

"Yes, Dad."

"Alex?"

No answer.

"Alex!"

"Present," Alex said, a loud crunch accompanying his voice. Apparently the snacking had already started.

"Zeno?"

"Loud and clear, boss."

"Everyone should be in position," Augustine said. "And like we talked about, a few of Tyrann's crew are helping to cover the area too. The train is set to leave the station in four minutes."

"Almost there." I grasped the last rung on the ladder and hoisted myself onto the rooftop. I wasn't excited about a couple of Tyrann's men helping us out, but Tyrann was. Augustine insisted that we needed extra help covering the area between the photography station and the crime lab. All he had to tell Tyrann was "we're sabotaging something Noble" and he was on board. Supposedly, he had sent two of his best men, Brick and Jonny. I'd worry about that later.

I walked in a crouch as I surveyed the surrounding buildings. Most in the area, like the one I had climbed, were relatively new— mostly made of glass and metal—but everything on this side of the tracks was vacant. I suspected it had something to do with the Sinisters not wanting to be too close to the Nobles, or vice versa. Consequently, the buildings right next to the Innerbelt acted like a kind of buffer zone.

I stayed low on the rooftop as I jogged to the other side. I checked out the other rooftops to my right and left. At first glance, both were empty, but I checked again to be sure; Augustine doubted they would appear, but the Sinistrali could be anywhere. Satisfied that both rooftops were clear, I peered over the ledge toward the Flats.

The sky was blue and uninterrupted by towering brick skyscrapers. I could see for miles, and I drank it in: Colorful homes connected by vibrant green grass dotted the horizon. Golden light reflected off the ubiquitous glass paneling. I couldn't believe how close we were to the Noble part of the city. I had almost forgotten how pristine everything looked.

"Three minutes," Augustine said.

The train station sprawled a few hundred feet below me, gleaming white in the morning sun. It was early, and there were virtually no people present. Most of the train station was automated, so there wouldn't be a need to camouflage my fall.

I shifted my gaze to the cars. Almost every car at the station had the same opaque gray walls. The transparent people carriers were much further up the line, closer to the terminal.

"You said it was the second from the back, right, Zeno?" I asked, surveying the cars that were set for departure. I had dressed mostly in black at Zeno's urging, and I had a small camera that relayed what I was seeing to Zeno's computer. It was almost invisible, but I could feel the spot where he had stuck it to my forehead. It itched terribly.

"Yeah, bro, but look a little to the left. More, more, a little more—there it is. I'm calling it 'the train of secrets,'" Zeno said. "TOS for short.'"

"Got it." I drew a mental X on the car in my mind. Second from the end.

"Two minutes," Augustine said. "And remember, you can also land on the cars in front or behind the senator's car. Both of them are empty."

"Right," I said. We had gone over the plan at least fifty times this morning. Or maybe it was only five, but it definitely *felt* like fifty.

"And when you land, make sure to get to the senator's train car quickly." I mouthed the words as he said them.

"Got it," I said.

I scratched at my arm through the gloves. The biokey seemed a little more agitated this morning. Maybe it mimicked how you felt.

"Thirty seconds," Augustine said, his voice tense.

I looked over the ledge again. I'd need to jump outward about twenty feet. If I overshot, I could spray a wall of Zeno's stuff out in front of me to keep me on course, but if I undershot, I'd be out of luck.

My heart started to race. This was it.

"Ten seconds until the train departs."

"Good luck," Daphne said softly.

I smiled to myself. Butterflies that had nothing to do with my impending swan dive appeared in my stomach.

"Thanks," I said, retreating from the ledge. I needed to time my jump just right.

"There it goes," Augustine said. "Victor, wait for Zeno's mark."

I watched in anticipation as the front part of the train started to move.

"All right, Captain V," Zeno said. "In three, two, one... Go for it!"

I bolted into action. Each powerful footfall propelled me forward. I leapt off the ledge with all the force and speed I could muster. My body careened forward into what I could only describe as perfect belly-flop position. I could see the train below me, inching its way down the line. Time seemed to slow as I soared through the air, my momentum fighting the earth's pull.

I reached the apex of my jump, and time sped back up. Gravity's firm fingers grasped my body and pulled me facedown through the air. However, my forward momentum had carried me further than I'd expected. I could hear words in my earpiece, probably Zeno, but the wind was so fierce that I couldn't make anything out. Not that it mattered. I knew what to do.

I kept my head down and watched the ground. The edge of the moving train came into view. I reoriented my wrists and closed my hands into fists. The now familiar sensation of being hit by an invisible cushion washed over me, gray beads materializing around me, and my forward momentum slowed considerably.

I kept my eyes fixed on the train below me as I descended through the sky. Perfect. Right on target. Except for one thing.

I was running out of train.

It was picking up speed, and I still needed to slow down and land without breaking every bone in my body.

One hundred feet left.

It would be close.

The train grew larger and larger as I sped toward it. I couldn't slow myself down yet. I could hear yelling in my ear, all of it unintelligible.

Avardi's car was directly under me.

Twenty-five feet.

I let out a long spray that my body obliterated, but I kept spraying. The senator's car passed below me, and I collided hard against the roof of the last car in a shower of gray beads.

I coughed and gasped for breath. I rolled over onto my back, still not breathing. A chorus of voices sounded in my ear.

"Victor!"

I moaned in response as I scattered some of the gray beads that surrounded me like a chalk outline.

"Victor!" It was Daphne's voice.

"Wooo! That's what I'm talking about!" Zeno shouted.

"Are you hurt?" Augustine asked.

Gingerly, I pushed myself up to a crouch and turned toward the front of the train.

I mentally checked my arms and legs. Nothing was broken, but I felt certain the whole front of my body would be bruised tomorrow.

"Victor, are you hurt?" Augustine's voice was sharp.

"I'm good," I said. "I'm good."

I had barely finished speaking when movement several cars up distracted me. A contingent of five police officers had appeared on the roof of the car.

"Guys, are you seeing this?" I said.

One of the policemen pulled a stunner from his hip and fired. The pulse of energy shot through the air. I barely had time to react.

I threw myself to the ground, but more stunner blasts were coming. I rolled to the side and threw up a wall of spray to shield myself, but I wasn't sure how long it would hold.

"Victor, get out of there!" Augustine yelled.

I grunted in anger. All the planning, all the practice, wasted. I searched for a way to make this work. Another wave of stunner fire lit up the air in front of me, and the outer layer of gray beads disappeared into the wind behind me. There was nothing left to do, but run.

"Zeno, tell me when and I'll jump for it."

The policemen barreled toward me, stunners still drawn.

"Four seconds and then go," he said. "I'll count you out."

"I don't know if I have four seconds," I said. The stunner fire was becoming more and more accurate by the second. My wall of spray was almost completely obliterated.

"Then go now, bro! Now!"

I sprung toward the train car's edge. The policemen were close. Streaks of lightning zipped past me, some in front and some behind, but I couldn't dodge. I couldn't change course. The edge was still fifteen feet away. I put all the strength I possessed into my legs, urging them to propel me faster. I looked over to see four stunner barrels far too close. And then everything went dark.

It was windy, very windy. Was I still on top of the train? My palms burned. I could hear voices. Daphne? Zeno?

"... waking up?"

"I don't know, the jolters should have kicked in by now." The voice was faint, but it sounded a bit like Zeno.

My hands convulsed with an electric charge, jarring me.

"What should we do with him, boss?" The unfamiliar voice caught me off guard.

I opened my eyes and stared up into five masculine faces, each one dressed in the customary white and blue of the police force, the wind whipping around their uniforms.

"Well, look who's awake. Nice to see you again, Mr. Wells."

I recognized *that* voice. I'd last heard it three days ago at the other end of a gun barrel.

This wasn't the police. This was the Left Hand. This was Harvesty.

I struggled to move, but the effects of the stunner hadn't worn off completely. I must have only been out for a few seconds. The wind whipped around me, and the steel roof of the train was cool against the side of my face. My right wrist dangled just over the edge of the train. I had been so close!

"Victor! Can you hear us?" Daphne's voice flooded my ear. I tried to answer, but the best I could do was grunt.

"Please, don't strain yourself, Victor," Harvesty said. "That's my job." He delivered a swift kick to my ribcage and smiled as I groaned in pain. With his foot, he rolled me onto my back. But the Harvesty I saw wasn't the one I remembered. Today he had decided to keep his mask on.

"That's better," Harvesty said, staring down at me. "I want you to see what's coming."

"Victor! Victor!" My earpiece emitted a scattered chorus of my name, and while I could feel pain, I still couldn't really move.

"I can hear you," I mumbled.

"What was that, Mr. Wells?" Harvesty glared down at me.

"I'm turning up the voltage in the gloves," Zeno said.

"What was that, Mr. Wells?" Harvesty repeated, his voice threatening. I didn't answer. "You were raised Noble. Didn't your mother teach you that it's impolite to ignore people?"

Harvesty grabbed my face and lifted my head so our faces were inches apart. "Didn't she?" I could smell the stench of his heavy breathing as he looked at me through manic eyes. "Oh, that's right, your mother's dead."

He slammed my head into the roof of the train. Stars exploded across my vision. My earpiece tumbled out, and I fought against unconsciousness.

"Looks like our friend here has some help," Harvesty said gleefully. "Too bad you won't be needing this anymore." With a large black boot, he kicked the earpiece over the edge of the train, the wind sweeping it far away as we hurtled in the opposite direction.

Suddenly, I felt another jolt of electricity in my palms, and then another. Feeling spread back into my extremities. I wiggled my fingers to be sure.

"You made a mess of things for me earlier this week," Harvesty said. "I'm going to give you one chance to tell me what I want to know." He reached to his hip and pulled out his gun, pointing it directly at my chest.

In the corner of my vision, something black descended from the sky and landed hard, sending a ripple through the metal roof of the car. Harvesty's eyes grew wide in rage as a new voice spoke.

"I can take it from here, Officers."

Kratos the Bounty Hunter stood behind Harvesty and his group of men, each of whom had drawn their stunners and looked to Harvesty for orders. Harvesty kept an eye on me.

"Mr. Bounty Hunter. So glad you've joined us." He nodded to his men and immediately, four stunners fired, each one connecting with the Bounty Hunter's torso. Kratos didn't move. I expected him to fall, but it was as if the stunner blasts had no effect on him.

"The Left Hand," he said, apparently unfazed. "And Victor Wells. Interesting." His cold eyes flitted to mine and then back to Harvesty.

I stared in awe. He was here again, just in time.

"Let's see if you can absorb this." Harvesty swung his gun around, and all thought of escape left my mind. I pushed myself forward and kicked out at Harvesty's legs. He stumbled, and the loud crack of his gun broke through the wind as Kratos dove sideways, rolled to his feet, and propelled himself into Harvesty's men.

I'd seen him fight before. The brief glimpse had been incredible. This wasn't any different. He pushed his first assailant into two of the others and came toward Harvesty with ferocity.

"Victor, get out of here!" Kratos yelled in between blows. Gray beads materialized all around him, showering me as the rush of wind took them away. One of Harvesty's men received an elbow to the head and fell unmoving to the ground. Now it was four on one.

"Don't let him get away!" Harvesty yelled.

One of the Sinistrali broke away from the melee and rushed toward me. Three on one. I pushed myself to my feet and ran the other way. A quick glance over my shoulder told me the man following me was close to my size. He had a long, thin saber strapped across his back, but he was reaching for his stunner.

I was tired of feeling helpless.

I changed tactics, planting both feet hard on the roof and launching myself toward the Sinistrali. With both fists closed, I kept a continuous spray going in front of my body as I rushed him. Lightning streaked in my direction but dissipated before it reached my torso. The man's eyes grew wide in surprise. I shouldered into him hard, batting away his stunner in the process. It clattered to the ground and was swept away by the air currents as another train whooshed past us.

He swung out with his left fist, catching me hard in my right shoulder. I stomached the pain and went low, diving for his feet. We crashed onto the steel roof of the train. I covered my head as he lashed out, my heavy gloves absorbing the bulk of the blows. I forced my knee hard into his gut. He doubled over, and a sharp blow from my elbow sent blood streaming down his face.

He moaned in pain, covering his broken nose with both hands. I ripped the saber from his back and sprung to my feet. Up ahead, Kratos was a whirlwind of limbs and gray beads as he fought three men at once. Now would be the perfect time to make my getaway, but this was twice now that Kratos had saved my life.

A nicely placed kick by Kratos sent Harvesty stumbling backwards, but he recovered and pulled out his gun.

"Watch out!" I yelled.

Another shot rang out, followed by a yell, but it wasn't from Kratos. It was Harvesty. A glint of metal flew through the air. The gun landed on the roof and slid toward me.

A yell of frustration sounded behind me, and the man with the broken nose came barreling toward me. Catching sight of the gun, he dove, but I was faster. My foot connected with the grip and it flew off the roof. The Sinistrali landed on my legs, his bloody hands leaving deep red marks on my pants. Anger blazed in his eyes as he swung out.

A quick bump on the butt of my saber, and the blade sparked to life. I blocked the oncoming punch, and the man's arm fell limp, only to be replaced with his other hand. Another quick thrust and I was free. I jumped to my feet and brought the triangular blade down hard. Without his arms to defend himself, his head was completely exposed. A crack sounded as metal hit bone, and he slumped to the ground.

I turned just in time to watch Kratos render Harvesty unconscious.

Now, only two Sinistrali remained, and neither of them had real guns.

I stumbled to the side as the train raced around a corner. Suddenly, we were bathed in shadows. A short stretch of the tracks ran through the Heights. Buildings surrounded me on both sides. My insides coiled up in fear as I searched the tracks. The buildings continued onward, like a long open-roofed tunnel. Until we were past them, I had no escape route. I had to get back to the ground, back to the Heights, and somehow figure out how to meet up with Augustine and the rest. And I had to do it before Kratos finished with the last two Sinistrali.

I turned just as another of Harvesty's men fell unconscious. I headed for the back of the train, trying to put as much space as possible between Kratos and myself. If only I had my earpiece, Zeno could tell me when the coast was clear.

Kratos's final assailant fell motionless to the ground.

I started to run.

"Stop!" Kratos yelled, already sprinting after me, but I couldn't. I couldn't let him take me in. I searched up and down the tracks, waiting for a break in the buildings. I leapt the crevice onto the final car. Kratos wasn't far behind, and I was out of room.

I kept my saber out and electrified as I turned to face him. Kratos slowed his approach to a jog, his masked face cold and expressionless.

"Victor Wells, I need you to come with me."

"I can't," I said. I thought back to our last conversation. Maybe I could reason with him. Maybe I could explain. Maybe he would let me go?

"I'm not going to turn you in," he said.

His words caught me off guard.

I looked into Kratos's harsh, unyielding eyes.

"And how am I supposed to believe that?" I asked. This could be a trap, a lie.

"We don't have time for this."

"I agree," I said. A change in the train's momentum almost made me stumble forward.

At the front of the train, sunlight broke through the buildings. I just needed to hold him off for ten more seconds.

With as much speed and force as I could muster, I brought my saber across my body in a sweeping motion. Instead of jumping back or dodging the strike, Kratos reached out and grabbed my blade out of the air. Electricity surged up and down the length of the blade but didn't seem to pass through his gloves.

"Don't make me use force," he said, his eyes taking on a steely glint. He ripped the saber from my grip and threw it into the wind. He took a step forward. "Come with me, I can help."

Five more seconds.

To my right, another contingent of police officers had climbed onto the roof and were running toward us. More Sinistrali or actual police? It didn't matter.

"Are they with you?" I said, nodding toward the oncoming officers. Kratos looked, and I acted. In one quick motion, I rammed into him and pushed off, using the momentum to propel me forward. Kratos stumbled and reached out, but wasn't quick enough to grab hold of me.

Sunlight flooded the rooftop as the train car cleared the buildings of the Heights. Freedom.

I sprinted as hard as I could toward the edge of the roof and jumped, my body flattening out as I sailed over the tracks below.

The ground was coming fast, but at a strange angle. Thanks to the momentum of the train, I was flying faster sideways than I was forward.

I threw a wall of spray to my left and plunged into it, the invisible particles turning into a shower of gray beads around me. With my momentum corrected, I fell almost straight down. A small puff of spray righted me, and another dose dampened my landing.

When I came to a stumbling stop, I turned to look back up at the train.

A black shadow was descending through the sky.

30

I started running. I had no idea where I was, and my earpiece was gone, so I couldn't ask for directions. Nothing was remotely familiar except for the tracks behind me, and I needed to get away from those, away from the Bounty Hunter, and into the Heights.

My feet pounded on the pavement as I dashed down a vacant street. Augustine, Daphne, and Alex were stationed periodically along the train's route, along with a couple of Tyrann's men. Hopefully, someone was close.

My breathing came in huffs. I didn't know my way through these empty streets, and I hoped that Kratos didn't either. It would have been easy to hide in one of the vacant buildings, but this close to the tracks, they would all have scanners, so I kept running.

My mind burned with questions. How had Kratos *and* the Left Hand known I would be on the train? I knew Kratos had ways of finding people, and the Left Hand had never failed to track someone down, but still. I was off the grid. How had they found me?

It was just like the fight at my house, except Kratos had been on my side that time. This time, I wasn't so sure.

He'd said that he'd help me survive the Left Hand's threats. Was that why he'd shown up on the train? Or was it like Alex had said—

he was after me and he was here to bring me in? Would he lie to me? Would he betray his government? I had seen his DNA readout—100 percent Noble—but I couldn't trust that anymore.

I kept running.

I took an arbitrary right turn. The tracks paralleled the road I was on, but there was no sign of anyone. No Alex. No Daphne. Where were they? I glanced behind me again just in time to see Kratos round a corner a few blocks behind me.

The cold feeling of dread threatened to steal my breath. I cut a hard left down the next street. Blood pounded in my ears. My lungs burned. My mind worked furiously, searching for a way out, an escape. It was clear that Kratos wasn't going to give up, and I wasn't going to get away.

I had two options. Prolong the inevitable, or stop and plead my case.

I made a decision.

I bought myself to a standstill in the middle of an abandoned street. Adrenaline pumped through my veins as my mind spun furiously. Could I reason with him, or would he be under the influence of the system that had branded me as something I wasn't?

I stood and waited. Seconds later, a billowing black figure came into view at an all-out sprint. He slowed his pace as he approached, walking the last few steps before stopping in front of me. He didn't slouch to catch his breath. Instead, he stood tall and pierced me with a stare. His hands were empty, and there was a comfortable amount of space between us. We locked eyes.

"What were you doing on the train?" he said.

What could I say? "Trying to break into a deceased man's car" wasn't a good answer.

"Trying to clear my name," I said.

Kratos continued to stare. "And what makes you so sure you're not guilty?"

"Because I'm not in league with the Left Hand," I said. "You saw them up there. They were trying to kill me."

Kratos didn't move. I took that as a good sign.

"My readout has been changed," I continued. "I checked my DNA using a scanner from a few years ago and compared it to a current readout. The DNA is the same, but the readout is different." I paused, but Kratos said nothing. "Look," I continued, "you were at my house when the Left Hand attacked. Something is going on, and I'm trying to figure out what it is."

H stood before me, immobile.

After a moment, he spoke again. "You need to come with me."

"No," I said. "I'm not letting you take me in." I couldn't go with him, to the government that had changed my DNA readout, not when we had come so far.

"Then you leave me no choice."

Kratos leapt forward. He swung for my head. I ducked his hook, but missed his knee. The wind left my lungs, and I doubled over. Kratos shoved me to the ground and took a step back.

"This ends the moment you stop resisting," he said as I scrambled to my feet. I couldn't win, but if I lasted long enough for someone else to show up, maybe I stood a chance.

Kratos advanced.

I jumped back and sprayed, gray beads materializing as he bounded after me. I landed in a crouch, my hands up and ready, but Kratos stayed where he was.

"Where did you get those?" He motioned to my gloves with his identical pair.

"From a friend."

"Give me a name," he commanded.

"The same guy who made your gloves," I said. "Zeno."

Kratos was impossible to read. He didn't respond for several seconds and instead stared at me with those piercing steely eyes. "He's working with you then?" he finally said.

"Yes," I said. "I used his scanners to check my DNA."

Kratos's stiff posture relaxed somewhat.

"I'm not a Sinister," I said. "Do you believe me?"

There was a long pause before he spoke.

"Unfortunately, I do," he said quietly.

I hadn't been expecting that.

"Wait, seriously?"

Kratos gave me a short nod.

Relief flowed through me. The government's own Bounty Hunter believed me.

Footsteps sounded nearby, and two men wearing sunglasses appeared on the street behind Kratos. He turned to look. They had to be Tyrann's men, Brick and Jonny.

"Who are they?" Kratos asked.

"Tyrann Kane's goons," I said. "Supposedly here to help."

Kratos didn't respond, but his posture shifted. He was ready to fight if need be.

"Well, what have we here, Jonny?"

The two men slowed to a walk. The one who talked, Brick, pocketed his sunglasses and flashed a set of ragged teeth the color of apple cider. "If it ain't our newest friend from the Flats, old Victor Wells. And would you look at that? The Bounty Hunter!" He reached inside his jacket and pulled out a gun, a real one. "Pleased to meet you."

"Those are outlawed," Kratos said.

"Just because the government outlaws something don't mean everyone listens," Brick said. As if to enforce his words, Jonny pulled out a stunner and trained it on Kratos.

"Where's everyone else?" I asked, keeping my eye on Brick's gun. "I thought Daphne and Augustine were closer."

"Turns out you're a little further up than they was expecting, so we're here to collect you. Mr. Kane told us to bring you to him if at all possible." He raised his gun and aimed it a few feet to my left. "And right now, it's lookin' like it's possible, so, Mr. Bounty Hunter, do you mind? We've got business to take care of."

Jonny kept his stunner aimed at Kratos as Brick made his way over.

I was surprised by Brick's brazen words. I was even more surprised that Kratos stood motionless at my side. But I *wasn't* surprised by Tyrann's betrayal.

"I'm not going with you," I said.

"The Heights belong to Mr. Kane. You're coming with us."

I caught Kratos shifting his weight.

"Tell Mr. Kane he can come get me himself if he's so interested."

Brick chuckled. "We got a talker! Been a while since we had to collect one of them." He smirked as he reached for my arm. Instinctively, I took a step backwards.

"Come on, boy, I don't bite," Brick said. He grabbed my arm. I pulled back, bringing him just within Kratos's reach.

Faster than I could blink, Kratos grabbed Brick's free arm and pulled hard. The gun clattered to the ground. Jonny fired, but Brick absorbed the blast, immediately slumping to the ground. There was a billowing of a black trench coat, two quick flashes of light, a grunt of pain, and Jonny joined Brick on the ground.

Kratos knelt next to Brick and picked up his gun. After examining it, he pulled out the clip and ejected all but one bullet. He shoved the clip back in place and cocked it.

"What are you..."

Kratos reached inside his coat and pulled out a small metal canister. A soft hiss sounded as he began coating the barrel of the gun with its contents. After a few seconds, he had coated the entire firearm in the spray, as well as his hand. Pointing the gun at nothing in particular, he pulled the trigger.

It was as if the firing mechanism was moving in slow motion. The hammer moved forward in a wake of gray beads. A muffled sound met my ears, and the barrel of the gun ballooned, the metal twisting and churning as it fought to let the explosion escape. A shower of gray beads fell around the Bounty Hunter's hand, and he tossed the now useless gun on the ground.

"I...that was awesome," I said.

Kratos looked at the gun with disdain. "Check the other body for one."

Jump off a building? Check.

Jump off a moving train? Check.

Join forces with Kratos the Bounty Hunter and rifle through an unconscious man's pockets at his urging? Check.

Alex would be so jealous.

I approached Jonny and got down on one knee. It was odd going through someone else's pockets, but Jonny didn't have anything more than a couple of wrappers for a discontinued candy.

"Nothing," I said.

"Good," Kratos said. "We're leaving."

"Wait, what?"

"We need to go. Now."

"Go where?" I asked. "Augustine and Daphne will be here any minute."

"The Pendletons cannot hide you as well as I can."

I glanced at the sliver of silver that showed above my gloves.

"I don't want to hide," I said.

Kratos paused but said nothing.

"The only way I'll be safe is if the Left Hand is gone," I said.

"It is not your fight."

"Whose is it then?" I said. "They put a timer on my life. I won't spend the rest of it hiding."

Kratos continued to stare at me. I took a chance.

"We might have found something that could expose whoever is behind the Left Hand, and we could use your help."

His eyes flicked to my gloves, lingering an extra moment on my left forearm, and then back to my eyes. A set of heavy footsteps sounded around the corner.

"Get behind me," Kratos said, taking a step toward the noise.

I started to spray an invisible protective wall for myself, but stopped as a hulking figure rounded the corner.

The footfalls belonged to Dax. Dax, who also worked with Tyrann, but Zeno trusted him, and for some reason, I trusted him too.

"I think we're good," I said, raising a hand in greeting.

Dax caught sight of Kratos and slowed his approach. "Everything all right, Victor?" he said, his British accent ringing through the silent street. He nodded to the two unconscious bodies on the ground.

"Yeah, I'm good," I said.

Kratos remained silent.

"Augustine's been in a right state. Earpiece not working?"

"I lost it on the train," I said.

"Dax!" Augustine's voice came around the corner.

"Over here," he said, regarding Kratos carefully.

Daphne rounded the corner, followed closely by Augustine. They stopped short when they saw the scene. I could only imagine how this looked.

"Victor, are you okay?" Augustine asked. Daphne's eyes flitted back and forth between me and Kratos.

"Yeah," I said, "but if he didn't show up when he did, I wouldn't be."

Augustine stared hard for a moment before speaking.

"Our business is not with you, Mr. Bounty Hunter. Hand Victor over, and we'll go our separate ways."

"No," Kratos said.

Daphne unsheathed her saber.

I turned to look at him. "You're not in charge here. I make my own choices."

Kratos scanned all the faces in the group. My guess was that he was calculating whether or not he could take us all. Four on one? It would probably be close.

"What do you hope to accomplish here?" Augustine said.

"I wish to ensure Victor's safety."

"Why?" Augustine said.

"I was with Victor when the Left Hand attacked him at his home. The news reports have been incorrect."

Augustine studied him. Dax and Daphne remained quiet. I looked back and forth between the two of them, not sure how this was going to go. Augustine was confronting a man who personified the government's system, a system he didn't believe in, a system that had wronged him. I stood beside a man who had saved my life twice.

"You're basing this course of action off of inaccurate news reports?" Augustine asked, somewhat skeptically.

"You do not know what I've seen." Kratos's reply was quick and sharp. "Something is amiss. I intend to help."

"How?" Augustine asked. "By turning Victor in?"

"Victor said you had information," Kratos said.

"And if we do?" Augustine's words were careful and slow.

"It depends on the nature of the information. If it is good and accurate," Kratos said, "I will help you."

"I haven't trusted the government for a long time now," Augustine said. "You've *just* learned that Victor's story doesn't add up, and you're willing to betray the people you represent?"

"Following truth is not betrayal," Kratos said.

"So you're saying you'll help us?" I asked. "Just like that?"

Kratos responded without hesitation. "Yes."

Augustine frowned. Daphne looked like she smelled something unpleasant.

It occurred to me that Kratos was just continuing to do his job. He went after bad guys. New information had come to light and he was following it.

"Look, I'm here and still conscious, aren't I?" I interjected. "He could have easily knocked me out and taken me away. Easily. But he didn't. I think he can help. Plus"—I met Daphne's eyes—"isn't this what you've been telling me about? People can make their own choices for good or for bad, regardless of their DNA?"

"This is a simple question of what is right and what is wrong," Kratos said. "Nothing more, nothing less."

"So what now?" Daphne said. "You swear yourself to secrecy and that's that, we can trust you?"

"I offer my help so long as our goals are in alignment. If things change, I will no longer be your ally."

Augustine stared at the Bounty Hunter, tight-lipped. "I believe in your principles, but I find it hard to put complete trust in your words." I gave Augustine a reproving look that he didn't see. This was the Bounty Hunter, and he was offering to help us!

Kratos nodded and took a step forward. "I agree that complete trust is necessary," he said and reached up behind his head. "And I assure you, I am trustworthy." In a single fluid motion, he peeled off his mask.

Daphne gasped. Even Dax looked surprised. To my knowledge, no one had ever seen the Bounty Hunter's actual face. It wasn't what I was expecting.

His pale, blurred features were suddenly olive-toned and sharp. Short golden hair framed his face. His eyes remained blue and piercing. My mind was still adjusting to the new image of Kratos when Augustine broke the stunned silence.

"I need to discuss this with Zeno," he said, his face unreadable. "But for now, you can come with us."

"Then I suggest we get going," Kratos said, looking over his shoulder. "It is possible that the Left Hand is still nearby."

Augustine nodded his assent.

"Augustine," I said, "where's Alex? I thought he was somewhere along the tracks."

"I thought we would have seen him by now. Pr—"

He stopped speaking and lifted his hand to his ear.

"Could you possibly walk any slower?" someone said angrily from around the corner.

"Yeah, I could," another person answered. "Wanna see?"

I heard a thud, and the subsequent stumble of someone being pushed.

"You know, for a pretty girl, you're pretty mean," Alex said as he came into view. He was followed by the brightly dressed Pria Kane. Tyrann had sent three of his men and one of his *daughters* to help us out?

Alex's face lit up when he saw us.

"Oh man, am I glad to see you guys! I couldn't hear anything you were saying, but seriously"—he pointed his thumb at Pria—"she gets a zero on my scale of cool..."

Pria looked at him in disgust as his voice trailed off and he stopped walking.

"Who's that?" Alex said, pointing to Kratos, who stood motionless in the street, dressed in all black with a silicone mask dangling from his hand. Alex's eyes widened as he put the pieces together. He opened his mouth to speak, but nothing came out.

"Oh, I bet you're one of those dreadful Followers, aren't you?" Pria said. "Clearly, it's the Bounty Hunter."

Alex continued to stare in shock.

"Alex, this is..." I glanced at the Bounty Hunter. "We've heard you go by Kratos."

He nodded.

I continued, looking back at Alex, "He's going to help us out." I figured it was best to get this stage of things over with quickly. The sooner Alex recovered from shock, the better.

"Good to see you again, Mr. Trabue," Kratos said.

"You remember me?" Alex said, a smile gripping his face like a vice.

Kratos looked mildly worried at Alex's state. He slid his mask back on. Out of habit or because he wanted to hide his expression, I wasn't sure, but it seemed to bring Alex a little closer to reality.

"He remembered..." Alex said softly. "He was at my house!"

"Yes, well, I suggest we get going," Augustine said.

"I need to get these two back as well." Dax motioned to Brick and Jonny. "Pria can come with me."

Pria didn't seem too pleased with the arrangement, but then again, she never seemed pleased with anything. Dax walked over and hoisted the two men onto his back, one over each shoulder. The act was effortless—I didn't even hear him grunt in exertion. "Right, this way, Pria," he said. Pria rolled her eyes and strode off down the road after him, making sure to throw Daphne an ugly look before she got too far.

"Okay, everyone," Augustine said, "this way."

We headed down the road in relative silence. Augustine led the way and seemed to be communicating with Zeno through his earpiece. At least that's what I assumed he was doing, not being able to listen in on the conversation myself. Alex trailed behind Kratos, which was a good thing, because if he had been in front, he would have been walking backwards and Kratos would have seen him drooling. Daphne walked alone off to the right. I sidled up next to her.

"Hey," I said.

"Hey," she said with a smile. "I'm glad you're okay."

Our fingers brushed as our arms swung. Daphne didn't pull away.

"Thanks, me too," I said, smiling back.

Daphne lowered her voice. "What do you think about the Bounty Hunter?"

"Kratos? I trust him," I said.

"Just like that?" she asked.

"He's saved my life twice," I said. "And he didn't knock me out and drag me back to the flats just now."

Daphne opened her mouth to respond, but our whispered conversation was cut short by Augustine.

"Mr. Bounty Hunter," he said, "Zeno gave me his strong opinion that we should offer you full disclosure."

Kratos nodded, but said nothing.

"We'll fill you in on the details when we arrive at my place," Augustine continued. "There are some platforms at the intersection up ahead. I assume you know how to ride them?"

"Yes," Kratos said.

"Good. Stay close. It's a straight shot back home, and we'll be moving fast. We've got some work to do."

31

I still couldn't believe Kratos was with us. He followed me as effort-lessly as if he'd ridden these platforms all his life. We flew past a Dr. Rosewood billboard that was more insulting graffiti than anything. It was easy enough to see that she was not well liked in the Heights. I turned my gaze back to the track to find Kratos staring at the bill-board, keeping his eyes on it until it was out of sight. Minutes later we dismounted from our platforms and made the short trek back to the events center.

After picking our way past the trash and a new barrage of threat-ening graffiti, we followed Augustine down the steps that led to the giant room behind the stage. Daphne and I were forced to stop as Kratos attempted to let Alex pass him for the umpteenth time. Alex walked into him. Again. It was getting a little ridiculous. I thought he had been taken with Daphne, but the attention he was giving Kratos bordered on worship.

We reached the landing and headed into the cavernous room. Zeno was seated at the long table, working furiously on what looked like a scanner, and was that a human hand?

"Zeno, what is th—"

"Nothing," he said, cutting me off and dropping his project into a box on the countertop.

"Mr. Bounty Hunter," Augustine started.

"Kratos is fine."

"Kratos," Augustine started again, "welcome. You of course already know Zeno."

"You've been gone a long time, Mr. Zeno," Kratos said, inclining his head in greeting.

"Yeah, it has been a minute. But it's good to see you, man. Although, if you could keep this whole thing"—Zeno waved his arms in an encompassing circular motion—"under wraps for me, that would be awesome."

Kratos nodded. "Of course."

"Perfect," Augustine said. "Now, we need to get you up to speed."

"Hold on," I said. There had been something itching at my mind since the moment the Sinistrali showed up on the train. "Before we start," I continued, "how did the Left Hand know I was going to be on the train? If someone is tipping them off, anything we plan is useless." I turned to Kratos. "How did *you* know I was going to be there?"

"Do not underestimate the resourcefulness of the Left Hand," Kratos said. "Even I don't know how they get their information, but I doubt they use informants like I do."

"Then how did you know Victor was going to be there?" Daphne asked.

"Proximity sensors," Kratos said. "The senator's train car is covered in them. Victor triggered them when he landed on the roof. I happened to be nearby."

"Seriously?" Zeno said. "I ran a scan for those, and they always show up, unless..." He trailed off and turned to face Kratos. "Unless they finally implemented my untraceable design?" Kratos nodded. "Man, what a day to do that." Zeno put his hands on his hips and looked at the ground. "I go in, try and help my government bros be more efficient, and what happens? It comes back to bite me." Zeno shook his head. "I'm glad I'm back in the private sector."

"This is the private sector?" Alex said.

Zeno shot him a look.

"Could it have been one of Tyrann's men who tipped off the Sinistrali?" I asked. "Or Pria?"

"I don't think it was Dax or Pria," Daphne said. "I wouldn't put it past Brick and Jonny, but I'm not sure they're smart enough to do something like that."

"I have to agree," Augustine said. "Kratos, any thoughts?"

"Did anyone here inform them?" he asked.

"Come on, man, this place is a Faraday cage. Nothing came out of here," Zeno said. "Not to mention, no one here would have done that. We're all on the same team."

"No one is above suspicion," Kratos said.

"Everyone here has a vested interest in what we're doing," Augustine said. "If this doesn't work, we all lose. No one here would sabotage that."

"You're certain?" Kratos said.

"Absolutely," I said, stepping forward.

"Then, as I said before, I do not know where they get it, but their information is always correct."

"But how?" Daphne asked. "Does this mean that regardless of what we plan, they're going to show up?"

"Guys," Alex said, "I think I know how they're doing it." All eyes turned to him. "It's called a remote DNA locator."

"A what?" Daphne said, squinting at him.

"A remote DNA locator. The message boards say that's how the Left Hand has a perfect record. They can find anyone anywhere as long as they have a sample of their DNA."

"I don't know if that technology exists yet, bro," Zeno said. "I mean, I haven't invented anything like that."

"Regardless," I said, "we'll just have to take into account that they might show up, right? We have to be prepared in ways they wouldn't expect."

"I like the way you're thinking, bro," Zeno said. "We need something crazy, something unpredictable! Maybe even..." That crazy glint returned to his eye and a smile took over his face.

"I agree, and we'll, um"—Augustine paused and looked at Zeno —"let Zeno take care of the unexpected." He turned to Kratos. "Well then, we need to get you up to speed. Time is short. Victor, your arm please."

I had been expecting this. I stepped forward and removed the glove from my hand, revealing the series of silver spherical splotches.

Kratos stared at it a moment before reacting. "A biokey? From Senator Supart?"

"Yes."

Man, he was quick.

"What does it unlock?" Kratos asked.

"We're not exactly sure," I said, "but it has to do with the Left Hand. Whatever it is, they want it."

"I see," Kratos said. It was impossible to guess what he was thinking, especially with his mask on. I could only hope he had an idea—a way to get us onto the train.

I checked my arm. "And we've only got one day, six hours, and a bunch of minutes and seconds before the biokey expires," I said. "So we've got to figure something out, and fast."

Kratos stood in silence for a moment. "I assume you want to get into the car before the sweep lab?"

Augustine nodded.

"I should be able to facilitate that."

"Just like that?" Daphne asked, skepticism written all over her face. Kratos turned to face her.

"Yes."

"Ideally," Augustine said, his eyes shifting back forth between Daphne and Kratos, "Victor would get on the train just after departure. That way, the car will be empty and he can bypass the train station completely."

"That won't be necessary," Kratos said.

"Seriously?" Daphne said. "What are you going to do, parade him around the station before boarding?"

Kratos didn't hesitate. "Victor will pose as my captive, and I will inform the head operator that I am transporting him back to head-quarters. That should be sufficient. I've transported people in a similar manner in the past. Once inside, we'll go to the senator's car. Victor will have until the next stop to find what he's looking for. I'll stand guard to ensure that he's not disturbed."

"Eh," Zeno said, tapping his chin with an index finger, "I give you six out of ten."

Kratos shot him an unreadable glance.

"Sorry, bro. Sounds like it'll go off without a hitch, but it lacks style." Zeno shook his head sadly. "I guess they're just not holding you to the same standard since I left."

"I'd prefer that it lacks style," Augustine said. "The simpler the better. However, Senator Supart's train car is second to last. Guarding one entrance will still leave the other vulnerable."

"You think we need another person to guard the other entrance?" I asked.

"I doubt the rear entrance will pose a threat, but it would be wise to have a lookout, just in case," Kratos admitted.

Alex's hand shot into the air.

"I'll do it!"

Kratos glanced at Alex, and then over to Augustine, who shrugged.

"Yeah," I said, "Alex would be perfect." Not to mention he'd get to live out his dream of working with the Bounty Hunter.

"It's decided then," Augustine said.

"Yes!" Alex gave a few fist pumps.

"But I have one last question about the plan," Augustine said. "The Left Hand appears to have infiltrated the police force. What if they've managed to get into the security team that's with the train?"

Kratos thought for a moment. I looked over at Daphne. I could see her mind was at work on something.

"In close quarters," Kratos said, "I should be able to hold off a team of six or sev—"

"What about a distraction?" Daphne asked, cutting him off.

"It would have to be big," Kratos said. "There are police officers in the train station as well. A small disturbance would have no effect on the personnel inside the train."

"This would be big," she said, nodding her head slowly. "If a building were to fall onto the tracks, for example, would that be big enough?"

"Assuming it was close by," Kratos said. "Protocol would mandate that all officers in the vicinity, including those on the train, attend to the situation." He paused, and I could hear a hint of surprise in his voice. "Could you make something like that happen?"

"Yes," Daphne said.

"Just like that?" Kratos asked.

Daphne smiled. "I know some people who might be interested in helping out."

"I'm impressed," Kratos said. "A distraction would be helpful."

"Then let's do it," I said.

Augustine nodded in agreement.

"Okay," Daphne said, then turned to Zeno. "They'll need some convincing."

"How much?" he asked.

"Not a lot. They like doing this sort of thing."

Alex spoke up. "You're amazing." His face immediately went red. At first, I thought he was talking about Kratos, but instead I found him staring at Daphne. Apparently the ability to knock over buildings ranked high on Alex's list of things he liked in a girl. Daphne stared back at him with her mouth half-open, seemingly not sure how to respond. Zeno looked back and forth between them.

"Well said, my man." Zeno stepped over and slapped Alex on the back, ending the awkward moment. "Now, any objections to the plan?"

We all shook our heads, except for Kratos, who didn't move.

"Excellent," Zeno said. He turned to Daphne. "Well, you should get going if you're planning to get everything ready by morning."

"Agreed," Daphne said. "Watch for my text."

Zeno nodded in reply, and Daphne headed out the door.

"See you all later tonight," she said, and then she was gone.

Alex waved a goodbye she didn't see.

"Ooo, I like this," Zeno said, his smile growing wider with every moment. "Yeah, I like this a lot. Somebody, Victor, can I get a fist bump please?"

We knocked knuckles, but there was still a crucial part of the plan that we hadn't discussed.

"How am I getting off the train after we have the information?"

"The same way we came in," Kratos replied. "We'll just need a meeting point, preferably in the Heights."

"I'll find us a spot," Augustine said. "And afterwards, we'll meet up back here."

I reviewed the plan in my head. It all sounded good to me. What would we have done without Kratos?

"Boom!" Zeno exclaimed. "Got it!" We all looked at him questioningly. Ignoring us, he stood up and headed for the door. "I'll be back in a bit!"

"What are you thinking, Zeno?" Augustine called.

"The unexpected!" he said, his afro zipping around the corner and out of sight.

After a moment, Augustine spoke. "Well I guess that just leaves the four of us. I think that's it for the afternoon, Kratos. Let's meet here at five a.m. tomorrow to go over everything."

Kratos nodded in reply and turned to leave.

"You're not staying?" I asked.

"I think it best if I stay elsewhere."

"Wait, what?" Alex said.

By the look on his face, either Alex had received word that donuts would no longer be made, or Kratos's words were just now registering.

"You should stay!" Alex blurted out. "I mean, it doesn't make sense for you to stay somewhere else if you're gonna be here so early tomorrow. Plus, it's not even dinnertime yet. Everyone's gotta eat."

"He does have a point," Augustine said, an uncomfortable expression playing on his features.

"Yeah, and I can show you around," Alex said, starting to walk toward one of the doors. "Or Augustine or Zeno can show you around. I've only been here for like a day."

"I must decline. I believe I know the way out." He nodded to each of us in turn and made a prompt exit. Augustine didn't look displeased at his retreat. He took a deep breath and exhaled before turning to us.

"Well, we have a few details to figure out," he said. "Let's get to it."

"And food?" Alex said, still staring at the door Kratos had walked out of.

"And food," Augustine said with a smile.

I smiled too. I was beginning to think that with Kratos's help, this just might work out after all.

Several hours later Daphne returned. Everything was in place. We all went to bed exhausted, but hopeful. Tomorrow we would find out what exactly Avardi had managed to uncover.

32

Kratos shoved me forward again. I stumbled but stayed on my feet.
Balancing was a little harder when your eyes were covered. Plus, my
wrists itched where they were manacled together behind my back,
and every time the cuffs touched the biokey, a tingle shot up my arm.

Every thirty seconds or so, I would hear someone gasp. I imag-
ined that Kratos had the same effect on the general population that
he did when I first saw him. Conversations ceased. Footsteps halted.
We walked forward undisturbed in a wave of silence.

I was sure that Alex was barely containing his excitement at
Kratos's side. Good thing he had a mask on. Kratos had offered to
bring Alex an extra mask, but Alex produced one out of his pocket.
Apparently, he always carried one with him. Who know when the
Bounty Hunter would call you into his service?

Kratos jerked me to a halt. Alex's footsteps stopped beside me.

"We are boarding this train. Are there any empty cars?" Kratos
said. I assumed he was speaking to the conductor. Public transit
trains didn't have them, but everything else did.

"L-let me ch-check the manifest." I heard the dull thuds of the
conductor's fingers on a glass screen as he checked for open compartments. "I-it looks like every train car i-is occupied. Sir."

"Do not lie to me. I know there are at least two empty train cars in this line."

"For-forgive me, Mr. Bounty Hunter, sir. The manifest shows the compartments as re-restricted."

"Not to me."

Kratos thrust me forward, and my feet made contact with a new surface. I didn't hear the conductor object.

"How long until the train departs?" Kratos asked.

There was a brief pause before the conductor spoke. "Four minutes, sir. And if I may, w-who is this?"

Kratos paused. I smiled under cover of the bag over my head. I knew the conductor wasn't talking about me, and I also knew that underneath Alex's mask, he was smiling.

"This is my protégé," he said slowly. I could hear the strain in his voice. It had been Alex's idea to protect his own identity. Begrudgingly, Kratos had relented. I was surprised Alex hadn't already exploded with joy.

"P-protege, sir?"

"Yes," he said shortly. "I need you to disable all of the security cameras throughout this line."

"Sir?"

"What is your name?" Kratos asked.

"W-Winston, sir."

"Winston, I have an individual of a sensitive nature in my company. While I am tasked with his or her capture, I am not uncivilized. This bag is as much for your protection as it is mine. At some point during the ride, I will remove it, and there can be no evidence of who is concealed beneath it. Turn off the cameras. I will not ask again."

"Y-yes, of course!" the conductor said. The sound of hurried retreating steps reached my ears.

Kratos shoved me again, and we headed toward the senator's compartment, or at least I assumed we did. He spoke quietly. "Daphne, now would be a good time."

Daphne's voice registered in my earpiece.

"Would you like a countdown?" she asked, her voice filled with excitement.

"That won't be necess—"

"Three, two, one!"

The explosion was deafening. The shockwave rattled the train.

The angry sound of brick breaking and steel bending rent the air. Muffled screaming made its way through the inch-thick glass that made up the windows of the train. The earth shook as thousands of pounds of brick, metal, and glass rained down from the sky.

An alarm sounded. Through the blackness of the bag, I could just make out the faint glow of a blinking red light. Kratos ushered me to the side as a wave of footsteps ran past us.

That should be the police presence leaving the train. Just like Kratos said.

"Mr. Bounty Hunter, sir!" The words came from Winston. "There has been an explosion and a building has fallen on the tracks!"

"Then I suggest we get moving. We don't want whoever did that to find this train."

"Y-you m-m-mean," he stuttered, "they, that, that was for u-us?"

"I suggest we depart. Immediately."

"Yes, d-d-depart." The conductor's footsteps raced away from us.

Kratos lowered his voice. "Two more train cars to pass through. Keep the bag on your head until I say so."

Kratos led me along far more gently than before. The alarm went silent. Winston must have been able to get the security system turned off.

"Ladies and gentlemen"—the conductor's voice sounded crisp in the overhead speakers—"for your continued safety, we have decided to leave early. Please remain calm and we will arrive at the next station in fourteen minutes."

Augustine's voice sounded in my earpiece. "Victor, that should give you plenty of time to search the senator's office. It's not large."

"Keep moving!" Kratos said, shoving me forward a few steps. A series of gasps met his words. He was good at keeping up the charade. I stumbled my way forward until he yanked me backwards a few steps. I felt like I was on a leash. He brushed past me, and I heard him unstrap a glove and place his hand on what I assumed was a scanner.

He ushered me through the now open door. The moment it closed, we were met with silence. I reached up to remove the bag.

"Wait," Kratos whispered.

Obediently, I stood motionless in silence.

"Go ahead."

I took the bag off my head. We were in a completely empty compartment. It was probably thirty feet long and twenty feet wide. Everything was gray, the walls, the floor, and even the ceiling, which was punctuated with a kind of subdued light. At the far end of the compartment, there stood a door with several keypads and scanners.

"I didn't think you'd be able to hold it together after that protégé comment," I said.

"You should have seen the looks people were giving us!" Alex exclaimed. He stood next to Kratos dressed in his Follower outfit from a few days before. Other than the height and build difference, the resemblance was uncanny.

"All right, let's go," Kratos said.

As we made our way over to the door, Augustine said, "Twelve minutes."

"Got it," I said. "And Daphne?"

"Yes?"

"That might have been the worst countdown I've ever heard."

She scoffed into her mic. "Just let me know the next time you blow up a building."

Kratos placed a hand on three separate scanners in succession, and the door slid open with a hiss.

"I'll knock on the door when it's time," he said. "Alex, stand guard on the outside of the far door. Keep your stunner out and alert me if you notice anything out of the ordinary."

"Roger that," Alex said as he unholstered his stunner. He peered down the sights, aiming first at the floor, then through the door. "Victor, stay there," he said and then passed through the open door, brandishing his stunner every which way. "Clear." He motioned me in.

I couldn't help but smile. There was no way Alex would be letting Kratos down today.

I stepped into the senator's train car and the door closed behind us. A metal sheet slid into place, followed by a glass one. The doors were double paned, I assumed for protection. The car was very different from the empty one we had come through. A large desk was bolted to the floor on one side, as were various cabinets and shelves. It really was a portable office. A large phone, several screens, and a computer were all secured in place as well.

Other than the bigger furniture, the room was sparsely decorated. A few pictures hung on the walls, but that was it.

"Good luck!" Alex said, jogging across to the other side of the room. The door opened, and he stepped into the last car in the line. If the Left Hand did somehow show up, Alex should still be okay. The door shut behind him, metal and then glass. I started my search.

"Ten minutes," Augustine said.

"So the safe could look like anything, right?" I said into my mic. "How exactly should I figure out what it is?"

"Just be happy I didn't finish my prototype of the invisible safe," Zeno said. "I'd start sweeping the biokey across stuff. Look for a sort of glowing indicator light when you do."

"Got it."

I held out my arm like a sensing rod police used to check people for weapons and waved it up and down over the first bookshelf, slowly making my way over to the desk.

Kratos's voice sounded in my ear. "We have incoming."

I jumped as a large thud sounded against the door to the senator's compartment. Another thump followed, and the sound of a body slumping to the floor reached my ears. My heart began to race as fear burned its way up my spine.

"I'll hold them off as long as I can," Kratos said, his voice strained. The metal part of the door suddenly jumped open, giving me a perfect and terrifying view of the battle outside. Smoke drifted toward the ceiling from the panels to the left of the door. A series of stunner-carrying rail employees rushed across the empty train car toward us. Lightning blasts lit up the air, but most dissipated as they reached Kratos's invisible shield.

The Left Hand had somehow made themselves part of the train's staff.

"Victor! Have you found it?" Augustine said.

"Not yet!" I said, frantically continuing my search.

Augustine's voice came through the earbud, "Alex, be prepared. The Left Hand is here."

Alex's gasp from just outside his door echoed in my earpiece.

Another thud sounded on the outside wall. I kept searching, stealing glances through the battle scene beyond the glass. Kratos was making quick work of his opponents.

A yell came from behind Alex's door. "Guys! They're here! And they're not getting past me!" Alex let out a battle cry. Two thuds sounded as bodies hit the floor. And then Alex spoke again. "I got two of them, but I think there's more. Oh crap, lots more. Taste my stunner, you murdering trash!"

I cast a look toward Kratos's side. He seemed to be doing fairly well. I hurriedly ran my arm over the second bookcase.

Still nothing.

"Victor, hurry, there's like a million of them. I don't know how much longer I can—"

Alex's voice was cut off. A thud echoed just outside the door.

"Alex!"

Augustine's voice was sharp in my ear. "Victor, you need to get out of—"

"No!" Zeno cut him off. "Victor, stay in the car. Make sure the other door doesn't open."

"What?" I jogged over to the far door as another thud sounded against it. "Alex is in there!"

"Zeno!" Augustine yelled.

"Trust me! It's the unexpected! Keep the door closed for another minute, and then do exactly as I say."

I paused. It looked like I was trapped. The only option I had was to stay where I was. Alex was unconscious on the other side of the door, and the Sinistrali were trying to break through. The moment they did, it was over.

"Victor! You with me?"

"What's the unexpected? And what about Alex?" I yelled back.

"Alex will be fine, trust me, and I'm going to get you out of there. I'm going to derail your car."

"*What?*"

"I'll explain later," Zeno said, the frantic click of a keyboard punctuating his words.

"Zeno, whatever you have planned, do it quickly," Kratos said. A quick glance through the glass showed me that the Sinistrali had abandoned their stunners and were advancing.

A loud clank sounded on Alex's side of the car, and I heard the groan of metal straining against the impact.

"I need thirty more seconds," Zeno said.

"Then you've got thirty seconds," Kratos said. He grabbed a pair of loose stunners off the floor and began firing into the advancing crowd.

"Twenty seconds," Zeno said. I searched frantically, but I knew I wasn't going to find anything. There wasn't enough time. And Alex was stuck behind the door. The Left Hand wouldn't kill him, would they?

Sparks flew across Alex's door, and the sliding metal part popped open. I could see light on the other side and a set of fingers trying to pull it the rest of the way open.

I continued to search. The metal let out an almighty groan, and Alex's door started to roll. Through the crack, I could see the tail of Alex's black trench coat lying across the floor.

"Keep them out, Vic!" Zeno said. "Fifteen seconds!"

The straining arms of a couple of Sinistralis pulled on the stubborn door, inching it backwards as it fought to close on them. The polished metal of a gun barrel nosed through the crack. I dove out of the way as the gun fired, exploding the glass part of the door into a thousand pieces.

I grabbed the only thing in the room not bolted to the ground—

the computer monitor—and charged the door. I swung and made contact with more than one set of hands. Yelps and curses were cut off as the door slid shut again and locked into place.

Zeno's voice reverberated in my ear.

"Victor! Get to the straps and hold on! It's about to get bumpy!"

I ran to the center of the room, grabbed hold of the straps hanging from the ceiling, shoved my feet in the footholds, and caught one last glance of Kratos.

He stood there in his trench coat, at least fifteen unconscious bodies at his feet, a pair of stunners aimed across the room.

"Hold on!" Zeno shouted into my ear.

The car jolted. The muscles in my hands and wrists tensed around the straps. My feet fought to stay in place. If the train had wheels, it would have been riding on only two of them. And then none of them. Kratos turned and watched as my doorframe rolled upwards past him. The car flipped off the tracks. I held on tighter than I ever had to anything before. Books flew off the shelves. The drawers of the desk jumped open. Paper fluttered through the air. And then I was weightless.

Gravity pulled on me, trying to force my body right, up, left, down.

The car tumbled through the air. I clung to the ceiling straps and footholds.

Zeno was in my ear, but I couldn't hear him. Fear paralyzed my senses. The inside of the car was a tornado of office supplies fueled by centrifugal force and gravity. Still I held on, but my feet were slipping.

I tried to reposition them in the loops.

I had just enough time to hear the misplaced sound of water colliding with metal, and then everything went black.

33

Voices. I could just make them out, but only in one ear. The words sounded blurry, but they were becoming clearer.

"... thinking?"

"Victor!"

It sounded like Augustine, or maybe Daphne? Hopefully Daphne.

"Victor!"

I groaned and got to my feet. It was dark, except for the faint green band of light that circled the floor of the room. I blinked as I attempted to orient myself. The train car. I was still inside the train car. And the voices were coming from my earbud.

"Victor!"

"I'm okay," I moaned.

A chorus of sighs sounded in my ear.

Zeno was the first to speak. "Bro! Just like I planned, the train car landed in the lake. You're partially underwater, but don't worry, those things are airtight."

I glanced at the door that had been on Alex's side. Despite the lack of glass, it seemed to be holding up.

"That explains the darkness," I said, bracing myself against the wall. "And did you say, 'just like I planned'? How did you jump the train off the tracks?" I started to pick my way across the car. Papers and pens and broken bits of glass littered the floor like the regurgitated contents of an office wastebasket.

"Glad you asked, bro!" Zeno said. "Big Brother has a system to get Kratos more of my special spray if he's running low, and they send it anywhere in the city in under a minute, so I hacked in using Daphne's password and ordered some more spray to be sent to the train. They're delivered by drones, and drones don't ask questions, well, at least not these ones..." He chuckled. "But I had them follow the senator's train car and put a few concentrated bursts on the tracks at just the right time. Basically, I created a ramp and sent your train car for a ride."

"A ride is right," I said, itching at the developing bump on my head. "What about Alex and Kratos? Are they okay?"

"The train cars on either side snapped together after yours was"—Augustine paused—"removed." In my mind's eye, he was glaring at Zeno. "Kratos got Alex out of there and off the train. Both of them are fine."

"Fine? How about awesome!" Alex said. "You should have seen it. I took down like ten Sinistralis and Kratos had to revive me and—"

"Later," came Kratos's crisp voice. "Victor, we're at the water's edge. Zeno, how do we get him out?"

"All in good time," Zeno said. I had the distinct impression that he was smiling. "And you just let my man Victor take care of getting himself out. But first, we've got to find that safe."

"Agreed," I said, holding my arm out over a pile of books on the floor. "I still haven't found it, but I'll keep searching. Zeno, is there any way to get more light in here? All I've got is this green glowing strip of light along the floor."

"You mean the ceiling?"

"Nope." I moved over to another pile of assorted office supplies. "I mean the floor."

There was a brief pause on the other side.

"So," Zeno said, "there is the possibility the car is, you know, upside down. Sorry about that."

I looked up, and sure enough, the darkened form of a desk was on the ceiling.

"Trajectory, speed, wind," Zeno continued, "the math was a little complicated on this one. But bro, you have to admit, getting it all done in under a minute? Not to toot my own horn, but—"

"Zeno!" Augustine said.

"Right, sorry. Anyways, the green light means the car is in emergency mode," Zeno continued. "The doors are all sealed, and everything is airtight. Don't worry though, you've got plenty of breathable air."

"Your optimism is inspiring," Daphne said. "You okay down there, Victor?"

"Yeah, I'm good," I said, making my way to the other side of the train car. "But what happened to all the Sinistrali? Did they follow us?"

"No," Kratos said. "No one followed us."

"Any chance the police will capture any of the Sinistralis you left behind?" Augustine asked.

"As soon as Victor's car derailed, I grabbed Alex and jumped off the back of the last train car," Kratos said. "There were a few conscious Sinistralis still on board. My guess is that they stayed behind to clean up."

His words were met with silence. I had had no idea just how powerful the Left Hand was. It seemed they were more resourceful and connected than I had ever thought possible. I waved my arm over another pile without any luck.

"Well, bro," Zeno said, filling the space. "I figure you've got twenty minutes before a team shows up to investigate the train car in the lake. As soon as you find what you're looking for, let me know. I'll work a little magic and open the door so you can swim to the surface. You can swim, right?"

"Yeah," I said, "but I've gone over just about everything on the floor. Still nothing. Anyone have any thoughts?"

"Maybe check all the bolted-down furniture?" Augustine offered.

I surveyed the car. The green band of light cast an eerie glow over the whole compartment.

The bookshelves were now empty. I walked over and pulled myself up to see if there was anything hidden there. A single book remained, almost like it was glued in place.

Could this be it?

I pulled it off the shelf.

"*Some Dark Holler*," I murmured, reading the title. I thumbed through the pages and waved my arm over it, but nothing happened. "I feel like I'm in some dark holler."

"What was that?" Augustine said.

"Nothing," I said. "Just a book." I waved my arm over the book-shelf again for good measure. "Nothing on the shelves." I let my eyes follow the band of green light around the room until they rested on the biggest fixture in the car. "We might have something in the desk though."

All the drawers were open and empty. All except one. I jumped and grabbed hold of the arms of the bolted-down chair, adjusting my grip so I could hang using only my right hand. I waved my left arm around in front of the only closed drawer, letting the silver embedded in my skin brush against the drawer's handle.

A small click sounded, and a jolt of electricity coursed through me. This had to be it.

I slid open the drawer, but did so slowly. A faint blue light shone out of it. I inched the drawer open a little further. A small blue cylinder, about the size of a pen, rested on the underside of the drawer.

"Guys, everyone, I've got something." With the pulsating cylinder in hand, I dropped back down to the paper-covered ceiling.

"My man!" Zeno said. "What's it look like?"

"It's a clear blue cylinder that pulses with light," I said. "It's about the size of my finger and feels like some sort of hard plastic."

"That must be it," Augustine said.

"All right, bro," Zeno said, "you ready to come topside?"

I gave one more look around the green-tinged compartment. "Absolutely."

"Kratos, Alex, can you still see the car?" Augustine asked.

"Yep!" Alex said.

"Yes, it has stayed stationary," Kratos said. "The roof looks to be about five feet underwater."

"Vic, after I open the door, wait until the car fills up with water before swimming out."

"What about the cylinder?"

"It should be fine. From what you're saying, I'm gonna guess it's waterproof and shatterproof."

"All right," I said, picking up my gloves and strapping them back on, "ready when you are."

"Stand back, man. Here comes the flood."

The airtight seal broke and water cascaded in. I jumped and grabbed hold of the chair arms again as water filled the car around me. I took a deep breath just before it reached my chin and let go, kicking out hard to swim through the open doorway. Moments later, my head broke the surface.

"Over here!" Alex's voice floated across the water. He and Kratos stood on the nearest bank. Alex waved me over. Kratos, stoic as usual, stood stationary.

I swam until my feet hit the bottom, and I walked the rest of the way. Alex met me with a fist bump.

"Man, you should have seen the train car flying through the air," he said, a huge grin on his face. "It was awesome."

"Weren't you unconscious?" I asked.

"Yeah, but you know, Zeno described it to me and I could see it all right here." He tapped his temple. "So where is it?"

I pulled out the sky-blue cylinder and held it up to the light.

"Whoa," Alex said. "That's it, huh?"

"Yep." I held it between my fingers.

"We need to get going," Kratos said. "And I'd pocket that if I were you."

I forced as much water out of my clothes as I could and secured the blue cylinder once more.

"Sounds good to me. Let's go."

With Zeno's aid, Kratos located some platforms. A windy twenty minutes later, the three of us were winding our way through the halls of the events center. We descended the stairs and passed through the doors behind the stage. Zeno, Daphne, and Augustine were waiting for us.

"Bros! Finally! Let's see it!" Zeno said as we walked through the door. "I mean, we're glad you're okay."

Daphne rushed over and gave both Alex and me hugs.

"You look awful," she said, taking a step back and looking me up and down.

She looked great as usual, except for a small cut beneath her eye.

"Whoa, what happened?" I pointed to my eye.

"Glass bottle. Some idiot threw it at me just before I got here."

"What? Why?"

"You saw all the graffiti outside, right?" she asked.

I nodded. How could I not? I had noticed a new addition to it on the way in, and it had only become more threatening.

"Yeah, well, the guy yelled something about telling my dad to turn you in so everyone could get back to their regular lives."

I stared at her. What kind of people would throw a bottle at a teenage girl?

"Don't worry," she said, motioning to her left. I noticed her saber sitting on the table beside her. "He won't be throwing anything else any time soon."

I gave her a weak smile and turned to face Augustine, fighting off the feeling of guilt.

"I'm sorry about all of this." I motioned to Daphne's cut. "And all the garbage and graffiti and—"

"Victor." Augustine spoke firmly. "That is not your problem. We have something far more pressing to consider."

"Yeah, bro, don't worry about it," Zeno said. "Now, where's this little blue cylinder?"

He was quick to change the subject, but the sick feeling remained. Putting myself in harm's way was one thing. Augustine and Daphne had already been uprooted once. I couldn't be the cause of that happening again. But Augustine was right—we had something we needed to figure out.

I reached down and pulled the blue cylinder out of my pocket. Zeno took it and brought it close to his face, examining every millimeter of it.

"Hmmm, interesting," Zeno said.

"What, is there something inside it?" Alex said.

"There most definitely is something."

"Do you have the necessary instruments to read it?" Kratos asked.

"Well, I'm guessing the human biokey is all we'll need."

I looked around the room. All eyes were on me.

"So what am I supposed to do? I was holding it earlier and it didn't do anything."

Zeno handed the blue vial back to me. "Maybe try rolling it across your arm?"

I unstrapped my gloves and set them down on the table. I took the vial in my right hand and did as he suggested. It felt cool to my skin as I rolled the glass cylinder down my forearm and into my palm.

This *had* to work. I fanned the fire of hope deep inside me into a blazing bonfire. We were about to find out why the Left Hand wanted me dead. We were about to find out who was behind it all.

The silver splotches covering my arm and hand went into a frenzy.

"Guys, something's happening!"

The countdown orientation disappeared, and my arm felt like it was lying on its own personal bed of nails. I watched as the silver changed from a mass of spherical shapes to letters and words, forming a short sentence of gleaming silver on my forearm.

My eyes widened. My stomach dropped.

"What is it?" Alex asked.

"We were wrong," I said in disbelief, holding up my arm for all to see.

Etched in my skin in unmistakable capital letters was a simple statement.

WRONG OFFICE.

34

The wrong office.

I stared at my arm. A stunned silence filled the room. There *were* no other offices.

Two minutes ago, I knew that we had done it. We had Avardi's info on the Left Hand in our possession. But the flame that had burned so brightly had become a fluttering candle, threatening to fizzle out.

"The wrong office?" Daphne said. "You've got to be kidding me."

I looked to Augustine. "What could it mean? You used to be in the senate. Is there another office, a secret one or something?"

Augustine shook his head. "I'm sorry, no. That's it. Kratos, any insight?"

"No," he said, a hint of surprise in his voice. "All senators have a single office, no exceptions."

"Victor," Alex said, "what's happening to your arm?"

The familiar tingle on my forearm returned. The silver of the biokey was rearranging itself, resuming its normal configuration.

"It's turning back into a clock," Daphne said, stepping over and taking my arm in her hands. An electric shock unrelated to the biokey shot up my arm. "It looks like it's resetting."

Two large splotches of silver rested on my forearm, accompanied by a few on my wrist and a couple dozen on my palm.

"Just over three days," I said slowly. "Until what? It expires again?"

"Bros," Zeno said. "I think we're getting a second chance."

"To find Avardi's office?" I asked. "I mean, to find his secret office? Does it even exist?"

"Of course it exists," Alex said. "Maybe 'office' was code for something, you know? We've just got to figure out what it means."

"I think he's right," Augustine said. "And the Left Hand wouldn't be after you if it weren't real."

"So we're back to square one," Daphne said, "with no idea of where to look." She turned to Zeno. "Any ideas?"

Zeno shook his head. "Nothing yet, Daph, but me and Gina can figure something out."

Suddenly, the giant projector screen blared to life, bathing the room in excess light.

"Gina, what's going on?" Zeno said.

Text rolled across the screen.

Pertinent news announcement.

"Impeccable timing as always," Zeno said. "Let's hope it's something good."

The text on the screen disappeared, and the practiced smile of Kelly Straunton gazed down upon us.

"...reminder that the top floor of the Ixlir Building will be closed later this week for the memorial of Senator Avardi Supart. His wife and son will have a day to view the tribute before it becomes open to the public to pay their respects." She paused. "In other news, President Keltan has asked all news outlets to share a message with the hope that it will reach Victor Wells, the T11D carrier who fled police custody a few days ago." She stared at a point somewhere off camera and touched her ear.

I knew everyone in the room was looking at me, but I couldn't tear my eyes away from the screen.

Kelly refocused on the camera and continued. "This is the message: Victor Wells, turn yourself in. Our interest is in keeping people safe, but we will pursue extreme measures if you do not comply. As a show of good faith, we are offering you one phone call to a family member: your grandfather, Ulysses Wells. To talk, call the number at the bottom of the screen." Ten digits appeared. "This message will be repeated every hour until tomorrow at noon." She let her hand drop from her ear and flashed another smile into the camera.

"And as always, a reminder of the reward for anyone who aids in the capture of a holder of T11D. For any Sinisters watching, Dr. Rosewood is offering real-time genetic enhancement for whoever captures Victor Wells. It's an experimental process, but if successful, your DNA readout could increase by up to fifteen points.

"Well, that's all we've got for this afternoon. Be sure to tune in later tonight when we discuss the effect of the recent Left Hand activity on the outcome of the Great Experiment. Fifty years is almost up. How will things chan—"

The screen went dead and text rolled across it.

Pertinent transmission ended.

Immediately, I turned to Zeno. All thoughts of breaking into the Capital had vanished.

"How do I make the call without being tracked?" If I could call him, he must be okay.

"Uhhh..." Zeno's eyes danced back and forth between me and Augustine.

"What?" I said. "You don't think I should call him?"

"Uhhh..."

"Are we going to talk about that reward?" Daphne asked. "Was I the only one who heard it? Capture Victor and get your genes modified to be more Noble? Is that even possible?"

I had no idea, but I did know that I finally had a chance to talk to Grandfather.

"We can talk about that later. Look, I need to talk to my grandfather. He knew Avardi really well. Maybe he can help us out!"

"Don't you find it odd that your grandfather reached out to you this way?" Augustine said, a somber expression on his face.

"No," I said, but I knew that Grandfather wasn't a fan of the media. He had steered himself out of the public spotlight years ago.

"Your grandfather is a smart man. I'm sure he figured out you found us. He doesn't need a citywide broadcast to get in touch with you," Augustine said.

"Then why wouldn't he just call?" I asked.

"That is the question, isn't it?" Augustine said pensively.

Kratos stood quietly in the corner of the room, unreadable.

"Hold on," Alex chimed in, "hear me out. The Left Hand is listening in on all his phone calls, and if he calls us here, they'll know exactly where to find us. And if that happens..."

"Alex does have a point," I said. "It's a crime to harbor someone with TɪɪD. What if he's just trying to protect you all?"

"I suppose," Augustine said, "but think ab—"

I cut him off. "Then he's probably just doing you a favor," I said a little more loudly than I intended. But they needed to get it. There was no reason I shouldn't talk to Grandfather; besides, he might be able to help us. Maybe he knew what Avardi meant by "wrong office."

I had to talk to him.

"Zeno, can I use your phone?" I asked. "It's untraceable, right?"

"Um, yeah," Zeno said slowly, glancing up at Augustine, who nodded. Zeno pulled the phone out of his pocket and held it in front of his eye. "I give Victor Wells complete access." A light shined across his face, and an audible beep sounded. "Your turn. Just say your name." Zeno stepped over and held the phone in front of my right eye.

"Victor Wells." A light shined in my eye and across my face. The phone beeped.

"There you go, man. That way all the encryption features are unlocked. You're good to go," Zeno said, handing his phone to me.

"Thanks," I said. "Do you mind if I talk to him by myself?"

"Of course not," Augustine said.

"Yeah, bro, it's all you." Zeno turned to Daphne. "Hey, Daph, I'm going to get some air. Wanna join?"

"Sure."

Alex stared at Kratos like he was waiting for the same invitation.

"Alex," Augustine said, "why don't you come with me? We'll grab some food from the kitchen."

"Okay," he said, slightly deflated, before turning to follow Augustine.

Kratos approached me from the corner. "My advice? Choose your words carefully."

I nodded. Kratos turned and followed Alex and Augustine.

I stood alone in the large room holding the phone. I was about to talk to Grandfather. The last time I had seen him, he had risked his life for me. So much had happened since then.

"Gina," I spoke loudly to the vacant screen. Text immediately appeared.

Yes?

"Can you bring up the number I need to dial to call my grandfather?"

Absolutely.

The numbers appeared on the screen. I dialed them and pressed the video button on the screen. It rang. The phone beeped at me. "Video call unavailable. Switching to audio."

I was a little disappointed, but maybe that was better. If someone was trying to track me through this phone call, having video would only make it easier.

The phone rang again. And again.

Finally, the line picked up.

"Grandfather?" I said.

I pressed the phone tightly against my ear.

"Victor." Grandfather's weary voice sounded through the speaker. It was the same way he talked after a long day—exhausted, but with a slight smile on his face. It felt so good to hear his voice.

"Grandfather! Are you okay? Where have you been?" I asked.

"Slow down, Victor, I'm fine, I'm fine. You've been making quite the stir from what I've been told."

I wished I could have seen him and talked face-to-face.

"I know," I said. "But none of it's true. And I have proof and—"

"Oh, Victor, we don't need to talk about that right now," Grandfather said. "Besides, you know that I care for you regardless of what everyone else thinks."

"I know," I said softly. Like Augustine and Daphne, status didn't matter to him.

"So tell me, Victor, how are you doing?" he said.

"I've had better days."

Grandfather paused for a moment and his tone changed. "Yes, but you've also had worse."

Worse? Worse than this? But it was something he had said before. When things became difficult, he reminded me I had survived worse. Losing my parents had been life wrenching, but I had made it through. Whatever situation I was in now, it couldn't be worse than that.

"You're right," I said.

Grandfather continued, his voice soft but firm. "And you got through them all right, didn't you?"

"Yes," I managed. "I did."

"And you'll make it through this," he said, the weariness leaving him for a moment. "Until we give up, hope is never lost!"

I wished I shared his fire. It seemed like there was no way out. Two more days had been put on the biokey, but what good did that do if we couldn't figure out where the "other office" was?

"Victor, we don't have much more time to talk," Grandfather continued, the weariness returning. "People are encouraging me to tell you to give up and turn yourself in." I could hear the strain in his voice.

"No," I said, "I can't do that."

"Good, Victor. That's good." I could picture his weary smile as he said it. "We in the Wells family, we never give up, do we?"

"No, we don't," I said. "And that's part of why I called. It might sound strange, but I need to know: did Avardi ever talk about having another office, one besides his regular office on the Innerbelt?"

There was a pause at the other end of the line. "Well, yes, he did," Grandfather said. My heart started to race. "But why do you want to talk about that?" he continued. "We need to talk about you. Wha—"

"Grandfather!" I said, cutting him off. "I need to know. Where is his other office?"

"Oh, well, most people call it the meeting place," Grandfather said. "You've been there before. It's the Ixlir Building. Avardi always said that he got more work done there than at his actual office."

"And you're sure?" I asked. I took a deep breath to steady myself.

The Ixlir Building, the right office, was inside the Capital.

"Yes, quite sure, but Victor," Grandfather said sadly, "they're telling me I have to go."

"Who's telling you that?" I asked. "Are you in a hospital?"

"No, no, somewhere else. But know that I love you, and remember, hope isn't lost until you give—"

The call ended suddenly.

Confused, I pulled the phone away from my ear and looked at the screen. It didn't look like anything had gone wrong. No interference, no lost signal, just "call ended."

I tried the number again.

It didn't even ring. I tried again with the same result. Why had it ended so suddenly? Was he given a specific allotment of time to talk to someone like me, a "Sinister"?

I contemplated what he had told me. The Ixlir Building. It was huge. If that really had been Avardi's other office, how was I going to search it? How was I going to get in?

I looked at Zeno's phone wistfully. Was there a way I could get in touch with Grandfather again? Maybe I could send him a text.

I unfolded one of the extra screens and brought up a new message. I typed out a few lines of text and pressed send. Moments later a notification popped up.

Number not available.

I tried again with the same result.

Strange, more than strange. Thoughts swirled in my mind like the beginnings of a storm. Why hadn't the number on the screen been Grandfather's actual number? What if the same people who had changed my readout had been in charge of the phone call? Maybe they were the ones who were telling him he had to go.

If that was the case, then the Left Hand had just heard every word.

I shook the thought from my mind. I was just being paranoid. Grandfather had sounded like himself, maybe a little tired, but still himself.

I looked back down at Zeno's phone. I canceled the message to Grandfather, and a list of Zeno's old texts appeared on the screen. One of them caught my eye. A text to Zeno from Daphne. It was dated several months back, but occupied the top spot on the screen.

I tapped on it guiltily. A lengthy conversation appeared.

What I read caught me off guard. The other night, Zeno had told me that he and Daphne were just friends. It looked like that hadn't always been the case.

Daphne and Zeno had feelings for each other, and had for a while by the looks of it. I tapped out of the text conversation and turned off the screen.

I had bigger things to worry about. My feelings could wait. I had to find a way into the Capital.

"Hey, Gina," I said, facing the enormous screen, "where's Ze—"

The sound of an explosion silenced my words.

"Gina! Where was that?" I yelled at the screen.

Augustine and Alex came rushing through the doors.

"What happened?" Alex said.

A video feed appeared on the giant projection screen, showing one of the outer walls of the events center, or, more accurately, what remained of it. Augustine glanced quickly at the screen.

"Victor, stay here. Alex, come on!"

"I'm coming with you," I said.

"This could have been meant for you. Stay here!"

Augustine dashed off with Alex in tow. I looked at the screen again. Brick debris littered the ground. A fire raged in the hole in the wall. I walked closer to the screen. I could have sworn I'd seen movement.

Barely inside the camera's view, I could make out Daphne stirring, partially obscured by brick and trash. Like a dropped dish that shattered on impact, Augustine's warning fell from my mind.

I raced through the doors, across the stage, up the stairs, and toward the exit. Alex and Augustine were pushing their way through the doors to the outside when I caught up to them.

Debris covered the ground. Chunks of brick and flaming trash littered the scene. From outside, you could see into one of the outer hallways of the events center, but I barely even glanced at it.

Daphne lay on the refuse-covered ground, coughing and holding her head.

"She's right here!" I yelled, spotting her before the others. I ran and knelt beside her. Kratos's black coat swished at my side. "Daphne!" I laid a hand on her shoulder. She opened her eyes and blinked several times. "Are you hurt?"

I searched her head and face for injuries, but found nothing. She had a couple of scrapes on her arms, but nothing serious. Kratos stood up without a word and started to scan the area.

"Zeno," she croaked, coughing again. Smoke hung overhead like a thick fog. Alex and Augustine arrived and crouched beside me.

"Where is he?" Augustine asked.

Daphne pointed and coughed again.

Alex jumped up and scoured the area. "Found him!" he yelled. "He's unconscious!"

Kratos rushed to Alex's side, bent down for a split second, and dashed off through the haze.

Augustine grabbed Daphne's hand. "Daphne, are you hurt?"

She shook her head and pushed herself into a sitting position. Augustine rushed over to examine Zeno. I held out my hand and Daphne took it, her fingers warm to the touch. I pulled her gently to her feet. She let go quickly and took off in a shaky jog toward the others.

"Don't worry guys, he's breathing," Alex said as we arrived. I looked down at Zeno. There were no obvious injuries, but he must have been closer to the blast than Daphne had.

Augustine's brow softened after checking his pulse. "The blast must have knocked him out. Daphne, did you see who did it?"

"No, Zeno and I were standing out here getting some air when the blast went off," she said. "Is Zeno okay?"

"He'll be fine once he comes to," Augustine said.

Alex knelt beside him again. "Well, that's easy. I saw this on a TV show once," he said, rubbing his hands together.

Before anyone could stop him, Alex brought his arm back in a mighty swing and slapped Zeno hard across the face.

"Alex!" Augustine turned to reprimand him, but stopped when Zeno moaned.

"Works every time," Alex said with a smile.

"You've had to do that before?" I said, surprised.

"Well no, this was my first time, so at this point, it's worked every time."

Zeno opened his eyes and coughed through the smoke.

"Zeno!" Daphne said.

"Oh hey, Daph, fancy meeting you here," he said, then coughed again.

Daphne smiled and shook her head.

"Zeno, are you hurt?" Augustine said.

"No, boss, I'm good, I think," Zeno said. "My ears are ringing, and I feel like I got hit in the face by something, but I'm good."

Alex hid his hand behind his back.

A comforting stream of relief washed over me. Both of them were okay.

Zeno pushed himself a little more upright and squinted through the haze.

"Did you ask Gina to help with this?" he said, motioning to the air. Augustine shook his head. "Well, come on, Gina!" Zeno said. "Help us out, girl!"

Almost immediately, what sounded like an old AC unit turned on. The haze began to clear. Alex reached out and helped Zeno to his feet.

"Did you see who did this?" Augustine asked.

Zeno rubbed his face where Alex had slapped him. "No, I didn't see anything, boss."

As the haze cleared, I looked around. Graffiti covered the walls around the hole the explosion had made.

Turn Victor Wells in.

The message was repeated a dozen different ways a hundred times over, but there was something new scrawled across the wall beside the hole in deep, blood-red text, bigger than everything else.

FINAL WARNING.

A hot, sticky feeling settled over me. Daphne and Zeno could have been killed. All because of me. I couldn't bear to think of what the locals would do next.

Kratos came back into view at a brisk jog, his black coat fluttering behind him. His eyes darted from the wall to me, and to everyone else. "There was no one to be found," he said. "The streets were empty."

I couldn't meet anyone's eyes.

This was all my fault.

35

I helped support Zeno as Augustine led a shaky Daphne back inside, down the stairs, and into the room behind the stage. I sat Zeno down next to Daphne while Kratos did a more thorough inspection of their injuries. They both appeared to be a little dazed. Zeno looked over and reached for Daphne's hand. She took it.

A jolt ran through me, but after reading their texts, I shouldn't have been surprised. Of course Zeno still had feelings for her, and how could he not? She probably still had feelings for him too.

I pushed the thoughts from my mind. I was just glad that no one was seriously hurt. They were lucky. Zeno and Daphne had come out of it remarkably unscathed, except for Zeno's rectangular afro, which now had a chunk missing.

"No, it's okay," Daphne said to Kratos. "I'm fine. I've had worse in saber fights."

Kratos turned his focus to Zeno, and Daphne continued to speak. "It's no coincidence this happened right after the reward was announced."

"And genetic modification as a prize to Sinisters?" Augustine said. "It's ludicrous!" He ran a hand through his hair and began to pace around the room.

"From what I understand," Kratos said, looking up from examining Zeno, "the science is close. There's talk that Dr. Rosewood is on the verge of a breakthrough. And Zeno, everything looks good."

"What do you mean, 'everything looks good'?" He pointed to his afro. "Eight months! *Eight* months!" He paused and then winked at me. It didn't make me feel better.

"I don't believe a word of it," Augustine said with a wave of his hand. He continued to pace. "It's just a ploy to get Victor captured or killed."

I watched Augustine walk back and forth. I knew he was mad about the announcement, but I didn't really care. My friends, the only people I had left, Daphne...I put them in danger. They could have died.

"Look," I said, "we can't do this again."

Augustine stopped pacing and turned to face me. The others did the same.

"Zeno and Daphne could have been killed," I continued. "Any of you could have. They're after me, not you."

Silence filled the room. I stood there, uncomfortable, but I met their gazes. I couldn't let them get hurt or die because of me. The Left Hand could strike at any moment. Someone else from the government could show up at any time. And now, apparently, any Sinister who wanted that reward could harm any one of us anywhere in the Heights.

"We're not giving up on this because it's dangerous." Daphne crossed her arms. "We live in the Heights—we're used to danger here."

"Yeah," Alex said, "and it's not like it'll be like this forever. The biokey expires in three days, right? After that, who knows?"

Daphne threw a glare Alex's way. He misinterpreted it and smiled back. She rolled her eyes.

"Alex has a point," Augustine said. "In three days' time, this could all be over."

"Except that we have no idea where this other office is," Daphne said.

"Actually, we do," I said, but without enthusiasm. "I talked to Grandfather. Avardi was referring to the Ixlir Building."

Alex let out a low whistle. Augustine rubbed at the stubble on his cheeks and chin.

I knew he was contemplating the Capital. I was sure he was more familiar with the place better than I was, but from what I knew, it was impenetrable. Walls, scanners, police, people, cameras. Augustine's face grew more grave in the silence.

Zeno set his glasses down on the table and rubbed his eyes. "So Kratos, tell me some good news, my man. Is there a way in?"

"No way," I answered for him. "You guys have been there. Even Nobles go through extra security checks. Not to mention we've got to actually get into the Capital district first."

Everyone grew quiet and solemn. They knew I was right. We were talking about breaking into the Capital, the one place where no Sinister had ever stepped. The people in the room with me were smart and talented, but there were some things that just couldn't be done. Not to mention, was it worth it, risking their lives on something that would most likely fail?

"Unfortunately, I agree with Victor," Kratos said. "I don't know of any way to get you inside undetected. Perhaps Alex could come, but without the biokey, our search would be futile."

If he didn't know how to get us in, what could we do? What could I do? I itched at my arm, the biokey tingling in response. Three days.

Three days and the biokey would expire. I looked at Zeno's battered afro and the fresh cuts and bruises scattered over Daphne's arms and face. Between the Left Hand and the locals, who knew how much longer we would last?

"All right," Alex said, clapping his hands and rubbing them together. "How are we gonna break into the Capital?"

His words were met with silence.

"No Sinister has ever broken into the Capital," Kratos said.

"What about when Senator Supart and Victor were Marked? They did it then," Alex said. "Look, if the Left Hand can do it, so can we."

"You know what, bro?" Zeno said. "That's probably the worst slogan I've ever heard, but I'm with you." He smiled. "Let's do it. Everybody in?"

"No!" I said. "Zeno, Daphne—you both could have died today. Alex, that could have been you. Heck, you could have died earlier today on the train. I'm not letting anyone else get hurt because of me."

"So you want to give up?" Augustine asked.

"We're dealing with the Left Hand!" I said. "They don't care who lives and who dies. The rest of the government is after me, and now every Sinister in the Heights is probably on the lookout too. And who knows what they'll do next?"

Did they not get it? The task in front of us was hopeless, and no one needed to get hurt because of me. No one needed to die.

"Look, man, other than this ringing in my ears, I'm cool," Zeno said. "And I was kidding earlier about my hair. It was time to take a little off the top. And the sides." Zeno pushed himself out of his chair and approached me. "We're good, man." He held out a fist. Reluctantly, I knocked knuckles with him.

"Me too, Victor," Daphne said. "We're not going to let you do this alone."

Her words almost made me reconsider, but the image of her and Zeno holding hands brought me back to reality.

"I suggest we start planning," Kratos said. "We don't have a lot of time to execute this. And I can promise you"—he turned to me—"no one will be dying while I'm here."

I looked down at the ground. All my life I had tried to be Noble, I had tried to be good. One thing the saber fights had taught me was that you fought your own battles. No one could fight them for you. And this was my fight, not theirs. Kratos was right—no one was dying while he was around.

The streets were deserted, but that was to be expected. It was night. I shivered beneath my jacket and pulled it tighter around me, picking up my pace as I did so.

We had spent the remainder of the evening hypothesizing ways to break into the Capital. Time was running out and things were looking bleak.

I checked over my shoulder. No one had followed me. I'd already checked several times. Not that it would have done them any good. I'd made up my mind.

I arrived at an intersection. Everything was black. Even the street-lights were out. But soon I'd reach the Innerbelt and cross it. Ten more minutes and I'd be in the hands of a Noble officer. Ten more minutes and my friends would be safe.

A light flickered on in one of the buildings, and I started. A man stood there, watching me. He was tall and well dressed. He looked like... *No,* I thought guiltily, *it can't be.* It couldn't be the Chairman. I rubbed my eyes and forced the thought out. I looked at the window again; the man had disappeared. My mind was tricking me. Fear of what I was about to do was playing games with my mind.

I thought back to my conversation with Grandfather. What would he think of what I was doing? When we were talking, I had no intention of turning myself in, but that was before my friends had almost been killed. I had abandoned Daphne once. I wouldn't be responsible for her death. I wouldn't be responsible for any of their deaths.

I walked on. The buildings were old here. Fire escapes dotted the sides of most of them. Broken and boarded-up windows abounded. Trash lay still in the calm night.

And then a worried yell pierced the cool air.

"Lucy!"

A small girl no older than six ran out into the street, leaving an open doorway that scattered dim golden light onto the pavement. She stopped when she saw me. Enough light shone from her house that I could see her face. Large brown eyes and long brown hair, like a miniature Daphne.

I could see it now. Other than location, she was indistinguishable from a Noble child of the same age. She was maybe a little dirtier and could stand to gain a few pounds, but she wasn't crazy or malnourished like the Noble news would lead you to believe. Daphne was right. She looked just as innocent, just as pure as any other child.

A silhouette of a woman hobbled into the doorway. In one hand she held a cane. With her other hand, she braced herself on the door. She must have had an injury to need something like that, an injury that couldn't be fixed in the Heights.

"Lucy, come back inside!" the woman yelled. But the little girl didn't listen. She continued to stare at me. I could tell the woman in the doorway was getting anxious, but she couldn't collect her daughter on her own, not without help.

A soft mechanical whirring met my ears, something familiar, but I couldn't quite place it. What was it?

The little girl continued to stare, as if she recognized me but wasn't sure why. She'd probably seen my face on the news.

"Lucy, come inside, now!"

The whirring became louder. Where was it coming from?

The mother's tone changed from impatience to panic. "Lucy!!"

I turned, and my heart almost stopped. I knew where I recognized the sound from.

"Sweeper, Lucy! Run! Run to me!"

The great mechanical beast came into view behind me, metal arms scrutinizing the street, snatching up every loose piece of matter. And I would be next if I didn't move.

The fire escapes. If I could get up one and get inside, I'd be safe.

I bolted for the hanging metal ladder, leaving the little girl standing motionless in the street.

It felt like déjà vu. The last person I had left in the street had been a man, a liar, a criminal. Daphne had said that the Chairman deserved to be swept away. But this little girl didn't deserve it. She was none of those things. She was just a child.

"Lucy, run!"

The sweeper continued, its metal arms reaching, cleaning up each piece of garbage. And when it got to the little girl, she would be considered garbage too.

Come on, move! I thought.

But she didn't. The girl's mother took a stumbling step forward and cried out.

I changed directions and sprinted toward the girl.

The sweeper was close, too close.

I scooped up the little girl, running toward the open door.

A long metal arm extended, reaching for me and the little girl in my arms. The mother had dropped her cane, both arms open to receive her daughter, but we weren't going to make it. The arm shot through the air, moving ever closer with electronically guided precision.

A thousand thoughts flew through my mind.

This was it, this was the end.

I would never have the chance to save my friends.

I stared into the terrified eyes of the little girl's mother.

I could at least save one life.

With all the strength I possessed, I threw the little girl to her mother. The viselike grip of the sweeper closed around my midsection as Lucy sailed through the air into her mother's arms.

And then my forward motion stopped.

The air was forced out of my lungs, and the sweeper jerked me backwards. The door to the house closed, leaving the moon as the only source of light, most likely the last light I'd ever see.

A dark shadow passed over me, and a collection of gray beads rained down from above.

Kratos, his trench coat billowing, soared over my head and landed just behind me on the retracting metal arm. A blast of blue light lit up the surrounding street, and the metal pincer of the sweeper opened, dropping me onto the ground. The arm retracted, and the sweeper turned and went back the way it had come.

I lay on the pavement, gasping for breath, fresh road rash on my arms and bruises on my back. A peculiar scent filled the air. Bleach. Alex had been right after all.

Kratos stood over me.

"Thanks," I coughed.

Kratos reached out his hand and helped me to my feet.

"What are you doing here?" I said. "And how'd you make the sweeper go away?"

"One of the perks of being me," he replied, then regarded me in silence for a moment. "I saw what you did back there. Saving that Sinister girl."

"There was a sweeper coming after her." I took a step to pass Kratos. "And not that I'm not grateful, but what are you doing here?"

Until I turned myself in, the others wouldn't be safe.

"Why did you do it?" he asked, stepping in front of me.

"Do what?" I tried to go around him again, but he cut me off.

"Save the Sinister girl."

I stopped trying to get past him and stood my ground. "I couldn't just let her die. She's just a kid! Anyone would have done the same."

"No," Kratos said quietly. "No, they wouldn't."

I peered up the street. The Innerbelt had to be close.

"I followed you," he added. "You were quite stealthy."

"Well thanks for saving me from the sweeper, but there's somewhere I need to be."

"In a government building?"

I resumed walking. As much as I hated the thought of it, yes, that was exactly where I needed to be. It was the only way they'd all be safe. I wouldn't have their blood on my hands.

"My job is justice, Victor. And this is not justice."

I stopped walking. The air was still. The night was dark. Dawn didn't bring with it the promise of new light or hope. Did he not understand? It wasn't about justice, it was about keeping the rest of them safe.

"It's the best alternative we have," I said.

"Giving up is not an alternative," he said quietly.

"I'm not giving up!" I yelled. "Don't you get it? My life for all of yours."

"So you think you display courage?" he said.

"Do you think this is easy for me? I'm accepting my fate so the rest of you don't die, so yes, I'm displaying courage."

"Then you are a fool." His words were quick and sharp.

I glared at him for a moment before responding, collecting my emotions, trying to rein in my frustration. "And why am I a fool?" I asked.

"Because this isn't about you," he said. "It never was. Your friends don't want to be saved; they want things to change. Outing the Left Hand, figuring out who is changing DNA readouts—that is what will cause change, not this."

I paused to consider his words. If by some miracle I could get into the Ixlir Building, unlock the safe, and get back out of the Capital alive, then maybe, just maybe, the Pendletons would no longer be outcasts. Maybe I wouldn't be an outcast.

"So what," I said, "I'm supposed to drag them along, and if they're captured or killed, then *oh well*?"

"You're rationalizing."

"What, that my life isn't worth the four of theirs?" I said.

"Yes."

I looked at him in disbelief.

"What you did tonight, saving that girl, that was courageous. That's what Daphne wants. That's what Augustine has been fighting for. Change. Most Nobles wouldn't think that child was worth saving. They wouldn't have risked their lives like you did."

"And a lot of good it will do her, growing up in this place." I kicked at the ground.

"Then fight for something better," he said. "Don't give up."

I had seen and learned much since I had been Marked. DNA status didn't matter. Nobles, Sinisters—we were all just people. We didn't need to be divided and segregated. We didn't need to hate each other. Could I really have a hand in changing all of that?

I regarded Kratos. He stood before me, calm and immovable, an adversary turned ally.

"Okay," I said. "If we're going to do this, we need a plan."

"Then come with me. We need all the help we can get."

36

"This is Kelly Straunton bringing you the top headlines for the day: 'The Feud Continues' and 'Do Train Cars Float?'

"Dr. Rosewood posted some harsh words for President Keltan regarding his handling of those carrying TɪɪD and Sinisters in general. Perhaps after yesterday's events, he'll change his tune.

"It would appear that the Left Hand has continuing interest in the recently deceased Senator Supart. Yesterday morning, the senator's personal train car was blown off the tracks. And yes, train cars do float, as was reported by those who arrived on the scene after it happened. No police were present due to the toppling of a nearby building by a group known as 'The Bombers.' Authorities are still working out the details of what exactly happened..."

Our failed attempt to find Avardi's information on the Left Hand was all over the news. Conspicuously absent from the news, however, was the explosion that could have killed Daphne and Zeno. I wondered how often tragedies in the Heights passed unnoticed by Nobles. Probably far too often. I tuned out the news and focused.

Daphne and I were locked in a fierce sparring match. I was surprised that she wanted to fight after the explosion yesterday, but this was our fourth match of the morning. I enjoyed it, but not as much as I would have two days ago. For some reason, I couldn't get the idea of her and Zeno holding hands out of my mind. I parried and jumped backwards, doing my best to catch her off balance, but our matches were merely a distraction.

I wanted to forget about what I had almost done last night. I owed Kratos a debt I wasn't sure I could repay. And unfortunately, he had left earlier this morning without giving me the opportunity to speak with him. I assumed he'd be back, but there was no telling when. We were hurting without his expertise.

We still hadn't figured out a way to get into the Capital.

Daphne and I clashed blades, sparks flying on contact. She insisted that we fight with electrified blades—something about it not being any fun unless there was some risk involved.

Augustine and Zeno had sequestered themselves in separate rooms, each brainstorming possible solutions to our problems. Meanwhile, Alex was seated at a table across from Daphne and me, moaning about the grim news playing on the screen.

"What's going on with the world?" he lamented. "Why is everybody dying?"

I let up my guard for a moment, and my saber clattered across the floor.

"Ha!" Daphne said. "That makes it two-two."

"Yeah, yeah," I said over my shoulder as I walked to the table. "What did you say, Alex? Someone else died?"

"The other two senators that got Marked."

"Both of them?" Daphne asked. "Already?" She de-electrified her saber and dropped it on the table.

A door burst open somewhere down the hall, and footsteps barreled toward us. "Augustine!" Zeno skidded through the doorway and stopped in front of us. His eyes were ablaze, and he wore that crazed smile again. The chunk that was missing from his afro only intensified his vibe. "Where's he at?"

"Not sure. His office, maybe," Daphne said.

"Thanks!" He turned on his heels and ran out.

"Wait, what did you figure out?" Daphne called after him.

"Later!"

She slumped into her chair, but I knew if it was anything important, we'd find out soon enough.

"Hey, I was going to ask you," I said, "those huge tracks we passed the other day. Where do they go? Ville?"

"As far as I know," Daphne said.

Alex looked up, his eyes like twin full moons. "Huge tracks going *south*?"

"Yep." I braced myself for one of his wild theories.

"Oh man," Alex said, "you should hear the stuff people are saying about Ville." He looked back and forth between us with great intensity.

"Any of it real?" Daphne raised an eyebrow.

"Probably not." Alex let his head droop.

"Have you ever been?" I asked, turning to Daphne.

"To Ville?" Daphne asked.

"Yeah."

"Well, you know, I spend the summers there," she said. "They've got a nice vacation scene."

"Wait, really?" Alex said, suddenly excited again.

"No, not really! I've been trying to figure out who changed our DNA readouts. I don't care about what's going on down there."

I had been hoping for more information, but it sounded like she knew just as little as I did. As far as I could tell, the leadership of Ville didn't get involved in our city for good or for bad, and hadn't in years.

We sat in silence for the next several minutes. My arm tingled as another hour passed. I was becoming more and more accustomed to the feeling, but this morning it felt especially sensitive, almost like the key knew as well as I did that time was short.

The message from yesterday was gone, and the usual series of silver blobs had replaced it. Two days, seven hours, fifty-nine minutes, and a handful of seconds.

I looked up to see Daphne staring at me. Alex had let his head drop onto the table. I thought I saw a puddle of drool forming around the corner of his mouth. Daphne crinkled her nose in disgust. We both turned to look when the back doors burst open, and a bald man in a well-tailored navy and orange suit strolled in.

"Well, would you look at that! My TɪɪD carrying friend Victor Wells in the flesh. Neither government nor Bounty Hunter has been able to catch you yet."

Tyrann Kane strode across the room toward us, a smile on his face.

"Who is that...?" Alex mumbled, pushing himself up.

"Tyrann Kane," I said softly.

Most of the color left Alex's face.

"What, no cronies with you today?" Daphne asked coolly.

"Cronies? I think you mistake the intentions of my friends. And no, no friends today, only family."

With that, Pria and Printh walked through the door. Daphne stiffened. Pria did the same, but then smiled at me. She was pretty when she wasn't pouting to her father or glaring at someone. I smiled back. After what Daphne had said about her, I figured she could use it.

Pria wore traditional loud colors, a loose, bright blue shirt and silver pants with streaks of gold on them, whereas Printh looked as gothic as ever. If not for the strand of pink and her pale skin, you could have mistaken her for a shadow.

Dax strode through the open doors a moment later.

"I thought you said 'only family,'" Daphne said.

"Oh, Dax? He qualifies," Tyrann said with a dismissive wave of the hand. "Men like him are hard to come by and just as good as family."

Dax inclined his head respectfully toward us as he came to a standstill a few feet behind Tyrann, but remained silent.

"Where is the good Mr. Pendleton?" Tyrann inquired, casting his eyes around the room. "I wanted to congratulate him on your handiwork from yesterday. Blowing a Noble car off the tracks?" He turned to me. "Nice work. It's only too bad there were no casualties. It would have been nice to see a little Noble blood in the lake."

None of us responded. Dax looked at the ground. Pria looked at the ceiling. Tyrann didn't seem to notice the awkward silence he had created. Or maybe he enjoyed it.

"But surely one of you could help me out. I've been trying to reach Augustine for hours now. I believe we have an account to settle."

"I don't know where he's at," Daphne said. "Looks like you'll just have to wait."

Alex turned completely white at this. He looked like he'd rather have been anywhere else—a pit of snakes, the dark side of the moon. My hands reflexively balled into fists.

"That sounds reasonable. I'm sure my daughters wouldn't mind the extra company."

Pria looked at Alex and Daphne like she definitely did mind, but Printh took the chair next to Alex, stoic as ever. Tyrann took the seat closest to me.

"Coming to our side bit by bit, I see," Tyrann said.

"What makes you say that?" I said, taken aback.

"That's an interesting mark on your arm." Tyrann nodded at the series of silver circles. "I'm not quite sure I've seen anything like that before."

I hastily pulled my glove back on. "It's a new kind of fluid tattoo," I said, hoping he wasn't familiar with them. It looked nothing like a fluid tattoo.

"Ah, wonderful!" he said, a mischievous smile stretching across his face. "I seem to recall hearing that Qinsari got something similar just before his act of heroism at the hospital. Tell me, who did the tattoo, Shranokof or Debue?"

Of course he knew about them.

"We, uh, kept our names out of it," I said, thinking fast. Daphne gave me a nervous glance. Dax remained stoic in the background.

"A wise move, especially for someone of your stature." Tyrann flicked an oily smile my way. "Though I do believe that I could be of great service to you with whatever you're planning. And if sending a Noble train car off the rails was act one, I can't wait to see what comes next!"

"All right, I'm going to go find my father," Daphne said.

"How terribly kind of you," he said.

"Yes, I don't want to be here any longer than I absolutely have to." Pria pouted.

"Well, in that case," Daphne said, sitting back down and folding her arms. Pria's eyes clouded with malice. Tyrann sat leisurely, absentmindedly staring off into space. Though I had the feeling that nothing he did was truly absentminded.

I tried to catch Daphne's eye, but her attention was on the ceiling, making certain Pria wasn't in her line of sight. Pria stared determinedly at her fingernails. But Alex was most uncomfortable of all. Printh sat nonchalantly next to him. I could tell he was trying his best to figure out how to put more space between the two of them without falling off his chair.

Fortunately, he was saved by Augustine's timely entrance.

Tyrann jumped to his feet. "You have impeccable timing, old friend! I have a few other items of business to attend to today, but I do believe it is time we settle a few things."

Augustine looked a little frazzled, but not defeated. Something had changed over the past couple of days, or maybe since Zeno's visit a few minutes ago, and it showed in his eyes.

"Is that so?" Augustine said. "Forgive me, but it will have to wait for another time."

"Oh?" Tyrann kept his grin plastered on his face, but his eyes turned cold.

"Yes. There are more pressing matters. And I'd like your help."

"And what could be so important as to take precedence over my business dealings?"

"The Left Hand. We're going to stop them."

"And why would I want them stopped?" Tyrann said with a frown. "They don't target Sinisters, they target Nobles. You know I don't like Nobles, Aug."

Alex fell off his chair.

"You don't have to help us stop them," Augustine said, "but that's what we're going to do. And we're going to have to be inside the Capital to do it."

"Oh," Tyrann said, his frown changing to a surprised smile. "I assume this was Mr. Wells's idea? Knock off the Left Hand so that you can be number one?" He nodded to me appreciatively. "A bold choice, Mr. Wells."

Zeno burst through the back doors.

"Boom!" he said, holding what looked like a drawer of junk as he rushed into the room. "I figured it out!" He paused when he caught sight of Tyrann and the rest of us staring at him. He shoved what appeared to be a few fleshy fingers back into his box. "What are you doing here?"

"Well, Mr. Zeno, ol' Aug here was just telling me about your need to get into the Capital," Tyrann said.

"Something that you've wanted to do for years," Augustine added.

"Oh, man!" Zeno smacked his hand against his forehead, sending a quiver up his afro. "I can't believe I didn't think of this before, but unless I'm way off about your ongoing project near the northern tracks, which I'm not, you can get us in."

"You sound so certain, Mr. Zeno. Such faith in me." He paused to allow another oily smile to seep across his features. "I admit it feels good."

"So you can do it?" I asked.

"Mr. Zeno is very perceptive," Tyrann said, shaking a finger at him. "You've managed to uncover one of my secrets, a work in progress for many years, something I'm very—"

"Get to it, Tyrann," Augustine said. "Can you, or can you not?"

Tyrann raised his eyebrows in surprise. Perhaps we were seeing a bit more of Augustine the senator than the man I'd met when I first arrived. Tyrann seemed to be impressed as well.

"I have effectively opened the door to the Capital," Tyrann said, "but I cannot pass through. Once I step foot inside..." He paused. "You know how Nobles are—alarms, sensors, cameras—I have no way to shut them off. However, if there was a way to do that..."

"Then we could get Victor inside the Capital without any trouble," Zeno finished.

"Get *Victor* into the Capital?" Tyrann turned to me. "A one-man job from the inside? When were you going to let me in on this little secret of yours?"

I didn't reply.

"Ah, yes. You play things close to the vest. I understand. Qinsari could have learned much from you. If he hadn't told everyone he talked to what his plans were, maybe he would have been able to take a few more Noble lives."

"Can you help or not, Tyrann?" Augustine said.

"Help get a TнD carrier inside the Capital? Absolutely. Assuming, of course, that Mr. Zeno will offer his services. I too will require access to the Capital."

"Look, as long as innocent people aren't hurt an—"

"Of course, of course, Mr. Zeno," Tyrann said, holding up a hand. "No innocent people will be harmed. I'm not a monster."

Daphne gave him an uncensored look of cynicism. Zeno looked to Augustine, who nodded.

"Then I'll do it," Zeno said.

"Excellent. This could be very beneficial. Very beneficial indeed. Of course, I mean mutually beneficial." Tyrann smiled. "Now, is there a timetable we are working with?"

"Two days," I said.

Tyrann raised his eyebrows in surprise, but not alarm. "Interesting. Yes, I think this should work quite nicely."

"We have a deal then?" Augustine said, extending his hand.

"To be absolutely clear, I will only offer a way in and out," Tyrann said. "No extra help inside the Capital, though I doubt you'll need it with Mr. Wells here. Agreed?"

"Agreed."

Tyrann and Augustine shook hands.

Augustine's face became more determined.

Tyrann adopted an even bigger smile than before. "Then I suggest we get started. My other business can wait. We're breaking into the Capital!"

37

"But I've been missing for three days," Alex said, looking up from his now spotless lunch plate. I sat next to him, still working on my food. Now that we had a way in, the plan was coming together quickly. Tyrann had left a while ago after establishing the necessary details for his part of the deal.

"Alex, don't worry about it, man," Zeno said. "We tested your DNA earlier this morning, and it's fine."

"That's not what I'm worried about," Alex said. "I'm talking backstory!"

"What about your father?" Daphne asked. "Isn't he worried about where you are?"

"No," Alex said matter-of-factly, "he's too busy in the senate. I left my ID card in my room at home just in case he decides to check in on me—which he won't. It hasn't been a week yet. That's usually about how long it takes him to check in."

The room fell silent for a moment, looks of pity coming from every angle, but Alex didn't seem to notice. It had been a fact of life for him as long as I'd known him. It was probably why we had become such good friends. He spent more time at my house than he did at his own. His father the senator—too busy doing good to spend time with his son.

Alex snatched a piece of fruit off my plate and popped it into his mouth. "I still think donuts are better," he said, chewing loudly, "but seriously, what do I say if someone asks me where I've been? I need a good backstory."

Kratos stepped forward. "You give them this." He handed Alex a slip of paper. "By the way, Zeno, the hologram projection works nicely." He had returned late last night and showed as much positive emotion about the plan as I had seen him show about anything.

"Come on, you old cynic," Zeno said. "I told you it was top notch. What did you expect?"

Alex peered at the paper Kratos had given him. "It just says 'Bounty Hunter.' Or at least I think it does." He squinted, turning the paper this way and that. "The penmanship is terrible."

Kratos growled out, "It matches about a hundred other autographs just like it that I gave out last night. Tell whoever asks that you were at the Followers convention."

"That's where you went?" I asked. "To sign autographs?"

"Yes, I still have other duties to attend to. So as not to appear suspicious, I fulfilled my obligations."

Alex let out a pitiful moan worthy of a dying dog and slumped onto the table. "That was yesterday? I was planning on going to that!"

"You've spent multiple days with him, you've got his autograph, and you're mad about missing a convention?" Daphne asked.

"Yeah, well, no, but...a little bit?" Alex looked bashful. "It's different. It's like I'm there with my people, you know? *My* people."

"You mean nerds?" Daphne asked, not bothering to mask her smile.

"Hey, you're coming with me for the first part, remember? Plus, look at Zeno and Dr. Rosewood. Nerds make the world go round, right, Zeno?"

Zeno's now shorter but perfectly manicured afro whipped around. "Easy, bro, I'm not a nerd. High-class intellectual with superbomb style and killer ideas, maybe," he said indignantly. "And I don't know if Rosewood is the best role model. She's like a thousand, man."

"But she doesn't look it, right? That's her deal, run the Great Experiment and live an extra hundred years?"

Kratos shifted his weight from his right foot to his left. Was that his version of fidgeting?

"I agree with Zeno," Augustine said, drawing my gaze away from Kratos, "but the question is this, Alex. For anyone who knows you, will that story work?"

Alex let out a sigh. "Yes, it'll work."

"And are we absolutely certain I have to go with him?" Daphne asked.

"Yes, Daphne," Augustine said, "it makes more sense this way."

"I still think Kratos would do a better job persuading them," Daphne said. "Plus, I have a few other things that need to be done too."

"Right," I said, "but not until later. And you'll be plenty persuasive, trust me."

Alex nodded vigorously.

Daphne glared.

I checked the clock. "Speaking of, it's probably time for you guys to get going."

"Now?" Alex said.

"Yes," Augustine answered. "In fact, the sooner the better."

Alex looked around, uncertain. "And how do you want me to get there exactly? Even though I've been here for a few days, I have no idea where we are."

"As you are very aware," Augustine said, motioning to his right, "Dax will take you where you need to go." At his words, Dax appeared alone in the doorway.

"Do I *have* to go with him?" Alex nodded toward the door. Augustine gave him a flat stare. Alex lowered his voice. "We've, uh, got a history."

Augustine leaned in. "And what history is that?"

"A history of him being huge and me being terrified."

"I think you'll find Dax's presence to be an advantage. Off you go. Daphne, don't forget your—"

"Yes, my glove. I've got it."

She reached into her bag and pulled out what looked like a very thin shell of a human hand. I had a similar one in my bag. Zeno had explained it to me earlier. There was a way to beat the scanners, and it was fairly simple, assuming you could get your hands on some Noble blood, which, unsurprisingly, Daphne could do. However, this time she wouldn't be using just *any* Noble blood. She'd be using mine.

"And you might want this," Zeno said, tossing a floppy piece of silicone through the air.

"Thanks." Daphne deftly caught the mask and placed it and her glove back into her bag, along with the dozen other gloves that were in there. "Come on, Alex," she said with a sigh as she headed toward the door. "Let's go."

Alex took a deep breath and grabbed the basket of treats, pastries, and fruits off the table and headed over to join them.

"Right, I'll get you lot to where you need to be." Dax nodded at Augustine, his deep British voice carrying through the room. "After Victor gets inside the Capital, you'll be on your own. I've got business to attend to elsewhere, but I'll meet up with Daphne on the outside to make sure everyone gets out all right."

I had no idea what Dax's business was, but I assumed it had to do with whatever Tyrann was going to do inside the Capital. I wasn't sure I wanted to know what that was.

"If anything suspicious happens, I'll be in touch," Dax said.

"Thanks, Dax, we appreciate it," Augustine said.

Dax nodded. Alex didn't look any happier about the arrangement. And he became even less so as he tried to sneak a piece of food from the basket. Dax swatted his hand away with blinding speed.

"Ouch!"

"Shame on you. Those are for a grieving family."

"No, they're so we can kidnap their son." Alex tried again.

Dax slapped his hand away once more. "Lucky for you, Daphne

doesn't have her saber close by, or I'd paralyze your hand right now. However"—Dax paused and looked down at Alex from his great height—"there are other ways to paralyze a man's hand."

Alex quickly shoved his hands in his pockets. Dax caught my eye and winked, the corner of his mouth twitching. I smiled back at him. It was odd. He felt a lot more like one of us than one of Tyrann's men.

"All right then, let's go," Dax said.

Daphne waved at me, which I halfheartedly returned as she headed out the door. Every time I saw her since I read Zeno's text, an image of Zeno and Daphne holding hands popped into my mind. I still liked her, but it was probably better to give her and Zeno some space.

After a stern look from Dax, Alex obediently followed him out the door, probably more out of fear than anything.

Kratos made to stand. "I must be going."

"So soon?" Augustine asked.

"I've stayed too long already."

"Ah, yes," Zeno said knowingly. "Bounty Hunter duties—more photoshoots and conventions."

Kratos let out a grumbling sound, as if the memory of the previous night caused him physical pain. He turned to me. "Before I go, could I have a word?"

"Uh, sure," I said, a little surprised.

I followed Kratos's sweeping black cloak out of the room and into the hallway. He stopped and removed his mask, for which I was thankful. He had started taking it off every once in a while when he was around us. I was getting more used to his real face, but it still surprised me every time his golden hair was exposed.

"Do you remember what I told you in the car the day that you were Marked?" he said, piercing me with eyes that seemed weighed down.

"Yeah," I said, taken slightly aback, "you told me how the Left Hand had never been beaten—"

"But," he interrupted.

"But..." I reached back in time to that moment. "It was something about, fighting for exceptions?"

"Yes."

I looked at him questioningly, but didn't speak. I knew there was a point to this. Kratos was a lot like Freddy. He didn't take superfluous actions, even in speech. Everything had a purpose.

"Our city is at war. I know you've heard of the war between us and other cities, but that's just the beginning. Tensions between Nobles and Sinisters run high. The Left Hand torments us with an unknown agenda. The Great Experiment is almost complete. So much contention, so much turmoil. I see it all." He paused for a moment, and I thought I was beginning to understand the look in his eyes.

He continued, "We have to believe that good can overcome evil. We have to hope for better things to come. If not, we have no reason to fight. No one has ever survived against the Left Hand as long as you have. Don't lose hope. You are the exception we're all fighting for."

I stayed silent and nodded. He nodded in return. With a swish of his coat, he strode off down the hall and disappeared around the corner.

I stood there alone, mulling over Kratos's words. *Don't lose hope.* The flame in my chest remained alight. I stoked it. I thought about Zeno and Augustine in the other room, and Dax, Daphne, and Alex on their way to the Flats.

A Marked man, a couple of traitor Nobles, and a group of Sinisters, I labeled everyone in my head. *We just might have what it takes.*

38

I sat on the edge of the bed in my room. The final details of planning had ended an hour or so earlier. Tomorrow morning, Jeffry Supart and his mom Lora would be going to the Ixlir Building to see Avardi's memorial. I would be going too and starting my search there. The memorial visit was my way in.

Kratos's words still played through my mind, and I couldn't help but hope this would be my last night sleeping here. I looked up as my door squeaked open and caught sight of a tall block of hair and glasses.

"Alex just dropped off the package," Zeno said. "Wanna see how it all comes together?"

"Sure," I said, grateful for the interruption. Sleep wasn't going to come easy tonight, and I was eager to see part of the plan in action.

I slid off the bed and followed Zeno down the wide corridors that ran through the building like a maze. I felt a little uncomfortable that I had read his and Daphne's texts, and the silence was killing me. Not to mention the image in my mind of him and her holding hands that I couldn't seem to shake.

"Hey, I was going to ask you a question about my gloves," I said, breaking the silence. Zeno glanced at me sideways. "The other day on the train after the Left Hand showed up, the gloves jolted me awake after I got stunned."

"Oh, yeah. Just a little safety feature I've been playing around with," he said. "I'm glad it worked. Your hands okay? Last time I tested them, the silicone turned to liquid."

"Yeah," I said slowly, "I think they're good." I glanced at my hands to double-check. I exhaled slowly.

Zeno chuckled and winked at me. "So, how are you holding up, my man?"

"A little nervous, but I feel good," I said.

"Good." He paused. "We're all fighting for you, bro. It'll work."

I looked at Zeno. His eyes were hard, but not in an angry or jaded way. They were resilient. He wasn't going to quit, and neither was I. It would work. It had to, as long as Tyrann didn't give us any trouble.

"Zeno, I've got a question for you."

"Anything, bro. Shoot."

"Why does Tyrann want to get into the Capital so badly? Do we need to be worried about him at all?"

We turned left down another corridor before he spoke.

"I'll be honest with you, bro, I'm a little unsure of Tyrann's agenda. He's been working on a way into the Capital for a while now, like, years. He's probably been waiting for an opportunity like this. But as far as him interfering with us, I don't think we have anything to worry about. I gotta think he'll be up to something nefarious while you're searching the Ixlir Building, but that's just something we're going to have to deal with, you know?"

"Yeah," I said, noticing the strained look on his face. I had forgotten that this whole undertaking weighed just as heavily on Zeno, Augustine, and Daphne as it did me.

"And here we are," Zeno said, ushering me into a smaller room filled with the faint blue glow of too many monitors.

On the biggest screen, I saw the freckled face of a teenager. Jeffry Supart, Avardi's son, picking out a pastry from the basket Alex and Dax had delivered.

"It looks like Alex did a good job," I said, moving closer. "And Dax kept him from eating all of the food."

"Yeah, the condolence basket worked great. The facial scans have already come in. We won't have to do anything tricky with your appearance, shoe lifts, stuff like that. You're built nearly identical. The mask is being printed now."

The soft whir of a machine in a nearby room caught my ear.

"Did Daphne leave with them?" I asked.

"No, she stayed behind."

I grinned. "She probably hated that."

"I am a hundred percent certain that is true," Zeno said, slightly distracted by the multitude of screens in the room, "but it's a good thing. I mean—and don't tell Daphne I said this—I know I'm a nerd, but Alex takes it to a whole new level." Zeno shook his head, and I knew he was thinking about the other Bounty Hunter Followers. "He was able to round up several of his, uh, friends after dropping the basket off. Daphne's had a bunch of time to persuade them and plan out her distraction for tomorrow."

I pictured the scene in my head: Daphne in a room full of boys all carrying inhalers and wearing glasses. I had to smile. And I was glad this wasn't the only thing she was doing. If it had been, I'm sure she would have gone crazy.

The image of her and Zeno popped back into my mind. Did they still have something going on, or were they really just friends? It had been eating at me all day. I needed to know.

"Zeno?" I said.

His gaze darted back and forth across the multitude of screens. His response was a little delayed. "Uh, yeah, bro, what's up?"

I wasn't sure quite how to phrase it, so I just let the words tumble out. "Do you and Daphne have a thing?" Zeno turned to me. "I mean, is there anything going on between you guys?" He continued to stare at me. He looked like he was fighting back an expression, I just wasn't sure which one, so I kept talking. "You know, like, romantically?"

"You read our texts, didn't you?"

I felt my face turn hot as guilt swelled up inside of me. "Yeah, I did. Man, I'm so sorry, I—"

"No sweat," Zeno said. "And to answer your, uh, well-posed question, you've got nothing to worry about, bro. A few months back, me and Daphne decided we were better as friends." His smile faded as he finished talking.

A strange feeling of relief flooded through me, like a stopped-up river that finally had an outlet. I wasn't sure what to say. Luckily, a beep sounded and saved me from the silence.

"It sounds like your mask is done," Zeno said. "Let's see what we've got."

I followed Zeno into an adjacent room. Inside of a glass container sat the finished product. A perfect facial replica of Jeffry Supart.

"Oh yeah, that came out nice," Zeno said, walking around the mask. "Yep, his own mother won't know the difference, well, unless you have to talk a lot."

"I can't talk?" I asked.

"I added some voice modulation tech in there, but it's not perfect. Passable, but not perfect. It might sound like he's got a cold if you talk too much."

"Gotcha." I stepped closer to examine the mask. The detail was incredible—the hair, the freckles. It was amazing, and a little creepy. "Zeno, this is awesome."

"You know that's right." He held out a fist and we bumped knuckles. "This is gonna work, bro—I can feel it."

I was nervous, but I hadn't been lying when I said I felt good. I was hopeful.

"Here, take this." Zeno reached into his pocket and pulled out an earbud.

"I thought we didn't need those until tomorrow?"

"This one is set to Daphne's frequency," he said, placing in my hand. "Just in case, you know, you guys want to chat."

"Thanks," I said, a little taken aback by the gesture.

"Don't mention it." He turned to the monitors. "But we've got an

early day tomorrow, so I'm gonna go catch a few Z's, and you probably should too."

I nodded and placed the earbud in my pocket.

He stood up straight and headed for the door.

"You know that goes in your ear, right?"

"Wha—oh, I mean, yeah."

Zeno winked at me. "Night, man. Good luck tomorrow."

"Thanks, you too."

Zeno left the room.

I pulled the earbud out of my pocket and placed it in my ear. No
sound came out of it, nor did I expect it to. It was late and we all
needed our rest for tomorrow.

I took one last look at the mask before leaving. The eyeholes were
noticeably blank and the cheeks were sunken in, but they wouldn't
be that way for long. In a few hours, I'd be wearing that mask.

39

I awoke with a start. I was alone in my room, but I heard voices. My hand flew to the saber concealed beneath a mountain of pillows, and I jumped out of bed, my feet landing softly on the thick carpet. Sleep had been fitful at best, but now I was wide awake. My eyes shot to the clock. It was barely midnight.

The Sinisters in the area had made it more than clear that I wasn't welcome. Had some of them broken in? Was everyone else okay?

I clicked the button that electrified the saber and made my way swiftly to the door, a series of sparks arcing across the blade partially lighting my way. And then I heard a voice again. It was saying my name.

"Victor!"

"Who's there?" I said evenly, brandishing my saber in front of me.

"Don't tell me you've picked up your saber and have decided to go all hero on us."

"Daphne?" I said, confused, looking around.

"Your earbud," she said, her voice taking on the tone of an eye roll.

I let my saber droop in front of me and de-electrified the blade, and my face started to burn. Thank goodness no one was here to see that. I brought my breathing back to normal, but even without an imminent threat, my heartbeat didn't want to slow down.

"I gathered," I said, trying to feign grogginess. I replaced the saber and sat down on the edge of the bed.

"Mm-hmm."

I smiled to myself. I was glad she had called. I wasn't sure if she would. Zeno had given me an earbud, the equivalent of his blessing, I guess. And now Daphne had called. Did it mean what I though it meant?

"So what are you doing up so late?" I asked, my heart continuing to beat faster than usual.

"Just getting everything ready for tomorrow."

"Your part or Alex's part?"

"My part. We finished Alex's hours ago."

"I'm not surprised," I said.

"And why's that?"

"Well," I said slowly, "because you had it easy."

"Easy?"

"Yeah, I mean, a pretty girl persuading a bunch of kids with glasses and inhalers—"

"Pretty?"

"Well, yeah," I said. "I think so. Everyone does. And I was thinking—"

"Victor—"

"I was thinking that I like you, and maybe after—"

"No, look, Victor," Daphne cut in. "We can't do this. Not right now, not with everything happening tomorrow."

The smile slid off my face like melting snow from a roof.

"We just need to be focused tomorrow," she said. "No distractions."

"Oh, okay."

So it was over before it even began.

"I don't mean to ruin everything, but it's for the best, isn't it?" she said, her voice strained.

"Um, yeah, I guess."

"So we're good?"

"Yeah, absolutely. We're good."

"Okay, good."

Silence.

"Well, good luck tomorrow," Daphne said.

"Yeah, you too," I replied, but the words were automatic.

"All right, good night."

"Night."

The line went dead. I sat on the edge of the bed, almost too stunned to sleep. What had just happened? It was like we were standing on opposite sides of a river, and the bridge had been taken out between us. Or more like Daphne had blown it up from her side.

How could I have been so stupid as to think that anything could go on between us while the Left Hand was after me? I could die at any time. The Sinistrali could show up tomorrow. I couldn't put her through that.

I let myself fall back onto the bed.

I understood what she was doing. No distractions. In a saber fight, distractions were equivalent to losing. However, she wouldn't have been a distraction. She would have been something to fight for.

I covered my eyes with my palms and dragged my fingers through my hair. I needed to sleep. I needed to prepare for tomorrow. I didn't need to worry about Daphne and our future, or even if there was a future. She was going to do her thing, and I was going to do mine. Tomorrow we were breaking into the Capital. Tomorrow we were going to expose the Left Hand. Then we could talk.

I closed my eyes and wished for sleep, but I couldn't stop my thoughts from coming. Why would Daphne do this? Why the night before? Why stop something before it began?

Those and a thousand other questions swirled around my mind until I finally succumbed to the less confusing unconsciousness of sleep.

40

"What incredible luck this turned out to be, wouldn't you agree, Mr. Wells? Only a week after going public and here we are, breaking into the Capital together. But I should have guessed, what with you carrying TɪɪD." Tyrann spoke almost in a singsong voice.

Luck was definitely not the word I would have used, not after last night, so I didn't reply. It was too early, there was too much at stake, and I disliked Tyrann too much to waste good, clean air on useless words. Especially in light of where we were going. Clean air was about to become a precious commodity.

"Daddy, you promised that the air would be clean down here, but I think I smell something."

Pria. For growing up in the Heights with her monster of a father, I wouldn't have thought she'd go to him with her complaints. Maybe she thought she had to make up for Printh's perpetual silence.

Tyrann stuck his nose into the air and sniffed in one long drag.

"Ah, it's just the stench of the Nobles, my dear. Or perhaps you're catching the Noble residue of Mr. Wells's disguise. He's trying so hard to be Noble this morning." Tyrann paused and turned to me. "The depths you go to in your subterfuge are, dare I say it, inspiring!"

The rest of us kept quiet. Anything that inspired Tyrann Kane was a bad thing in my book. But he did have a point. I was trying hard to be a Noble, very hard. Today I'd dressed as a normal kid would if they were going to school. My clothes were pressed, my hair was combed, but I had one extra accessory—a mask.

We passed a puddle of water on the ground. I caught a glimpse of myself on its still surface.

I stared into the face of Jeffry Supart. *Weird.*

A voice sounded in my ear. "Victor, can you spray some of my stuff around Pria's head so we don't have to listen to the daddy-daughter commentary all morning? It's murder on the ears, bro." We all wore one of Zeno's earbuds, but apparently he could decide which of us he wanted to talk to.

I smiled to myself but didn't answer. I would have liked to spray some around my own ears. Tyrann was in a better mood than I had ever seen him, which did nothing to improve his already unbearable attitude.

"Nobles beware, we're almost there!" he said cheerfully.

"What happened to not hurting anyone?" I asked.

"I promised Zeno no physical harm would be done," Tyrann said with a smile. "And I intend to keep that promise."

I wasn't so sure, but we were in too deep to turn back now.

I looked back at Augustine, who was bringing up the rear of our procession. Apparently he hadn't heard Tyrann's latest little rhyme. Or he had decided not to hear it. Instead, he had his head back and eyes up, taking in our surroundings.

It was a strange place that we found ourselves in, and quiet too. Ours were the only footsteps I could hear, broken only by the occasional faint whoosh of the train as it flew by in the distance. We were in the northernmost section of the Heights. It was a ghost town.

I breathed in deep through my nose. The air smelled a little different here. I was told that Sinisters didn't like this part of town due to its proximity to the Capital. Maybe that explained the strange odor. The scent reminded me a bit of stagnant water, or air that had gone undisturbed for too long.

"Ah, here we are at last," Tyrann said, coming to a stop about thirty feet from the fence that guarded the Innerbelt.

"Not to sound rude," I said, casting my eyes around in front of me, "but I don't see anything." There was nothing spectacular about where we had stopped, just more of the same broken road we had been walking on, more of the decayed, derelict buildings that surrounded us, and more of the wide expanse of tracks in front of us.

"And that's just the point!" Tyrann rubbed his hands together in anticipation. "I think you'll enjoy this! Careful now, mind the first step, and follow me." With that, Tyrann strode forward and disappeared, right into the ground.

I stood there, rooted to the spot. He had *literally* disappeared.

Printh followed suit. Pria was next, each of them moving without hesitation. I received a whiff of Pria's perfume as she pranced by, a surprisingly pleasant break from the dank air.

"This is really well done," Augustine said as we approached the spot where the others had disappeared. "I almost didn't catch it, but you can see a slight shimmer of light next to that brown rock on the left." Augustine smiled bitterly. "Leave it to Tyrann to surprise you. This may be the best hologram I've seen. After you." He rested a hand on my shoulder and ushered me forward.

My mind rushed backwards almost a week in time. I was jogging down an alleyway. There was a wall up ahead, and I passed right through it, and what was it that I had thought? Only a Sinister would fall for a holographic wall?

A lot could change in a week.

I took one step through the mirage, expecting my foot to make contact with the ground, but it never did. I attempted to stifle a yell, but was only partially successful as I plunged into the darkness. Immediately, the temperature dropped ten degrees, the air took on the fresh ferric scent of dirt, and I found myself sliding down a steep incline toward a bright light at the end of a tunnel. Out of instinct, I tried to activate Zeno's spray, but the gloves were tucked into the waistband of my pants.

I slid on my back at a blistering pace through the darkness, finally slowing down as the incline flattened out. At the bottom of the slide, the Kane clan stood waiting for Augustine and me.

"Well done, Mr. Wells," Tyrann said. "And welcome." He held his arms out wide as Augustine came sliding to a stop behind me. Pria stood next to her father with a wrinkled nose. Printh had become almost invisible in the darkness. "Impressive, isn't it?" Tyrann looked at me to gauge my reaction. I nodded approvingly. It really was impressive.

I guessed we had fallen at least four stories. The walls, though made of dirt, were completely smooth, almost like they had been compacted and then coated with a glassy, reflective material, and this was just the receiving area. I knew the important part was still to come.

"Shall we continue on then?" Augustine said, brushing himself off and peering around the room.

"Absolutely! If you'll follow me, I'll point you in the right direction before we part ways," Tyrann said with a smile, gesturing as if he were about to give us a tour of his home. "I can't wait to see what you do on the other side!"

Tyrann had probably said that same phrase a dozen times this morning. He hadn't asked many questions about what we were going to do once we got into the Capital. He had "wanted to be surprised," he said. I just hoped that whatever he did while he was there wasn't a surprise as well.

Soft blue lights interrupted the top of a perfect circular hallway through which Tyrann was now beckoning.

"I'm impressed, though I can't say surprised," Augustine said, dragging a hand across the nearest wall.

"Oh yes, it's a most incredible feat," Tyrann said in his humblest tone. "Fifty feet down to avoid detection and damage to the Innerbelt, a reception chamber large enough for anything, and a perfect ten-foot sphere to walk through for our pleasure. A hallway for a king as we pass from society to society."

Zeno buzzed in my ear, "Man, it is way too early for poetry. In fact, it's always too early for poetry."

"As I said, impressive." Augustine spoke as he admired the wall. "Where were you able to find a machine capable of su—"

"Please hold all compliments and comments to the end," Tyrann said offhandedly, cutting Augustine short. He was enjoying himself far too much.

"And hold your breath to the end," Pria muttered, wrinkling her nose.

"What?" I didn't smell anything at first, but then it hit me. Like a colony of flies, harmless, but annoying, the stench of human waste filled the tunnel. Printh, expressionless as ever, didn't seem to mind.

We walked for another minute or so before the tunnel came to a T where the underground landscape changed. The lights remained blue, but the tunnel changed from a ten-foot circle to an eight-by-fifteen-foot rectangle.

Tyrann came to a halt and faced us.

"I present to you the Capital district," he said.

I looked at the shift in the tunnels in front of us. Tyrann had been working for years on this project, yet he had never gotten past where we now stood. Until today. Sensors guarded the interior walls of the sewer, and prior to this morning, Tyrann didn't have Zeno to help him bypass the security tech.

"Once we step into that corridor, we'll be the only Sinisters inside." He looked up and smiled. "Aug, I never thought we'd share an experience like this, yet here we are. Today is a momentous day!" Augustine said nothing in return. Tyrann continued on undaunted. "Mr. Zeno, is everything in place?"

"Yep," Zeno said, his voice coming in through my earbud. "The motion detectors have all been deactivated. I'll put the cameras on a loop as soon as you give the word."

"Excellent." Tyrann looked like a smug little kid on Christmas morning, getting everything he had ever wanted.

"Do I have to go with them, Daddy?" Pria said.

"Yes," he said, turning to her, "and you should consider it an honor to accompany a carrier of TɪɪD." He let his disapproving gaze linger on her.

"So we've got fifteen minutes until we're supposed to be there," I said, directing myself to Tyrann. "The fourth left, the eighth right after that, and then follow it until the fifth cover?" I didn't really need to double-check, but we needed to go and Pria needed some saving.

"Righto, Victor!" Tyrann said, finally turning away from Pria. "She may not be good for much, but Pria does know the layout of these tunnels very well." As soon as his back was turned, she pierced him with an ugly look. "And I believe the time for us to go our separate ways is at hand! Mr. Zeno, are you ready?"

"I am chomping at the virtual bit," Zeno said flatly.

"Then off we go!" Tyrann said.

He and Printh entered the corridor and turned left. We were going to head to the right.

I adjusted the bag on my back and turned to Augustine and Pria. "Let's go."

Pria threw one last sharp glance at her father before falling into step behind me. Augustine brought up the rear.

"I'll see you on tonight's news broadcast!" Tyrann said, his cheery tones floating down the tunnel behind us.

I shook my head and kept walking. I was glad to be rid of him, but not knowing what he had planned made me a little uneasy. I glanced back at Pria. She gave me a tight-lipped nod, but quickly opened her mouth to breathe. The smell was worsening.

I would have preferred someone else to accompany us, but like Tyrann had said, Pria apparently knew her way around down here, and just in case things went south, we would need her expertise.

Dax and Alex were inside the Capital. Daphne was just outside of it. And after our conversation last night, it would have been a little weird if Daphne were here. Tyrann had indicated that it was necessary for Printh to go with him, which was just fine with us. Zeno played the role of eyes in the sky. Thanks to the "truenoble" password and Zeno's knack for computers, he basically had universal access to anything and everything to help us out.

The tunnel moving forward had a significant upward grade to it, bringing us nearer and nearer to the surface. With each step, the putrid smell seemed to intensify.

"Everyone doing okay?" I looked over my shoulder.

Pria's face was wrinkled in such a fashion that I wasn't sure it would ever fully recover. Augustine didn't seem overly perplexed by the smell, though his eyebrows were knit closely together, almost as if he were concentrating very hard on something. I was certain he was. What we were about to do was just as important to him as it was to me, if not more so.

Thoughts of Daphne threatened to force their way into my mind, but I did my best to shut them out. The stench actually helped with that. Something else to concentrate on. No distractions.

"All right, Alpha team," Zeno's voice chimed in my ear, "you're getting close. The tunnel should be flattening out up ahead."

"Tyrann didn't demand to be the Alpha team?" I asked.

"Come on, bro, we're the good guys. We're always the Alpha team."

My left arm tingled, a reminder of the passage of time. I picked up my pace.

Finally, the tunnel flattened out, and the layout changed completely. The floor was divided in half by a small channel that ran down the center. An opaque housing covered the channel, which I knew was the source of the stench. Too bad the covering didn't mask the smell.

I chose the left side. Glancing down to my right, I noticed a series of miniature pipes that flowed from the covering, into the walkway, and finally disappeared into the wall.

"I know it smells terrible, but the system is fairly ingenious." Augustine studied the covering and the small pipes with mild fascination. "All the homes and buildings use the methane in the excrement as a heat source. The small pipes suck out the gas and store it where it can be burned."

"You mean to tell me that my whole life, my house was heated by a load of crap?"

"Like I said, ingenious."

"The ingenious part would have been to make the covering smell proof." I pulled out one of my gloves and sprayed some of Zeno's creation in front of my nose. Immediately, his voice sounded in my ear.

"Did you just do what I think you did?"

"Know anyone else who has this stuff?"

"Did it work?"

I began a deep breath in through the nose, which resulted in me gagging.

Zeno chuckled. "Bro, it absorbs energy, not smells."

"If we weren't relying on you so much, I'd turn you off right now," I said, still gagging.

Pria's voice cut through the sulfuric air. "Ugh, can you keep it down? It's hard enough dealing with this horrific smell without having to block out your voice too."

"Man, the girl is a monster, isn't she?" Zeno said.

I didn't respond. Daphne had once said that if I really got to know Pria, I wouldn't think so poorly of her. After seeing how Tyrann treated her, I think I was beginning to see what she meant.

"All right, everybody, one last mic check," Zeno said. "Can everyone hear me?"

He must have opened the channel to everyone because a series of voices cascaded through my earpiece—Daphne, Dax and Alex included.

"Yep," I added my voice to the chorus.

"Good, everyone is accounted for. Now, remember, once Victor is inside, I'll be muting his earpiece. We'll still be able to talk, but he won't hear anything unless he requests it."

"Roger that, train traffic controller, Zeno," Daphne said.

"It's captain train traffic controller, thank you," he said.

I didn't want to get in on their back and forth.

"Here's the first cover," I said, bringing us back on track. Up ahead sat a small array of black cones arranged in a circle. The cones were angled toward a central spot on the ceiling, sending magnetic waves to stabilize a manhole cover. A dial on the first cone managed the intensity of the waves, allowing the manhole cover to be raised and lowered.

"I remember when the Capital switched over to this system." Augustine's voice changed pitch like he was about to give a history or science lesson. "It was years ago, one of the first things I voted on, I think."

"You should have voted to do something about the smell down here," I said.

I checked my watch. The sooner we were in position, the better. The longer everyone else had to wait, the greater their chance of being caught.

"Come on, we're almost there." I picked up the pace.

"Daphne, I think right about now would be prime time for you to get going," Zeno said. "I'll keep you updated on the police's progress."

"Perfect. I'll tell the rest of them. It's been a while since I've run through the Flats."

"Well then, this is your captain speaking," Zeno said, "instructing you to have a good time! And don't get caught. That's going to be crucial."

"I agree," Augustine said. "Good luck, Daphne."

I elected to stay quiet. No distractions. Zeno had supplied Daphne and a few of Tyrann's men with silicone gloves to beat the scanners. Each of the gloves was injected with my blood. Daphne was currently making her way through the Flats. Soon, she'd start hitting scanners. Police and Sinistrali would be alerted of her location immediately. Hopefully, they would draw enough attention to flush some of the police presence and the Sinistrali out of the Capital and make my job easier.

"Thanks," Daphne said. "I'll see you on the other side."

"She's going on her own channel"—Zeno paused and a few buttons clicked—"now. Victor, what's it looking like down there?"

"Two more covers to go and we'll be there," I said.

We continued walking. I did my best to breathe through my mouth, expelling thoughts of Daphne with each breath, but I couldn't block out the smell, or the thoughts, completely.

Two minutes later, we arrived. I knelt down and unslung the case I had been carrying. The metallic clicks of the zipper gave way to a polished blade.

"I have the same model," Pria said, eyeing the saber.

"Really? This is my favorite kind," I said. "You must have good taste."

Pria smiled and looked away. It was probably the first real smile I had seen from her, and it was transformative. I couldn't help but stare. It was like her beauty had been magnified.

"All right, everyone, we're in position," I said, directing my attention to the task at hand. We assumed a tripod arrangement around the black cones on the floor, Augustine to my right and Pria to my left.

"Excellent," Zeno said. "Perfect timing. The Supart car is on its way now. Another two minutes, and it should be there. Alex?"

"We're ready." Alex's voice came in immediately, firm and determined.

The next minute and a half passed mostly in silence, leaving us all to our thoughts. I reviewed the plan again in my mind. It wasn't too complicated. This was going to work. It had to.

"Alpha team, get ready. Here it comes!" Zeno said.

"All right, guys, I see the car," Alex said, his voice wavering a little with anticipation.

"Alex, wait for my mark," Zeno said. "Dax, be ready, it's almost there. Make sure the car stops." Zeno paused. "In three, two, one, now!"

Up above, I visualized what I knew was happening. Dax's enormous form was stepping out in front of Supart's car, bringing it to a halt just outside the Ixlir Building.

"Perfect," Zeno said. "Alex, the door should be opening any moment. You ready, bro?"

"Ready."

It was an odd situation, an odd feeling, sitting there in the quiet, odorous sewer system knowing things were happening above us but not being able to see them.

"All right, Victor," Alex said, "I'm thinking that as soon as we go, I can give you thirty seconds, maybe a little more."

"Got it," I said.

"Everyone got their inhalers?" Alex said, and then quickly added, "Sorry, guys, that wasn't for you."

"Get ready," Augustine said, nodding to Pria. With a determined look on her face, she whipped out a gun-like instrument. On one end stood an inch-long silver needle. In the area where the bullets would be was an empty vial. She pulled out a lighter with her other hand and flamed the needle.

I raised an eyebrow.

"What?" she said. "We just want his blood, not for him to come out of this diseased."

I opened my mouth to reply, but Zeno's voice sounded in my ear. "And the car door is opening."

I grasped my saber and pushed the button to electrify it. Paralyzing lightning raced up and down the blade. Augustine nodded at me. Pria stared fixedly on the manhole cover in the ceiling, the needle gun grasped loosely in her right hand.

"He's stepping out," Zeno said.

"I can see him," Alex said.

"As soon as the door closes, go," Zeno said.

"Alex," came Kratos's voice. "Good luck."

Those words would be immortalized in Alex's memory forever.

"Followers," Alex said, his voice now surging with confidence, "are you ready? Charge!"

I couldn't see it, but the battle cry Alex let out gave me enough to go on. A hundred inhaler-propelled adolescent feet pounded the pavement as they raced across the street and surrounded the car in a tornado of black trench coats. Dust fell from the ceiling. I stiffened in anticipation. Any second.

Zeno yelled.

"Victor, now!"

I reached down and spun the dial on the magnetic array. The manhole cover dropped like a rock.

41

I reached up with my left arm and showered the room in a concentrated blast of energy-absorbing particles. Someone yelped, but the sound was cut off as the invisible beads absorbed the vibrations in the air. I brought my saber up in a wide arc as the manhole cover came to a hard stop a mere inch above the array and brought it down swiftly but softly against the newcomer's head.

Jeffry Supart's eyes stayed wide open as he slumped off of the manhole cover, unconscious. Pria sprung into action, pulling Jeffry off to the side. I stepped into his place and looked up through the hole in the ceiling. It was midday, but no daylight shone through. Fabric from several black trench coats obscured the way.

"I can't hold this up much longer!" Alex's voice was strained.

"Nor can I." Kratos's crisp voice showed a hint of surprise, but what could you expect when you got a bunch of teenagers and put them within fifty feet of their idol?

Kratos was attempting to keep his fans in one spot, blocking the giant hole in the ground from view.

"Twenty more seconds tops!" Alex huffed.

Augustine rushed over, took off the blue jacket Jeffry was wearing, and tossed it to me. I caught it and shoved my gloves into my back pockets, hoping the jacket would cover them all the way. Augustine propped Jeffry's unconscious body up for Pria. The small vial of her needle gun was three-quarters full of blood.

"Come on, Pria!" I tossed my saber to the side, shoved my arms through the holes of the jacket and held out my hand. Like we knew it would, the jacket fit perfectly.

"Don't rush me!"

I stood on the platform with my arm outstretched.

"Annnnd got it!" She stood up, leapt onto the manhole cover, and grabbed my arm at the wrist. She pushed a button on the side of her needle gun. There was a metallic click, and the needle automatically replaced itself. With practiced hands, she brought the needle almost parallel to the surface of my palm.

"What, no flame for me?"

"No time." With a smile, Pria inserted the needle into my hand with practiced precision. I didn't feel a thing. She pulled the trigger, and I watched as the freshly drawn blood flowed directly into the synthetic liner that covered my hand. Perfectly executed.

Pria jumped back and reached for the manhole controls. "Good luck," she said, our eyes locking momentarily. I smiled.

"Thanks." I turned my attention skyward. "Alex, I'm coming up!"

I heard the almost imperceptible click of the dial, and the manhole cover shot through the air, carrying me up to the street above. I dropped to my knees before I arrived aboveground and found myself in the middle of an incredibly crowded street. Black trench coats fluttered around me like I was in a tornado of overweight bats.

I pushed myself to my feet, pretending to have been knocked over in the melee. There were at least a hundred trench coat-clad Followers swarming around me and the Supart car. We weren't more than thirty feet from the door to the Ixlir Building.

"There he is!"

I caught sight of Kratos twenty feet in front of me, but he immediately disappeared and reappeared fifty feet to my left.

"No, he's over there!"

The Followers shouted and shifted directions, running madly like a pack of disoriented dogs toward their prize. Everyone was putting on a great show, Kratos included.

"Everybody stop!" An officer arrived on the scene, his fingers playing with the stunner in his holster.

"Police!" a Follower near me shrieked.

Four more officers approached at a run, hands on their stunners.

"Stop!"

The Followers scattered.

Kratos disappeared again and reappeared nearby, coming to a stop in front of the oncoming Followers. He had been using a hologram of himself before, but this looked like the real thing. The Followers surged toward him. He stood immobile, surveying the stampede.

"Stop or we'll shoot!" The policemen took aim. I ducked down in anticipation of the blasts.

The Followers were less cautious. Several small blasts of electricity charged the air around me. Five bodies immediately slumped to the ground.

"Stand down! I'll grab their leader!" The words came from the front of the group. The blasts stopped, and Kratos sprinted at the oncoming superfans. He thrust out his hand and directed an invisible wedge into the crowd. He dodged and jumped, advancing nimbly through the Followers, picking his way through the frenzy until he scooped one of them up—Alex.

Immediately, they all dispersed, running in different directions. Kratos continued running hard and disappeared down a side street.

I breathed a sigh of relief. Alex was safe. So far so good. The mass of Followers had thinned out around me, and I found myself suddenly caught in an embrace.

"Oh Jeffry, are you hurt, my dear?"

I looked into the slightly puffy eyes of a woman I knew very well. She had dark brown hair and dark brown eyes that had recently seen tears. Jeffry's mother—Lora Supart. Concern was etched into the lines on her face as if she had been practicing the expression for a week. I was sure she had.

I hugged my right elbow and forced my face into a grimace, but nodded my head all the same. I felt a pang of guilt as she hugged me tight and dusted me off. She had just lost her husband, and she didn't know it at the moment, but her son lay unconscious fifteen feet below us. She didn't need to feel any more pain.

"That was the strangest thing I think I've ever seen inside the Capital." Her words were distracted as she watched the last few stragglers disappear from view. I quickly tugged my jacket down around me, making sure my gloves were hidden from view.

"Ma'am, are you and your son all right?"

The small contingent of officers jogged up, each one wearing an expression of mild bewilderment.

"Yes, yes, we're fine, Officers." She grabbed the lapels of my jacket and straightened them. "Just on our way to the senate offices."

Recognition and comprehension dawned on the officer's face. "Of course, Mrs. Supart. We'll ensure there are no more distractions for you."

"Oh no, Officers, that won't be necessary."

"No"—the officer closest to us held up his hand—"we insist. We've just gotten word that Victor Wells has resurfaced somewhere in the Flats. Other units are on their way to get to him, but we'll help make sure everything goes smoothly for you today." He turned to his partner. "Stevens, let the captain know that Coughlin and I will be following the Suparts to ensure they are undisturbed this afternoon."

"You got it, Bachman."

Like an unbalanced scale, my stomach dropped and my guilt climbed. The added police weren't going to do me any favors. Officer Stevens retreated, leaving Coughlin and Bachman standing at attention, ready to serve. *Great.*

"Victor, they shouldn't be a problem. They won't be in the room with you," Augustine's voice chimed in my ear. "They'll stand guard outside—you'll be fine." I hoped he was right, but it didn't do anything to loosen the knot in my stomach.

"Thank you, Officers." Lora placed her hand on my back and gently guided me around the vehicle toward the entrance. The Ixlir Building was the second tallest in the area at five stories high. "Oh, Jeffry, would you run back and lock the car, dear?" Lora asked. "It's probably fine, but with all those Followers, who knows?"

My pulse quickened. Zeno had assured me that the super-slim glove I wore worked very well against regular scanners. He hadn't said anything about cars. I nodded and walked back to the car, remembering what had happened the last time I had used a car window scanner.

Here goes nothing.

I placed my hand on the sun-warmed window of the car. The familiar beads of light snaked their way around my hand, outlining it briefly until Jeffry's DNA, hopefully, was verified.

The usual blur of moments stretched into an agonizing waiting period. Finally, the scanning finished, and a portion of the window lit up. Red. A large word filled the screen.

Error.

My heart rate jumped. I kept quiet. Surprise. I needed to show surprise.

"Hm, odd. Don't worry dear, I'll take care of it." Lora walked over and placed her hand on the front passenger window. A moment later, I heard the soft click of the door locks closing, and the light pulsed green.

"Come, Jeffry."

I turned and followed her, my mind racing.

If my glove didn't work on the car, would it work on the scanner to get into the building? Did Pria fill my glove properly?

My heart pounded as we made our way toward the large glass doors in front of us. I did my best to keep my expression neutral.

"Zeno, is this going to work?" Augustine's voice was soft, but intense.

"Cars are a little finicky, you know that. Ever since they stopped letting me work on them...but that's the government for you."

"Zeno!"

"Sorry, no, we shouldn't have any problems. As long as the glove was filled correctly, we should have nothing to worry about."

"Are you *questioning* me?" Pria said.

"You'll know in a minute," Zeno said.

"Wonderful," she said. "It's not like this is my first time, you know."

I wanted to tell them all to shut up and try to build some confidence. I chanced a glance at my hand. I didn't see any erroneous blood outside of the glove. My hand looked normal. She had to have filled it properly.

"Kratos, are you in position?" Augustine said.

"I am."

It was tough having everyone's voices in my head without being able to respond. But it was comforting knowing that Kratos was somewhere nearby, waiting, just in case. I couldn't see him, but that was probably a good thing.

The officers followed us from several feet back, giving "our family" a little privacy. Lora placed a hand on my back and ushered me toward the entrance.

Alex's voice came through my earbud. "Everyone is out. Dax and I are on our way back to the Heights."

Good, I thought, drawing near to the entrance. This was good. This was going to work.

"Come, Jeffry," Lora said, a hint of melancholy in her voice. She had already placed her hand on the scanner and was through the glass doors. Protocol dictated that I scan my hand too, and I knew the officers weren't going to bend the rules today, not with "Victor Wells" on the loose and the Left Hand Marking people all over the place.

I covered the remaining distance to the scanner. The two police officers held their position five feet behind me. I paused before reaching the scanner, noticing the large screen embedded in the wall of the building and the familiar face of a reporter.

"Police are responding to two separate scans that detected T11D. It would appear that Victor Wells has returned to the Flats. Thus far he

is still on the run, but the police are hopeful that he will be appre-
hended short—"

Kelly Straunton touched her finger to her ear, a look of confusion
occupying her face.

"And I have just received word that Victor Wells's DNA has been
scanned in two more places. One near the Capital, and one near the
southern border. Opposite ends of the city. I'm told the scans
happened within seconds of each other. It can't be possible," she said.
"Theories on that and more when we come back."

She smiled uncertainly into the camera, and the video feed
changed to a commercial.

Daphne taking a sample of my blood had paid off after all.

"Let's go, Jeffry, we don't need to listen to that," Lora said.

I nodded and placed my hand on the scanner as calmly and
surely as I could. I knew Jeffry well, but I hadn't studied his mannerisms outside of the saber fights, so I wasn't sure what to mimic. Hopefully, anybody watching me would assume that today was merely a
difficult day for a boy who had just lost his father, and any nuances
would be excusable.

I waited, my hand sweating beneath the slim silicone glove I wore.
The screen lit up the color of blood. Error. I could hear the fidgeting
of the officers behind me. I lifted my hand, let the screen clear and
replaced it.

Red. Error.

I could feel color and heat rising in my face. I was standing near
two police officers who didn't know they were mere feet away from
the most wanted man in the city, but if this didn't work, it was only a
matter of time. I just hoped Zeno's voice modulator was good enough
to not raise suspicion. It was time to talk.

"Is the scanner broken?" I asked, looking back at the officers. My
heart pounded in my chest. I thought my voice sounded good, but
Lora would be the judge of that. She was the one I had to fool. Augustine's voice erupted into my earbud.

"Zeno, it's not working. Kratos, are you ready?"

"You give the word."

"This is our only shot!" Zeno cut in. "We can't pull him out yet!"

I agreed with Zeno—this was our only chance. We didn't have another day, we didn't have time to orchestrate another elaborate plan, and we didn't have much more time until the biokey expired.

"As far as I can tell, everything is in order. Give your other hand a try," the other officer suggested.

I hesitated.

"Kratos, move now!" Augustine said.

"Wait!" Pria said. "I can help!"

"Then help!" Zeno said. "He can't afford anymore wasted time!"

The officers began to approach.

"Victor, you owe me one for this," she said.

"Pria!" Augustine yelled.

"Yes, yes, I know," Pria said calmly. "The blood in the glove needs to spread out evenly through the material. Have you seen anyone clap their hands together before placing them on the scanner?"

Of course I had. People did it all the time, especially when it was cold outside. It was supposed to help the blood get to the surface, but it was frowned upon by most of the Nobles as a hallmark gesture of Sinisters.

"That's what you need to do. Then try again. It should do the trick."

The officers were close, and Lora stared at me through a half-opened door. I clapped my hands hard twice and rubbed them together quickly before thrusting my hand back onto the scanner.

Lora rolled her eyes and the officers halted their progress. My heart hammered in my chest. The glass felt cool to the touch, even through the glove, a brief reprieve from the sweat on my hands.

The light on the screen snaked its way around my fingers.

Come on, work. Work!

I took my gaze away from the screen and looked up into the eyes of Jeffry's mother. Even from several feet away I could see the sadness in them, but it wasn't directed at me. She was in pain, and it was all because of the Left Hand. And that's who I was after. This had to work. It was the only way.

The screen emitted a tone. The scan was complete.

"See, Bach? I told you it works. It's not just some gimmick the Sinisters do." Coughlin peered over my shoulder at the now green screen.

A chorus of cheers erupted in my earbud.

Silently, I exhaled and removed my shaking hand from the screen.

"Yeah, well it looks ridiculous," Bach said.

"I couldn't agree more," Lora said from inside the door. "Jeffry, this way."

I glanced one last time at the news screen on the wall. The commercial had been replaced with a life-size picture of me, complete with a caption.

"If you see Victor Wells, do not approach. Alert the authorities immediately."

"Thanks, Pria," I muttered under my breath, stepping through the large glass doors, followed closely by the two officers.

"He's in," Kratos said.

And so I was, a lone Sinister inside the Ixlir Building.

42

"Would you like us to accompany you inside, Mrs. Supart?"

Lora glanced at me, her face displaying a smile of both nostalgia and sadness.

"No, no, Officers, I think we'd like a few minutes alone."

"A couple of officers will be outside your door, just in case."

"Thank you. Come, Jeffry."

The officers nodded and turned their backs to us, leaving us to ourselves in front of the elevator. Lora placed a gentle hand on my shoulder and ushered me slowly toward the large glass doors. Other than Dr. Rosewood's research tower, at five floors, the Ixlir Building was the tallest in the Flats. Lora pressed the button for the fifth floor.

The gentle ride up took only a few seconds, and thankfully, passed in silence. The doors opened and we headed down a hallway. With each step my nerves grew.

"Here we are, dear."

With Lora's hand on my back and my heart pounding with anticipation, I pushed through the large wooden door, but I wasn't prepared for what I saw. In the middle of the room on a giant easel sat an almost life-size family portrait of Avardi, Lora, and Jeffry. A hundred candles of varying heights and colors had been placed around it, each one giving off a bright glow that helped to light up the smiles of the Suparts in the picture. I had only seen a few candles in my life—they were antiques—but they were often the only light source used at funerals.

I fought back the emotion. Avardi was gone, really gone. Jeffry was fatherless. Lora, husbandless. I took a shuddering breath and tried to compose myself.

I was here for the biokey safe. I was here to expose the Left Hand.

I wiped at my eyes and looked around the room. Lora had shut the door behind us and sat down in a large leather armchair near the wall.

Photographs had been placed all around the room and on a large table behind the family picture. Notable accomplishments had been framed, but clearly it had been the people in Avardi's life that had mattered the most. More often than not, the pictures displayed his family.

A pang of guilt struck me. This was supposed to be a nice, sentimental visit for the Suparts. I only hoped it would stay that way for Lora. And I could only hope that Jeffry would forgive me for robbing him of this experience.

I faintly remembered the day when I had walked through my parents' house for the last time. It was something I didn't think about often, mostly because it was a painful experience, but it was something I had needed to do. It brought closure. I could only hope the real Jeffry would have the chance to do so too.

"Jeffry, I don't know if I've told you this before," Lora said, her voice airy and light, "but this was your father's favorite chair in the whole room. Comfortable, a perfect view out the far window, and just beneath the armrest..." She paused and I heard the rustling of leather fabric. "There is a perfect hiding place for this."

I turned to face her.

In her hand she held a police-grade stunner, and it was pointed at my chest.

"There's no use running. The only exit is blocked by two police officers." She stared at me with hard eyes. "I will warn you that I am a very good shot. I require an explanation. You are not my son. Who are you? What are you doing here?"

Her voice wasn't angry, but it also wasn't afraid. I could tell by the look in her eyes that she was no stranger to situations where the stakes were high.

My gut told me to tell her the truth, but I hesitated. If I judged this wrong, I was dead.

"Either give me an answer or I'll shoot you and alert the guards."

I made up my mind.

"Lora," I said slowly. She raised her eyebrows in surprise. "It's me, Victor. Jeffry is safe. I'm sorry he's not here with you."

A sliver of relief showed through her fierce stare. She kept the stunner leveled at my torso and smiled.

"I never thought I'd find myself in this situation. My husband's stunner pointed at my son's friend. I always knew you as a level-headed boy, but why are you here and why have you kidnapped my son?"

How could I explain it?

I rolled up the sleeve on Jeffry's jacket, exposing the fluid silver of the biokey. "Because of this. It led me here."

The barrel of her stunner dropped a few inches. "From my husband?"

I nodded.

"So he did get one," she murmured, more to herself than me. She appeared lost in thought for a moment. I held my tongue. She could still shoot me. "And you're sure you were supposed to come here, and not the other off—" She paused. "You're the reason his office went into the lake, aren't you?"

"Sorry about that."

Lora waved her hand dismissively. "He never liked that office anyways. He spent far more time here." Lora rose to her feet, but kept the stunner in hand. "Well then, we haven't much time. Let's find that safe."

"That's it?" I asked. "No more questions?"

"You expect me to believe that garbage they throw around on the news about you?"

"Everyone else seems to."

"Where would he hide it?" she mumbled to herself, peering around the room. "Well, everyone is a lot more trusting of the government than I am. I know your grandfather and I knew your father—both very good men. I never had a chance to thank you for saving Avardi. Those last few days were more valuable than you know."

I paused, not knowing exactly what to say.

"Well don't just stand there," she said while tearing the cushions off the couch. "We don't have much time. Start looking!"

"Are you sure it's here on this floor?" I asked.

"If the biokey led you to this building, this floor is the only one it would be on. *That* I know for certain."

"Okay, great," I said. I decided it was time to break radio silence. I tapped my earbud. "Augustine, any ideas?"

"Pendleton?" Lora said, looking up. "Another good man. I assumed you had help to get a mask like that and get past the scanners. Avardi always spoke highly of Augustine. Such a shame what happened to that family..." She dropped to her hands and knees, searching the underbody of a couch.

"Ask Mrs. Supart if there are any new fixtures in the room, furniture or otherwise," Augustine said. "Zeno, do you see anything obviously out of place?"

I had almost forgotten that Zeno had implanted a micro camera into the mask.

"No. Well, yes, everything, but there's nothing there that shouldn't be."

"Lora, are there any new fixtures in the room?"

She looked around carefully. "I'm not sure. I didn't spend a lot of time here, my dear." She continued peering around the room and then turned to face me. "Do you mind taking off your mask? It's an eerie thing seeing Jeffry but knowing it's not him. You can put it back on before you leave."

I hesitated. My mask was my shield; I understood for a moment how Kratos must feel. But it was the least I could do after kidnapping her son.

"Of course." I peeled the mask off my face. Lora continued to stare at me, not like I was a TııD-carrying fugitive, but like a mother would before letting her child leave for the day.

"You're missing something. Considering the nature of what we're after, you need some protection." She paused, the barrel of her stunner resting on her bottom lip, much like any normal person would do with a finger while in thought. "Jeffry goes on and on about how gifted you are with a saber. There should be one to your liking in there." She motioned with her stunner to a large wooden closet situated to the left of the window at the other end of the room. Either she was entirely too comfortable with a stunner, or she didn't really know what she was doing. I had a feeling it was the former.

I walked over and pulled open the door. Inside stood an array of sabers. Some were old and fashioned entirely of wood. My eyes gravitated toward a saber in the corner of the closet, one that could be electrified. In case things went poorly, I couldn't be fighting with wood only.

"Choose any one you like. I think there are cases in there too."

I pulled the saber out, examining it before placing it inside the thin case and throwing it over my shoulder.

"Good, now let's find that safe."

Augustine's voice came over my earpiece again. "Victor, check the big table behind the family picture. Look for something out of place, maybe something that doesn't belong."

Zeno cut in. "Or something very important or very unimportant. Remember, bro, it could be anything."

"Got it," I said. "Lora, let's ch—"

A knock sounded at the door. Lora looked up in alarm. I felt all the blood leave my face. I still held the Jeffry mask in my hands.

The door began to move, slowly inching its way open.

"Mrs. Supart, everything okay in there?" It was one of the officers.

She rushed over and grabbed the door, halting its progress.

"Yes, Officer," she said, slightly out of breath, "everything is fine." I could tell the officer was puzzled, probably due to the aggressive stop of the door and the slightly winded woman behind it.

"Well, uh, let us know if you need anything. With Victor Wells somewhere in the Flats, we just want to be sure."

"Of course. Thank you, Officer." She closed the door and made her way back across the room. "Hurry! Traditionally, these visits are fairly short."

I nodded and headed for the table. "Look for anything out of place."

Lora nodded in understanding and set about the room, scouring the bookshelves for anything out of the ordinary. I stared at the table before me. Pictures covered the entire thing, some without frames and some with them. The metal-framed picture of Avardi, Lora, and Jeffry sat at the head of the table, much larger than any of the other pictures.

"There are more like us, you know," Lora said suddenly. I looked over, past the large picture on the table, and locked eyes with her. She must have noted my confusion. "Being where you are, you don't strike me as the kind of person who believes in all this Sinister-Noble nonsense. There are more people who think like we do. Not all Nobles believe all Sinisters are bad or inferior. Some, though they hide it, believe we all have choices to make regardless of our DNA." She continued to pierce me with her stare. "Your parents were some of those people, if you didn't know."

I didn't. I let the words sink in. If I had only known. But now, I did think like them. Now, it was like being connected to them. I thought like my parents, and it felt good.

"Why are you telling me this?"

"Because I believe change is coming, and it won't be easy. The Great Experiment...goodness, well it's almost up, isn't it? And I think a great deal of disruption is coming. I know you have help, but you need to know you're not alone in this. Help will come from unlikely places."

She went back to searching.

My eyes strayed to the Supart family picture on the table, an idea striking me. The frame was made of metal, and ornately designed.

"I wonder," I murmured to myself, reaching for the picture. I rolled up my left sleeve again, exposing the biokey. The moment my fingers made contact, the metal frame began to glow the same color as the cylinder from the train car. "I think I found it!"

A chorus of exclamations made their way through my earpiece as Lora hurried over to my side. And then a knock sounded at the door.

"Mrs. Supart, is everything okay in there?" The officer cracked the door open again.

"Yes! Don't come in!"

The light from the frame grew brighter. My arm burned like it was being scalded by hot water. I tried to look, but the light was too bright.

"What's going on in there?" The officer attempted to open the door further.

"No, I said stay out!" Lora crossed the room swiftly, but she wasn't quick enough.

Officer Coughlin opened the door wide. He paused, taking in the scene—the office, the light, and finally, me. His eyes widened in recognition. He reached for his stunner and touched his earpiece. "Victor Wells is in the Capital, I repeat, Vic—"

A flash of light exploded from Lora's stunner and Coughlin fell to the floor unconscious.

"Coughlin!" Bachman yelled, rushing into the room. Another flash of light and he fell unconscious next to his partner.

"Is that thing done?" Lora half yelled, half grunted as she dragged the two bodies inside the door, shut it, and turned the lock.

Light continued to shine throughout the room. The blue was so intense that I had to shut my eyes against it.

"I don't know, is it supposed to do this?" I grunted through the pain.

"No idea. He bought this one on his own."

I felt a vibration run through the metal frame, and then, as abruptly as it had started, the light died out completely. The pain in my arm ceased. There was a soft click, and a small groove appeared on the back of the frame.

I inspected my arm—the silver was gone. In its place the skin was splotchy and red.

Lora returned to the desk and examined the picture. "My favorite picture of us," she said. "He spent so much time here. Avardi always kept this picture in the building. He said it was how he kept Jeffrey and me close." Lora paused and looked away. I looked at the ground, not sure what to say. "Well, I say open the thing up, grab the information inside, and get out of here. I doubt you have more than a minute before this office is swarming with police."

"I'd give you two minutes," Zeno said in my ear. "Daphne's got a pretty good contingent of officers after her."

"They say we've got two minutes," I said.

"I assume you have a backup exit strategy?" She raised an accusatory eyebrow, as if she would be disappointed if my plan to kidnap her son and break into her dead husband's office wasn't well-thought-out.

"Yes." I looked toward the window, the one I'd be shattering in the near future. "But, are you sure you don't want what's in there? I mean your husba—"

"Oh heavens no, dear!" she interrupted. "No one can know that I know anything, so off you get." She pushed the frame into my hands and retreated toward the front of the room. "I'm going to stun myself and blame it on you. I do apologize, but I believe it's necessary for my safety. Unfortunately, I'll have to tell them that you forced me to stun them." She nodded toward the unconscious officers.

I had known Lora for years, but only as the lady who made incredible cookies. She was an interesting woman, a good woman. A smile took hold of my face.

"There's no time to go around grinning like an idiot!" She waved her stunner at the officers on the ground and then pointed it back at me. "They'll be back up in a few moments—reinforced police suits and all. After I stun myself, come take the gun away from me. I won't make you shoot an old lady." She winked and inverted the stunner. "Next time I see you, I want this back, you understand?"

"I do. And Lora?"

"Yes, dear?" She looked down briefly and locked eyes with me. The officers had begun to stir and moan.

"Thank you."

"No dear, thank you. Oh, for heaven's sake." Two quick flashes of light silenced the groans of the officers. "That's better. Well, you'd better be going. Here's to making waves and changing the world." She winked and smiled. "Now get going!"

Without another word, the blue light of the stunner illuminated her features and sent her limp body to the floor next to the officers. I rushed over, grabbed the stunner, and shoved it into the waistband of my pants. I pulled out my gloves and slipped them on as quickly as I could.

A few quick steps brought me back to the desk. I grabbed the picture frame and dug my fingernails into the small groove on the back. A cover piece popped off. What looked like a thin metallic flake dropped onto the table—a data chip—followed by a single fluttering sheet of paper. This was it. The identity of the Left Hand's leader. This was what Avardi had died protecting, and we finally had it!

I snatched the piece of paper off the desk and unfolded it quickly. I knew I didn't have much time before more officers arrived. A few hurried lines had been scratched onto the paper. My eyes blazed over them, and the thrill of victory, of finally getting here, vanished. I read the lines again.

With shaking hands, I folded the paper and stuffed it into my pocket. The last words I saw before it disappeared from view stayed in my mind like a tattoo.

Dr. Victoria Rosewood. The proof is on the chip.

The leader of the Left Hand was Dr. Victoria Rosewood, the savior of our city.

43

"Open up! It's the police!"

The words jarred me from my spot, but my mind fought for understanding. Dr. Rosewood? There was no way. Or was there? Who else was in a perfect position to change my DNA status?

I picked up the gray metal chip and slipped it into a hidden pocket on the side of my glove.

A loud thump sounded against the large wooden door. Zeno's voice chimed in my ear.

"Bro, did you get it? I can't see anything from the camera in your mask."

Another loud thump.

"Yeah," I said, my mind still reeling, "but it changes things." The only person with more power than her was President Keltan.

"You read it?" Augustine asked.

"There was a slip of paper, but—"

I looked back as another loud thump shook the door.

"Tell us later!" Augustine said. "Get out of there!"

Without another word, I went to plan B.

I grabbed the chair behind the table, lifted it, and swung out with all the force I could muster.

The window exploded and showered me and the street below in transparent debris. A few muffled cries reached my ears as I stepped out on the window ledge. The wind whipped around my back.

Another concussive blow sounded in the senator's office, and the door splintered. One look told me the door couldn't handle another hit like that.

"Kratos!" I tapped on my earbud.

"I see you. Go now. I'll meet you on the street."

The door gave way.

I jumped into the exhilarating arms of free fall and plummeted toward the ground below.

After a few well timed sprays, I hit the ground running, my shoes crunching the broken glass beneath my feet.

Kratos fluttered down from an adjacent building and landed in front of me. As he paced toward me, the few people who had stopped to stare fled.

"I've got him," Kratos said, a finger on his earpiece. He nodded to me. "Let's go." We took off running down the street.

"Good," Augustine said. "Victor, what did you find? We assumed there would be some sort of data card."

"There was, and I've got it in my glove, but there was a piece of paper too," I said in between breaths. "It said Dr. Rosewood is behind the Left Hand."

"Wait, what?" said Alex.

In front of me, Kratos stiffened.

"Man, I told you there was something wrong with that hundred-year-old woman!" Zeno said.

"My goodness," Augustine said slowly.

"Wait, you believe it?" I asked. "I mean, it makes sense, I guess, but—"

Kratos cut me off and spoke quickly. "Victor, be ready to spray behind you if I tell you to."

"What?"

"Raise your hands." He nodded behind me. "Raise them now." I cast a glance up over my shoulder. A small team of officers peered out over the street, stunners drawn and pointed in my direction. "Keep them up. I may have to hit or tackle you, and if I do, I want you to fall over like you're unconscious. I'll drag you into the alleyway, and we'll go from there. Deal?"

I nodded and froze with my hands above my head. Augustine, Zeno, and Alex continued to talk back and forth.

"Everyone quiet!" Kratos hissed. My earbud went silent. He had never raised his voice before. Behind his ever-expressionless mask, pain showed through his eyes. "Victor, get ready."

The officers behind me needed to see the Bounty Hunter taking me down. I assumed they were still approaching, acting as backup if needed. I watched Kratos's eyes. They widened.

He launched himself at me. His chest caught me in the face, his arms spread wide. Flashes of blue shot over my head and to my side. I barely had time to hear the imperceptible hiss of his gloves before I hit the pavement.

I landed hard on my back. My earbud flew out of my ear. Kratos threw his weight off of me and jumped into a crouch. Light flooded my vision, but it wasn't the kind of light someone might see before they pass out or die. This was the blue dissipating light of stunner fire.

My earbud lay two feet away. I reached for it, but stunner fire lit up the area like a fireworks display. I retracted my hand as one of the blasts caught my earbud and short-circuited it.

Kratos crouched over me, gray beads raining from his outstretched arms. The air around us buzzed with bright blue light.

"Victor!" Kratos yelled.

His arms were still outstretched. Beyond the almost continuous blinding flashes of light, I could make out a line of men wearing police uniforms, each with weapons pointed toward us.

The truth of the situation dawned on me. Despite the heat of the waning day, I felt a chill run through my body. The Left Hand was here, again. Maybe Alex was right—maybe they could track me anywhere.

The street was deserted except for us and the advancing Sinistrali. At least fifteen of them walked toward us in a line, their stunners more active than lightning rods in a storm. I looked quickly behind me, hoping against hope that we weren't surrounded.

The street was clear, but the moment Kratos quit spraying, we were dead. I just hoped he had enough of Zeno's spray to hold them off.

"Victor!" Kratos said. "In my jacket pocket, there are several small cylinders."

I whipped my head back around. I couldn't see a way out of this.

"Victor!"

I scrambled forward.

"Which pocket?"

"Either one! Just grab one of the cylinders. When I tell you, throw it in front of my hands."

I reached into the pockets of his trench coat and pulled out two silver metal cylinders.

"You have them?" he asked.

"Yes!" I had one in each hand. They were roughly the size of a water bottle and matched the silver beads from Zeno's spray in color.

"Zeno, I'm going to need you to open the nearest manhole cover in just a few seconds," Kratos said.

I assumed Zeno was responding, but without my earbud, I was deaf to the conversation.

"I just need it open, I don't need it timed perfectly!"

Kratos cast a glance at me. "When I say now, throw the cylinder out into the stunner fire and follow me."

I nodded.

The line of Sinistralis continued to advance. The flashes from their stunners only seemed to intensify. I didn't know how much longer we could hold them like this.

"Now!"

I let the silver cylinder fly. It glinted in the sunlight as it arced over Kratos's head, almost as if it were in slow motion. The moment the cylinder disappeared into the river of blue light, it exploded. A white steam jettisoned outward and upward, forming a protective curtain that disappeared into the air. Stunner fire continued, but it dissipated when it reached the now invisible curtain. With each impact, the protective barrier turned slightly more gray. The stunner fire increased. Kratos spun around.

"Go!" he shouted. "Zeno, manhole!"

I broke into a sprint behind him. A hundred feet down the road lay the nearest manhole cover.

"Eight seconds, Zeno! Get it open!"

The manhole cover dropped out of sight, leaving an opening for us to escape.

I felt a surge of hope...until the hole in the road became obscured by something closer, something dressed in a police uniform.

"Victor, get behind me!"

Immediately, I jumped to my right. A stunner shot sailed past me, soaring along the path my head had been on a microsecond before. I counted no less than four bodies prepared to receive us. Each of them fired their stunners at us in rapid succession. Kratos absorbed them all.

And then they were upon us.

Kratos jumped, his trench coat trailing him through the air like a black ribbon of death. He caught two of them with a scissor kick and a third with an elbow, but the fourth was untouched. And I was exposed.

Reflex kicked in.

My hand flew to the saber protruding from the case on my back. I brought it out and electrified it in a single swift movement.

I lunged forward, my crackling blade slicing through the air. My opponent leapt back, but not fast enough. My blade caught him in the leg, and he immediately collapsed. A quick blow to the head rendered him unconscious.

I looked over to find three bodies strewn about Kratos's feet.

"Come on! That won't hold much longer!"

I glanced back at the invisible barrier to find a curtain of gray that had become almost black. A lone stunner blast broke through the curtain, and the barrier exploded. Millions of particles showered the area in a blizzard of gray. The line of Sinistrali charged.

"Run!"

Bright blue blasts filled the air around us. Adrenaline fueled my movements, ushering me forward faster and faster.

"Come on!"

I willed my legs to move faster. Kratos sprinted fifteen feet ahead of me, his trench coat flapping in his wake. I watched him slide into the hole in the ground and disappear from view.

The stunner fire concentrated on me even more heavily. I re-angled my free hand behind my head and let loose a continuous stream of spray, and not a second too soon. Several charged bolts fizzled out directly behind my ears.

Ten feet.

I jumped.

I brought my free arm around in front of me and let out a small burst of spray. It stopped me in midair. I tucked in my arms and fell straight down the hole.

44

"Are you hurt?" Kratos said.

I pushed myself to my feet and stepped gingerly, testing my legs. I looked up as something banged against the resealed manhole cover.

"I think I'm good," I said.

"Here." Kratos reached into his pocket and pulled out a syringe full of a thick, purple liquid. "In case one of us gets hurt. It will take away any pain for a short period of time."

He handed it to me and I pocketed it.

Another bang on the manhole cover. Kratos didn't even look up.

"Where are Augustine and Pria?" I asked. "Are they close?"

"We're not meeting up with them," Kratos said.

"Wait, why?" I said. "What happened?"

"Nothing. We're going to test your information, and we're going now."

"What, now? How are we going to do that? And why?"

"I know where Dr. Rosewood is. We are going to confront her. We are going to end it."

I stared at him. I didn't have words. Was he crazy?

He continued to talk. "I've made my decision," Kratos said, looking up at the ceiling. He was either talking to Augustine or Zeno.

If only I had my earpiece. "Yes, it is wise. It is the one play she will not expect. You can either help or I can do it on my own," he continued. "Yes. I'll keep you updated."

Another metallic bang sounded against the manhole cover.

Kratos eyed me.

"Are you coming?"

"Coming with you? To Dr. Rosewood?" I asked.

He nodded.

It was crazy. Pursued by the Sinistrali, and he wanted to go to their potential leader? But I had to consider it. I knew Kratos was used to doing things alone. The fact that he had invited me to come with him must mean something. Maybe he wasn't sure what he would find. And I owed him. Not to mention, I wanted to know more than anyone who was after me.

"What about the others?" I asked.

"They'll be waiting for us in the Heights."

We locked eyes. I nodded.

"Okay, I'm in."

"Good, then follow me."

He took off down the passageway.

I sprinted after Kratos as he ran beneath the blue lights of the sewers. I struggled to keep pace with him. He ran so fast it was like he had spent time down here before.

Ahead of me, Kratos came to an abrupt stop. "Zeno, do you have my position? Can you lower this manhole cover?"

I didn't hear a response to his question, but after a moment of silence, the manhole cover sunk through the air like it was resting in transparent quicksand.

"My earbud's gone," I said.

"I'll keep my mic on so everyone can hear you. I'll go first."

Kratos stepped onto the magnetically suspended metal disk.

"Send me up," he said.

The manhole cover ascended to the ceiling, carrying Kratos up with it. My mind filled with questions. Why was he so intent on confirming my info? There had to be a reason.

The metal disk descended from street level once again, now empty.

"It's all clear. Come quickly." Kratos's voice came from above as a whisper.

I stepped onto the metal manhole cover and rose through the air. I had the odd feeling that the sewer was somehow regurgitating me, spitting me back up into the daylight like it didn't want me there.

A series of gasps met my appearance. The street we had arrived at had been sparsely populated, but with our appearance, everyone had scattered.

"Stay close." Kratos was already moving. I blinked a few times in the sunlight and stepped off the manhole cover to jog after him. On either side of us, tall metal walls stood like sentinels guarding the path. Upon seeing Kratos, people who exited the buildings immediately reentered them, leaving the streets deserted except for us.

A few blocks away, I could make out Dr. Rosewood's research tower over the tops of nearby buildings. White stone, gray metal, and tinted glass towered over any other edifice in the area. Was that where we were going?

We took several turns without stopping. I stayed close to Kratos, not familiar with this part of the Capital, but he knew where we were. Every turn was made without hesitation.

Kratos had said we were going to test my info. How? Just walk into the tower and ask? And what if the paper I had read was a code? What if it actually wasn't Dr. Rosewood? I couldn't help but think that we should have stuck with the original plan.

A shiver raced through me at the thought. My mind jumped back to what seemed like a far distant memory: Dr. Rosewood being ushered into the back of a car immediately after my Marking. She had been just as eager to get out of there as everyone else, hadn't she?

Finally, the research tower appeared before us in its entirety, a massive structure. The Nobles liked their space—each floor probably had fifteen-foot ceilings—making the fifty-story structure dominate the skyline.

And then the skyline exploded.

Flames shot out of the front right corner of the building about halfway up. The force of the explosion knocked me off my feet. My stunner and saber clattered on the ground next to me, neither weapon making a noise to my deafened ears.

Blood ran down my arms where I had attempted to catch myself on the ground. Dazed, I lay there for a moment, trying to make sense of what had just happened. I pushed myself to my feet and blinked against the pain. Kratos was already up. I looked around. People streamed out of the research building like water out of a constricted hose. Glass covered the ground and bits of melted metal littered the street. My ears rang, but I was starting to process normal sounds again. Kratos's voice next to me was faint.

"Victor, are you okay?"

I nodded in response, taking note of something I had never seen before in the cold eyes of my ally. Fear.

He seemed to be on the brink of indecision. For some reason, I could tell he desperately wanted—no, needed—to go into the research building, flaming hole notwithstanding.

"Yes," I said, "but the explosion—Dr. Rosewood—would she have survived?"

"It wasn't for her," he said.

"Then who was it for?" I asked. Something was weird about the timing of the explosion. It wasn't a coincidence.

"It was meant for a DNA database."

"There's one here?"

"Not anymore," Kratos said, gazing at the hole in the building.

My mind strained to put the pieces together. Rumor had it that there were multiple DNA centers—databanks that contained all the genetic information that separated the Nobles from the Sinisters. The thing was, no one knew where they were.

We didn't detonate the bomb. Who else had access to explosives? The Left Hand? No, they only ever killed people, and they liked to take credit. Their insignia was nowhere to be found. Who could do this? Who had access to a detonator?

And then it hit me.

"Tyrann."

Kratos nodded.

"But why?"

But I knew why—it was obvious. He was finally making a play against the Nobles.

"Right now, that doesn't matter. Now, we must go."

I stared at the wreckage of the building. He had said he wasn't going to hurt anyone. I looked back to Kratos. His eyes hardened.

"We're still going in there?" I asked.

He gave me a solemn look. The street filled up with people behind him. Screams and emergency sirens filled the air. I was sure police units were on their way, if not just around the corner.

"Yes."

I ran my hand through my hair, letting it come to rest on the back of my head. There was a fierceness in his eyes that I couldn't explain, but I knew Kratos needed me.

I bent over and grabbed my saber and stunner off the ground.

"Well, no time like the present."

Kratos turned, his trench coat whipping out behind him as we ran against the flow of terrified Nobles.

45

Police sirens weren't far behind us, but their progress wasn't as fast as ours. Kratos cut a wedge through the crowd with some concentrated bursts of spray, causing the hysterical people to bounce off of it left or right, clearing a space for us.

No one we passed looked hurt. I didn't see any blood, I just saw terror. Wide, lost eyes blew past us like raindrops in a hurricane, but there were no injuries.

Was it a victimless explosion? Maybe Tyrann hadn't lied?

The crowd thinned out the closer we got to the entrance, the majority of people already having escaped to the street. The building was no longer on fire.

We skirted the side of the smoldering debris and headed for the front doors. This was supposed to be one of the most heavily guarded places in the city. Security had to be somewhere.

"Shouldn't there be guards?" I asked.

Kratos didn't break stride as he spoke. "The only security guards we care about will be closer to the roof."

The roof?

He didn't hesitate as we crossed the threshold. The main lights were still on, but the reddish hue of the emergency lights overshadowed the lobby—a warning of danger ahead—and the building appeared to be empty except for a few stragglers who rushed past us.

"What else is in here?" I asked. "Where are all the people?"

"It's a research building. Everyone is outside."

"No, I mean, there was an explosion. Shouldn't there be, I don't know, casualties or something?"

Kratos didn't respond, but instead walked over to a pair of glass elevator doors.

I had ridden on these elevators once before. A school trip several years ago had brought us here. However, the last time I approached these doors, they opened automatically for us. This time they held their ground.

"Are they broken?"

"No, just nonfunctional in emergencies." Kratos looked around. "But we need to get inside. It will be much quicker than the stairs."

I unsheathed my saber and examined the tip.

This should work.

I lodged the saber in the crevice where the two ends of the glass door met. The doors parted, and Kratos heaved them the rest of the way open and stepped inside. I re-sheathed the saber and followed him in.

"So if they're not working, what are we doing in here?"

"I had something installed in the elevator shaft. Boost me up to that ceiling panel." He pointed at the large rectangle in between the two lights. He popped the panel off and disappeared.

Moments later, his hand appeared and I was pulled into the faint lighting on top of the elevator. I never thought I'd ride an elevator again, much less be on top of one. I looked straight up. The shaft seemed to go on forever, with dim lights breaking up the darkness every fifteen feet or so.

I couldn't help wondering if Kratos had done this before. Why would he have something installed in this particular elevator?

He rummaged around behind me. I turned to find his face bathed in the pale red light coming in from below. He looked even more ominous than usual.

"Did Zeno show you how to use one of these?" He held up a small motorized contraption similar to the one I had used to climb a building several times.

"Yes."

He hoisted the machine onto the nearest cable and secured it in place. "This will take us to the fiftieth floor. It contains living quarters. There's a separate staircase to the roof from there." He pierced me with a serious gaze, the only face he knew how to make. "Dr. Rosewood usually has a contingent of security with her. I can't promise it will be safe from here on out. Be on your guard."

"We left 'safe' a long time ago," I said. "And I'm with you, but we need a plan."

"The plan is for you to do what I say."

"I need to know what we're dealing with," I said. "What are we going to find up there?"

"Answers."

I didn't have a chance to respond before he went flying through the semidarkness, leaving me standing there in silence. Kratos didn't seem to be himself; coming here felt rushed and impulsive, maybe even emotional. Also, he seemed strangely familiar with this place.

A minute later the machine returned, coming to rest just below eye level. I looked up. The darkness seemed to extend forever, covering Dr. Rosewood's living quarters in the blackness of the unknown. I made sure the small data chip was securely fastened in my glove and took a deep breath.

I was about to go see Dr. Rosewood. No, I was about to interrogate Dr. Rosewood, with Kratos. I exhaled and gripped the handholds on the machine.

I zipped up the cable like a piece of dust being sucked up through a vacuum. The cool air felt good on my skin, but it didn't shake the hot feeling in my gut. Forty seconds later, I arrived at the top. Kratos stood by, waiting.

I joined him next to a large set of steel doors that only added to the foreboding darkness and silence that greeted us. Kratos disturbed the imposing atmosphere with a whisper.

"Wait three seconds, then follow."

"No," I whispered. Kratos looked back, his eyes hard. "We *need* a plan."

"There will be four guards inside this room," he said. "They are well trained. On the far east wall, there is a staircase leading to the roof. That's where we're headed."

I pulled my saber from my back.

"Get past the guards, and get to the stairs," I said. "Got it. Anything else?"

"Yes. It will be dark inside. I will turn the lights on and immediately turn them back off—that will disorient the guards. Keep your eyes closed until they go back off. I'll meet you at the stairs."

Kratos pressed his palm to the scanner next to the door. The access-granting light glowed a dim green before the steel doors retracted silently into the walls.

He held up a hand with three fingers as a reminder.

Three seconds.

Kratos bounded through the opening into the dark room beyond.

One, two, three.

I closed my eyes just in time for the blinding light to illuminate the apartment. Immediately, the room went dark.

I drew my stunner with my left hand and brandished my saber with my right, and entered the room at a crouch. It was huge, spanning what I realized must be the entire width of the building.

A series of rapid-fire thuds met my ears, followed by the sound of a body dropping to the floor.

Kratos stood over the unconscious body. Two men materialized and ran toward Kratos. He became a blur of limbs, fighting both at once. I sprinted over, electrified my saber, and swung.

No one had time to react. I caught the first man in the back of his legs. He yelled out in pain as he crumpled. Kratos landed a hard blow to the side of his head, and he slumped unconscious to the floor.

The second man dove at me.

A small hiss escaped Kratos's gloves, and the man nearly stopped in midair. I smashed my saber into his skull. He fell unmoving to the ground.

I looked around.

"Where's the last—"

Kratos yanked my stunner out of my hand and fired a shot over my shoulder. I turned just as the fourth security guard fell, his momentum carrying him belly-first across floor.

"There." Kratos nodded to the ground.

He trudged over to the nearest wall and flipped on a light switch.

"Thanks," I said, blinking against the light.

"Let's go. The staircase is over here." Kratos started walking.

"Should we be worried about any more of these guys?" I said, catching up with him and doing a quick sweep of the floor. "And how do you know this place so well?"

"No, she never has more than four guards in her residence."

I waited for the answer to my second question, but it didn't come.

The staircase wasn't hard to see. A stainless steel railing lined transparent glass steps that appeared to go right into the ceiling. As far as I could tell, there was no opening. We stopped a few steps short of the bottom stair, I assumed to strategize, but I was wrong.

"I want you to stay here." Kratos's voice was taut.

"No," I said flatly.

"For your own safety, st—"

"How about for your safety?" I said, cutting him off. "What are you going to do up there? Interrogate her? And then what? What if there are more guards?"

"There will only be one—her personal bodyguard. I'll handle him, if need be."

"If need be?" I said. "Kratos, what aren't you telling me?"

"Dr. Rosewood is most likely attempting to leave the building after the explosion," he said. "We need to get to her before she does."

"And I'm coming," I said.

Kratos locked eyes with me. "Fine. Stay immediately behind me. Do not say a word. If I say go, you jump off the building and get to safety without hesitation. Do you understand?"

My heart began to race anew. What was he expecting to find up there?

"Victor!"

An odd sound I'd never heard before shook the ceiling. It was definitely motorized, but it sounded like a storm was raging outside. I could hear the air currents whipping around above us. Kratos's eyes went wide.

"We have to get up there now!"

He turned and sprinted up the glass steps.

"What is that?" I shouted, two steps behind. The noise was deafening. And then, just as quickly as it had arrived, it was gone.

Kratos slowed as he reached the top of the stairs, his head almost touching the ceiling.

"A helicopter. Stay close, and remember what I said."

He reached up and placed his hand on the ceiling. As if his touch was magic, a square panel slid out of the way, granting us access to the roof.

46

We emerged from Dr. Rosewood's living quarters into the bright sunlight. My eyes were met with elements of a scene that didn't quite fit together. A great metal monstrosity perched on top of the roof, its multiple stationary rotors jutting out in the air. Its side door was open, but the helicopter looked vacant. The edges of the roof had no walls and no guardrails, just a small raised lip and then fifty stories of open air. Near the far edge of the roof sat a woman in a lounge chair drinking what looked to be a glass of lemonade through a straw, peering unconcernedly out over the Capital.

Dr. Rosewood.

She was an austere woman with a strict face, dressed in regal white, the color of Nobility, and looked only a fraction of her age. She had an air of complete calm, as if no afternoon had been more pleasant, even though part of her building had just exploded beneath her.

Kratos stepped out onto the roof and strode toward her. I stayed a handful of steps behind him, feeling very exposed on the open roof. Dr. Rosewood continued to stare out over the Capital. Only when Kratos spoke did she notice us.

"Mother," he said.

I almost choked on the breath I had been taking.

Mother?

Dr. Rosewood turned, her face changing rapidly from smile to frown as she noticed me standing behind her *son*.

"I need to know the truth," he said.

"It looks like you've brought a guest, and a wanted one at that," she said, ignoring his request completely. She set her half-finished lemonade on the ground, uncrossed her legs, and stood up.

"I have information tying you to the Left Hand."

I watched Dr. Rosewood's expression. I had expected her to laugh, to brush it aside as completely off-base, silly, or crazy. Instead, her expression remained mostly neutral. A few crease lines appeared at the corners of her eyes.

"Interesting," she said, folding her arms.

"You don't deny it?" Kratos stood his ground, unmoving, like a black-cloaked boulder.

Dr. Rosewood regarded us, eyes cool and calculating, just like Kratos's. This was serious. The implications of the situation started to sink in. If Dr. Rosewood really was the leader of the Left Hand, what did that say about the Great Experiment, not to mention our current situation?

"You'll be happy to know that the information must be false. I am not affiliated with the Left Hand, nor have I ever been. I am your mother. I thought you would know that."

At that moment, a man emerged from the open door of the helicopter. He paused the moment he caught sight of us, attempting to hide in the shadow of the helicopter, but he was too late.

Harvesty.

"Liar!" Kratos yelled.

Dr. Rosewood glanced at him, her young features molding into a soft frown. "Oh, Harvesty, I wish you would have worn your mask."

Harvesty stepped out of obscurity, a glint of polished metal preceding his advance.

"So the family business is all out in the open now, is it?" he growled, the barrel of his gun leveled at Kratos.

"Victor, stay behind me," Kratos said as he moved sideways,

mirroring Harvesty's movements.

"No, Mr. Wells, stay where you are," Dr. Rosewood said. "And drop your weapons."

"Do as she says." Harvesty's voice held a deadly tone. I tossed the saber and stunner to the ground. "And Bounty Hunter"—he motioned with the barrel of his gun—"move."

Kratos obeyed.

With blinding speed.

He dove left. Harvesty fired, but missed.

Kratos rolled, reached inside his coat, and hurled a silver cylinder at Harvesty's torso. It exploded on contact, showering him in gray beads and sending him stumbling backwards. Another gunshot went wide as Kratos tackled Harvesty to the ground. The gun flew out of Harvesty's grasp, and Kratos's fist connected with Harvesty's head. His eyes closed, and Kratos let him slip to the ground.

Dr. Rosewood watched the events unfold like a passive spectator. She clapped politely as Kratos stood, breathing heavily.

"Impressive as ever," she said. "You should really join me. We would be unbeatable."

I picked up the stunner and trained it on her.

"I would never join the Left Hand," Kratos said, his eyes blazing.

"A shame, really. You would find what we do very interesting."

"I do find what you do interesting. Why did you send the Left Hand after Victor?"

Rosewood turned her attention to me.

"It's simple really," she started, eyeing me. "Saving the senator was the first strike against him. We knew Avardi Supart had been compiling information against us, but had hidden it somewhere. After his Marking, we learned that he'd given Victor the key to it. Naturally, he had to be eliminated." Dr. Rosewood smiled. "I changed his DNA readout so the government would be after him too. If they caught him, I would have easy access to him. In hindsight, the TııD part was a bit much. Just being Sinister worked well enough on the Pendletons, and others. I don't know if I will do that again in the future."

Kratos's eyes were furious.

"You're going to call them off," he said. "The Left Hand will not be after Victor any longer."

"Is that so?" Dr. Rosewood said.

I fired a blast from the stunner at the ground in front of her feet. She looked over at me in mild surprise.

"Yes," I said. "Call them off."

"And make it irreversible," Kratos said. "They are not to continue on after you've been put in prison."

Dr. Rosewood stood there dressed in white against the backdrop of a pale blue sky. Her expression was unreadable.

"Okay, I will do as you say." She held her hands up. "I'm reaching for my phone," she said as she pulled it out.

"We want to hear," I said.

"Put it on speaker," Kratos said.

"Of course."

The phone began to ring. A click sounded and a male voice answered on the other side.

"Hello?"

"Yes, it's me. I'm removing the hit from Victor Wells."

"And when would you like it reinstated?" the man said, sounding confused.

"Never," Rosewood said. "Get the word out to the others. He will never be a target of interest again. Do you understand?"

"Yes," the man said, still sounding perplexed.

"Goodbye." Dr. Rosewood closed her phone. She looked back and forth between the two of us. "Satisfied?"

"Yes," Kratos said, moving toward her. "Now, you're coming with us." I kept my stunner trained on her, just in case she tried anything.

I nodded to Kratos. We had done it. The Left Hand had been called off. We had their leader in our custody.

"Not so fast," a new voice said from behind me. The hairs on the back of my neck rose. A man stood on the top stair leading up from Dr. Rosewood's apartment.

Wilkes.

I recognized him from the night he had shown up at my house with Harvesty. In his hand, he held a gun.

Harvesty began stirring on the ground. Kratos stopped in his tracks, halfway between Harvesty and Dr. Rosewood.

"Drop the stunner," Wilkes said, motioning toward the ground with the barrel of his gun. I let it clatter to the ground. Harvesty groaned and began pushing himself to his feet.

"You're late," Dr. Rosewood said.

"Looks like it's a good thing," Wilkes said, nodding to Harvesty. "Bounty Hunter get the best of you again?"

"For the last time," Harvesty said as he stooped over to pick up his gun. He stared hungrily at us like a beaten dog about to get revenge. Wilkes made his way over, gun trained on me. Harvesty kept his pointed at Kratos.

"Get over there," Harvesty snarled at Kratos, motioning toward the far edge of the roof.

"Oh Harvesty, don't be so dramatic," Dr. Rosewood said, taking a few steps back. "But yes, Kratos, some space would be nice. I need to have a chat with Mr. Wells." Harvesty ushered Kratos backwards. She turned to me. "It was a good effort, what you and my son have managed to do. You were so close!" She glanced at Wilkes, who had moved to her side. "Then again, not really."

I hated her. She had killed countless people, caused widespread fear and panic. And she was going to get away with it, again.

"Now, on to what I want," she continued. "I know you found Senator Supart's information or else you would not be here. I also know that you came straight here after finding it. I want it. Give it to me."

She couldn't win.

"No," I said.

"No?" she said. Wilkes took half a step forward, the barrel of his gun pointed directly at my face.

I stood my ground.

"Oh good, defiance in the face of danger—how Noble." She rolled her eyes and turned to Wilkes. "Go retrieve the machine, and Kratos, hands up, or Harvesty will shoot you." Wilkes nodded and disappeared back down the stairs. Harvesty kept his gun trained on Kratos as he raised his hands. Moments later, Wilkes returned carrying a chrome metal box with a screen on top, which he handed to Dr. Rosewood.

"Thank you, Wilkes," she said without looking at him. "Mr. Wells, I won't order the Left Hand after you again, because clearly you're idiotic enough to die for something." She paused and looked at me. Almost a hundred years of conniving lived behind those eyes.

"Now, Mr. Wells, who is it that you care so much about? Your grandfather? Daphne and Augustine Pendleton? Mr. Zeno? And of course Alex Trabue?" She made a series of taps on the screen and then tilted it toward me. Each of their pictures was displayed on the screen. "You may be wondering what this is, and since your time in this world is short, I'll tell you:

"It is a global positioning DNA tracker. Simply load a DNA sequence, and that person, dead or alive, will be pinpointed anywhere on a map. I would have sent my Sinistrali after you while you were bunking with the Pendletons, but we wouldn't have been able to find out just how much Senator Supart knew." She set the metal box down. "So now the question lies with you, Mr. Wells. Are you prepared to give me Senator Supart's microchip, or should I send my Sinistrali after one of your friends? I promise they wouldn't suffer long. I'm sure they'll be dead within the hour."

My mind felt like ice. We had failed. Desperation strangled my insides. Hand over the microchip or hand over my friends. An impossible choice.

"I can see you're having trouble deciding who you should condemn first. I'd be happy to choose for you, or you can simply hand over the chip, and I'll let your friends go on their merry way."

"Why are you doing this?" Kratos said. His gaze danced back and forth between the gun in Harvesty's hands and his mother as he took another step backwards. Behind him, the ledge loomed closer. "What do you have to gain?"

Dr. Rosewood sighed.

"Oh, Kratos, you haven't put it together yet?" she said. "I thought I raised you better than that. I am a carrier of TɪɪD."

I watched Kratos. His eyes were wide in shock and betrayal.

"Don't look so surprised," she said. "It makes sense, doesn't it? That's why I created the Left Hand. I needed a way to eliminate any trace of the truth, and that included people who knew or who suspected anything. If I hadn't taken action, I would have died long ago, or maybe been put to death even, who knows?

"I feared people would begin to ask questions once the Left Hand had killed every other scientist on our task force except for me, but instead, I was heralded as a hero, a survivor." She smiled. "But I've taken far too long, and the day is not yet over." She turned to me. "So now is the time, Mr. Wells. Give me the chip or everyone you hold dear will die."

What was I supposed to do? My mind raced through the options, but there were none. She could kill everyone, and if I didn't talk, she would torture and kill me. Either way, she would get what she wanted. And I would be dead.

I reached down and unzipped my glove.

"Victor, no!" Kratos said.

"Shut your mouth," Harvesty growled, shoving the barrel of his gun closer to Kratos's chest.

"She'd kill us all anyways," I said, holding out the microchip for Dr. Rosewood. She plucked it from my fingers.

"Now you're catching on," she said, tossing the chip to the ground and stomping on it. "And Harvesty, if you're going to shoot someone, shoot Mr. Wells. He's of no further use to us. Wilkes, go start the helicopter."

With a nod, Wilkes headed over to the giant flying machine.

Harvesty grinned. "It's about time." He aimed his gun at me. "I even got a special set of bullets made, just for you."

I felt my insides tighten. Could I get to my stunner before he pulled the trigger? Could Zeno's spray stop a bullet?

No, I realized, there was no stopping this.

"Any last words?" Harvesty said.

I stared down the barrel of his gun. We had been so close.

Instead, I would die. The Left Hand would win.

"No?" Harvesty said. "Good. I hate when people beg."

Kratos moved quickly in my periphery. He reached inside his jacket, cocked his arm back, and a gunshot rang out.

I jumped at the noise, but there was no pain. I opened my eyes.

Smoke drifted out the end of Harvesty's gun and was swept away in the breeze of the rooftop. It was pointed at Kratos.

Kratos stood motionless near the ledge. His hands went to his chest. Blood blossomed around his fingertips. Off balance, he took a step backwards.

"No!" I yelled.

He took another step backwards. My body responded of its own accord.

I shouldered hard into Harvesty and scooped the stunner off the ground, my index finger glued to the trigger. Concentrated bursts of electricity exploded from the muzzle of the gun as I aimed at Dr. Rosewood and Harvesty. I sprinted harder than I ever had, but I wasn't fast enough.

It happened in slow motion.

Kratos stumbled back. The edge of the ledge caught him just above his ankles. His eyes registered shock. He was leaning—too far. Then his feet were off the ground, the open space beyond the ledge attempting to swallow him up. And then it did.

I turned briefly and caught sight of Dr. Rosewood's face. She looked on sadly, though not with remorse.

I jumped over the edge, and she too disappeared from view.

Time sped back up.

Kratos was falling limply some distance below me. I was acutely aware of gravity's pull on both of us. I willed myself to fly faster through the air, making myself as aerodynamic as possible. The sound of the helicopter starting back up barely registered as I flew toward the ground at a hundred miles per hour. I was mere feet away from Kratos now, his fluttering trench coat barely beyond my grasp.

Fifty stories wasn't enough.

47

My fingers brushed against his fluttering jacket. I reached as far as I could, stretching my arms to the limit. I knew somewhere in the back of my mind that if I didn't start spraying soon, we were both dead, but I couldn't give up. Not yet.

Finally, my hand closed around a fistful of fabric. I yanked hard, pulling myself even faster toward the ground and wrapping my arms around the unconscious form of my friend. I had never started spraying so late.

Gray beads materialized immediately and pelted me in the arms and face. I kept spraying.

Our progress slowed, but not enough.

I closed my eyes, spraying until the final moment.

A sickening crunch sounded, and I *felt* the breaking of Kratos's bones beneath my weight as we collided with the pavement.

Stars burst before my eyes and I fought for consciousness, but the pain kept me in reality.

I couldn't breathe, I couldn't speak, and I was sure my ribs were broken. I rolled off of Kratos's corpse-like form and onto my back.

My mind refused to accept what had just happened. Shock, pain —I couldn't think. My lungs burned for air, and my mind screamed for relief. My diaphragm stopped spasming mere seconds before I lost consciousness, but the first breath of air only granted me greater access to my pain and injuries.

Kratos lay immobile on the ground next to me, blood starting to pool around him.

"Krato—ah!" I yelled, the pain in my chest cutting off my cry of remorse. I pushed myself up and checked for a pulse.

Please be alive.

It was faint, but present. I exhaled a painful breath. My knees felt damp. I looked down and saw red. I needed to stop the bleeding.

Gingerly, I rolled Kratos onto his back. Blood flowed freely from a single hole in his stomach, but there was something I hadn't noticed before. A stiff, black material covered his torso. It seemed to be sealing off the wounded area, but there was so much blood.

My hands shook. I placed them over the bullet hole and pressed. Instantly, pain shot throughout my body. I gasped for air. I wanted to yell for help. I looked around, but there was no one. Police lights shimmered in the distance, blocking either end of the street. I needed to get us out of here.

I tried to push myself to my feet, but I could hardly stand, let alone support Kratos. If I let the police get here, they could help. But the police—the Flats, the whole city—they believed in Dr. Rosewood. To them I was a Sinister, I carried TⅡD. If I left Kratos, maybe he would live. Maybe the police would get here in time.

"Help!" I tried to yell, but it came out as more of a whisper.

A man stood nearby, maybe fifty feet away. He was tall and well-dressed—the Chairman. But it couldn't be. My mind was playing tricks on me. We had left him...

I closed my eyes and tried to clear my mind. When I opened them again, the Chairman was gone. I blinked a few more times and tried to take a steadying breath.

I couldn't leave Kratos for the police. Dr. Rosewood would silence him in an instant.

I looked around. Ten feet away was a manhole cover. If I could just get Kratos over to it, maybe Zeno could lower it for us.

Zeno, of course.

With a grunt of pain, I moved over to Kratos's head. His earbud was nestled securely in his ear. With bloodstained fingers, I pulled it out and shoved in my own ear.

"Zeno," I croaked, "I need help."

Immediately, Zeno's voice came through.

"Victor! Where are you? What happ—"

"Kratos has been shot."

Augustine was quick to interject. "What do you mean, shot? Stunned?"

"No, shot," I grunted. "With a gun." My bloodstained hands shook harder. I checked Kratos's wound again. The bleeding had slowed, but it hadn't stopped. The cold reality of my situation tried to dawn on me. My mind resisted. He couldn't die.

"Bro, where are you?" Zeno asked. I could hear the rapid clicking of his fingers on the keyboard.

I looked up to see Dr. Rosewood's helicopter take off and fly through the sky.

She wasn't going to get away with this.

"On the street outside the research tower," I said, doing my best to keep my breathing shallow.

"Victor, are you hurt?" Augustine said.

"I'll survive," I said. "But Kratos might not."

"Bro, if you can get to a manhole cover, I'll lower you down. Pria's on her way."

I looked at the manhole cover. I didn't know if I could get myself there, let alone drag a full-grown man with me.

"Okay," I grunted. I couldn't give up.

A memory sparked in my mind. Kratos had given me something in case of injury.

I searched my pockets. I pulled out the syringe with the purple liquid. Miraculously, it hadn't broken.

I uncapped the needle and plunged it into the flesh next to Kratos's bullet wound. I pressed the plunger until the cartridge was three-fourths empty and retracted the needle. I wiped it off on my shirt. I didn't know what it would do, but if I was going to get Kratos over to the manhole cover, I needed all the help I could get. I pushed the needle into my leg and emptied the rest of the cartridge.

The purple liquid burned as it coursed into my veins, but the pain was only momentary. And then there was no pain at all, anywhere. Not in my chest, or my back, or my leg. It was all gone. The relief was intoxicating.

Maybe we'd survive this after all.

I grabbed a fistful of Kratos's jacket and shoved it into his wound, readjusting one of his arms to keep it in place. I grabbed both of his feet and starting dragging him.

"You there, bro?"

"Almost," I said, grunting from exertion. "All right, we're here."

"Going down," Zeno said.

Moments later, the street had swallowed us up. I pulled Kratos off the manhole cover and sent it back up, closing us off from the Flats. Never before had I been so happy to be in a sewer.

"Victor!" Pria's voice ricocheted around the dimly lit hallways.

"Over here," I yelled back.

Seconds later, she whipped around the nearest corner, her silver hair tied back and a small bag over her shoulder. She knelt down next to us.

"How bad is it?" she asked.

I uncovered the bullet hole. Her eyes widened.

"And we fell off a building."

She looked at me.

"Seriously? Why do you seem fine?"

"I had a syringe full of some purple liquid," I said. "Not sure what it was, but I don't feel pain anymore."

"Did you give any to him?"

"Yeah," I said. "Three-quarters of the cartridge."

"And a quarter for you?" she asked.

I nodded.

"Good," she said, examining the wound. I had never seen her so focused. "We're going to need these."

Pria opened her bag and pulled out a series of black discs.

"Put these underneath him. They'll stick to his clothes," she said, handing them to me. "One under his head, two under his back, and one under each limb. Be careful. We don't know what's broken."

I did so while she went to work on Kratos's gunshot wound. Her hands flew over the wound with practiced movements. By the time I was done placing the discs, she had bandaged him up. Bits of blood-stained gauze protruded from his stomach like white and red blossoms on a dead tree. She grabbed a set of small spheres that matched the discs I had placed on Kratos and arranged them on the ground.

"Help me pick him up," she said.

Together, we lifted Kratos's body and placed the discs over the spheres. I could feel the magnetic push against his body. We let go and stepped back. His body floated two feet off the ground—the perfect levitating stretcher.

"Pria," I said, "this is amazing."

"We'll have time for compliments later," she said. "I've patched him up the best I can, but he needs more than that." She looked over at me. "Can you run?"

"I think so," I said.

"Good. Try to keep up."

48

We finally emerged from the sewers. The giant dirt slide loomed in front of us, the top disappearing into the darkness beyond. It was a foreboding backdrop for our welcoming party.

Augustine stood there alone waiting for us. He rushed over the moment we came into view.

"How is he?" Augustine's face was grave.

"Not good," Pria said. "He's lost a lot of blood. And I think the bullet is still lodged inside him."

"We can treat him back at the events center," Augustine said.

Pria nodded and kept pressure on the wound.

"Where's everyone else?" I asked. "Where's Daphne?"

"Zeno, is she still evading the police?" Augustine asked.

Zeno popped into my ear.

"Yeah, boss, the news has the police following five different Victor Wells paths, but I've got Daphne about thirty seconds out. She'll be topside by the hologram by the time you guys get up there."

At least one part of the plan was going like it was supposed to.

"Everyone else is already back at the events center," Augustine said, glancing up. "And you're sure no one followed you?" He scoured the entrance to the sewers.

Pria looked up from checking Kratos's bandage. "No one followed us. And if they had, they would have gotten lost down there." The gauze she had packed was now completely soaked in blood. She fished more out of her bag and packed it over the wound.

"And how, exactly, are we going to get back up there?" I asked.

She nodded toward the darkness to our right.

"I can't fathom why my father didn't use it to begin with," she said, "but there's an elevator over there that will take us to the top."

Two glass doors stood open, waiting to receive us.

We crowded into the elevator, taking care with Kratos. With a bandage in place, he looked like he still had a chance. His chest moved up and down slowly.

The elevator made a quick ascent. I looked to Pria. I owed her big time. Daphne had been right—I liked her more the better I got to know her.

The doors slid open, and we were greeted by an empty road.

"Everyone, this way," Pria said and took off at a jog. Kratos's body floated along with her. Augustine and I followed.

We passed through the hologram that disguised the entrance to find Daphne standing there waiting for us, face flushed, breathing hard.

"How's he doing?" she asked as soon as we appeared.

"Not good," Pria answered. For a moment, it looked like the animosity between them had been forgotten.

Daphne peered down at Kratos's limp figure. Some of the color drained from her face.

"But you got out all right?" Augustine asked. "No more police following you?"

"Yeah," Daphne said, tearing her eyes away from Kratos. "It went just like we planned it."

"I'm glad you made it back," I said, though I immediately regretted it. It felt awkward. We weren't out of the woods yet. No distractions.

Daphne nodded and gave me a tight-lipped smile.

"We need to go," Pria said. "Now."

Daphne stole a quick glance at Pria, who avoided her gaze. The tension increased.

Augustine nodded. "Let's go then."

49

"He's still bleeding, but it's slowed significantly. He's more or less stable, for now," Pria said, hurrying this way and that. We all stood around the stainless-steel table—Alex, Daphne, Zeno, Augustine, Pria, and me. Kratos lay still on its cold, gleaming surface. His mask had been removed, but there wasn't much color in his face. A dull beep could be heard every time his heart beat.

I stared at his lifeless face as conversation happened around me.

"What if we reached out to Mrs. Supart?" Augustine said.

"You think there's a backup?" Zeno asked, then shook his head. "I don't know, boss. I mean, with how well protected it was, I've gotta think that was the only copy."

"But there must be evidence *somewhere*," Augustine said. "Victor, what do you think? You know the Suparts well—would they have kept a backup? Victor?"

I tore my eyes away from Kratos. Alex continued to stand nearby, eyes closed, head slightly inclined. Kratos's current state had hit him hard.

"What? Sorry, I don't know if they'd have a backup," I said.

Besides, did it even matter?

"We could search their home," Daphne said. "It wouldn't be hard.

Or, Victor, maybe you could talk to Mrs. Supart. From what you said, she would probably help us if we asked."

"Yeah, bro! I bet I could work some magic if I got onto their server." Zeno cracked his knuckles. Daphne looked at me with hopeful eyes, but I couldn't bring myself to return her look. Not with Kratos lying half-dead on the table in front of us.

"Victor," Daphne said, "this isn't over. We're not just going to give up. We know who is behind the Left Hand. We can do something with that!"

"Yeah? And who will believe us?" I said, raising my voice. Pria looked up from redressing Kratos's wound. "Don't you get it? The only proof in existence—she took it. Then she crushed it. It's gone. She won."

"It's not over, Victor," Augustine said softly.

"Isn't it?" I motioned to Kratos. "Look what Rosewood did to her own son. That was us getting off lucky."

The screen on the wall emitted a tone.

Pertinent news announcement. Do you wish to view it?

"I thought we'd be getting one of these," Zeno said with a sigh. "Fine, Gina. Go ahead."

The screen came to life with Kelly Straunton front and center.

"... Surprisingly, there were no casualties following the explosion that decimated several floors of Dr. Rosewood's research tower. Dr. Rosewood herself was able to safely evacuate the scene." Kelly Straunton had adopted a more somber expression for this segment. "Criminal mastermind and TııD carrier Victor Wells is thought to be behind the day's events, sending dozens of police officers on a wild goose chase while he carried out some unfinished business inside the Capital.

"The widow of Senator Avardi Supart maintains that Victor Wells kidnapped her son, Jeffry, and then, posing as him, accompanied her to her husband's memorial earlier this afternoon, making him the first Sinister in history to break into the Capital. Jeffry Supart was recently found unharmed and unconscious in the middle of the street just outside the Ixlir Building. Authorities are still trying to determine Wells's point of entry." She brought a finger to her earpiece. "And now, a message from President Keltan."

The screen shifted, and President Keltan was seen standing at a podium in a room full of reporters.

"I wish I were addressing you under different circumstances," he said, his face both tired and full of worry. "This is an attack unparalleled in recent years. For months now, I have resisted the urging of Dr. Rosewood to take measures to help keep the Flats safe. I think it is time that I listen to her sage advice. Therefore, effective immediately, I am instituting a mandate that all Sinisters are to stay in the Heights. The Flats, not just the Capital, will be declared a Sinister-free zone. Anyone found not in compliance with this measure will be punished severely. It is for our safety, for order, that we must—"

"Turn that off, Gina," Zeno said.

The screen went dead.

"Oh, for goodness sake!" Pria said. Kratos's new bandage had started to turn crimson. She reached into her bag and rushed over just as the back door swung open.

"There they are! Men of action!" Tyrann said, striding toward us, a grin on his face. "And you, Mr. Wells, are becoming something of a celebrity!"

"What are you doing here, Tyrann?" Augustine said, straightening up.

"Checking in on my daughter, of course," he said, his gaze finally landing on her. He stopped short. "Is that...the Bounty Hunter?" His grin grew wider. "I expected much from you, but to capture and wound the Bounty Hunter? Bravo!" He nodded appreciatively before letting his features go cold. "Pria, what do you think you're doing?"

"Trying to stop the bleeding, obviously," she said without looking up.

Tyrann turned incredulous. "No daughter of mine will save the life of a Noble!" He moved toward her.

I knew Tyrann was crazy, but did he really just order his daughter to let someone die?

Alex had finally opened his eyes. Last I knew he was terrified of Tyrann, but now, he looked murderous.

"Tyrann! Every life is worth saving," Augustine said sharply.

"And I asked her to do it," I said. Tyrann stopped and looked at me, his face a mixture of confusion and anger, but both melted away. A knowing smile replaced them.

"Ah, keep him alive to bargain with? I see." He nodded. "Very wise, Mr. Wells, very wise." He chuckled to himself as he turned his back on Pria.

I glanced at her. We locked eyes, but she quickly looked away.

"Now that you've checked on your daughter," Augustine said, "is there anything else we can help you with?"

"No, I don't believe so," Tyrann said, folding his arms. "Although, I have been dying to trade stories with Victor here. However, blowing up part of a building sounds a little mundane next to capturing the Bounty Hunter."

Augustine clenched his fists. I knew he felt partially responsible. He had given Tyrann the detonator, after all.

"Oh, don't seem so angry, Aug. I did it as a service to mankind. It was for the Experiment. I've been feeling very philanthropic as of late."

"For the Experiment? An explosion like that? How is that a service?"

"I assure you, no Nobles were killed," Tyrann said, "as you no doubt learned from the news. I'll have to plan better next time."

"Next time?" Augustine asked.

"Well, two more times," Tyrann said.

"What, why?" Augustine sputtered.

"The DNA centers," I said. I had skipped over this detail earlier. "That's what was in the research tower. The Bounty Hunter told me." I didn't feel comfortable calling him "Kratos" in front of Tyrann.

"But why?" Augustine asked.

"To destroy Dr. Rosewood's research and records," Tyrann said. "Without those, the system will be crippled and the Nobles will lose their power. But enough business for one day. Time for a celebration!" He turned to his daughter. "Come, Pria. We have much to prepare, starting with washing all that Noble blood off of you." He gave Kratos a look of repulsion.

"I'm staying," Pria said, her eyes fixed on Kratos's chest.

Tyrann looked at her in disbelief.

"She has the best medical knowledge of anyone here," Augustine said. "We could use her help."

Tyrann adopted a quick smile that left his eyes cold.

"I see." He paused. "Just be sure to not make him too healthy again," he said, staring at Pria. She didn't look up. "Well then, I must be off. Congratulations again on your prize, Mr. Wells."

I didn't trust myself to respond. He thought this was some great victory, a win for the Sinisters. My friend was lying on the table in front of me, nearly dead, and I knew who was responsible.

Tyrann strode out the door without another word. The door shut behind him before any of us spoke.

"No offense, Pria," Zeno said. "But your dad is crazy."

"As if I didn't already know," she muttered.

I watched her as she monitored Kratos's vitals.

"Thanks, Pria," I said. "I know you don't have to do this and it'll probably cause some problems later, but th—"

I stopped mid-sentence as I doubled over. The pain from earlier was returning, only this time it was much worse. I groaned and fell to my knees, finally slumping to the ground. My breathing was shallow. I couldn't fully inhale.

The pain—it hurt so much.

"Pria! What's happening?" Augustine said.

She rushed to my side and placed two fingers on my neck, cradling my head with her other hand.

"His injection wore off," she said, staring into my eyes.

Then Daphne's, Zeno's, Alex's, and Augustine's faces were all floating above me, concern written across each one.

I coughed, and fresh pain rolled over me. I shut my eyes against it, blocking it out.

Then everything faded away.

50

I awoke to the sound of slow, persistent beeping. It was mostly dark, just the dim glow of a nearby lamp to light the room. I was in my bed at the events center, I realized. A comfy armchair from another room had been brought in. Silver hair spilled over one of the cushy arms, glinting softly in the lamplight.

Pria.

I pushed myself up on my elbows. No pain. I took a deep breath and exhaled. No pain again. Pria stirred in the chair. I poked myself in the ribs just to be sure. Still no pain.

She's a miracle worker!

I stretched my arms, and the leads attached to my finger came unplugged from the portable heart monitor. Instantly, the repetitive beeps turned into one long, continuous tone.

Pria's eyes snapped open.

"Sorry!" I said, reaching for the fallen cord.

"I'll get it." She got up and reattached the leads to my finger. The beeping resumed. She ran her hands through her hair and then threw it back into a ponytail. "How are you feeling?"

"Honestly, great," I said. "It feels like I'm all healed."

"If we were in the Flats, you would be," she said, "but we're here, so you've still got some recovering to do." She moved back to the chair and sat down.

"What time is it?" I asked. "Was I out long?"

"It's the middle of the night," she said, yawning.

"Seriously?" I asked.

"It took them literally forever, but Daphne and Zeno tracked down some of that purple stuff. I gave you a dose of it about an hour ago."

That made sense. With a sinking feeling, I realized that the pain would return. Pria let her head fall back against the chair cushion and closed her eyes.

"How is Kratos?" I asked. "Did the bleeding ever stop?"

"Not completely," she said, not bothering to open her eyes or sit up. "But I can't figure out why. I gave him a transfusion, but Daphne's watching him now."

I stared at Pria as she shifted in her chair.

"How did you learn to do all of this?" I asked.

"So we're not going to quietly go back to sleep then?" She glared at me.

"I hardly know you, and here you are, in my room, taking care of me. It's just a question," I said.

With a sigh, Pria sat up. "So what do you want to know? My whole life story?"

"How about just part of it, for starters?" I said. "Seriously though, you probably saved Kratos's life. How'd you know what to do?"

Pria hesitated, her eyes searching my face. "I've wanted to be a doctor since I was little," she finally said. "I studied and read everything I could. Printh told me not to let our father know, so I mostly did it in secret."

"She talks?" I asked.

"Of course she talks," Pria said. "She just doesn't think any of you are worth talking to, that's all."

"Ouch," I said. "But wait, Tyrann doesn't want you to be a doctor? Are there not doctors in the Heights?"

Pria laughed bitterly. "Oh, if you only knew. People would have to think we were worth saving for there to be doctors for us."

"I do."

"Right," she said skeptically.

"Look, without you, Kratos would probably be dead somewhere in the sewers underneath the Capital. And I'd probably still be unconscious."

"I'm starting to think that's a better option." Pria smiled.

"Ha ha," I said. "Really though, even if you didn't know how to save us, I'm still glad you're here. It's like Augustine said earlier—everyone is worth saving."

"So you've bought into their way of thinking, I take it?"

"You haven't?" I said.

Pria didn't respond. The silence hung in the air between us.

After a long while, she spoke again. "So what are you going to do now? The Left Hand isn't after you anymore, but you're still a wanted man. Are you going to go after her?"

"Rosewood?" I asked.

She nodded.

"I don't know." I broke eye contact and looked down at the floor. "But what's the point? We have no proof. She's been killing people and hiding her trail for years. Kratos and I got lucky. Who knows what she'd do if we showed up again?"

Pria opened her mouth to respond, but an alarm sounded.

"What in the world is that?" Pria said, looking around at the ceiling.

"I don't know," I said, "but it can't be good."

I threw off my covers and jumped out of bed. I opened the door to the hallway and the sound intensified. It must have been shrieking throughout the entire building. I felt a tightness in my chest that had nothing to do with my injuries.

"What did you do with my saber?" I asked.

Pria reached behind the door. "It's right here."

I held my hand out for it.

"Are you kidding me?" she said. "Who knows when that purple

stuff will wear off? You could collapse at any second. Besides, you want to get to the room behind the stage, right? I know a shortcut."

She shouldered past me, electrified the saber, and took off at a jog.

A short series of twists and turns later, and we arrived. Augustine and Zeno were already there.

Daphne entered the room at the same time we did. "What is it?" she said.

Alex blundered through the door, looking like he had been woken from a deep sleep. "Wazgoing on?" he said, rubbing the sleep from his eyes.

"I don't know," Zeno said between sirens. "Gina! Shut that thing off and tell us what's going on!"

Immediately, the sound ceased.

Text appeared on the overhead screen.

Sweeper incoming.

"What? Here?" Zeno said. "Show me the cameras, now!"

The screen populated with several different live feeds. All were devoid of movement, except one.

"There!" Daphne said, pointing at it.

"Enlarge it!" Zeno said.

The feed took over the whole screen. The scene was surreal. I could see the sweeper clearly. Its tentacle-like arms shot in every direction with computer-guided rigidness, devouring anything in its path. Its lights illuminated the street.

It came to a stop just outside of the building.

The arms retracted.

The lights turned off.

The sweeper quit moving.

"What's it doing?" I asked. "Powering down?"

"I don't know," Zeno said slowly. "Gina, what do you think? Is it safe?"

The sweeper appears to be deactivated. All systems have been shut down.

"What does that mean?" Augustine asked.

The key has been turned off. The batteries are not using any power. There is no electricity.

"Girl, he wasn't talking to you," Zeno said, then turned to Augustine. "I don't know, boss. I've never see anything like this before. Daphne, Pria?"

Pria shook her head. So did Daphne.

"I think we're being invited out," Alex said.

"What makes you say that?" Augustine said.

He pointed at the screen. One of the metal arms appeared to be waving at us, beckoning us to it.

"What do we do?" Alex said.

No one spoke. I looked around the room. There was only one option.

"We go out," I said.

"Seriously?" Daphne asked.

"Yes," I said firmly. I started toward the door.

"Victor, wait!" Daphne said.

"For what?" I asked.

"We're coming with you!"

Moments later, I pushed open the door that led outside.

The looming figure of the motionless sweeper sat before us. It looked dead. The air smelled of bleach. Why was it here?

The lights of the sweeper blared to life.

I shielded my eyes. My heart raced, but the metal arms didn't move.

The sound of metal scraping against metal grated against the silent night, and a hatch on the sweeper opened up.

The form of a man stepped out, hands raised in greeting.

"Sorry, sorry, it's just a little too dark for my taste."

I recognized that voice.

But it couldn't be.

He continued walking forward until I could make out his face.

"You—how are you here?" Daphne said. "We thought you were dead."

"Daphne, who is this?" Augustine whispered.

The Chairman smiled.

"You can call me the Chairman," he said. "And clearly, I am not dead, but so nice to have such a wonderful reception."

"How are you here?" I asked. "And why?"

"I would have thought the first part of that was obvious," he said, motioning behind him. "And for your second question, I've been watching you. But you knew that already, didn't you, Victor?"

All eyes turned to me.

"What do you mean?"

"I mean that you saw me, didn't you? I tried to make it fairly obvious."

"Victor, what is he talking about?" Augustine said.

"I thought I was hallucinating," I said slowly. "I didn't think we'd ever see him again, not after the sweeper took him."

"Pria knows him," Daphne said suddenly, turning to her. "Who is he?"

"I only know that he calls himself the Chairman," she said. "And that he likes to gamble."

"Yes," the Chairman said. "Unfortunately, we kept our relationship very business oriented, but I wouldn't mind if that changed." He smiled in Pria's direction. I could feel her recoil next to me.

"He's the one who gave us the 'truenoble' password," I said. "And I've seen him twice since"—I paused and looked over at Daphne —"once a couple of days ago and then again after Kratos got shot. I thought I was seeing things." I turned back to the Chairman. "So it really was you?"

"Oh, yes." He nodded.

"You were there after the Bounty Hunter got shot?"

"You mean your good friend, Kratos? Indeed, I was."

"How do you know his name?" Zeno asked.

"I know a lot of things," the Chairman said. "For example, I know that Kratos hasn't stopped bleeding and Pria here doesn't know why." He paused and smiled. "But I do." His last few words were in singsong.

"Then tell me," Pria demanded. The Chairman turned to me instead.

"Did Harvesty say anything to you about his bullets? I assume it was Harvesty who shot him?"

I thought back to the moments before it happened, the rage in Harvesty's eyes as he pointed his gun at me.

"He said he had a special set made, just for me."

"Special indeed," the Chairman said. "They were laced with poison, a poison that you are not equipped to deal with here."

Pria's eyes grew wide. I turned back to the Chairman.

"Wait, you knew they were poisoned?" I asked, my voice rising. The Chairman nodded. "You were there right after it happened and you didn't help? We could have died!"

The Chairman held up his hands.

"I have to watch how things play out, at least to a certain extent, you see. I wanted to make sure you were made of the right stuff before I offered my help."

"Help?" Daphne said. "I wouldn't trust anything you tried to give us."

"Oh, Daphne, always playing hard to get." He smiled as if it was an inside joke. Augustine's eyebrows knit together. "The good news is that you passed my test. I am here to help!" He held his arms out wide and smiled. "You are free to reject my help, of course," the Chairman continued, "but without it your friend, Kratos, will die. And I always choose to help the winning side."

"The winning side of what?" Zeno asked.

"Everything."

We stood there in silence, bathed in the lights of a sweeper.

"Who are you?" Augustine asked.

He looked at each of us in turn, a mysterious expression on his face.

"I am the Chairman, the leader of Ville, and operator of the sweepers," he said. "And I just might know how to help you expose Dr. Victoria Rosewood."

I hope you enjoyed The Left Hand, but I hate to break to you —it's over.

Or is it...?

Nope, no it is not. Victor Wells will return! But in the meantime, a gift for the discerning reader, and lover of stories.

FREE EBOOK ALERT!

As a thank you for reading, here's a freebie, on me. It's a short story—over fifty pages of exclusive content you can't get anywhere else (even on Amazon). It sheds light on the origin of the esteemed Dr. Rosewood and the Great Exp—well, maybe I've said too much. Anyways, it's awesome, and you'll enjoy seeing how Dr. Rosewood became Dr. Rosewood.

To get your completely gratis eBook, simply go to jordanallenmedia.com, click on "free eBook," and the magic of the internet will send you the ebook, entitled "A Life Worth Saving," right to your inbox! You're welcome.

Now, it truly is the end. Thanks for reading. I can't wait to join you for the next one.

- JA

ACKNOWLEDGMENTS

No man is a island, it takes a village, um, what else? What I'm trying to say is that I couldn't have done this alone. Well maybe, but if it would have been just me, my book would have been poorly written, filled with punctuation and grammatical errors, the cover would have most likely been a pencil sketch with stick figures, and let's be serious, the manuscript would still be in a semi-finished, rough draft form in some long-neglected file on my computer.

Like most things in life, it's the wonderful people around you that can take something ordinary and make it great. With that in mind, here comes the gratitude.

First and foremost on the list is my very talented wife, Britton. I couldn't have done this without her unwavering support and long-standing patience. She endured my late nights and early mornings, listened to me ramble on about stuff I was just making up, and somehow still loves me even though my hair appears to be thinning. How did I ever get so lucky?

Next up are my parents. My dad, unknowingly, has been urging me to write a book ever since I was a little kid. If I ever took a long time to do something, he would always ask me, "Son, what are you doing, writing a book?" I'd laugh, then he'd laugh. And now I laugh again. Yes, Dad, that's exactly what I was doing.

But it was really my mom who instilled in me a love of books. Because of her I've lived more lives and been on more journeys than I ever thought possible. What a joy that has been, and will continue to be.

I'd like to thank the other members of our illustrious, self-titled group known (though, not widely or officially) as The Magnificent Seven- Aaron, Adam, Luke, Ricky, Seth, and Tye. Gentlemen, without your camaraderie, I never would have made it out of that dark dungeon on 305 W. 12th Street. Well, at the time of writing this, I'm still here, but if all goes to plan, we'll all be free in a few months time.

I'd like to give special thanks to my good friend Luke Bauserman. You both blazed the way and helped me make a dream reality. Also of note, we've spent nearly a thousand hours riding together in the car over the last four years. You wanna keep carpooling next year at work?

I'd like to thank the members of the Third Sunday Writing Club —Luke, Austin, and Sadie—for their critique and feedback. Your thoughts and suggestions took things to another level.

And how could I forget those other yay-hoos over at Lock10 Press? I couldn't ask for a better publishing team.

I'd like to give a shout out to Matt Bird for his dedication to the craft of storytelling. If the Mona Lisa were a book, he'd know the reason for her smile. Thanks for sharing some of those secrets of story with me.

Thanks to Therin Knite for her keen mind and sharp eye, and for helping me to not sound like an idiot.

Thanks to Stephanie Parent—you caught the things the rest of us missed. I'll be forever grateful.

Thanks to Mike Corley, the artist responsible for the cover. You, sir, are a man of both character and creativity. Thanks for making things look awesome.

A page in a book doesn't do justice to how I feel, but suffice it to say that I am extremely grateful. I feel fortunate beyond measure to have this opportunity. So, one last time before I close—to those named and unnamed—thank you.

    -Jordan

ABOUT THE AUTHOR

Raised in Idaho where the locals say, "if you don't like the weather, wait a minute," Jordan grew up and moved to Ohio where he found the locals say the same thing. He now resides with his wife, two dogs, and upcoming child in a place with a shockingly similar climate.

Jordan Allen was born in Utah, raised in Idaho, and now claims to be a resident of Ohio (allegedly) with his wife and two dogs. A lover of chocolate chip cookie dough ice cream, sharp suits, a still morning on the golf course, and using his mind to battle hair loss, Jordan spends his days drilling on teeth, attempting to start a work out regimen, and disliking healthy smoothies.

Jordan has been bucked off a donkey, chased by an emu, smothered by his two golden doodles and blinded by the beauty and charm of his wife. He has also had a staring contest with a llama, mediated on a mountain top, swam less than a mile, and lost his lunch on an airplane.

After a lifetime of adventure, he now lives in Ohio with his lovely wife and two dogs and will shortly be celebrating the birth of their first child (but only if you're reading this in the first half of 2018, otherwise the child has come and we have effectively broken the internet due to cuteness overload).

Jordan is a dentist by day, asleep at night, and groggy in the mornings. He enjoys a good pint of cookie dough ice cream (daily, if possible), whipped cream with a little bit of pumpkin pie (but only around Thanksgiving), and the taste of gatorade when dehydrated (honestly, there's nothing better). He married way out of his league and has thus far managed to keep that secret from his wife for over half of a decade. When he's not spending time making children cry or extolling the virtues of flossing, he hangs out with his wife and two dogs, practices his short game, and practices his long game. He can occasionally be seen practicing his medium game as well. He is constantly on the lookout for well-made suits, the perfect crepe pan, and an eccentric pair of socks.

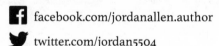 facebook.com/jordanallen.author

twitter.com/jordan5504

 instagram.com/jallen5504